The Adventures of
DON QUIXOTE,
MAN OF
LA MANCHA

The Adventures of
DON QUIXOTE, MAN OF LA MANCHA

by MIGUEL De CERVANTES

Abridged for modern readers from the translation by JOHN ORMSBY

Illustrated by JOSÉ LLOBERA

GROSSET & DUNLAP / PUBLISHERS / NEW YORK

Contents

Part I

v

Contents

Part II

Illustrations

DON QUIXOTE

PART I

CHAPTER 1

The Gentleman of La Mancha

IN A VILLAGE of La Mancha, there lived one of those gentlemen that keep a lance in the lance-rack, a lean horse, and a greyhound for coursing. An olla of rather more beef than mutton, a salad on most nights, lentils on Fridays, and a pigeon or so extra on Sundays, made away with three-quarters of his income. The rest of it went in a doublet of fine cloth and velvet breeches and shoes to match for holidays, while on weekdays he made a brave figure in his best homespun. He had in his house a housekeeper past forty, a niece under twenty, and a lad for the field and market place. The age of this gentleman of ours was bordering on fifty; he was of a hardy habit, spare, gaunt-featured, a very early riser and a great sportsman. He was called Quexana.

The above-named gentleman whenever he was at leisure (which was mostly all the year round) gave himself up to reading books of chivalry with such ardor and avidity that he almost entirely neglected the pursuit of his field sports, and even the management of his property; and to such a pitch did his infatuation go that he sold many an acre of tillageland to buy books of chivalry to read, and brought home as many of them as he could get. But of all there were none he liked so well as those of the famous Feliciano de Silva, for their lucidity of style, particularly when in his reading he came upon passages like *"the reason of the unreason with which my reason is afflicted so weakens my reason that with reason I murmur at your beauty."* Over conceits of this sort the poor gentleman lost his wits, and used to lie awake striving to worm the meaning out of them; what Aristotle himself could not have

3

made out had he come to life again for that special purpose. He was not at all easy about the wounds which the knight Don Belianis gave and took, because it seemed to him that, great as were the surgeons who had cured him, he must have had his face and body covered all over with seams and scars.

Many an argument did he have with the curate of his village (a learned man, and a graduate of Siguenza) as to which had been the better knight, Palmerin of England or Amadis of Gaul. Master Nicholas, the village barber, however, used to say that neither of them came up to the Knight of Phœbus.

In short, our gentleman became so absorbed in his books that he spent his nights from sunset to sunrise, and his days from dawn to dark, poring over them; and what with little sleep and much reading his brains got so dry that he lost his wits. His fancy grew full of what he used to read about in his books: enchantments, quarrels, battles, challenges, wounds, wooings, loves, agonies, and all sorts of impossible nonsense; and it so possessed his mind that the whole fabric of invention and fancy he read of was true, that to him no history in the world had more reality in it.

His wits being quite gone, he hit upon the strangest notion that ever madman in this world hit upon, and that was that he fancied it was right and requisite, as well for the support of his own honor as for the service of his country, that he should make a knight-errant of himself, roaming the world over in full armor and on horseback in quest of adventures, and putting in practice himself all that he had read of as being the usual practices of knights-errant; righting every kind of wrong, and exposing himself to peril and danger from which he was to reap eternal renown and fame. And so, led away by the intense enjoyment he found in these pleasant fancies, he set himself forthwith to put his scheme into execution.

The first thing he did was to clean up some armor that had belonged to his great-grandfather, and had been for ages lying forgotten in a corner eaten with rust and covered with mildew. He scoured and polished it as best he could and then proceeded to inspect his hack, which, with more blemishes than the steed of the jester, Gonela, surpassed in his eyes the Bucephalus of Alexander. Four days were spent in thinking what name to give him, because (as he said to himself) it was not right that a horse belonging to a knight so famous should be without some distinctive name; for it was only reasonable that, his master taking a new character, he should take a new name, and that it should be a distinguished one, befitting the new calling he was about to follow. And so, after having composed, struck out, rejected, added to, un-

4

made, and remade a multitude of names out of his memory and fancy, he decided upon calling him Rocinante.

Having got a name for his horse so much to his taste, he was anxious to get one for himself, and he was eight days more pondering over this point, till at last he made up his mind to call himself Don Quixote. Recollecting, however, that the valiant Amadis was not content to call himself curtly Amadis and nothing more, but added the name of his kingdom and country to make it famous, and called himself Amadis of Gaul, he, like a good knight, resolved to add on the name of his, and to style himself Don Quixote of La Mancha.

So then, his armor being furbished, his hack christened, and he himself confirmed, he came to the conclusion that nothing more was needed now but to look for a lady to be in love with; for a knight-errant without love was like a tree without leaves or fruit, or a body without a soul. As he said to himself, "If, by good fortune, I come across some giant hereabouts, a common occurrence with knights-errant, and overthrow him in one onslaught, or cleave him asunder to the waist, or, in short, vanquish him, will it not be well to have someone I may send him to as a present, that he may come in and fall on his knees before my sweet lady, and in a humble, submissive voice say, 'I am the giant Caraculiambro, lord of the island of Malindrania, vanquished in single combat by the never sufficiently extolled knight Don Quixote of La Mancha, who has commanded me to present myself before your Grace, that your Highness dispose of me at your pleasure'?" Oh, how our good gentleman enjoyed the delivery of this speech, especially when he had thought of someone to call his Lady!

There was, in a village near his own, a very good-looking farm girl with whom he had been at one time in love, though, so far as is known, she never knew it nor gave a thought to the matter. Her name was Aldonza Lorenzo, and upon her he thought fit to confer the title of Lady of his Thoughts; and after some search for a name which should not be out of harmony with her own, and should suggest and indicate that of a princess and great lady, he decided upon calling her Dulcinea del Toboso—she being of El Toboso—a name, to his mind, musical, uncommon, and significant, like all those he had already bestowed upon himself and the things belonging to him.

5

CHAPTER 2

Don Quixote Sets Out

THESE PRELIMINARIES SETTLED, he did not care to put off any longer the execution of his design, urged on to it by the thought of all the world was losing by his delay, seeing what wrongs he intended to right, grievances to redress, injustices to repair, and abuses to remove. So, without giving notice of his intention to anyone, and without anybody seeing him, one morning before the dawning of the day (which was one of the hottest of the month of July) he donned his suit of armor, mounted Rocinante with his patched-up helmet on, braced his buckler, took his lance, and by the back door of the yard sallied forth upon the plain in the highest contentment at seeing with what ease he had made a beginning with his grand purpose. But scarcely did he find himself upon the open plain, when a terrible thought struck him, one all but enough to make him abandon the enterprise at the very outset. It occurred to him that he had not been dubbed a knight, and that according to the law of chivalry he neither could nor ought to bear arms against any knight. These reflections made him waver in his purpose, but his craze being stronger than any reasoning, he made up his mind to have himself dubbed a knight by the first one he came across, following the example of others in the same case, as he had read in the books that brought him to this pass. And so comforting himself, he pursued his way, taking that which his horse chose, for in this he believed lay the essence of adventures.

Thus setting out, our new-fledged adventurer paced along, talking to himself and saying, "Who knows but that in time to come, when the history of my famous deeds is made known, the sage who writes it, when he has to set forth my first sally in the early morning, will do it after this fashion? 'Scarce had the rubicund Apollo spread o'er the face of the broad spacious earth the golden threads of his bright hair, when the renowned knight Don Quixote of La Mancha, quitting the lazy down, mounted his celebrated steed Rocinante and began to traverse the ancient and famous Campo de Montiel' "; which in fact he was actually traversing.

Presently he broke out again, as if he were love-stricken in earnest, "O Princess Dulcinea, lady of this captive heart, a grievous wrong hast thou done me to drive me forth with scorn, and with inexorable obduracy banish me from the presence of thy beauty. O lady, deign to hold in remembrance this heart, thy vassal, that thus in anguish pines for love of thee."

So he went on stringing together these and other absurdities, all in the style of those his books had taught him, imitating their language as well as he could; and all the while he rode so slowly and the sun mounted so rapidly and with such fervor that it was enough to melt his brains if he had any. Nearly all day he traveled without anything remarkable happening to him, at which he was in despair, for he was anxious to encounter someone at once upon whom to try the might of his strong arm.

Towards nightfall his hack and he found themselves dead tired and hungry, when, looking all around to see if he could discover any castle or shepherd's shanty where he might refresh himself and relieve his sore wants, he perceived not far out of his road an inn, and quickening his pace he reached it just as night was setting in. At the door were standing two young women on their way to Seville with some carriers who had chanced to halt that night at the inn. And as, happen what might to our adventurer, everything he saw seemed to him to happen after the fashion of what he had read of, the moment he saw the inn he pictured it to himself as a castle with its four turrets and pinnacles of shining silver, not forgetting the drawbridge and moat and all the belongings usually ascribed to castles of the sort. To this inn, which to him seemed a castle, he advanced, and at a short distance from it he checked Rocinante, hoping that some dwarf would show himself upon the battlements, and by sound of trumpet give notice that a knight was approaching the castle. But seeing that they were slow about it, and that Rocinante was in a hurry to reach the stable, he made for the inn door, and perceived the two gay damsels who were standing there, and who seemed to him to be two fair maidens or lovely ladies taking their ease at the castle gate.

7

At this moment it so happened that a swineherd who was going through the stubbles collecting a drove of pigs gave a blast of his horn to bring them together, and forthwith it seemed to Don Quixote to be what he was expecting, the signal of some dwarf announcing his arrival. So with prodigious satisfaction he rode up to the inn and to the ladies, who, seeing a man approaching in full armor and with lance and buckler, turned in dismay into the inn. Don Quixote, guessing their fear by their flight, with courteous bearing and gentle voice addressed them: "Your ladyships need not fly or fear any rudeness, for the order of knighthood to which I profess offers that to no one, much less to highborn maidens as your appearance proclaims you to be."

The girls were looking at him and straining their eyes to make out the features which the clumsy visor obscured, but when they heard themselves so described, they could not restrain their laughter, which made Don Quixote wax indignant, and say, "Modesty becomes the fair, and moreover laughter that has little cause is great silliness; this, however, I say not to pain or anger you, for my desire is none other than to serve you."

The incomprehensible language of our cavalier only increased the ladies' laughter, and that increased his irritation, and matters might have gone farther if at that moment the landlord had not come out. He, being a very fat man, was a very peaceful one. Seeing this grotesque figure clad in armor that did not match any more than his saddle, bridle, lance, buckler, or corselet, he was not at all indisposed to join the damsels in their manifestations of amusement; but, in truth, standing in awe of such a complicated armament, he thought it best to speak to him politely, so he said, "Señor Caballero, if your worship wants lodging, excepting the bed (for there is not one in the inn) there is plenty of everything else here." Don Quixote, observing the respectful bearing of the Alcaide of the fortress (for so innkeeper and inn seemed in his eyes), answered, "Sir Castellan, for me anything will suffice, for

'My armor is my only wear,
My only rest the fray.' "

The host fancied he called him Castellan because he took him for a "worthy of Castile," though he was in fact an Andalusian, and as crafty a thief as Cacus and as full of tricks as a student or a page. "In that case," said he,

" 'Your bed is on the flinty rock,
Your sleep to watch alway';

8

and if so, you may dismount and safely reckon upon any quantity of sleeplessness under this roof for a twelvemonth, not to say for a single night."

So saying, he advanced to hold the stirrup for Don Quixote, who got down with great difficulty (for he had not broken his fast all day), and then charged the host to take great care of his horse, as he was the best bit of flesh that ever ate bread in this world. The landlord eyed the beast, but did not find him even half as good as Don Quixote said; and putting him up in the stable, he returned to see what might be wanted by his guest, whom the damsels, who had by this time made their peace with him, were now relieving of his armor. While they were doing this, taking the baggages for ladies of high degree belonging to the castle, he said to them with great sprightliness:

> "Oh, never, surely, was there knight
> So served by hand of dame,
> As served was he, Don Quixote hight,
> When from his town he came;
> With maidens waiting on himself,
> Princesses on his hack—

—or Rocinante, for that, ladies mine, is my horse's name, and Don Quixote of La Mancha is my own; though I had no intention of declaring myself until my achievements in your service and honor had made me known. A time, however, will come for your ladyships to command and me to obey, and then the might of my arm will show my desire to serve you."

The girls, who were not used to hearing this sort of talk, had nothing to say in reply; they only asked him if he wanted anything to eat.

"I would gladly eat a bit of something," said Don Quixote, "for I feel it would come very seasonably." The day happened to be a Friday, and in the whole inn there was nothing but some pieces of the fish they call "troutlet"; so they asked him if he thought he could eat troutlet, for there was no other fish to give him. "If there be troutlets enough," said Don Quixote, "they will be the same thing as a trout; for it is all one to me whether I am given eight reals in small change or a piece of eight."

They laid a table for him at the door of the inn for the sake of the air, and the host brought him a portion of ill-soaked and worse cooked stockfish, and a piece of bread as black and moldy as his own armor.

While he was dining there came up to the inn a sowgelder, who, as he approached, sounded his reed pipe four or five times, and thereby completely convinced Don Quixote that he was in some famous castle, and that they were regaling him with music, and that the stockfish was trout, the bread the whitest, the wenches ladies, and the landlord the castellan of the castle; and consequently he held that his enterprise and sally had been to some purpose. But still it distressed him to think he had not been dubbed a knight, for it was plain to him he could not lawfully engage in any adventure without receiving the order of knighthood.

CHAPTER 3

Knighthood Is Attained

HARASSED BY THIS REFLECTION, Don Quixote made haste with his scanty supper, and having finished it called the landlord, and shutting himself into the stable with him, fell on his knees before him, saying, "From this spot I rise not, valiant knight, until your courtesy grants me the boon I seek, one that will redound to your praise and the benefit of the human race." The landlord, seeing his guest at his feet and hearing a speech of this kind, stood staring at him in bewilderment, not knowing what to do or say, and entreating him to rise, but all to no purpose until he had agreed to grant the boon demanded of him.

"I looked for no less, my lord, from your High Magnificence," replied Don Quixote, "and I have to tell you that the boon I have asked is that you shall dub me knight tomorrow morning, and that tonight I shall watch my arms in the chapel of this your castle; thus tomorrow, as I have said, will be accomplished what I so much desire, enabling me lawfully to roam through all the four quarters of the world seeking adventures on behalf of those in distress, as is the duty of chivalry and of knights-errant like myself."

The landlord, who was something of a wag, and had already some suspicion of his guest's want of wits, was quite convinced of it on hearing talk of this kind from him, and to make sport for the night he determined to fall in with his humor. So he told him he was quite right in pursuing the object he had in view; and that he himself in his younger days had followed the same honorable calling, roaming in quest of adventures in various parts of the world, where he had proved the nimbleness of his feet and the lightness of his fingers, doing many wrongs, cheating many widows, ruining maids and swin-

11

dling minors, and, in short, bringing himself under the notice of almost every tribunal and court of justice in Spain; until at last he had retired to this castle of his, where he was living upon his property and upon that of others. He told him, moreover, that in this castle of his there was no chapel in which he could watch his armor, as it had been pulled down in order to be rebuilt, but that in a case of necessity it might, he knew, be watched anywhere, and he might watch it that night in a courtyard of the castle. In the morning, God willing, the requisite ceremonies might be performed so as to have him dubbed a knight, and so thoroughly dubbed that nobody could be more so. He asked if he had any money with him, to which Don Quixote replied that he had not a farthing, as in the histories of knights-errant he had never read of any of them carrying any. On this point the landlord told him he was mistaken; for, though not recorded in the histories, because in the author's opinion there was no need to mention anything so obvious and necessary as money and clean shirts, it was not to be supposed therefore that they did not carry them, and he might regard it as certain and established that all knights-errant took care to see that their squires were provided with money and other requisites; and when it happened that knights had no squires (which was rarely the case) they themselves carried everything in cunning saddlebags that were hardly seen on the horse's croup. He therefore advised him never from that time forth to travel without money and the usual requirements, and he would find the advantage of them when he least expected it.

Don Quixote promised to follow his advice scrupulously, and it was arranged forthwith that he should watch his armor in a large yard at one side of the inn; so, collecting it all together, Don Quixote placed it on a trough that stood by the side of a well, and bracing his buckler on his arm he grasped his lance and began with a stately air to march up and down in front of the trough, and as he began his march night began to fall.

The landlord told all the people who were in the inn about the craze of his guest, the watching of the armor, and the dubbing ceremony he contemplated. Full of wonder at so strange a form of madness, they flocked to see it from a distance, and observed with what composure he sometimes paced up and down, or sometimes, leaning on his lance, gazed on his armor without taking his eyes off it for ever so long; and as the night closed in the light from the moon was so brilliant that everything the novice knight did was plainly seen by all.

Meanwhile one of the carriers who were in the inn thought fit to water his team, and it was necessary to remove Don Quixote's armor as it lay on the trough; but he seeing the other approach hailed him in a loud voice, "O thou, whoever thou art, rash knight that comest to lay hands on the armor of the most valorous errant that ever girt on sword, have a care what thou dost; touch it not unless thou wouldst lay down thy life as the penalty of thy rashness."

The carrier gave no heed to these words, but seizing it by the straps flung the armor some distance from him. Seeing this, Don Quixote raised his eyes to heaven and exclaimed, "Aid me, lady mine, in this the first encounter that presents itself to this breast which thou holdest in subjection; let not thy favor and protection fail me in this first jeopardy"; and, with these words, dropping his buckler he lifted his lance with both hands and with it smote such a blow on the carrier's head that he stretched him on the ground, so stunned that had he followed it up with a second there would have been no need of a surgeon to cure him. This done, Don Quixote picked up his armor and returned to his beat with the same serenity as before.

Shortly after this, another carrier, not knowing what had happened (for the first still lay senseless), came with the same object of giving water to his mules, and was proceeding to remove the armor in order to clear the trough, when Don Quixote, without uttering a word, or imploring aid from anyone, once more dropped his buckler and once more lifted his lance, and without actually breaking the second carrier's head into four pieces, made more than three of it. At the noise all the people of the inn ran to the spot, and among them the landlord. The comrades of the wounded, perceiving the plight they were in, began from a distance to shower stones on Don Quixote, who screened himself as best he could with his buckler, not daring to quit the trough and leave his armor unprotected. The landlord shouted to them to leave him alone, for he had already told them that he was mad, and as a madman he would not be held accountable even if he killed them all. Still louder shouted Don Quixote, calling them knaves and traitors, and the lord of the castle, who allowed knights-errant to be treated in this fashion, a villain and a low-born knight whom, had he received the order of knighthood, he would call to account for his treachery.

"But of you," he cried, "base and vile rabble, I make no account; fling, strike, come on, do all ye can against me, ye shall see what the reward of your folly and insolence will be." This he uttered with so much spirit and boldness that he filled his assailants with a terrible fear, and as much for this reason as at the persuasion of the landlord they left off stoning him, and he allowed them to carry off the wounded, and with the same calmness and composure as before resumed the watch over his armor.

13

But these fancies of his guest were not much to the liking of the landlord, so he determined to cut matters short and confer upon him at once the wretched order of knighthood before any further misadventure could occur. Going up to him, he apologized for the rudeness which, without his knowledge, had been offered him by these low people, who, however, had been well punished for their audacity. As he had already told him, he said, there was no chapel in the castle, nor was it needed for what remained to be done, for, as he understood the ceremonial of the order, the whole point of being dubbed a knight lay in the accolade and in the slap on the shoulder, and that could be administered in the middle of a field; and that he had now done all that was needful as to watching the armor, for all requirements were satisfied by a watch of two hours only, while he had been at it more than four. Don Quixote believed it all, and told him he stood there ready to obey him, and to make an end of it with as much dispatch as possible; for, if he were again attacked, and felt himself to be dubbed knight, he would not, he thought, leave a soul alive in the castle, except such as out of respect he might spare at his bidding.

Thus warned, the landlord forthwith brought out a book in which he used to enter the straw and barley he served out to the carriers, and, with a lad carrying a candle-end, and the two damsels already mentioned, he returned to where Don Quixote stood, and bade him kneel down. Then, reading from his account book as if he were repeating some devout prayer, in the middle of his delivery he raised his hand and gave him a sturdy blow on the neck, and then, with his own sword, a smart slap on the shoulder, all the while muttering between his teeth as if he was saying his prayers. Having done this, he directed one of the ladies to gird on his sword, which she did with great self-possession and gravity, and not a little was required to prevent a burst of laughter at each stage of the ceremony; but what they had already seen of the novice knight's prowess kept their laughter within bounds. On girding him with the sword, the lady said to him, "May God make your worship a very fortunate knight, and grant you success in battle."

Having thus, with speed, brought to a conclusion these ceremonies, Don Quixote was on thorns until he saw himself on horseback sallying forth in quest of adventures; and saddling Rocinante at once, he mounted, and embracing his host, as he returned thanks for his kindness in knighting him, he addressed him in language so extraordinary that it is impossible to convey an idea of it or report it. The landlord, to get him out of the inn, replied with no less rhetoric though with shorter words, and without even calling upon him to pay the reckoning let him go with a Godspeed.

14

CHAPTER 4

What Happened on Leaving

DAY WAS DAWNING when Don Quixote quitted the inn, so happy, so gay, so exhilarated at finding himself now dubbed a knight, that his joy was like to burst his horse-girths. However, recalling the advice of his host, he determined to go home and provide himself with money and shirts, and also with a squire, for he reckoned upon securing a farm laborer, a neighbor of his, a poor man with a family, but very well qualified for the office of squire to a knight. With this object he turned his horse's head towards his village, and Rocinante, thus reminded of his old quarters, stepped out so briskly that he hardly seemed to tread the earth.

He had not gone far, when out of a thicket on his right there seemed to come feeble cries as of someone in distress, and the instant he heard them he exclaimed, "Thanks be to heaven that it so soon offers me an opportunity of fulfilling the obligation I have undertaken. These cries, no doubt, come from some man or woman in want of help, and needing my aid and protection." Wheeling, he turned Rocinante in the direction whence the cries seemed to proceed. He had gone but a few paces into the wood, when he saw a mare tied to an oak, and tied to another, and stripped to the waist, a youth of about fifteen years of age, from whom the cries came. Nor were they without cause, for a lusty farmer was flogging him with a belt and following up every blow with scoldings and commands; while the youth answered, "I won't do it again, master mine; I won't do it again, and I'll take more care of the flock another time."

Seeing what was going on, Don Quixote said in an angry voice, "Discourteous knight, it ill becomes you to assail one who cannot defend himself; mount your steed and take your lance" (for there was a lance leaning against the oak to which the mare was tied), "and I will make you know that you are behaving as a coward." The farmer, seeing before him this figure in full armor brandishing a lance over his head, gave himself up for dead, and made answer meekly, "Sir Knight, this youth that I am chastising is my servant, employed by me to watch a flock of sheep, and he is so careless that I lose one every day, and when I punish him for his carelessness and knavery he says I do it out of niggardliness, to escape paying him the wages I owe him, and before God, and on my soul, he lies."

"Base clown!" said Don Quixote. "By the sun that shines on us I have a mind to run you through with this lance. Pay him at once without another word; if not, by the God that rules us I will make an end of you on the spot; release him instantly."

The farmer hung his head, and without a word untied his servant, of whom Don Quixote asked how much his master owed him.

He replied, nine months at seven reals a month. Don Quixote added it up, found that it came to sixty-three reals, and told the farmer to pay it immediately, if he did not want to die.

The trembling clown replied that as he lived and by the oath he had sworn (though he had not sworn any) it was not so much; for there were to be taken into account and deducted three pairs of shoes he had given the lad, and a real for two blood-lettings when he was sick.

"All that is very well," said Don Quixote, "but let the shoes and the blood-lettings stand as a set-off against the blows you have given him without any cause; for if he spoiled the leather of the shoes you paid for, you have damaged that of his body, and if the barber took blood from him when he was sick, you have drawn it when he was sound; so on that score he owes you nothing."

"The difficulty is, Sir Knight, that I have no money here; let Andres come home with me, and I will pay him all."

"I go with him!" said the youth. "Nay, God forbid! No, señor, not for the world; for once alone with me, he would flay me alive."

"He will do nothing of the kind," said Don Quixote. "I have only to command, and he will obey me; and as he has sworn to me by the order of knighthood which he has received, I leave him free, and I guarantee the payment."

"Consider what you are saying, señor," said the youth. "This master of mine is not a knight, nor has he received any order of knighthood; for he is Juan Haldudo the Rich, of Quintanar."

"That matters little," replied Don Quixote. "Everyone is the son of his works."

"That is true," said Andres, "but this master of mine—of what works is he the son, when he refuses me the wages of my sweat and labor?"

"I do not refuse, brother Andres," said the farmer. "Be good enough to come along with me, and I swear by all the orders of knighthood there are in the world to pay you as I have agreed."

"See that you do as you have sworn," said Don Quixote; "if not, by the same oath I swear to come back and hunt you out and punish you. And if you desire to know who it is lays this command upon you, know that I am the valorous Don Quixote of La Mancha, the undoer of wrongs and injustices."

So saying, he gave Rocinante the spur and was soon out of reach. The farmer followed him with his eyes, and when he saw that he had cleared the wood and was no longer in sight, he turned to the boy Andres, and said, "Come here, my son, I want to pay you what I owe you, as that undoer of wrongs has commanded me."

"My oath on it," said Andres, "your worship will be well advised to obey the command of that good knight—may he live a thousand years—for, as he is a valiant and just judge, if you do not pay me, he will come back and do as he said."

"My oath on it, too," said the farmer; "but as I have a strong affection for you, I want to add to the debt in order to add to the payment." And seizing him by the arm, he tied him up again, and gave him such a flogging that he left him for dead.

"Now, Master Andres," said the farmer, "call on the undoer of wrongs; you will find he won't undo that, though I am not sure that I have quite done with you, for I have a good mind to flay you alive." But at last he untied him, and gave him leave to go look for his judge in order to put the sentence pronounced into execution.

Andres went off in a hurry, swearing he would go to look for the valiant Don Quixote of La Mancha and tell him exactly what had happened, and that all would have to be repaid him sevenfold. But for all that, he went off weeping, while his master stood laughing.

Thus did the valiant Don Quixote right that wrong, and, thoroughly satisfied with what had taken place, as he considered he had made a very happy and noble beginning with his knighthood, he took the road towards his village in perfect self-content.

He now came to a road branching in four directions, and immediately he was reminded of those crossroads where knights-errant used to stop to consider which road they should take. In imitation of them he halted for a while, and after having deeply considered it, he gave Rocinante his head, submitting his own will to that of his hack, who followed out his first intention, which was to make straight for his own stable.

After he had gone about two miles Don Quixote perceived a large party of people, who, as afterwards appeared, were some Toledo traders, on their way to buy silk at Murcia. There were six of them coming along under their sunshades, with four servants mounted, and three muleteers on foot. Scarcely had Don Quixote descried them when the fancy possessed him that this must be some new adventure. So with a lofty bearing and determination he fixed himself firmly in his stirrups, got his lance ready, brought his buckler before his breast, and planting himself in the middle of the road, stood waiting the approach of these knights-errant, for such he now considered them to be; and when they had come near enough to see and hear, he exclaimed with a haughty gesture, "All the world stand, unless all the world confess that in all the world there is no maiden fairer than the Empress of La Mancha, the peerless Dulcinea del Toboso."

The traders halted at the sound of this language and the sight of the strange figure that uttered it, and from both figure and language at once guessed the craze of their owner. They wished, however, to learn quietly what was the object of this confession that was demanded of them, and one of them, who was rather fond of a joke, said to him, "Sir Knight, we do not know who this good lady is; show her to us, for if she be of such beauty as you suggest, with all our hearts we will confess the truth that is on your part required of us."

"If I were to show her to you," replied Don Quixote, "what merit would you have in confessing a truth so manifest? The essential point is that without seeing her you must believe, confess, affirm, swear, and defend it; else ye have to do with me in battle, ill-conditioned, arrogant rabble that ye are; and come ye on, one by one as the order of knighthood requires, or all together as is the custom and vile usage of your breed, here do I bide and await you, relying on the justice of the cause I maintain."

"Sir Knight," replied the trader, "I entreat your worship in the name of this present company of princes, that your worship will be pleased to show us

18

Battered in body as he was, to rise was beyond his power.

some portrait of this lady, though it be no bigger than a grain of wheat. And in this way we shall be satisfied, and you will be content; nay, I believe we are already so far agreed with you that even though her portrait should show her blind of one eye, and distilling vermilion and sulphur from the other, we would nevertheless, to gratify your worship, say all in her favor that you desire."

"She distills nothing of the kind, vile rabble," said Don Quixote, burning with rage, "nothing of the kind, I say; and ye must pay for the blasphemy ye have uttered against beauty like that of my lady."

And so saying, he charged with leveled lance against the one who had spoken, with such fury that, if Rocinante had not stumbled midway and come down, it would have gone hard with the rash trader. Down went Rocinante, and over went his master, rolling along the ground for some distance; and when he tried to rise he was unable, so encumbered was he with lance, buckler, spurs, helmet, and the weight of his old armor; and all the while he was struggling to get up he kept saying, "Fly not, cowards and caitiffs! Stay, for not by my fault, but my horse's, am I stretched here."

One of the muleteers in attendance, who could not have had much good nature in him, hearing the poor prostrate man blustering in this style, was unable to refrain from giving him an answer on his ribs; and coming up to him he seized his lance, and having broken it in pieces, with one of them he began so to belabor our Don Quixote that, in spite of his armor, he milled him like a measure of wheat. His masters called out not to lay on so hard and to leave him alone, but the muleteer's blood was up, and he did not care to drop the game until he had vented the rest of his wrath, and gathering up the remaining fragments of the lance he threw them all upon the unhappy victim, who all through the storm of sticks that rained on him never ceased threatening heaven, and earth, and the brigands, for such they seemed to him.

At last the muleteer was tired, and the traders continued their journey, taking with them matter for talk about the poor fellow who had been cudgeled. He when he found himself alone made another effort to rise; but if he was unable when whole and sound, how was he to rise after having been thrashed and well nigh knocked to pieces? And yet he esteemed himself fortunate, as it seemed to him that this was a regular knight-errant's mishap, and entirely, he considered, the fault of his horse. However, battered in body as he was, to rise was beyond his power.

CHAPTER 5

The Knight Is Brought Home

FINDING, then, that he could not move, he thought of his usual remedy, which was to think of some passage in his books, and his craze brought to his mind that about Baldwin and the Marquis of Mantua, when Carloto left him wounded on the mountain side, a story known by heart by the children, not forgotten by the young men, and lauded and even believed by the old folk. This seemed to him to fit exactly the case in which he found himself, so, making a show of severe suffering, he began to roll on the ground and with feeble breath repeat the very words which the wounded knight of the wood is said to have uttered:

> "Where art thou, lady mine, that thou
> My sorrow dost not rue?
> Thou canst not know it, lady mine,
> Or else thou art untrue."

And so he went on with the ballad as far as the lines:

> "O noble Marquis of Mantua,
> My Uncle and liege lord!"

As chance would have it, when he had got to this line there happened to come by a peasant from his own village, a neighbor of his, who had been with a load of wheat to the mill, and he, seeing the man stretched there, came up to him and asked him who he was and what was the matter with him that he complained so dolefully.

The Knight Is Brought Home

Don Quixote was firmly persuaded that this was the Marquis of Mantua, his uncle, so the only answer he made was to go on with his ballad, in which he told the tale of his misfortune, and of the loves of the Emperor's son and his wife all exactly as the ballad sings it.

The peasant stood amazed at hearing such nonsense, and relieving him of the visor, already battered to pieces by blows, he wiped his face, which was covered with dust, and as soon as he had done so he recognized him and said, "Señor Quexana, who has brought your worship to this pass?" But to all questions the other only went on with his ballad.

Seeing this, the good man removed as well as he could the breastplate and backpiece to see if he had any wound, but he could perceive no blood nor any mark whatever. He then contrived to raise him from the ground, and with no little difficulty hoisted him upon his ass, which seemed to him to be the easiest mount for him; and collecting the arms, even to the splinters of the lance, he tied them on Rocinante, and leading him by the bridle and the ass by the halter he took the road for the village, very sad to hear what absurd stuff Don Quixote was talking. Nor was Don Quixote less so, for what with blows and bruises he could not sit upright on the ass, and from time to time he sent up sighs to heaven. The peasant went along cursing his fate that he had to listen to such a lot of nonsense. However, he came to the conclusion that his neighbor was mad, and so made all haste to the village.

They reached it just as night was beginning to fall, but the peasant waited until it was a little later, that the belabored gentleman might not be seen riding in such a miserable state. When it was what seemed to him the proper time he entered the village and went to Don Quixote's house, which he found all in confusion, and there were the curate and the village barber, who were great friends of Don Quixote, and his housekeeper was saying to them in a loud voice, "What does your worship think can have befallen my master, Señor Licentiate Pero Perez?" for so the curate was called; "it is two days now since anything has been seen of him, or the hack, or the buckler, lance, or armor. Miserable me! I am certain of it, these accursed books of chivalry he reads so constantly, have upset his reason; for now I remember having often heard him saying to himself that he would turn knight-errant and go all over the world in quest of adventures. To the devil with such books, that have brought to ruin in this way the finest understanding there was in all La Mancha!"

The niece said the same and, indeed, more: "You must know, Master Nicholas"—for that was the name of the barber—"it was often my uncle's way to stay two days and nights together poring over these unholy books of misventures, after which he would fling the book away and snatch up his sword and fall to slashing the walls; and when he was tired out he would say he had killed four giants like four towers. But I take all the blame upon myself for never having told your worships of my uncle's vagaries, that you might put a stop to them before things had come to this pass, and burn all these accursed books—for he has a great number—that richly deserve to be burned like heretics."

All this the peasant heard, and from it he understood at last what was the matter with his neighbor, so he began calling aloud, "Open, your worships!"

At his words they all hurried out, and when they recognized their friend, master, and uncle, who had not yet dismounted from the ass because he could not, they ran to embrace him.

"Hold!" said he, "for I am badly wounded through my horse's fault; carry me to bed, and if possible send for the wise Urganda to cure and see to my wounds."

"See there! Plague on it!" cried the housekeeper at this, "did not my heart tell the truth as to which foot my master went lame of? To bed with your worship at once, and we will contrive to cure you here without fetching that Hurgada. A curse I say once more, and a hundred times more, on those books of chivalry that have brought your worship to such a pass."

They carried him to bed at once, and after searching for his wounds could find none, but he said they were all bruises from having had a severe fall with his horse Rocinante when in combat with ten giants, the biggest and the boldest to be found on earth.

They put a host of questions to Don Quixote, but his only answer to all was—give him something to eat, and leave him to sleep, for that was what he needed most. They did so, and the curate questioned the peasant at great length as to how he had found Don Quixote. He told him, and the nonsense he had talked when found and on the way home, all which made the curate the more eager to do what he did the next day, which was to summon his friend the barber, Master Nicholas, and go with him to Don Quixote's house.

CHAPTER 6

Knight and Squire Go Forth

A<small>T THE INSTANT</small> of their arrival the following morning, Don Quixote began shouting out, "Here, here, valiant knights! here is need for you to put forth the might of your strong arms, for they of the Court are gaining the mastery in the tourney!"

When they reached Don Quixote he was already out of bed, and was still shouting and raving, and slashing and cutting all round, as wide awake as if he had never slept.

They closed with him and by force got him back to bed, and when he had become a little calmer, addressing the curate, he said to him, "Of a truth, Señor Archbishop, it is a great disgrace for us who call ourselves the Twelve Peers, so carelessly to allow the knights of the Court to gain the victory in this tourney."

"Hush, friend," said the curate. "Please God, the luck may turn, and what is lost today may be won tomorrow; for the present let your worship have a care of your health, for it seems to me that you are overfatigued, if not badly wounded."

"Wounded no," said Don Quixote, "but bruised and battered."

They gave him something to eat, and once more he fell asleep, leaving them marveling at his madness.

That night, all the books that were in the whole house were burned to ashes; and some must have been consumed that deserved preservation in ever-lasting archives; and so in them was verified the proverb that the innocent suffer with the guilty.

One of the remedies which the curate and the barber immediately applied to their friend's disorder was to wall up and plaster the room where the books had been, so that when he got up they might say that a magician had carried them off, room and all; and this was done with all dispatch. Two days later Don Quixote got up, and the first thing he did was to go and look at his books, and not finding the room where he had left it, he wandered from side to side looking for it. He came to the place where the door used to be, and tried it with his hands, and turned and twisted his eyes in every direction without saying a word; but after a good while he asked his housekeeper whereabouts was the room that held his books.

The housekeeper, who had been already well instructed in what she was to answer, said, "There are neither room nor books in this house now, for the devil himself has carried all away."

"It was not the devil," said the niece, "but a magician who came on a cloud one night after the day your worship left, and he entered the room, and what he did there I know not, but after a little while he made off, flying through the roof, and left the house full of smoke; and when we went to see what he had done we saw neither book nor room: but we remember very well, the housekeeper and I, that on leaving, the old villain said in a loud voice that, for a private grudge he owed the owner of the books and the room, he had done mischief in that house that would be discovered by and by."

"It must have been Friston," said Don Quixote, "and he is a sage magician, a great enemy of mine, because he knows by his arts and lore that I am to engage in single combat with a knight whom he befriends and that I am to conquer, and he will be unable to prevent it."

"But, uncle," said the niece, "who mixes you up in these quarrels? Would it not be better to remain at peace in your own house instead of roaming the world looking for better bread than ever came of wheat, never reflecting that many go for wool and come back shorn?"

"Oh, niece of mine," replied Don Quixote, "how much astray art thou in thy reckoning."

The two were unwilling to make any further answer, as they saw that his anger was kindling.

In short, then, he remained at home fifteen days very quietly without showing any signs of a desire to take up with his former delusions, and during this time he held lively discussions with his two friends, the curate and the barber, on the point he maintained, that knights-errant were what the world stood most in need of. The curate sometimes contradicted him, sometimes agreed with him, for if he had not observed this precaution he would have been unable to bring him to reason.

Meanwhile Don Quixote worked upon a farm laborer, a neighbor of his, an honest man (if indeed that title can be given to him who is poor), but with very little wit in his pate. In a word, he so talked him over, and with such persuasions and promises, that the poor clown made up his mind to sally forth with him and serve him as esquire. Don Quixote, among other things, told him he ought to be ready to go with him gladly, because any moment an adventure might occur that might win an island in the twinkling of an eye and leave him governor of it. On these and the like promises Sancho Panza (for so the laborer was called) left wife and children, and engaged himself as esquire to his neighbor.

Don Quixote next set about getting some money; and selling one thing and pawning another, and making a bad bargain in every case, he got together a fair sum. He provided himself with a buckler, which he begged as a loan from a friend, and, restoring his battered helmet as best he could, he warned his squire Sancho of the day and hour he meant to set out, that he might provide himself with what he thought most needful. Above all, he charged him to take saddlebags with him. The other said he would, and that he meant to take also a very good ass he had, as he was not much given to going on foot. About the ass, Don Quixote hesitated a little, trying to recall any knight-errant taking with him an esquire mounted on ass-back, but no instance occurred to his memory. For all that, however, he determined to take him, intending to furnish him with a more honorable mount when a chance of it presented itself, by appropriating the horse of the first discourteous knight he encountered.

All being done, without taking leave, Sancho Panza of his wife and children, or Don Quixote of his housekeeper and niece, they sallied forth unseen by anybody from the village one night, and made such good time that by daylight they held themselves safe from discovery, even should search be made for them.

Sancho rode on his ass like a patriarch, longing to see himself soon governor of the island his master had promised him. Don Quixote decided upon taking the same route and road he had taken on his first journey, that over the

Campo de Montiel, which he traveled with less discomfort than on the last occasion, for, as it was early morning and the rays of the sun fell on them obliquely, the heat did not distress them.

And now Sancho Panza said to his master, "Your worship will take care, Señor Knight-errant, not to forget about the island you have promised me, for be it ever so big I'll be equal to governing it."

To which Don Quixote replied, "Friend Sancho Panza, if thou livest and I live, it may well be that before six days are over, I may have won some kingdom that has others dependent upon it, which will be just the thing to enable thee to be crowned king of one of them."

"In that case," said Sancho Panza, "if I should become a king, Teresa, my wife, would come to be queen and my children infantes."

"Well, who doubts it?" said Don Quixote.

"I doubt it," replied Sancho Panza, "because for my part I am persuaded that though God should shower down kingdoms upon earth, not one of them would fit the head of Teresa. Let me tell you, señor, she is not worth two maravedis for a queen; countess will fit her better, and that only with God's help."

"Leave it to God, Sancho," returned Don Quixote, "for he will give her what suits her best; but do not undervalue thyself so much as to come to be content with anything less than being governor of a province."

"I will not, señor," answered Sancho, "especially as I have a man of such quality for a master in your worship, who will know how to give me all that will be suitable for me and that I can bear."

CHAPTER 7

Tilting at Windmills

AT THIS POINT they came in sight of thirty or forty windmills on the plain, and as soon as Don Quixote saw them he said to his squire, "Fortune is arranging matters for us better than we could have shaped our desires ourselves, for look there, friend Sancho Panza, where thirty or more monstrous giants present themselves, all of whom I mean to engage in battle and slay, and with whose spoils we shall begin to make our fortunes; for this is righteous warfare, and it is God's good service to sweep so evil a breed from off the face of the earth."

"What giants?" said Sancho Panza.

"Those thou seest there," answered his master, "with the long arms."

"Look, your worship," said Sancho, "what we see there are not giants but windmills, and what seem to be their arms are the sails that turned by the wind make the millstone go."

"It is easy to see," replied Don Quixote, "that thou art not used to this business of adventures. Those are giants; and if thou art afraid, away with thee out of this and betake thyself to prayer while I engage them in fierce and unequal combat."

So saying, he gave the spur to his steed Rocinante, heedless of the cries his squire Sancho sent after him, warning him that most certainly they were windmills and not giants he was going to attack. He, however, was so positive they were giants that he neither heard the cries of Sancho, nor perceived, near as he was, what they were, but made at them shouting, "Fly not, cowards and vile beings, for a single knight attacks you."

27

A slight breeze at this moment sprang up, and the great sails began to move, seeing which Don Quixote exclaimed, "Though ye flourish more arms than the giant Briareus, ye have to reckon with me."

So saying, and commending himself with all his heart to his lady Dulcinea, he charged at Rocinante's fullest gallop and fell upon the first mill that stood in front of him; but as he drove his lance-point into the sail the wind whirled it round with such force that it shivered the lance to pieces, sweeping with it horse and rider, who went rolling over on the plain, in a sorry condition. Sancho hastened to his assistance as fast as his ass could go, and when he came up found him unable to move, with such a shock had Rocinante fallen with him.

"God bless me!" said Sancho, "did I not tell your worship to mind what you were about, for they were only windmills? And no one could have made any mistake about it but one who had something of the same kind in his head."

"Hush, friend Sancho," replied Don Quixote, "the fortunes of war more than any other are liable to frequent fluctuations; and moreover I think that that same sage Friston who carried off my study and books, has turned these giants into mills in order to rob me of the glory of vanquishing them."

"God order it as he may," said Sancho Panza, and helping him to rise got him up again on Rocinante, whose shoulder was half out; and then, discussing the late adventure, they followed the road to Puerto Lapice, for there, said Don Quixote, they could not fail to find adventures in abundance and variety, as it was a great thoroughfare.

"Be that as God will," said Sancho, "I believe it all as your worship says it; but straighten yourself a little, for you seem all on one side, maybe from the shaking of the fall."

"That is the truth," said Don Quixote, "and if I make no complaint of the pain it is because knights-errant are not permitted to complain of any wound."

"If so," said Sancho, "I have nothing to say; but God knows I would rather your worship complained when anything ailed you. For my part, I confess I must complain however small the ache may be; unless this rule about not complaining extends to the squires of knights-errant also."

Don Quixote could not help laughing at his squire's simplicity, and he assured him he might complain whenever and however he chose, just as he liked, for, so far, he had never read of anything to the contrary in the order of knighthood.

"What we see are not giants but windmills!"

Sancho bade him remember it was dinnertime, to which his master answered that he wanted nothing himself just then, but that *he* might eat when he had a mind. With this permission Sancho settled himself as comfortably as he could on his beast, and taking out of the saddlebags what he had stowed away in them, he jogged along behind his master munching deliberately, and from time to time taking a pull at the bota with a relish that the thirstiest tapster in Malaga might have envied; and while he went on in this way, gulping down draft after draft, he never gave a thought to any of the promises his master had made him, nor did he rate it as hardship but rather as recreation going in quest of adventures, however dangerous they might be. Finally they passed the night among some trees, from one of which Don Quixote plucked a dry branch to serve him after a fashion as a lance, and fixed on it the head he had removed from the broken one.

All that night Don Quixote lay awake thinking of his Dulcinea, in order to conform to what he had read in his books, how many a night in the forests and deserts knights used to lie sleepless supported by the memory of their ladies. Not so did Sancho Panza spend it, for having his stomach full of something stronger than chicory water he made but one sleep of it, and, if his master had not called him, neither the rays of the sun beating on his face nor all the cheery notes of the birds welcoming the approach of day would have had power to waken him. On getting up he tried the bota and found it somewhat less full than the night before, which grieved his heart because they did not seem to be on the way to remedy the deficiency readily. Don Quixote did not care to break his fast, for, as has been already said, he confined himself to savory recollections for nourishment.

They returned to the road they had set out with.

"Now, brother Sancho Panza," said Don Quixote, "we may plunge our hands up to the elbows in what they call adventures; but observe, even shouldst thou see me in the greatest danger in the world, thou must not put a hand to thy sword in my defense, unless indeed thou perceivest that those who assail me are rabble or base folk; for in that case thou mayest very properly aid me; but if they be knights it is on no account permitted or allowed thee by the laws of knighthood to help me until thou hast been dubbed a knight."

"Most certainly, señor," replied Sancho, "your worship shall be fully obeyed in this matter; all the more as of myself I am peaceful and no friend to mixing in strife and quarrels: it is true that as regards the defense of my own person I shall not give much heed to those laws, for laws human and divine allow each one to defend himself against any assailant whatever."

"That I grant," said Don Quixote, "but in this matter of aiding me against knights thou must put a restraint upon thy natural impetuosity."

"I will do so, I promise you," answered Sancho, "and will keep this precept as carefully as Sunday."

While they were thus talking there appeared on the road two friars mounted on two mules. They wore traveling spectacles and carried sunshades; and behind them came a coach attended by four or five persons on horseback and two muleteers on foot. In the coach there was, as afterwards appeared, a Biscay lady on her way to Seville. The friars, though going the same road, were not in her company; but the moment Don Quixote perceived them he said to his squire, "Either I am mistaken, or this is going to be the most famous adventure that has ever been seen, for those black-robed bodies we see there doubtless are magicians who are carrying off some stolen princess in that coach, and with all my might I must undo this wrong."

"This will be worse than the windmills," said Sancho. "Look, señor, those are friars of St. Benedict, and the coach plainly belongs to some travelers: I tell you to mind well what you are about and don't let the devil mislead you."

"I have told thee already, Sancho," replied Don Quixote, "that on the subject of adventures thou knowest little. What I say is the truth, as thou shalt see presently."

So saying, he advanced and posted himself in the middle of the road along which the friars were coming, and as soon as he thought they had come near enough to hear what he said, he cried aloud, "Devilish beings, release instantly the highborn princess whom you are carrying off by force in this coach, else prepare to meet a speedy death as the just punishment of your evil deeds."

The friars drew rein and stood wondering at the appearance of Don Quixote as well as his words, to which they replied, "Señor Caballero, we are not devilish, but two brothers of St. Benedict following our road, nor do we know whether or not there is any captive princess coming in this coach."

"No soft words with me, for I know you, lying rabble," said Don Quixote, and without waiting for a reply he spurred Rocinante and with leveled lance charged the first friar with such determination that, if the friar had not flung himself off the mule, he would have been brought to the ground against his will, and sore wounded, if not killed outright. The second brother, seeing how his comrade was treated, drove his heels into his mule and made off across the country faster than the wind.

Sancho Panza, when he saw the friar on the ground, dismounting briskly from his ass, rushed towards him and began to strip off his gown. At that instant the friars' muleteers came up and asked what he was stripping him for. Sancho answered them that this fell to him lawfully as spoil of the battle which his lord Don Quixote had won. The muleteers, who did not understand all this about battles and spoils, seeing that Don Quixote was some distance off talking to the travelers in the coach, fell upon Sancho, knocked him down, and leaving hardly a hair in his beard, belabored him with kicks and left him stretched breathless and senseless on the ground; and without any more delay helped the friar to mount, who, trembling, terrified, and pale, as soon as he found himself in the saddle, spurred after his companion, who was standing at a distance looking on; then, not caring to wait for the end of the affair just begun, they pursued their journey making more crosses than if they had the devil after them.

Don Quixote was, as has been said, speaking to the lady in the coach: "Your beauty, lady mine," said he, "may now dispose of your person as may be most in accordance with your pleasure, for the pride of your ravishers lies prostrate on the ground through this strong arm of mine; and lest you should be pining to know the name of your deliverer, know that I am called Don Quixote of La Mancha, knight-errant and adventurer, and captive to the peerless and beautiful lady Dulcinea del Toboso: and in return for the service you have received of me I ask no more than that you should return to El Toboso, and on my behalf present yourself before that lady and tell her what I have done to set you free."

One of the squires in attendance upon the coach, a Biscayan, was listening to all Don Quixote was saying, and, perceiving that he would not allow the coach to go on, but was saying it must return at once to El Toboso, he made at him, and seizing his lance addressed him in bad Castilian, "Begone, caballero, and ill go with thee; by the God that made me, unless thou quittest coach, I shall slay thee!"

Don Quixote answered him very quietly, "If thou wert a knight, as thou art none, I should have already chastised thy folly and rashness, miserable creature." To which the Biscayan returned, "I no gentleman!"

"You will see presently," replied Don Quixote; and throwing his lance on

31

the ground he drew his sword, braced his buckler on his arm, and attacked the Biscayan, bent upon taking his life.

The Biscayan, when he saw him coming on, though he wished to dismount from his mule, in which, being one of those sorry ones let out for hire, he had no confidence, had no choice but to draw his sword; it was lucky for him, however, that he was near the coach, from which he was able to snatch a cushion that served him for a shield; and they went at one another as if they had been two mortal enemies. The others strove to make peace between, but could not.

The lady in the coach, amazed and terrified at what she saw, ordered the coachman to draw aside a little, and set herself to watch this severe struggle, in the course of which the Biscayan smote Don Quixote a mighty stroke on the shoulder over the top of his buckler, which, given to one without armor, would have cleft him to the waist. Don Quixote, feeling the weight of this prodigious blow, cried aloud, saying, "O lady of my soul, Dulcinea, flower of beauty, come to the aid of this your knight, who, in fulfilling his obligations to your beauty, finds himself in this extreme peril." To say this, to lift his sword, to shelter himself well behind his buckler, and to assail the Biscayan was the work of an instant, determined as he was to venture all upon a single blow. The Biscayan, seeing him come on in this way, was convinced of his courage by his spirited bearing, and resolved to follow his example, so he waited for him, keeping well under cover of his cushion, being unable to execute any sort of maneuver with his mule, which, dead tired and never meant for this kind of game, could not stir a step.

On came Don Quixote against the wary Biscayan, with uplifted sword and a firm intention of splitting him in half, while on his side the Biscayan waited for him sword in hand, and under the protection of his cushion. With trenchant swords upraised and poised on high, it seemed as though the two valiant and wrathful combatants stood threatening heaven, and earth, and hell, with such resolution and determination did they bear themselves. The fiery Biscayan was the first to strike a blow, which was delivered with such force and fury that had not the sword turned in its course, that single stroke would have sufficed to put an end to the bitter struggle and to all the adventures of our knight.

But that good fortune which reserved him for greater things, turned aside the sword of his adversary, so that although it smote him upon the left shoulder, it did him no more harm than to strip all that side of its armor, carrying

32

away a great part of his helmet with half of his ear, all which with fearful ruin fell to the ground, leaving him in a sorry plight.

Good God! Who is there that could properly describe the rage that filled the heart of our Manchegan when he saw himself dealt with in this fashion? All that can be said is, it was such that he again raised himself in his stirrups, and, grasping his sword more firmly with both hands, he came down on the Biscayan with such fury, smiting him full over the cushion and over the head, that—even so good a shield proving useless—as if a mountain had fallen on him, he began to bleed from nose, mouth, and ears, reeling as if about to fall backwards from his mule, as no doubt he would have done had he not flung his arms about its neck; at the same time, however, he slipped his feet out of the stirrups and then unclasped his arms, and the mule, taking fright at the terrible blow, made off across the plain, and with a few plunges flung its master to the ground. Don Quixote stood looking on very calmly, and, when he saw him fall, leaped from his horse and with great briskness ran to him, and, presenting the point of his sword to his eyes, bade him surrender, or he would cut his head off. The Biscayan was so bewildered that he was unable to answer a word, and it would have gone hard with him, so blind was Don Quixote, had not the ladies in the coach, who had hitherto been watching the combat in great terror, hastened to where he stood and implored him with earnest entreaties to grant them the great grace and favor of sparing their squire's life; to which Don Quixote replied with much gravity and dignity, "In truth, fair ladies, I am well content to do what ye ask of me; but it must be on one condition and understanding, which is that this knight promise me to go to the village of El Toboso, and on my behalf present himself before the peerless lady Dulcinea, that she deal with him as shall be most pleasing to her."

The terrified and disconsolate ladies, without discussing Don Quixote's demand or asking who Dulcinea might be, promised that their squire should do all that had been commanded.

"Then, on the faith of that promise," said Don Quixote, "I shall do him no further harm, though he well deserves it of me."

33

CHAPTER 8

Rocinante Forgets Himself

AFTER DON QUIXOTE took his leave, he and his squire turned off the road and passed into a wood and came to a halt in a glade covered with tender grass, beside which ran a pleasant cool stream that invited them to pass there the hours of the noontide heat, which by this time was beginning to come on oppressively. Don Quixote and Sancho dismounted, and turning Rocinante and the ass loose to feed on the grass that was there in abundance, they ransacked the saddlebags, and without any ceremony, very peacefully and sociably, master and man made their repast on what they found in them. Sancho had not thought it worth while to hobble Rocinante, feeling sure, from what he knew of his staidness, that all the mares in the Cordova pastures would not lead him into an impropriety.

Chance, however, and the devil, who is not always asleep, so ordained it that feeding in this valley there was a drove of Galician ponies belonging to certain Yanguesan carriers, whose way it is to take their midday rest with their teams in places and spots where grass and water abound; and where Don Quixote chanced to be suited the Yanguesans' purpose very well. It so happened, then, that Rocinante took a fancy to disport himself with their ladyships the ponies, and abandoning his usual gait and demeanor as he scented them, he, without asking leave of his master, got up a briskish little trot and hastened to make known his wishes to them. They, however, it seemed, preferred their pasture to him, and received him with their heels and teeth to such effect that they soon broke his girths and left him naked without a saddle

34

to cover him; but what must have been worse to him was that the carriers, seeing the violence he was offering to their mares, came running up armed with stakes, and so belabored him that they brought him sorely battered to the ground.

By this time Don Quixote and Sancho, who had witnessed the drubbing of Rocinante, came up panting, and said Don Quixote to Sancho:

"So far as I can see, friend Sancho, these are not knights but base folk of low birth: I mention it because thou canst lawfully aid me in taking due vengeance for the insult offered to Rocinante before our eyes."

"What the devil vengeance can we take," answered Sancho, "if they are more than twenty, and we no more than two, or, indeed, perhaps not more than one and a half?"

"I count for a hundred," replied Don Quixote, and without more words he drew his sword and attacked the Yanguesans, and incited and impelled by the example of his master, Sancho did the same; and to begin with, Don Quixote delivered a slash at one of them that laid open a great portion of his shoulder. The Yanguesans, seeing themselves assaulted by only two men while they were so many, betook themselves to their stakes, and driving the two into the middle they began to lay on with great zeal and energy. In fact, at the second blow they brought Sancho to the ground, and Don Quixote fared the same way, all his skill and high mettle availing him nothing, and fate willed it that he should fall at the feet of Rocinante, who had not yet risen; whereby it may be seen how furiously stakes can pound in angry boorish hands. Then, seeing the mischief they had done, the Yanguesans with all the haste they could loaded their team and pursued their journey, leaving the two adventurers a sorry sight and in sorrier mood.

Sancho was the first to come to, and finding himself close to his master he called to him in a weak and doleful voice, "Señor Don Quixote, ah, Señor Don Quixote!"

"What wouldst thou, brother Sancho?" answered Don Quixote in the same feeble suffering tone as Sancho.

"In how many days does your worship think we shall have the use of our feet?" asked Sancho Panza.

"For myself I must say I cannot guess how many," said the battered knight Don Quixote; "but I take all the blame upon myself, for I had no business to put hand to sword against men who were not dubbed knights like myself, and so I believe that in punishment for having transgressed the laws of chivalry

35

the God of battles has permitted this chastisement to be administered to me. For which reason, brother Sancho, when thou shalt see rabble of this sort offering us insult thou art not to wait till I draw sword against them, for I shall not do so at all; but do thou draw sword and chastise them to thy heart's content, and if any knights come to their aid I will take care to assail them with all my might; and thou hast already seen by a thousand proofs what the might of this strong arm of mine is equal to"—so uplifted had the poor gentleman become through the victory over the stout Biscayan.

But Sancho did not fully approve of his master's admonition. "Señor," he replied, "I am a man of peace, and I can put up with any affront because I have a wife and children to support; so let it be a hint to your worship, as it cannot be a mandate, that on no account will I draw sword either against clown or against knight, and that here before God I forgive the insults that have been offered me, whether they have been, are, or shall be offered me by high or low, rich or poor, noble or commoner."

To which his master said in reply, "I wish the pain I feel on this side would abate so as to let me explain to thee, Panza, the mistake thou makest. Come now, sinner, suppose the wind of fortune should turn in our favor, filling the sails of our desires so that we put into port in one of those islands I have promised thee. How would it be with thee if on winning it I made thee lord of it? It is essential that the new possessor should have good sense to enable him to govern, and valor to attack and defend himself, whatever may befall him."

"In what has now befallen us," answered Sancho, "I'd have been well pleased to have that good sense and that valor your worship speaks of, but I swear on the faith of a poor man I am more fit for plasters than for arguments. See if you worship can get up, and let us help Rocinante, though he does not deserve it, for he was the main cause of all this thrashing. I never thought it of Rocinante, for I took him to be a virtuous person and as quiet as myself. After all, they say right that it takes a long time to come to know people, and that there is nothing sure in this life. Who would have said that, after such mighty slashes as your worship gave that unlucky knight-errant, there was coming at the very heels of them, such a great storm of sticks as has fallen upon our shoulders?"

"Know, friend Sancho," answered Don Quixote, "that the life of knights-errant is subject to a thousand dangers and reverses. And I would have thee know also, Sancho, that wounds caused by any instruments which happen by chance to be in hand inflict no indignity, and this is laid down in the law of

Chance was conducting their affairs for them from good to better.

the duel in express words. I say this lest thou shouldst imagine that because we have been drubbed in this affray we have therefore suffered any indignity; for the arms those men carried, with which they pounded us, were nothing more than their stakes, and not one of them, so far as I remember, carried rapier, sword, or dagger."

"They gave me no time to see that much," answered Sancho. "And thinking of whether all those stake-strokes were an indignity or not gives me no uneasiness, which the pain of the blows does, for they will remain as deeply impressed on my memory as on my shoulders."

"No more of that: pluck strength out of weakness, Sancho, as I mean to do," returned Don Quixote, "and let us see how Rocinante is, for it seems to me that not the least share of this mishap has fallen to the lot of the poor beast."

"There is nothing wonderful in that," replied Sancho, "since he is a knight-errant too; what I wonder at is that my beast should have come off scot-free where we come out scotched."

"Fortune always leaves a door open in adversity in order to bring relief to it," said Don Quixote. "This little beast may now supply the want of Rocinante, carrying me hence to some castle where I may be cured of my wounds. So, friend Panza, say no more, but get up as well as thou canst and put me on top of thy beast, and let us go hence ere night come on and surprise us in these wilds."

Sancho raised himself, stopping halfway bent like a Turkish bow without power to bring himself upright, but with all his pains he saddled his ass, who too had gone astray somewhat, yielding to the excessive license of the day. He next raised up Rocinante, and as for him, had he possessed a tongue to complain with, most assuredly neither Sancho nor his master would have been behind him.

Sancho fixed Don Quixote on the ass and secured Rocinante with a leading rein, and taking the ass by the halter, he proceeded more or less in the direction in which it seemed to him the high road might be. And, as chance was conducting their affairs for them from good to better, he had not gone a short league when the road came in sight, and on it he perceived an inn, which to his annoyance and to the delight of Don Quixote must needs be a castle. Sancho insisted that it was an inn, and his master that it was not one, but a castle, and the dispute lasted so long that before the point was settled they had time to reach it, and into it Sancho entered without any further controversy.

37

CHAPTER 9

Sancho Gets the Blanket

THE INNKEEPER, seeing Don Quixote slung across the ass, asked Sancho what was amiss with him. Sancho answered that it was nothing, only that he had fallen down from a rock and had his ribs a little bruised. The innkeeper had a wife whose disposition was not such as those of her calling commonly have, for she was by nature kind-hearted, and so she at once set about tending Don Quixote, and made her young daughter, a very comely girl, help her in taking care of her guest. There was besides in the inn, a servant, an Asturian lass with a broad face and snub nose, blind of one eye and not very sound in the other. This graceful lass, then, helped the young girl, and the two made up a very bad bed for Don Quixote in a garret that showed evident signs of having formerly served for many years as a straw-loft.

On this accursed bed Don Quixote stretched himself, and the hostess and her daughter soon covered him with plasters from top to toe, while Maritornes, the Asturian maid, held the light for them; and while plastering him, the hostess, observing how full of weals Don Quixote was in some places, remarked that this had more the look of blows than of a fall.

It was not blows, Sancho said, but that the rock had many points and projections, and that each of them had left its mark. "Pray, señora," he added, "manage to save some plasters, as there will be no want of someone to use them, for I too am rather sore."

"Then you must have fallen too," said the hostess.

"I did not fall," said Sancho Panza, "but from the shock I got at seeing my master fall, my body aches so that I feel as if I had had a thousand whacks."

"How is the gentleman called?" asked Maritornes, the Asturian.

"Don Quixote of La Mancha," answered Sancho Panza, "and he is a knight-adventurer, and one of the best and stoutest that have been seen in the world this long time past."

"What is a knight-adventurer?" said the lass.

"Are you so new in the world as not to know?" answered Sancho Panza. "Well, then, you must know, sister, that a knight-adventurer is a thing that in two words is seen drubbed and emperor, that is today the most miserable and needy being in the world, and tomorrow will have two or three crowns of kingdoms to give his squire."

"Then how is it," said the hostess, "that belonging to so good a master as this, you have not, to judge by appearances, even so much as a county?"

"It is too soon yet," answered Sancho, "for we have not been long going in quest of adventures. However, if my master Don Quixote gets well of this wound, or fall, and I am left none the worse of it, I would not change my hopes for the best title in Spain."

To all this conversation Don Quixote was listening very attentively, and sitting up in bed as well as he could, and taking the hostess by the hand he said to her, "Believe me, fair lady, you may call yourself fortunate in having sheltered my person, which is such that if I do not myself praise it, it is because self-praise debaseth. I shall preserve forever inscribed on my memory the service you have rendered me in order to tender you my gratitude while life shall last me."

The hostess, her daughter, and Maritornes listened in bewilderment to the words of the knight-errant, and wondered to themselves, for he seemed to them a man of a different sort from those they were used to. Thanking him for his civility, they left him, while the Asturian gave her attention to Sancho, who needed it no less than his master.

For a while Don Quixote with the pain of his ribs had his eyes as wide open as a hare's. The inn was all in silence, and in the whole of it there was no light except that given by a lantern that hung burning in the middle of the gateway. Presently the knight slept and lay sleeping several hours, at the end of which he awoke and felt very great bodily relief and so much ease from his bruises that he thought himself quite cured. He was eager to take his departure at once in quest of adventures, as it seemed to him that all the time he loitered there was a fraud upon the world and those in it who stood in need of his help and protection; so he saddled Rocinante himself and put the pack-saddle on his squire's beast, whom likewise he helped to dress and mount the ass; after which he mounted his horse and turning to a corner of the inn he laid hold of a pike that stood there, to serve him by way of a lance. All who were in the inn, more than twenty persons, stood watching him.

As soon as they were both mounted, at the gate of the inn, Don Quixote called to the host and said in a very grave and measured voice, "Many and great are the favors, Señor Alcaide, that I have received in this castle of yours, and I remain under the deepest obligation to be grateful to you for them all the days of my life. If I can repay them in avenging you of any arrogant foe who may have wronged you, only tell me of it, and I promise you by the order of knighthood to procure you satisfaction and reparation to the utmost of your desire."

The innkeeper replied to him with equal calmness, "Sir Knight, I do not want your worship to avenge me of any wrong, because when any is done me I can take what vengeance seems good to me. The only thing I want is that you pay me the score that you have run up in the inn last night, as well for the straw and barley for your two beasts, as for supper and beds."

"Then this is an inn?" said Don Quixote.

"And a very respectable one," said the innkeeper.

"I have been under a mistake all this time," answered Don Quixote, "for in truth I thought it was a castle, and not a bad one. But since it appears that it is not a castle but an inn, all that can be done now is that you should excuse the payment, for I cannot break the rule of knights-errant, who I know never paid for lodging or anything else in the inn where they might be; for any hospitality that might be offered them is their due by right in return for the insufferable toil they endure in seeking adventures by night and by day, exposed to all the inclemencies of heaven and all the hardships of earth."

"I have little to do with that," replied the innkeeper; "pay me what you owe me, and let us have no more talk of chivalry, for all I care about is to get my money."

"You are a stupid, scurvy innkeeper," said Don Quixote, and putting spurs to Rocinante and bringing his pike to the slope he rode out of the inn before anyone could stop him, and pushed on some distance without looking to see if his squire was following him.

The innkeeper, when he saw him go without paying him, ran to get payment of Sancho, who said that as his master would not pay neither would he,

40

because, being as he was squire to a knight-errant, the same rule and reason held good for him as for his master. At this the innkeeper waxed very wroth, and threatened if he did not pay to compel him in a way that he would not like. To which Sancho made answer that by the law of chivalry his master had received he would not pay a rap, though it cost him his life.

Unfortunately for Sancho, there were among the company in the inn four woolcarders from Segovia, three needlemakers from the Colt of Cordova, and two lodgers from the Fair of Seville, lively fellows, tenderhearted, fond of a joke, and playful, who, almost as if moved by a common impulse, came to Sancho and dismounted him from his ass, while one of them went in for the blanket of the host's bed. But on flinging him into it they looked up, and seeing that the ceiling was somewhat lower than what they required for their work, they decided to go out into the yard, which was bounded by the sky, and there, putting Sancho in the middle of the blanket, they began to raise him high.

The cries of the poor blanketed wretch were so loud that they reached the ears of his master, who, halting to listen attentively, was persuaded that some new adventure was coming, until he clearly perceived that it was his squire who uttered them.

Wheeling about, he came up to the inn at a laborious gallop, and finding it shut went round it to see if he could find some way of getting in; but as soon as he came to the wall of the yard, which was not very high, he discovered the game that was being played with his squire. He saw him rising and falling in the air with such grace and nimbleness that, had his rage allowed him, it is my belief he would have laughed. He tried to climb from his horse on to the top of the wall, but he was so bruised and battered that he could not even dismount; and so from the back of his horse he began to utter such maledictions and objurgations against those who were blanketing Sancho as it would be impossible to write down accurately. They, however, did not stay their laughter or their work for this, nor did the flying Sancho cease his lamentations, mingled now with threats, now with entreaties but all to little purpose, or none at all, until from pure weariness they left off. They then brought him his ass, and mounting him on top of it they put his jacket round him; and the compassionate Maritornes, seeing him so exhausted, thought fit to refresh him with a jug of water, and that it might be all the cooler she fetched it from the well. Sancho took it, and began drinking; but as at the first sup he perceived it was water he did not care to go on with it, and begged Maritornes to fetch him some wine, which she did with right good will, and paid for it with her own money.

When Sancho had done drinking he dug his heels into his ass, and the gate of the inn being thrown open he passed out very well pleased at having paid nothing and carried his point, though it had been at the expense of his usual sureties, his shoulders. It is true that the innkeeper detained his saddlebags in payment of what was owing to him, but Sancho took his departure in such a flurry that he never missed them. The innkeeper, as soon as he saw him off, wanted to bar the gate close, but the blanketeers would not agree to it, for they were fellows who would not have cared two farthings for Don Quixote, even had he been really one of the knights-errant of the Round Table.

CHAPTER 10

Two "Armies" Meet

SANCHO REACHED his master so limp and faint that he could not urge on his beast. When Don Quixote saw the state he was in he said, "I have now come to the conclusion, good Sancho, that this castle or inn is beyond a doubt enchanted, because when I was by the wall of the yard witnessing the acts of thy sad tragedy, it was out of my power to mount upon it, nor could I even dismount from Rocinante, because they no doubt had me enchanted; for I swear to thee that if I had been able to climb up or dismount, I would have avenged thee in such a way that those braggart thieves would have remembered their prank forever."

"I would have avenged myself too if I could," said Sancho, "and for my part I believe those who amused themselves with me were not enchanted, as your worship says, but men of flesh and bone like ourselves; so that, señor, your not being able to leap over the wall of the yard or dismount from your horse came of something else besides enchantments; and what I make out clearly from all this is, that these adventures we go seeking will in the end lead us into such misadventures that we shall not know which is our right foot; and that the best and wisest thing, according to my small wits, would be for us to return home, now that it is harvesttime, and attend to our business."

"How little thou knowest about chivalry, Sancho," replied Don Quixote. "Have patience; the day will come when thou shalt see what an honorable thing it is to pursue this calling; nay, tell me, what delight can equal that of winning a battle, and triumphing over one's enemy? None, beyond all doubt."

"Very likely," answered Sancho, "though we have never won any battle ex-

43

cept the one with the Biscayan, and even out of that your worship came with half an ear and half a helmet the less."

Thus talking, Don Quixote and his squire were going along, when, on the road they were following, Don Quixote perceived approaching them a large and thick cloud of dust, on seeing which he turned to Sancho and said:

"This is the day, O Sancho, on which I shall do deeds that shall remain written in the book of fame for all ages to come. Seest thou that cloud of dust which rises yonder? Well, then, all that is churned up by a vast army composed of various and countless nations that comes marching there."

"According to that there must be two," said Sancho, "for on this opposite side also there rises just such another cloud of dust."

Don Quixote turned to look and found that it was true, and rejoicing exceedingly, he concluded that they were two armies about to engage and encounter in the midst of that broad plain. Now the cloud of dust he had seen was raised by two great droves of sheep coming along the same road in opposite directions, which, because of the dust, did not become visible until they drew near, but Don Quixote asserted so positively that they were armies that Sancho was led to believe it and say, "Well, and what are we to do, señor?"

"What?" said Don Quixote: "give aid and assistance to the weak and those who need it; and thou must know, Sancho, that this which comes opposite to us is conducted and led by the mighty emperor Alifanfaron, lord of the great isle of Trapobana; this other that marches behind me is that of his enemy Pentapolin, the king of the Garamantas."

"But why are these two lords such enemies?"

"They are at enmity," replied Don Quixote, "because this Alifanfaron is a pagan and is in love with the daughter of Pentapolin, who is a very beautiful and moreover gracious lady, and a Christian, and her father is unwilling to bestow her upon the pagan king."

"By my beard," said Sancho, "but Pentapolin does quite right, and I will help him as much as I can."

"In that thou wilt do what is thy duty, Sancho," said Don Quixote, "for to engage in battles of this sort it is not requisite to be a dubbed knight."

They placed themselves on a rising ground from which the two droves that Don Quixote made armies of might have been plainly seen if the clouds of dust they raised had not obscured them; nevertheless, seeing in his imagination what did not exist, he began thus in a loud voice:

"That knight whom thou seest yonder in yellow armor, who bears upon his

44

shield a lion crowned crouching at the feet of a damsel, is the valiant Laurcalco, lord of the Silver Bridge; that one in armor with flowers of gold, who bears on his shield three crowns argent on an azure field, is the dreaded Micocolembo, grand duke of Quirocia."

And so he went on naming a number of knights of one squadron or the other out of his imagination. Sancho Panza hung upon his words without speaking, and from time to time turned to try if he could see the knights and giants his master was describing, and as he could not make out one of them he said to him:

"Señor, devil take it if there's a sign of any man you talk of, knight or giant, in the whole thing; maybe it's all enchantment."

"How canst thou say that!" answered Don Quixote. "Dost thou not hear the neighing of the steeds, the braying of the trumpets, the roll of the drums?"

"I hear nothing but a great bleating of ewes and sheep," said Sancho; which was true, for by this time the two flocks had come close.

"The fear thou art in, Sancho," said Don Quixote, "prevents thee from seeing or hearing correctly, for one of the effects of fear is to derange the senses and make things appear different from what they are; if thou art in such fear, withdraw to one side and leave me to myself, for alone I suffice to bring victory to that side to which I shall give my aid." And so saying he gave Rocinante the spur, and putting the lance in rest, shot down the slope like a thunderbolt. Sancho shouted after him, crying, "Come back, Señor Don Quixote; I vow to God they are sheep and ewes you are charging! Come back! What madness is this!"

But not for all these entreaties did Don Quixote turn back; on the contrary he went on shouting out, "Ho, knights, ye who fight under the banners of the valiant emperor Pentapolin, follow me all; ye shall see how easily I shall give him his revenge over his enemy."

So saying, he dashed into the midst of the squadron of ewes, and began spearing them with as much spirit as if he were transfixing mortal enemies in earnest. The shepherds and drovers accompanying the flock shouted to him to desist; seeing it was no use, they ungirt their slings and began to salute his ears with stones as big as one's fist. Don Quixote gave no heed to the stones, but, letting drive right and left, kept saying:

"Where art thou, proud Alifanfaron? Come before me!" Here came a rock from the brook that struck him on the side and buried a couple of ribs in his body. Then came two more stones which struck him on the hand and on the

45

face, knocking three or four teeth and grinders out of his mouth, and sorely crushing two fingers of his hand. Such was the force of the first blow and of the second, that the poor knight in spite of himself came down backwards off his horse. The shepherds came up, and felt sure they had killed him; so in all haste they collected their flock together, took up the dead beasts, of which there were more than seven, and made off without waiting to ascertain anything further.

All this time Sancho stood on the hill watching the crazy feats his master was performing, and cursing the hour and the occasion when fortune had made him acquainted with him. Seeing him, then, brought to the ground, and that the shepherds had taken themselves off, he ran to him and found him in very bad case, though not unconscious; and said he:

"Did I not tell you to come back, Señor Don Quixote; and that what you were going to attack were not armies but droves of sheep?"

"That's how that thief of a sage, my enemy, can alter and falsify things," answered Don Quixote. "It is a very easy matter for those of his sort to make us believe what they choose; and this malignant being who persecutes me, envious of the glory he knew I was to win in this battle, has turned the squadrons of the enemy into droves of sheep. But come hither, Sancho, and see how many of my teeth and grinders are missing, for I feel as if there was not one left in my mouth."

Sancho put his fingers in Don Quixote's mouth, and feeling about, asked him, "How many grinders used your worship to have on this side?"

"Four," replied Don Quixote, "besides the back tooth, all whole and quite sound."

"Mind what you are saying, señor."

"I say four, if not five," answered Don Quixote, "for never in my life have I had tooth or grinder drawn, nor has any fallen out."

"Well, then," said Sancho, "in this lower side your worship has no more than two grinders and a half, and in the upper neither a half nor any at all, for it is all as smooth as the palm of my hand."

"Luckless that I am!" said Don Quixote, hearing the sad news his squire gave him. "I had rather they despoiled me of an arm, so it were not the sword-arm; for I tell thee, Sancho, a mouth without teeth is like a mill without a millstone, and a tooth is much more to be prized than a diamond; but we who profess the austere order of chivalry are liable to all this."

Sancho ran to his ass to get something wherewith to relieve his master's pain out of his saddlebags; but not finding them, he well nigh took leave of his senses, and cursed himself anew, and in his heart resolved to quit his master and return home, even though he forfeited the wages of his service and all hopes of the promised island.

Don Quixote now rose, and putting his left hand to his mouth to keep his teeth from falling out altogether, with the other he laid hold of the bridle of Rocinante, who had never stirred from his master's side—so loyal and well-behaved was he—and betook himself to where the squire stood leaning over his ass with his hand to his cheek, like one in deep dejection. Seeing him in this mood, looking so sad, Don Quixote said to him:

"Bear in mind, Sancho, it is impossible for good or evil to last forever; and hence it follows that the evil having lasted long, the good must be now nigh at hand; so thou must not distress thyself at the misfortunes which happen to me, since thou hast no share in them."

"How have I not?" replied Sancho; "was he whom they blanketed yesterday perchance any other than my father's son? And the saddlebags that are missing today with all my treasures, did they belong to any other but myself?"

"What! Are the saddlebags missing, Sancho?" said Don Quixote.

"Yes, they are missing," answered Sancho.

"In that case we have nothing to eat today," replied Don Quixote.

"It would be so," answered Sancho, "if there were none of the herbs your worship says you know in these meadows, those with which knights-errant as unlucky as your worship are wont to supply such-like shortcomings."

"For all that," answered Don Quixote, "I would rather have just now a loaf of bread than all the herbs described. Nevertheless, Sancho the Good, mount thy beast and come along with me, for God, who provides for all things, will not fail us."

"Well, be it as your worship says," replied Sancho. "Let us be off now and find some place of shelter for the night, and God grant it may be somewhere where there are no blankets, nor blanketeers, nor phantoms, nor enchanted Moors; for if there are, may the devil take the whole concern."

"Ask that of God, my son," said Don Quixote, "and do thou lead on where thou wilt, for this time I leave our lodging to thy choice."

CHAPTER 11

Don Quixote Saves a Corpse

SANCHO PROCEEDED in the direction in which he thought they might find refuge without quitting the high road, which was there very much frequented. As they went along, night overtook them before they had discovered any place of shelter; and what made it still worse was that they were dying of hunger, for with the loss of the saddlebags they had lost their entire larder; and to complete the misfortune they met with an adventure which without any invention had really the appearance of one. It so happened that the night closed in somewhat darkly, but for all that they pushed on, Sancho feeling sure that as the road was the king's highway they might reasonably expect to find some inn within a league or two. Going along, then, they saw coming towards them on the road they were traveling a great number of lights which looked exactly like stars in motion. Sancho was taken aback at the sight of them, nor did Don Quixote altogether relish them: the one pulled up his ass by the halter, the other his hack by the bridle, and they stood still, watching anxiously to see what all this would turn out to be, and found that the lights were approaching them, and the nearer they came the greater they seemed, at which spectacle Sancho began to shake, and Don Quixote's hair stood on end; he, however, plucking up spirit a little, said:

"This, no doubt, Sancho, will be a most mighty and perilous adventure, in which it will be needful for me to put forth all my valor and resolution."

"Unlucky me!" answered Sancho; "if this adventure happens to be one of phantoms, as I am beginning to think it is, where shall I find the ribs to bear it?"

"For all that," replied Don Quixote, "I entreat thee, Sancho, to keep a good heart, for experience will tell thee what mine is."

"I will, please God," answered Sancho, and the two retiring to one side of the road set themselves to observe closely what all these moving lights might be; and very soon afterwards they made out some twenty *encamisados,* all on horseback, with lighted torches in their hands, the awe-inspiring aspect of whom completely extinguished the courage of Sancho. His heart sank and his teeth chattered when they perceived distinctly that behind them there came a litter covered over with black and followed by six more mounted figures in mourning down to the very feet of their mules. And as the *encamisados* came along they muttered to themselves in a low plaintive tone. This strange spectacle at such an hour and in such a solitary place was quite enough to strike terror into Sancho's heart, but it was just the opposite with his master, whose imagination immediately conjured up all this to him vividly as one of the adventures of his books.

He took it into his head that the litter was a bier on which was borne some sorely wounded or slain knight, to avenge whom was a task reserved for him alone; and without any further reasoning he laid his lance in rest, fixed himself firmly in his saddle, and with gallant spirit and bearing took up his position in the middle of the road where the *encamisados* must of necessity pass; and as soon as he saw them near at hand he raised his voice and said:

"Halt, knights, or whosoever ye may be, and render me account of who ye are, whence ye come, where ye go, what it is ye carry upon that bier, for, to judge by appearances, either ye have done some wrong or some wrong has been done to you, and it is fitting and necessary that I should know, either that I may chastise you for the evil ye have done, or else that I may avenge you for the injury that has been inflicted upon you."

"We are in haste," answered one of the *encamisados,* "and the inn is far off, and we cannot stop to render you such an account as you demand"; and spurring his mule he moved on.

Don Quixote was mightily provoked by this answer, and seizing the mule by the bridle he said, "Halt, and be more mannerly, and render an account of what I have asked of you; else, take my defiance to combat, all of you."

The mule was shy, and was so frightened at her bridle being seized that

49

rearing up she flung her rider to the ground over her haunches. An attendant who was on foot, seeing the *encamisado* fall, began to abuse Don Quixote, who now moved to anger, without any more ado, laying his lance in rest charged one of the men in mourning and brought him badly wounded to the ground, and as he wheeled round upon the others the agility with which he attacked and routed them was a sight to see, for it seemed just as if wings had that instant grown upon Rocinante, so lightly and proudly did he bear himself. The *encamisados* were all timid folk and unarmed, so they speedily made their escape from the fray and set off at a run across the plain with their lighted torches. The mourners, too, enveloped and swathed in their skirts and gowns, were unable to bestir themselves, and so with entire safety to himself Don Quixote belabored them all and drove them off against their will, for they all thought it was no man but a devil from hell come to carry away the dead body they had in the litter.

Sancho beheld all this in astonishment at the intrepidity of his lord, and said to himself, "Clearly this master of mine is as bold and valiant as he says he is."

A burning torch lay on the ground near the first man whom the mule had thrown, by the light of which Don Quixote perceived him, and coming up to him he presented the point of the lance to his face, calling on him to yield himself prisoner, or else he would kill him; to which the prostrate man replied, "I am prisoner enough as it is; I cannot stir, for one of my legs is broken. I entreat you, if you be a Christian gentleman, not to kill me, which will be committing grave sacrilege, for I am a licentiate and I hold first orders."

"Then what the devil brought you here, being a churchman?" said Don Quixote.

"What, señor?" said the other. "My bad luck."

"Then still worse awaits you," said Don Quixote, "if you do not satisfy me as to all I asked you at first."

"You shall be soon satisfied," said the licentiate. "My name is Alonzo Lopez. I come from the city of Baeza with eleven others, priests, the same who fled with the torches, and we are going to the city of Segovia accompanying a dead body which is in that litter, and is that of a gentleman who died in Baeza, where he was interred; and now, as I said, we are taking his bones to their burial-place, which is in Segovia, where he was born."

"And who killed him?" asked Don Quixote.

"God, by means of a malignant fever that took him," answered the bachelor.

"In that case," said Don Quixote, "the Lord has relieved me of the task of avenging his death had any other slain him. I would have your reverence know that I am a knight of La Mancha, Don Quixote by name, and it is my calling to roam the world righting wrongs and redressing injuries."

"I do not know how that about righting wrongs can be," said the bachelor, "for from straight you have made me crooked, leaving me with a broken leg that will never see itself straight again all the days of its life. I entreat you, sir knight-errant, whose errand has been such an evil one for me, to help me to get from under this mule that holds one of my legs caught between the stirrup and the saddle."

"I would have talked on till tomorrow," said Don Quixote. "How long were you going to wait before telling me of your distress?"

He at once called to Sancho, who, however, had no mind to come, as he was just then engaged in unloading a sumpter mule, well laden with provender which these worthy gentlemen had brought with them. Sancho made a bag of his coat, and, getting together as much as he could, and as the bag would hold, he loaded his beast, and then hastened to obey his master's call, and helped him to remove the licentiate from under the mule; then putting him on her back he gave him the torch, and Don Quixote bade him follow the track of his companions, and beg pardon of them on his part for the wrong which he could not help doing them.

And said Sancho, "If by chance these gentlemen should want to know who was the hero that served them so, your worship may tell them that he is the famous Don Quixote of La Mancha, otherwise called the Knight of the Rueful Countenance."

The licentiate took his departure, without making any reply. Don Quixote asked Sancho what had induced him to call him the "Knight of the Rueful Countenance" more then than at any other time.

"I will tell you," answered Sancho; "it was because I have been looking at you for some time by the light of the torch held by that unfortunate, and verily your worship has got of late the most ill-favored countenance I ever saw: it must be either owing to the fatigue of this combat, or else to the want of teeth and grinders."

51

Don Quixote laughed at Sancho; nevertheless he resolved to call himself by that name, and have his shield painted as he had devised.

Don Quixote would have looked to see whether the body in the litter were bones or not, but Sancho would not have it, saying:

"Señor, you have ended this perilous adventure more safely for yourself than any of those I have seen: perhaps these people, though beaten and routed, may bethink themselves that it is a single man that has beaten them, and feeling ashamed of it may take heart and come in search of us and give us trouble enough. The ass is in proper trim, the mountains are near at hand, hunger presses, we have nothing more to do but make good our retreat, and, as the saying is, the dead to the grave and the living to the loaf."

And driving his ass before him he begged his master to follow, who, feeling that Sancho was right, did so without replying; and after proceeding some little distance between two hills they found themselves in a wide and retired valley, where they alighted, and Sancho unloaded his beast; and stretched upon the green grass, with hunger for sauce, they breakfasted, dined, lunched, and supped all at once, satisfying their appetites with more than one store of cold meat which the dead man's clerical gentlemen (who seldom put themselves on short allowance) had brought with them on their sumpter mule. But they had no wine to drink, nor even water to moisten their lips. And as thirst tormented them, Sancho, observing that the meadow where they were was full of green and tender grass, said:

"It cannot be, señor, but that this grass is a proof that there must be hard by some spring or brook to give it moisture, so it would be well to move a little farther on, that we may find some place where we may quench our thirst."

The advice seemed good to Don Quixote, and, he leading Rocinante by the bridle and Sancho the ass by a halter, they advanced up the meadow.

CHAPTER 12

Unparalleled Achievement

FEELING THEIR WAY, for the darkness of the night made it impossible to see anything, they had not gone two hundred paces when a loud noise of water, as if falling from great high rocks, struck their ears. The sound cheered them greatly; but halting to make out by listening from what quarter it came they heard unseasonably another noise which spoiled the satisfaction the sound of the water gave them, especially for Sancho, who was by nature timid and faint-hearted. They heard strokes falling with a measured beat, and a certain rattling of iron and chains that, together with the furious din of the water, would have struck terror into any heart but Don Quixote's. They had happened to reach a spot in among some tall trees, whose leaves stirred by a gentle breeze made a low ominous sound; so that, what with the solitude, the place, the darkness, the noise of the water, and the rustling of the leaves, everything inspired awe and dread; more especially as they perceived that the strokes did not cease, nor the wind lull, nor morning approach. But Don Quixote, supported by his intrepid heart, leaped on Rocinante, and bracing his buckler on his arm, brought his pike to the slope, and said, "Friend Sancho, know that I by Heaven's will have been born in this our iron age to revive in it the age of gold, or the golden as it is called; I am he for whom perils, mighty achievements, and valiant deeds are reserved; I am, I say again, he who is to revive the Knights of the Round Table, and to consign to oblivion the whole herd of famous knights-errant of days gone by, performing in these in which I live such exploits, marvels, and feats of arms as shall obscure their brightest deeds. Thou dost mark well, faithful and trusty squire, the gloom of this night, its strange silence, the awful sound of that water and that incessant hammering that wounds and pains our ears. Well, then, all this that I put before thee is but an incentive to my spirit; therefore tighten Rocinante's girths a little, and God be with thee; wait for me here three days and no more, and if in that time I come not back, thou canst return to our village, and thence, to do me a favor, thou wilt go to El Toboso, where thou shalt say to my incomparable lady Dulcinea that her captive knight hath died in attempting things that might make him worthy of being called hers."

When Sancho heard his master's words he began to weep in the most pathetic way, saying:

"Señor, I know not why your worship wants to attempt this so dreadful adventure; it is night now, no one sees us here, we can easily turn about and take ourselves out of danger, even if we don't drink for three days to come; and as there is no one to see us, all the less will there be anyone to set us down as cowards; besides, I have many a time heard the curate of our village, whom your worship knows well, preach that he who seeks danger perishes in it. And if this does not soften that hard heart, let this thought move it, that you will have hardly quitted this spot when from pure fear I shall yield my soul up to anyone that will take it. I left home and wife and children to come and serve your worship, trusting to do better and not worse; but as covetousness bursts the bag, it has rent my hopes asunder, for just as I had them highest about getting that wretched unlucky island your worship has so often promised me, I see that instead you mean to desert me now in a place so far from human reach: for God's sake, master mine, deal not so unjustly by me, and if your worship will not entirely give up attempting this feat, at least put it off till morning, for the lore I learned when I was a shepherd tells me it cannot be three hours till dawn now."

"It shall not be said of me now or at any time," replied Don Quixote, "that tears or entreaties turned me aside from doing what was in accordance with knightly usage; and so I beg of thee, Sancho, to hold thy peace, for God, who has put it into my heart to undertake now this terrible adventure, will take care to watch over my safety and console thy sorrow; what thou hast to do is to tighten Rocinante's girths well, and wait here, for I shall come back shortly, alive or dead."

Sancho perceiving it his master's resolve, and how little his entreaties pre-

54

vailed with him, determined to have recourse to his own ingenuity and compel him, if he could, to wait till daylight; and so, while tightening the girths of the horse, he quietly and without being felt, with his ass's halter tied both Rocinante's legs, so that when Don Quixote strove to go he was unable as the horse could only move by jumps. Seeing the success of his trick, Sancho Panza said:

"See there, señor! Heaven, moved by my prayers, has so ordered it that Rocinante cannot stir; and if you will be obstinate, and spur him, you will only provoke fortune, and kick, as they say, against the pricks."

Don Quixote at this grew desperate, but the more he drove his heels into the horse, the less he stirred him; and not having any suspicion of the tying, he resigned himself to wait till daybreak or until Rocinante could move, firmly persuaded that all this came of something other than Sancho's ingenuity. So he said to him, "As it is so, Sancho, and as Rocinante cannot move, I am content to wait till dawn smiles upon us, even though I weep while it delays its coming."

"There is no need to weep," answered Sancho, "for I will amuse your worship by telling stories from this till daylight, unless you would like to dismount and lie down to sleep a little on the green grass after the fashion of knights-errant, so as to be fresher when day comes and the moment arrives for attempting this extraordinary adventure you are looking forward to."

"What art thou talking about dismounting or sleeping for?" said Don Quixote. "Am I, thinkest thou, one of those knights that take their rest in the presence of danger? Sleep, thou who art born to sleep, or do as thou wilt, for I will act as I think most consistent with my character."

"Be not angry, master mine," replied Sancho, "I did not mean to say that." And coming close to him he laid one hand on the pommel of the saddle and the other on the cantle, not daring to separate a finger's width from him; so much afraid was he of the strokes which still resounded with a regular beat. Don Quixote bade him tell some story to amuse him as he had proposed, to which Sancho replied that he would if his dread of what he heard would let him. "Still," said he, "I will strive to tell a story which, if I can manage to relate it, and nobody interferes with the telling, is the best of stories, and let your worship give me your attention, for here I begin.

"I say then," continued Sancho, "that in a village of Estremadura there was a goat-shepherd—that is to say, one who tended goats—which shepherd

55

or goatherd, as my story goes, was called Lope Ruiz, and this Lope Ruiz was in love with a shepherdess called Torralva, which shepherdess called Torralva was the daughter of a rich grazier, and this rich grazier—"

"If that is the way thou tellest thy tale, Sancho," said Don Quixote, "repeating twice all thou hast to say, thou wilt not have done these two days; go straight on with it, and tell it like a reasonable man, or else say nothing."

"Tales are always told in my country in the very way I am telling this," answered Sancho, "and I cannot tell it in any other, nor is it right of your worship to ask me to make new customs."

"Tell it as thou wilt," replied Don Quixote; "and as fate will have it that I cannot help listening to thee, go on."

"And so, lord of my soul," continued Sancho, "as I have said, this shepherd was in love with Torralva the shepherdess, a wild buxom lass. And in course of time, the devil, who never sleeps, contrived that the love the shepherd bore the shepherdess turned into hatred, and the reason, according to evil tongues, was some little jealousy she caused him that crossed the line and trespassed on forbidden ground; and so much did the shepherd hate her from that time forward that, in order to escape from her, he determined to quit the country and go where he should never set eyes on her again. Torralva, when she found herself spurned by Lope, was immediately smitten with love for him, though she had never loved him before."

"That is the natural way of women," said Don Quixote, "to scorn the one that loves them, and love the one that hates them: go on, Sancho."

"It came to pass," said Sancho, "that the shepherd carried out his intention, and driving his goats before him took his way across the plains of Estremadura to pass over into Portugal. Torralva, who knew of it, went after him, and on foot followed him at a distance. The shepherd, they say, came with his flock to cross over the river Guadiana, which was at that time swollen and almost overflowing its banks, and at the spot he came to there was neither boat nor anyone to carry him or his flock to the other side, at which he was much vexed, for he perceived that Torralva was approaching and would give him great annoyance with her tears and entreaties. However, he went looking about so closely that he discovered a fisherman who had alongside of him a boat so small that it could only hold one person and one goat; but for all that he spoke to him and agreed with him to carry himself and his three hundred goats across. The fisherman got into the boat and carried one goat over; he came back and carried another over; he came back again, and again brought

"What art thou talking about dismounting for?"

over another—let your worship keep count of the goats the fisherman is taking across, for if one escapes the memory there will be an end of the story, and it will be impossible to tell another word of it. To proceed, I must tell you the landing place on the other side was slippery, and the fisherman lost a great deal of time in going and coming; still he returned for another goat, and another, and another."

"Take it for granted he brought them all across," said Don Quixote, "and don't keep going and coming in this way, or thou wilt not make an end of bringing them over this twelvemonth."

"How many have gone across so far?" said Sancho.

"How the devil do I know?" replied Don Quixote.

"There it is," said Sancho, "what I told you, that you must keep a good count; well then, by God, there is an end of the story, for there is no going any farther."

"So, then," said Don Quixote, "the story has come to an end?"

"As much as my mother has," said Sancho.

"In truth," said Don Quixote, "thou hast told one of the rarest stories, tales, or histories, that anyone in the world could have imagined, and such a way of telling it and ending it was never seen nor will be in a lifetime; though I expected nothing else from thy excellent understanding. But I do not wonder, for perhaps those ceaseless strokes may have confused thy wits."

With this and other talk of the same sort master and man passed the night, till Sancho, perceiving that daybreak was coming on, very cautiously untied Rocinante. As soon as Rocinante found himself free, though by nature he was not at all mettlesome, he seemed to feel lively and began pawing—for as to capering, begging his pardon, he knew not what it meant. Don Quixote, then, observing that Rocinante could move, took it as a good sign and a signal that he should attempt the dread adventure. By this time day had fully broken and everything showed distinctly, and Don Quixote saw that he was among some tall trees, chestnuts, which cast a very deep shade. He also perceived that the sound of the strokes did not cease, but could not discover what caused it, and so without any further delay he let Rocinante feel the spur, and once more taking leave of Sancho, he told him to wait for him there three days at most.

Sancho began to weep afresh on again hearing the affecting words of his good master, and resolved to stay with him until the final issue and end of the business. The feeling he displayed touched his master somewhat, but not so much as to make him show any weakness; on the contrary, hiding what he felt as well as he could, he began to move towards that quarter whence the sound of the water and of the strokes seemed to come.

Sancho followed him on foot, leading by the halter, as his custom was, his ass, his constant comrade in prosperity or adversity; and advancing some distance through the shady chestnut trees they came upon a little meadow at the foot of some high rocks, down which a mighty rush of water flung itself. At the foot of the rocks were some rudely constructed houses from among which came, they perceived, the din and clatter of blows, which still continued without intermission. Rocinante took fright at the noise of the water and of the blows, but quieting him Don Quixote advanced step by step towards the houses, commending himself with all his heart to his lady, imploring her support in that dread pass and enterprise, and on the way commending himself to God, too, not to forget him. Sancho, who never quitted his side, stretched his neck as far as he could and peered between the legs of Rocinante to see if he could now discover what it was that caused him such fear and apprehension. They went it might be a hundred paces farther, when on turning a corner the true cause, beyond the possibility of any mistake, of that dread-sounding and to them awe-inspiring noise that had kept them all the night in such fear and perplexity, appeared plain and obvious; and it was six fulling hammers which by their alternate strokes made all the din.

When Don Quixote perceived what it was, he was struck dumb and rigid from head to foot. Sancho glanced at him and saw him with his head bent down upon his breast in manifest mortification; and Don Quixote glanced at Sancho and saw him with his cheeks puffed out and his mouth full of laughter, and evidently ready to explode with it, and in spite of his vexation he could not help laughing at the sight of him; and when Sancho saw his master begin he let go so heartily that he had to hold his sides with both hands to keep himself from bursting with laughter. Four times he stopped, and as many times did his laughter break out afresh with the same violence as at first, whereat Don Quixote grew furious, above all when he heard Sancho say mockingly, " 'Thou must know, friend Sancho, that of Heaven's will I was born in this our iron age to revive in it the golden or age of gold; I am he for whom are reserved perils, mighty achievements, valiant deeds.' " And here he went on repeating the words that Don Quixote uttered the first time they heard the awful strokes.

Don Quixote, then, seeing that Sancho was turning him into ridicule, was

58

so mortified and vexed that he lifted up his pike and smote him two such blows that if, instead of catching them on his shoulders, he had caught them on his head there would have been no wages to pay, unless indeed to his heirs. Sancho seeing that he was getting an awkward return in earnest for his jest, and fearing his master might carry it still further, said to him very humbly, "Calm yourself, sir, for by God I am only joking."

"Well, then, if you are joking I am not," replied Don Quixote. "Look here, my lively gentleman, if these, instead of being fulling hammers, had been some perilous adventure, have I not, think you, shown the courage required for the attempt and achievement?"

"No more señor," returned Sancho. "I own I went a little too far with the joke. But tell me, your worship, now that peace is made between us, was it not a thing to laugh at, and is it not a good story, the great fear we were in?— at least that I was in; for as to your worship I see now that you neither know nor understand what either fear or dismay is."

"I do not deny," said Don Quixote, "that what happened to us may be worth laughing at, but it is not worth making a story about, for it is not everyone that is shrewd enough to hit the right point of a thing."

"At any rate," said Sancho, "your worship knew how to hit the right point with your pike, aiming at my head and hitting me on the shoulders, thanks be to God and my own smartness in dodging it."

CHAPTER 13

The Helmet of Mambrino

I T NOW BEGAN to rain a little, and Sancho was for going into the fulling mills, but Don Quixote had taken such an abhorrence to them on account of the late joke that he would not enter them on any account; so turning right, they came upon another road, different from that which they had taken the night before. Shortly afterwards Don Quixote perceived a man on horseback who wore on his head something that shone like gold, and the moment he saw him he turned to Sancho and said:

"I think, Sancho, there is no proverb that is not true, all being maxims drawn from experience itself, the mother of all the sciences, especially that one that says, 'Where one door shuts, another opens.' I say so because if last night fortune shut the door of the adventure we were looking for against us, cheating us with the fulling mills, it now opens wide another one for another, better adventure. If I mistake not, there comes towards us a man on a dappled gray steed who wears on his head the helmet of Mambrino."

"What I see," answered Sancho, "is only a man on a gray ass like my own, who has something that shines on his head."

"Well, that is the helmet of Mambrino," said Don Quixote. "Stand to one side and leave me alone with him; thou shalt see how, without saying a word, to save time, I shall possess myself of the helmet I have so longed for."

"I will take care to stand aside," said Sancho; "but God grant, I say once more, that it be not fulling mills."

"I have told thee, brother, on no account to mention those fulling mills to me again," said Don Quixote, "or I vow—and I say no more—I'll *full* the soul out of you."

60

Sancho held his peace in dread lest his master should carry out the vow he had hurled like a bowl at him.

The fact of the matter as regards the helmet, steed, and knight that Don Quixote saw, was this. In that neighborhood there were two villages, one of them so small that it had neither apothecary's shop nor barber, which the other that was close to it had, so the barber of the larger served the smaller, and in it there was a sick man who required to be bled and another man who wanted to be shaved, and on this errand the barber was going, carrying with him a brass basin; but as luck would have it, as he was on the way it began to rain, and not to spoil his hat, which probably was a new one, he put the basin on his head, and being clean it glittered at half a league's distance. He rode upon a gray ass, as Sancho said, and this was what made it seem to Don Quixote to be a dapple-gray steed and a knight and a golden helmet.

When he saw the poor knight draw near, without entering into any parley with him, at Rocinante's top speed he bore down upon him with the pike pointed low, fully determined to run him through, and as he reached him, without checking the fury of his charge, he cried to him:

"Defend thyself, miserable being, or yield me of thine own accord that which is so reasonably my due."

The barber, who saw this apparition coming down upon him, had no other way of saving himself from the stroke of the lance but to let himself fall off his ass; and no sooner had he touched the ground than he sprang up more nimbly than a deer and sped away across the plain faster than the wind, leaving the basin on the ground.

Don Quixote told Sancho to pick up the helmet, and he, taking it in his hands, said:

"By God the basin is a good one, and worth a real of eight if it is worth a maravedi," and handed it to his master, who immediately put it on his head, turning it round, now this way, now that, trying to make it fit. "Clearly," he said, "the pagan to whose measure this famous headpiece was first forged must have had a very large head; but the worst of it is half of it is wanting."

When Sancho heard him call the basin a headpiece he was unable to restrain his laughter, but remembering his master's wrath he checked himself in the midst of it.

"What art thou laughing at, Sancho?" said Don Quixote.

"I am laughing," said he, "to think of the great head the pagan must have had who owned this helmet, for it looks exactly like a regular barber's basin."

"Dost thou know what I suspect, Sancho?" said Don Quixote; "that this

61

wonderful piece of this enchanted helmet must by some strange accident have come into the hands of someone who was unable to recognize its value, and who, not knowing what he did, and seeing it to be of the purest gold, must have melted down one half for the sake of what it might be worth, and of the other made this which is like a barber's basin as thou sayest; but be it as it may, to me who recognize it, its transformation makes no difference, for I will set it to rights at the first village where there is a blacksmith."

"Putting that aside," said Sancho, "will your worship tell me what are we to do with this dapple-gray steed that looks like a gray ass, which that Mambrino that your worship overthrew has left deserted here? For, from the way he took to his heels and bolted, he is not likely ever to come back for it; and by my beard but the gray is a good one."

"I have never been in the habit," said Don Quixote, "of taking spoil of those whom I vanquish, nor is it the practice of chivalry to take away their horses and leave them to go on foot. Therefore, Sancho, leave this horse, or ass, or whatever thou wilt have it to be; for when its owner sees us gone hence he will come back for it."

"God knows I should like to take it," returned Sancho, "or at least to change trappings."

"On that head I am not quite certain," answered Don Quixote, "and the matter being doubtful, pending better information, I say thou mayest change them, if so be thou hast urgent need of them."

"So urgent is it," answered Sancho, "that if they were for my own person I could not want them more." And forthwith, fortified by this license, he effected the change, rigging out his beast to the ninety-nines and making quite another thing of it. This done, they broke their fast on the remains of the spoils of war plundered from the sumpter mule, and, all anger and gloom removed, they mounted and, without taking any fixed road, they set out, guided by Rocinante's will, which carried along with it that of his master, not to say that of the ass, which always followed him wherever he led, lovingly and sociably; nevertheless they returned to the high road, and pursued it without any other aim.

CHAPTER 14

The Galley Slaves

PRESENTLY Don Quixote raised his eyes and saw coming along the road they were following some dozen men on foot strung together by the neck, like beads, on a great iron chain, and all with manacles on their hands. With them there came also two men on horseback and two on foot; those on horseback with wheel-lock muskets, those on foot with javelins and swords, and as soon as Sancho saw them he said:

"That is a chain of galley slaves, on the way to the galleys by force of the king's orders."

"How by force?" asked Don Quixote. "Is it possible that the king uses force against anyone?"

"I do not say that," answered Sancho, "but that these are people condemned for their crimes to serve by force in the king's galleys."

"In fact," replied Don Quixote, "however it may be, these people are going where they are taking them by force, and not of their own will."

"Just so," said Sancho.

"Then if so," said Don Quixote, "here is a case for the exercise of my office, to put down force and to succor and help the wretched."

"Recollect, your worship," said Sancho, "Justice, which is the king himself, is not using force or doing wrong to such persons, but punishing them for their crimes."

The chain of galley slaves had by this time come up, and Don Quixote in very courteous language asked those who were in custody of it to be good enough to tell him the reason or reasons for which they were conducting these

63

people in this manner. One of the guards on horseback answered that they were galley slaves belonging to his majesty, that they were going to the galleys, and that was all that was to be said and all he had any business to know.

"Nevertheless," replied Don Quixote politely, "I should like to know from each of them separately the reason of his misfortune."

"Come and ask them," said the guard. "They can tell if they choose, and they will, for these fellows take a pleasure in doing and talking about rascalities."

With this permission, which Don Quixote would have taken even had they not granted it, he approached the chain and asked the first for what offenses he was now in such a sorry case.

He made answer that it was for being a lover.

"For that only?" replied Don Quixote. "Why, if for being lovers they send people to the galleys I might have been rowing in them long ago."

"The love is not the sort your worship is thinking of," said the galley slave. "Mine was that I loved a washerwoman's basket of clean linen so well, and held it so close in my embrace, that if the arm of the law had not forced it from me, I should never have let it go of my own will to this moment; I was caught in the act, there was no occasion for torture, the case was settled, they treated me to a hundred lashes on the back, and three years of *gurapas* besides, and that was the end of it."

"What are *gurapas?*" asked Don Quixote.

"*Gurapas* are galleys," answered the galley slave, who was a young man of about four-and-twenty.

Don Quixote asked the same question of the second, who made no reply, so downcast and melancholy was he; but the first answered for him, and said, "He, sir, goes as a canary, I mean as a musician and a singer."

"What!" said Don Quixote, "for being musicians and singers are people sent to the galleys too?"

"Yes, sir," answered the galley slave, "for there is nothing worse than singing under suffering."

"On the contrary, I have heard say," said Don Quixote, "that he who sings scares away his woes."

"Here it is the reverse," said the galley slave; "for he who sings once weeps all his life."

"I do not understand it," said Don Quixote, but one of the guards said to him, "Sir, to sing under suffering means to confess under torture; they put

64

this sinner to the torture and he confessed his crime, which was being a cattle-stealer, and on his confession they sentenced him to six years in the galleys, besides two hundred lashes that he has already had on the back; and he is always dejected and downcast because the other thieves that march here despise him for confessing and not having spirit enough to say nay; for, say they, 'nay' has no more letters in it than 'yea,' and a culprit is well off when life or death with him depends on his own tongue and not on that of witnesses or evidence; and to my thinking they are not very far out."

"And I think so too," answered Don Quixote; then passing on to the third he asked him what he had asked the others, and the man answered very readily and unconcernedly, "I am going for five years to the *gurapas* for the want of ten ducats."

"I will give twenty with pleasure to get you out of that trouble," said Don Quixote.

"That," said the galley slave, "is like a man having money at sea when he is dying of hunger and has no way of buying what he wants; I say so because if at the right time I had had those twenty ducats that your worship now offers me, I would have greased the notary's pen and freshened up the attorney's wit with them, so that today I should be in Toledo, and not on this road coupled like a greyhound. But God is great; patience—there, that's enough of it."

Don Quixote went on and asked another what his crime was, and the man answered with no less but rather much more sprightliness than the last one.

"I am here because I carried the joke too far with a couple of cousins of mine, and with a couple of other cousins who were none of mine; in short, I carried the joke so far with them all that it ended in such a complicated increase of kindred that no accountant could make it clear: it was all proved against me, I got no favor, I had no money, I was near having my neck stretched, they sentenced me to the galleys for six years, I accepted my fate, it is the punishment of my fault; I am a young man; let life only last, and with that all will come right. If you, sir, have anything wherewith to help the poor, God will repay it to you in heaven, and we on earth will take care in our petitions to him to pray for the life and health of your worship, that they may be as long and as good as your amiable appearance deserves."

This one was in the dress of a student, and one of the guards said he was a great talker and a very elegant Latin scholar.

Behind all these there came a man of thirty, a very personable fellow, except that when he looked his eyes turned in a little, one towards the other. He was bound differently from the rest, for he had to his leg a chain so long that it was wound all round his body, and two rings on his neck. Don Quixote asked why this man carried so many more chains than the others. The guard replied that it was because he alone had committed more crimes than all the rest put together, and was so daring a villain, that though they marched him in that fashion they did not feel sure of him, but were in dread of his making his escape.

"What crimes can he have committed," said Don Quixote, "if they have not deserved a heavier punishment than being sent to the galleys?"

"He goes for ten years," replied the guard, "and all that need be said is that this good fellow is the famous Gines de Pasamonte, otherwise called Ginesillo de Parapilla."

"Gently, señor commissary," said the galley slave at this, "let us have no fixing of names or surnames; my name is Gines de Pasamonte, not Parapilla as you say; let each one mind his own business, and he will be doing enough. And you, sir, if you have anything to give us, give it to us at once, and God speed you, for you are becoming tiresome with all this inquisitiveness about the lives of others; if you want to know about mine, let me tell you I am Gines de Pasamonte, whose life is written by these fingers."

"He says true," said the commissary, "for he has himself written his story as grand as you please, and has left the book in the prison in pawn for two hundred reals."

"And I mean to take it out of pawn," said Gines, "though it were in for two hundred ducats."

"Is it so good?" said Don Quixote.

"So good is it," replied Gines, "that all I will say about it is that it deals with facts, and facts so neat and diverting that no lies could match them."

"And how is the book entitled?" asked Don Quixote.

"The 'Life of Gines de Pasamonte,'" replied the subject of it.

"And is it finished?" asked Don Quixote.

"How can it be finished," said the other, "when my life is not yet finished? All that is written is from my birth down to the point when they sent me to the galleys this last time."

"Then you have been there before?" said Don Quixote.

"In the service of God and the king I have been there for four years now," replied Gines, "and it is no great grievance to me to go back to them, for

66

there I shall have time to finish my book; I have still many things left to say, and in the galleys of Spain there is more than enough leisure; though I do not want much for what I have to write, for I have it by heart."

"You seem a clever fellow," said Don Quixote.

"And an unfortunate one," replied Gines, "for misfortune always persecutes good wit."

"It persecutes rogues," said the commissary.

"I told you already to go gently, master commissary," said Pasamonte; "their lordships yonder never gave you that staff to ill-treat us wretches here, but to take us where his majesty orders you; and now let us march on, for we have had quite enough of this entertainment."

The commissary lifted his staff to strike Pasamonte, but Don Quixote came between them, and begged him not to ill-use him, as it was not too much to allow one who had his hands tied to have his tongue a trifle free; and turning to the whole chain of them he said:

"From all you have told me, dear brethren, I make out clearly that though they have punished you for your faults, perhaps this one's want of courage under torture, that one's want of money, the other's want of advocacy, and lastly the perverted judgment of the judge may have been the cause of your failure to obtain the justice you had on your side. All which presents itself now to my mind, compelling me to demonstrate in your case the purpose for which Heaven sent me into the world and caused me to make profession of the order of chivalry to which I belong. Sirs of the guard," Don Quixote went on, "these poor fellows have done nothing to you; let each answer for his own sins yonder; there is a God in Heaven who will not forget to punish the wicked or reward the good; and it is not fitting that honest men should be the instruments of punishment to others. This request I make thus gently and quietly, that, if you comply with it, I may have reason for thanking you; and, if you will not voluntarily, this lance and sword together with the might of my arm shall compel you to comply with it by force."

"Nice nonsense!" said the commissary. "A fine piece of pleasantry he has come out with at last! He wants us to let the king's prisoners go, as if we had any authority to release them, or he to order us to do so! Go your way, sir, and good luck to you; put that basin straight that you've got on your head, and don't go looking for three feet on a cat."

" 'Tis you that are the cat, rat, and rascal," replied Don Quixote, and acting on the word he fell upon him so suddenly that without giving him time to defend himself he brought him to the ground sorely wounded with a lance-thrust; and lucky it was for him that it was the one that had the musket. The other guards stood thunderstruck and amazed at this unexpected event, but recovering presence of mind, those on horseback seized their swords, and those on foot their javelins, and attacked Don Quixote, who was waiting for them with great calmness; and no doubt it would have gone badly with him if the galley slaves, seeing the chance before them of liberating themselves, had not effected it by contriving to break the chain on which they were strung. Such was the confusion that the guards, now rushing at the galley slaves who were breaking loose, now to attack Don Quixote, who was waiting for them, did nothing at all that was of any use. Sancho, on his part, gave a helping hand to release Gines de Pasamonte, who was the first to leap forth upon the plain free and unfettered, and who, attacking the prostrate commissary, took from him his sword and the musket, with which, aiming at one and leveling at another, he, without ever discharging it, drove every one of the guards off the field, for they took to flight, as well to escape Pasamonte's musket, as the showers of stones the now released galley slaves were raining upon them. Sancho was greatly grieved at the affair, because he anticipated that those who had fled would report the matter to the Holy Brotherhood, who at the summons of the alarm bell would at once sally forth in quest of the offenders; and he said so to his master, and entreated him to leave the place at once, and go into hiding in the sierra that was close by.

"That is all very well," said Don Quixote, "but I know what must be done now"; and calling together all the galley slaves, who were now running riot, and had stripped the commissary to the skin, he collected them round him to hear what he had to say, and addressed them as follows: "To be grateful for benefits received is the part of persons of good birth, and one of the sins most offensive to God is ingratitude. Sirs, ye have already seen the benefit ye have received of me; in return for which I desire ye at once proceed to the city of El Toboso, and there present yourselves before the lady Dulcinea del Toboso, and say to her that her knight, he of the Rueful Countenance, sends to commend himself to her; and that ye recount to her in full detail all the particulars of this notable adventure, up to the recovery of your longed-for liberty; and this done ye may go where ye will, and good fortune attend you."

Gines de Pasamonte made answer for all, saying, "That which you, sir, our deliverer, demand of us, is impossible to comply with, because we cannot go together along the roads, but only singly and separate, and each one his own way, endeavoring to hide ourselves to escape the Holy Brotherhood, which, no doubt, will come out in search of us. What your worship may do, and fairly do, is to change this service and tribute as regards the lady Dulcinea del Toboso for a certain quantity of ave-marias and credos which we will say for your worship's benefit, and this is a condition that can be complied with by night as by day, running or resting. But to imagine that we are going now to set out for El Toboso, is to imagine that it is now night, though it is not yet ten in the morning, and to ask this of us is like asking pears of the elm tree."

"Then by all that's good," said Don Quixote, now stirred to wrath, "Don Ginesillo de Paropillo, or whatever your name is, you will have to go yourself alone!"

Pasamonte, who was anything but meek (being by this time thoroughly convinced that Don Quixote was not quite right in his head as he had committed such a vagary as to set them free), finding himself abused in this fashion, gave the wink to his companions, and falling back they began to shower stones on Don Quixote at such a rate that he was quite unable to protect himself with his buckler, and poor Rocinante no more heeded the spur than if he had been made of brass. Sancho planted himself behind his ass, and with him sheltered himself from the hailstorm that poured on both of them. Don Quixote was unable to shield himself so well but that more pebbles struck him full on the body with such force that they brought him to the ground; and the instant he fell the student pounced upon him, snatched the basin from his head, and with it struck three or four blows on his shoulders, and as many more on the ground, knocking it almost to pieces. They then stripped him of a jacket that he wore over his armor, and from Sancho they took his coat, leaving him in his shirt-sleeves. And dividing among themselves the remaining spoils of the battle, they went each one his own way, intent upon keeping clear of the Holy Brotherhood.

The ass and Rocinante, Sancho and Don Quixote, were all that were left upon the spot; the ass with drooping head, serious, shaking his ears from time to time as if he thought the storm of stones that had assailed them was not yet over; Rocinante stretched beside his master, for he too had been brought to the ground by a stone; Sancho stripped, and trembling with fear of the Holy Brotherhood; and Don Quixote fuming to find himself so treated by the very persons for whom he had done so much.

CHAPTER 15

In the Sierra Morena

SEEING HIMSELF served in this way, Don Quixote said to his squire, "I have always heard it said, Sancho, that to do good to boors is to throw water into the sea. If I had believed thy words, I should have avoided this trouble; but it is done now, it is only to have patience and take warning for the future."

"Your worship will take warning as much as I am a Turk," returned Sancho; "but, as you say this mischief might have been avoided if you had believed me, believe me now, and a still greater one will be avoided; for I tell you chivalry is of no account with the Holy Brotherhood, and they don't care two maravedis for all the knights-errant in the world; and I can tell you I fancy I hear their arrows whistling past my ears this minute."

"Thou art a coward by nature, Sancho," said Don Quixote, "but lest thou shouldst say I am obstinate, and that I never do as thou dost advise, this once I will take thy advice, and withdraw out of reach of that fury thou so dreadest; but it must be on one condition, that never, in life or in death, thou art to say to anyone that I retired or withdrew from this danger out of fear, but only in compliance with thy entreaties."

"Señor," replied Sancho, "to retire is not to flee, and there is no wisdom in waiting when danger outweighs hope, and it is the part of wise men to preserve themselves today for tomorrow, and not risk all in one day; so repent not of having taken my advice, but mount Rocinante if you can, and if not I will help you; and follow me, for my mother-wit tells me we have more need of legs than hands just now."

70

In the Sierra Morena

Don Quixote mounted without replying, and, Sancho leading the way on his ass, they entered the side of the Sierra Morena, which was close by, as it was Sancho's design to cross it entirely and come out again at Almodóvar del Campo, and hide for some days among its crags so as to escape the search of the Brotherhood should they come to look for them. He was encouraged in this by perceiving that the stock of provisions carried by the ass had come safe out of the fray with the galley slaves, a circumstance that he regarded as a miracle, seeing how they pillaged and ransacked.

That night they reached the very heart of the Sierra Morena, where it seemed prudent to Sancho to pass the night and even some days, at least as many as the stores he carried might last, and so they encamped between two rocks and among some cork trees; but destiny, which, according to the opinion of those who have not the true faith, settles everything in its own way, so ordered it that Gines de Pasamonte, the famous thief whom Don Quixote had released from the chain, driven by fear of the Holy Brotherhood, which he had good reason to dread, resolved to hide in the mountains; and his fate and fear led him to the same spot to which Don Quixote and Sancho Panza had been led by theirs, just in time to recognize them and leave them to fall asleep: and as the wicked are always ungrateful, and immediate advantage overcomes all considerations of the future, Gines, who was neither grateful nor well-principled, made up his mind to steal Sancho Panza's ass, not troubling himself about Rocinante, as being a prize that was no good either to pledge or sell. While Sancho slept he stole his ass, and before day dawned he was far out of reach.

Aurora made her appearance bringing gladness to the earth but sadness to Sancho Panza, for he found that his Dapple was missing, and seeing himself bereft of him he began the saddest and most doleful lament in the world, so loud that Don Quixote awoke at his exclamations and heard him saying, "O son of my heart, born in my very house, my children's plaything, my wife's joy, the envy of my neighbors, relief of my burdens, and lastly, half supporter of myself, for with the six-and-twenty maravedis thou didst earn me daily I met half my charges."

Don Quixote, when he heard the lament and learned the cause, consoled Sancho with the best arguments he could, entreating him to patient, and promising to give him a letter of exchange ordering three out of five ass-colts that he had at home to be given to him. Sancho took comfort at this, dried his tears, suppressed his sobs, and returned thanks for the kindness shown him

71

by Don Quixote. He on his part was rejoiced to the heart on entering the mountains, as they seemed to him to be just the place for the adventures he was in quest of. Sancho marched behind his master laden with what Dapple used to carry, emptying the sack and packing his paunch, and so long as he could go that way, he would not have given a farthing to meet with another adventure.

While so engaged he raised his eyes and saw that his master had halted, and was trying with the point of his pike to lift some bulky object that lay upon the ground, on which he hastened to help him. It was a saddle-pad with a valise attached to it, half or rather wholly rotten and torn; but so heavy were they that Sancho had to help to take them up, and his master directed him to see what the valise contained. Sancho did so with great alacrity, and though the valise was secured by a chain and padlock, from its torn and rotten condition he was able to see its contents, which were four shirts of fine holland, and other articles of linen no less curious than clean; and in a handkerchief he found a good lot of gold crowns, and as soon as he saw them he exclaimed:

"Blessed be all Heaven for sending us an adventure that is good for something!"

Searching further he found a little memorandum book richly bound; this Don Quixote asked of him, telling him to take the money and keep it for himself. Sancho kissed his hands for the favor, and cleared the valise of its linen, which he stowed away in the provision sack. Considering the whole matter, Don Quixote observed:

"It seems to me, Sancho—and it is impossible it can be otherwise—that some strayed traveler must have crossed this sierra and been attacked and slain by footpads, who brought him to this remote spot to bury him."

"That cannot be," answered Sancho, "because if they had been robbers they would not have left this money."

"Thou art right," said Don Quixote, "and I cannot guess what this may mean; but stay; let us see if in this memorandum book there is anything written by which we may be able to discover what we want to know."

He opened it, and the first thing he found in it, written roughly but in a very good hand, was a letter.

Don Quixote turned the page and said, "This seems to be a love letter."

"Then let your worship read it aloud," said Sancho, "for I am very fond of love matters."

"With all my heart," said Don Quixote, and reading it aloud as Sancho had requested him, he found it ran thus:

Thy false promise and my sure misfortune carry me to a place whence the news of my death will reach thy ears before the words of my complaint. Ungrateful one, thou hast rejected me for one more wealthy, but not more worthy; but if virtue were esteemed wealth I should neither envy the fortunes of others nor weep for misfortunes of my own. What thy beauty raised up thy deeds have laid low; by it I believed thee to be an angel, by them I know thou art a woman. Peace be with thee who hast sent war to me, and Heaven grant that the deceit of thy husband be ever hidden from thee, so that thou repent not of what thou hast done, and I reap not a revenge I would not have.

When he had finished the letter, Don Quixote said, "There is little to be gathered from this, except that he who wrote it is some rejected lover"; and turning over the pages of the book he found more letters and verses, some of which he could read, while others he could not; but they were all made up of complaints, laments, misgivings, desires and aversions, favors and rejections, some rapturous, some doleful. While Don Quixote examined the book, Sancho examined the valise, not leaving a corner in the whole of it that he did not search.

Don Quixote was still very anxious to find out who the owner of the valise could be, conjecturing from the letter, from the money in gold, and from the fineness of the shirts, that he must be some lover of distinction whom the scorn and cruelty of his lady had driven to some desperate course; but as in that uninhabited spot there was no one to be seen of whom he could inquire, he saw nothing else for it but to push on, taking whatever road Rocinante chose—which was where he could make his way—firmly persuaded that among these wilds he could not fail to meet some rare adventure. As he went along, then, occupied with these thoughts, he perceived on the summit of a height that rose before their eyes a man who went springing from rock to rock and from tussock to tussock with marvelous agility. As well as he could make out he was unclad, with a thick black beard, long tangled hair, and bare legs and feet. His thighs were covered by breeches apparently of tawny velvet but so ragged that they showed his skin in several places. He was bareheaded, and notwithstanding the swiftness with which he passed as has been described, the Knight of the Rueful Countenance observed all these trifles, and though he made the attempt, he was unable to follow him. Don Quixote at once came to the conclusion that this was the owner of the saddle-pad and of the valise, and made up his mind to go in search of him, even though he should have to wander a year in those mountains before he found him, and so he directed Sancho to take a short cut over one side of the mountain, while he himself went by the other, and perhaps by this means they might light upon this man who had passed so quickly out of their sight.

"I could not do that," said Sancho, "for when I separate from your worship fear at once lays hold of me, and assails me with all sorts of panics and fancies; and let what I now say be a notice that from this time forth I am not going to stir a finger's width from your presence."

"It shall be so," said he of the Rueful Countenance, "and I am very glad that thou art willing to rely on my courage; so come on now behind me slowly as well as thou canst, and make lanterns of thine eyes; perhaps we shall light upon this man that we saw, who no doubt is no other than the owner of what we found."

To which Sancho made answer, "Far better would it be not to look for him, for, if we find him, and he happens to be the owner of the money, it is plain I must restore it; it would be better, therefore, that without taking this needless trouble, I should keep possession of it until in some other less meddlesome way the real owner may be discovered; and perhaps that will be when I shall have spent it, and then the king will hold me harmless."

"Thou art wrong there, Sancho," said Don Quixote, "for now that we have a suspicion who the owner is, and have him almost before us, we are bound to seek him and make restitution; and if we do not see him, the strong suspicion we have as to his being the owner makes us as guilty as if he were so; and so, friend Sancho, let not our search for him give thee any uneasiness, for if we find him it will relieve mine."

And so saying he gave Rocinante the spur, and Sancho followed him on foot and loaded, and after having partly made the circuit of the mountain they found lying in a ravine, dead and half devoured by dogs and pecked by jackdaws, a mule saddled and bridled, all which still further strengthened their suspicion that he who had fled was the owner of the mule and the saddle-pad.

As they stood looking at it they heard a whistle like that of a shepherd watching his flock, and suddenly on their left there appeared a great number of goats and behind them on the summit of the mountain the goatherd in

74

charge of them, a man advanced in years. Don Quixote called aloud to him and begged him to come down to where they stood.

The goatherd descended, and reaching the place where Don Quixote stood, he said, "I will wager you are looking at that hack mule that lies dead in the hollow there, and, faith, it has been lying there now these six months; tell me, have you come upon its master about here?"

"We have come upon nobody," answered Don Quixote, "nor on anything except a saddle-pad and a little valise that we found not far from this."

"I found it too," said the goatherd, "but I would not lift it for fear of some ill-luck or being charged with theft."

"That's exactly what I say," said Sancho; "I found it too, and I would not go within a stone's throw of it."

"Tell me, good man," said Don Quixote, "do you know who is the owner of this property?"

"All I can tell you," said the goatherd, "is that about six months ago, there arrived at a shepherd's hut three leagues, perhaps, away from this, a youth of well-bred appearance and manners, mounted on that same mule which lies dead here, and with the same saddle-pad and valise which you say you found and did not touch. He asked us what part of this sierra was the most rugged and retired; we told him that it was where we now are. On hearing our answer the youth turned about and made for the place we pointed out to him, leaving us all charmed with his good looks, and wondering at his question and the haste with which we saw him depart in the direction of the sierra; and after that we saw him no more, until some days afterwards he crossed the path of one of our shepherds, and without saying a word to him, came up to him and gave him several cuffs and kicks, and then turned to the ass with our provisions and took all the bread and cheese it carried, and having done this made off back again into the sierra with extraordinary swiftness. When some of us goatherds learned this we went in search of him for about two days through the most remote portion of this sierra, at the end of which we found him lodged in the hollow of a large thick cork tree. He came out to meet us with great gentleness, with his dress now torn and his face so burned by the sun that we hardly recognized him. He saluted us courteously, and in a few well-spoken words he told us not to wonder at seeing him going about in this guise, as it was binding upon him in order that he might work out a penance which for his many sins had been imposed upon him. We asked him to tell

75

us who he was, but we were never able to find out from him: we begged of him too, when he was in want of food, which he could not do without, to come and ask it of us and not take it by force from the shepherds. He thanked us for the offer, begged pardon for the late assault, and promised for the future to ask it in God's name without offering violence to anybody.

"But in the midst of his conversation he stopped and became silent, keeping his eyes fixed upon the ground for some time, during which we stood still waiting anxiously to see what would come of this abstraction; and with no little pity, for we could perceive plainly that a fit of madness of some kind had come upon him; and before long he showed that what we imagined was the truth, for he arose in a fury from the ground where he had thrown himself, and attacked the first he found near him with such rage that if we had not dragged him off him, he would have beaten him to death, all the while exclaiming, 'Oh, faithless Fernando, here, here shalt thou pay the penalty of the wrong thou hast done me'; and to these he added other words all in effect upbraiding this Fernando and charging him with treachery and faithlessness.

"We forced him to release his hold with no little difficulty, and without another word he left us, and rushing off plunged in among these brakes and brambles, so as to make it impossible for us to follow him; from this we suppose that madness comes upon him from time to time, and that someone called Fernando must have done him a wrong of a grievous nature such as the condition to which it had brought him seemed to show. This, sirs, is all I can say in answer to what you have asked me; and be sure that the owner of the articles you found is he whom you saw pass by with such nimbleness."

Don Quixote resolved, as he had done before, to search for the madman all over the mountain, not leaving a cave unexamined until he had found him. But chance arranged matters better than he expected or hoped, for at that very moment, in a gorge on the mountain that opened where they stood, the youth he wished to find appeared, coming along muttering to himself.

Approaching them, the youth greeted them in a hoarse voice but with great courtesy. Don Quixote returned his salutation with equal politeness, and dismounting from Rocinante advanced with well-bred bearing to embrace him, as if he had known him for a long time. The other, whom we may call the Ragged One of the Sorry Countenance, after submitting to the embrace pushed him back a little and, placing his hands on Don Quixote's shoulders, stood gazing at him as if seeking to see whether he knew him, not less amazed, perhaps, at the sight of Don Quixote than Don Quixote was at the sight of him.

CHAPTER 16

Cardenio's Story

The first to speak after embracing was the Ragged One.

"Of a surety, señor, whoever you are, I thank you for the proofs of kindness and courtesy you have shown me, and would I were in a condition to requite them; but my fate does not afford me any other means of returning kindnesses done me save the hearty desire to repay them."

"Mine," replied Don Quixote, "is to be of service to you. And if your misfortune should prove to be one of those that refuse admission to any sort of consolation, it was my purpose to join you in lamenting over it, so far as I could; for it is still some comfort in misfortune to find one who can feel for it. And I entreat you, señor, to tell me who you are and the cause that has brought you to live or die in these solitudes. And I swear," added Don Quixote, "by the order of knighthood which I have received, and by my vocation of knight-errant, if you gratify me in this, to serve you with all the zeal my calling demands of me."

The Knight of the Thicket, hearing him of the Rueful Countenance talk in this strain, did nothing but stare at him, and survey him from head to foot; and when he had thoroughly examined him, he said to him:

"If you have anything to give me to eat, for God's sake give it me, and after I have eaten I will do all you ask in acknowledgment of the good will you have displayed towards me."

Sancho from his sack, and the goatherd from his pouch, furnished the Ragged One with the means of appeasing his hunger, and what they gave him

77

he ate so hastily that he took no time between mouthfuls, gorging rather than swallowing; and while he ate neither he nor they who observed him uttered a word. As soon as he had done he made signs to them to follow him, which they did, and he led them to a green plot which lay a little farther off round the corner of a rock. On reaching it he stretched himself upon the grass, and the others did the same, all keeping silence, until the Ragged One, settling himself in his place, said:

"If it is your wish, sirs, that I should disclose in a few words the surpassing extent of my misfortunes, you must promise not to break the thread of my sad story with any interruption, for the instant you do so the tale I tell will come to an end."

Don Quixote gave the promise for himself and the others, and with this assurance he began as follows:

"My name is Cardenio, my birthplace one of the best cities of this Andalusia, my family noble, my parents rich, my misfortune so great that my parents must have wept and my family grieved over it without being able by their wealth to lighten it; for the gifts of fortune can do little to relieve reverses sent by Heaven. In that same country there was a heaven in which love had placed all the glory I could desire; such was the beauty of Luscinda, a damsel as noble and as rich as I, but of happier fortunes, and of less firmness than was due to so worthy a passion as mine. This Luscinda I loved, worshipped, and adored from my earliest and tenderest years, and she loved me in all the innocence and sincerity of childhood. Our parents were aware of our feelings, and were not sorry to perceive them, for they saw clearly that as they ripened they must lead at last to a marriage between us, a thing that seemed almost prearranged by the equality of our families and wealth.

"We grew up, and with our growth grew the love between us, so that the father of Luscinda felt bound for propriety's sake to refuse me admission to his house. But though they enforced silence upon our tongues they could not impose it upon our pens, which can make known the heart's secrets to a loved one more freely than tongues.

"At length growing impatient and feeling my heart languishing with longing to see her, I resolved to ask her of her father for my lawful wife, which I did. To this his answer was that he thanked me for the disposition I showed to do honor to him and to regard myself as honored by the bestowal of his treasure; but that as my father was alive it was his by right to make this demand, for if it were not in accordance with his full will and pleasure, Lus-

"It is your wish, sirs, that I should disclose my misfortunes."

cinda was not to be taken or given by stealth. I thanked him for his kindness, reflecting that there was reason in what he said, and that my father would assent to it as soon as I should tell him, and with that view I went the very same instant to let him know what my desires were. When I entered the room where he was I found him with an open letter in his hand, which, before I could utter a word, he gave me, saying, 'By this letter thou wilt see, Cardenio, the disposition the Duke Ricardo has to serve thee.' This Duke Ricardo, as you, sirs, probably know already, is a grandee of Spain. I took and read the letter, which was couched in terms so flattering that even I myself felt it would be wrong in my father not to comply with the request the duke made in it, which was that he would send me immediately to him, as he wished me to become the companion, not servant, of his eldest son, and would take upon himself the charge of placing me in a position corresponding to the esteem in which he held me. On reading the letter my voice failed me, and still more when I heard my father say, 'Two days hence thou wilt depart, Cardenio, in accordance with the duke's wish, and give thanks to God who is opening a road to thee by which thou mayest attain what I know thou dost deserve'; and to these words he added others of fatherly counsel. The time for my departure arrived; I spoke one night to Luscinda, I told her all that had occurred, as I did also to her father, entreating him to allow some delay, and to defer the disposal of her hand until I should see what the Duke Ricardo sought of me: he gave me the promise, and she confirmed it.

"Finally, I presented myself to the duke, and was received and treated by him very kindly. But the one to whom my arrival gave the greatest pleasure was the duke's second son, Fernando by name, a gallant youth, of noble, generous, and amorous disposition, who very soon made so intimate a friend of me that it was remarked by everybody. It so happened, then, that as between friends no secret remains unshared, he made all his thoughts known to me, and in particular a love affair which troubled his mind a little. He was deeply in love with a peasant girl, a vassal of his father's, the daughter of wealthy parents, and herself so beautiful, modest, discreet, and virtuous, that no one who knew her was able to decide in which of these respects she was most highly gifted or most excelled. The attractions of the fair peasant raised the passion of Don Fernando to such a point that, in order to overcome her virtuous resolutions, he determined to pledge his word to her to become her husband. Bound to him as I was by friendship, I strove by the best arguments I could think of to dissuade him from such a course; but perceiving I produced no effect I resolved to make the Duke Ricardo, his father, acquainted with the matter; but Don Fernando, being sharp-witted and shrewd, foresaw this, perceiving that by my duty as a good servant I was bound not to keep concealed a thing so much opposed to the honor of my lord the duke; and so, to mislead me, he told me he could find no better way of effacing from his mind the beauty that so enslaved him than by absenting himself for some months, and that he wished the absence to be effected by our going, both of us, to my father's house under the pretence, which he would make to the duke, of going to see and buy some fine horses that there were in my city, Cordova, which produces the best in the world. When I heard him say so, even if his resolution had not been so good a one I should have hailed it as one of the happiest that could be imagined, seeing what a favorable opportunity it offered me of returning to see my Luscinda. With this thought and wish I commended his idea, advising him to put it into execution as quickly as possible, as, in truth, absence produced its effect in spite of the most deeply rooted feelings. But, as afterwards appeared, when he said this to me, he had already pledged himself to the peasant girl; and as with young men love is for the most part nothing more than appetite, and that which seemed to be love takes to flight, as it cannot pass the limit fixed by nature, which fixes no limit to true love, his passion had subsided and his eagerness cooled; and if at first he feigned a wish to absent himself in order to cure his love, he was now in reality anxious to go to avoid keeping his promise.

"The duke gave him permission, and ordered me to accompany him; we arrived at my city, and my father gave him the reception due to his rank; I saw Luscinda without delay, and my love gathered fresh life. To my sorrow I told the story of it to Don Fernando, for I thought that in virtue of the great friendship he bore me I was bound to conceal nothing from him. I extolled her beauty, her gaiety, her wit, so warmly that my praises excited in him a desire to see a damsel adorned by such attractions. To my misfortune I yielded to it, showing her to him one night by the light of a taper at a window where we used to talk to one another. As she appeared to him in her dressing gown, she drove all the beauties he had seen until then out of his recollection; speech failed him, his head turned, he was spellbound, and in the end love-smitten. It is true, and I own it now, that though I knew what good cause Don Fernando had to praise Luscinda, it gave me uneasiness to hear these praises from his mouth, and I began to feel distrust of him; not that I feared any change in the constancy or faith of Luscinda; but Don Fernando contrived always to read the letters I sent to Luscinda and her answers to me, under the pretense that he enjoyed the wit and sense of both. It so happened, then, that Luscinda having begged of me a book of chivalry to read, one that she was very fond of, Amadis of Gaul—"

Don Quixote no sooner heard a book of chivalry mentioned, than he said: "Had your worship told me at the beginning of your story that the Lady Luscinda was fond of books of chivalry, no other laudation would have been requisite to impress upon me the superiority of her understanding. And I wish your worship had, along with Amadis of Gaul, sent her the worthy Don Rugel of Greece, for I know the Lady Luscinda would greatly relish Queen Madasima and Elisabad, and the shrewd sayings of the shepherd Darinel. But pardon me for having broken the promise we made not to interrupt your discourse; for when I hear chivalry or knights-errant mentioned, I can no more help talking about them than the rays of the sun can help giving heat, or those of the moon moisture."

While Don Quixote was saying this, Cardenio allowed his head to fall upon his breast, and seemed plunged in deep thought. After some time he raised his head and said, "I cannot get rid of the idea, nor will anyone in the world make me think otherwise—than that that arrant knave Master Elisabad made free with Queen Madasima."

"That is not true, by all that's good," said Don Quixote in high wrath, turning upon him angrily; "and it is a very great slander. Queen Madasima was a very illustrious lady, and it is not to be supposed that so exalted a princess would have made free with a quack; and whoever maintains the contrary lies like a great scoundrel, and I will give him to know it, on foot or on horseback, armed or unarmed, by night or by day, or as he likes best."

Cardenio was looking at him steadily, and his mad fit having now come upon him, he had no disposition to go on with his story, nor would Don Quixote have listened to it. Cardenio, then, being, as I said, now mad, when he heard himself given the lie, and called a scoundrel and other insulting names, snatched up a stone that he found near him, and with it delivered such a blow on Don Quixote's breast that he laid him on his back. Sancho Panza, seeing his master treated in this fashion, attacked the madman with his closed fist; but the Ragged One received him in such a way that with a blow of his fist he stretched him at his feet, and then mounting upon him crushed his ribs to his own satisfaction; the goatherd, who came to the rescue, shared the same fate; and having beaten and pummeled them all he left them and quietly withdrew to his hiding place on the mountain. Sancho rose, and with the rage he felt at finding himself so belabored without deserving it, ran to take vengeance on the goatherd, accusing him of not giving them warning that this man was at times taken with a mad fit. The goatherd replied that he had said so, and that if he had not heard him, that was no fault of his. Sancho retorted, and the goatherd rejoined, and the altercation ended in their seizing each other by the beard, and exchanging such fisticuffs that if Don Quixote had not made peace between them, they would have knocked one another to pieces.

Don Quixote again asked the goatherd if it would be possible to find Cardenio, as he felt the greatest anxiety to know the end of his story. The goatherd told him, as he had told him before, that there was no knowing of a certainty where his lair was; but that if he wandered about much in that neighborhood he could not fail to fall in with him either in or out of his senses.

CHAPTER 17

The Knight Does Penance

DON QUIXOTE TOOK LEAVE of the goatherd, and once more mounting Rocinante bade Sancho follow him, which he, having no ass, did very discontentedly. They proceeded slowly, making their way into the most rugged part of the mountain.

"Señor," said Sancho, "is it a good rule of chivalry that we should go astray through these mountains without path or road, looking for a madman who when he is found will perhaps take a fancy to finish what he began, not his story, but your worship's head and my ribs, and end by breaking them altogether for us?"

"Peace, Sancho," said Don Quixote, "for let me tell thee it is not so much the desire of finding that madman that leads me into these regions as that which I have of performing among them an achievement wherewith I shall win eternal name and fame throughout the known world."

"And is it very perilous, this achievement?"

"No," replied he of the Rueful Countenance, "but all will depend on thy diligence."

"On my diligence!" said Sancho.

"Yes," said Don Quixote, "for if thou dost return soon from the place where I mean to send thee, my penance will be soon over, and my glory will soon begin. But as it is not right to keep thee in suspense, I would have thee know, Sancho, that the famous Amadis of Gaul was one of the most perfect knights-errant—I am wrong to say he was one; he stood alone, the first, the only one, the lord of all that were in the world in his time. This, then, being

83

so, I consider, friend Sancho, that the knight-errant who shall imitate him most closely will come nearest to reaching the perfection of chivalry. Now one of the instances in which this knight most conspicuously showed his endurance, fortitude, and love, was when he withdrew, rejected by the Lady Oriana, to do penance upon the Peña Pobre. So, as this place is so well suited for a similar purpose, I must not allow the opportunity to escape which now so conveniently offers me its forelock."

"What is it in reality," said Sancho, "that your worship means to do in such an out-of-the-way place as this?"

"Have I not told thee," answered Don Quixote, "that I mean to imitate Amadis here, playing the victim of despair, the madman, the maniac, so as at the same time to imitate the valiant Don Roland, when at the fountain he had evidence of the fair Angelica having disgraced herself and through grief thereat went mad. Or perhaps I shall content myself with the simple imitation of Amadis, who without giving way to any mischievous madness but merely to tears and sorrow, gained as much fame as the most famous."

"It seems to me," said Sancho, "that the knights who behaved in this way had provocation and cause for those follies and penances; but what cause has your worship for going mad? What lady has rejected you, or what evidence have you found to prove that the lady Dulcinea del Toboso has been trifling with Moor or Christian?"

"There is the point," replied Don Quixote, "and that is the beauty of this business of mine; no thanks to a knight-errant for going mad when he has cause; the thing is to turn crazy without any provocation, and to let my lady know. And so, friend Sancho, waste no time in advising me against so rare, so happy, and so unheard-of an imitation; mad I am, and mad I must be until thou returnest with the answer to a letter that I mean to send by thee to my lady Dulcinea; and if it be such as my constancy deserves, my insanity and penance will come to an end; and if it be to the opposite effect, I shall become mad in earnest, and, being so, I shall suffer no more. But tell me, Sancho, hast thou got Mambrino's helmet safe? for I saw thee take it up from the ground when that ungrateful wretch tried to break it in pieces but could not, by which the fineness of its temper may be seen."

To which Sancho made answer, "By the living God, Sir Knight of the Rueful Countenance, I cannot bear with patience some of the things that your worship says; and from them I begin to suspect that all you tell me about chivalry, and winning kingdoms and empires, and giving islands, must be all

84

made up of wind and lies, and all pigments or figments, or whatever we may call them; for what would anyone think that heard your worship calling a barber's basin Mambrino's helmet? I have the basin in my sack all dented, and I am taking it home to have it mended, to trim my beard in it, if, by God's grace, I am allowed to see my wife and children some day or other."

"Look here, Sancho," said Don Quixote, "by him thou didst swear by just now I swear thou hast the most limited understanding that any squire in the world has or ever had. Is it possible that all this time thou hast been going about with me thou hast never found out that all things belonging to knights-errant are represented not as they seem but as what they ought to be? Not because it really is so, but because there is always a swarm of enchanters in attendance upon us that change everything with us, and turn things as they please, and according as they are disposed to aid or destroy us; thus what seems to thee a barber's basin seems to me Mambrino's helmet, and to another it will seem something else. Keep it safe, my friend, for just now I have no need of it; indeed, I shall have to take off all this armor and remain as naked as I was born, if I have a mind to follow Roland rather than Amadis in my penance."

Thus talking they reached the foot of a high mountain which stood like an isolated peak among the others that surrounded it. Past its base there flowed a gentle brook, all around it spread a meadow so green and luxuriant that it was a delight to the eyes to look upon it, and forest trees in abundance, and shrubs and flowers added to the charms of the spot. Upon this place the Knight of the Rueful Countenance fixed his choice for the performance of his penance, and as he beheld it exclaimed in a loud voice as though he were out of his senses:

"This is the place, oh, ye heavens, that I select and choose for bewailing the misfortune in which ye yourselves have plunged me: this is the spot where the overflowings of mine eyes shall swell the waters of yon little brook, and my deep and endless sighs shall stir unceasingly the leaves of these mountain trees, in testimony and token of the pain my persecuted heart is suffering. Oh, Dulcinea del Toboso, star of my fortune, may Heaven grant thee in full all thou seekest of it; bethink thee of the condition to which absence from thee has brought me, and make that return in kindness that is due to my fidelity! Oh, thou, my squire, pleasant companion in my prosperous and adverse fortunes, fix well in thy memory what thou shalt see me do here, so that thou mayest relate and report it to the sole cause of all"; and so saying he dismounted from Rocinante, and in an instant relieved him of saddle and bridle, and giving him a slap on the croup, said, "He gives thee freedom who is bereft of it himself."

Seeing this, Sancho said, "Indeed, Sir Knight of the Rueful Countenance, if my departure and your worship's madness are to come off in earnest, it will be as well to saddle Rocinante again in order that he may supply the want of Dapple, because it will save me time in going and returning: for if I go on foot I don't know when I shall get there or when I shall get back, as I am, in truth, a bad walker."

"I declare, Sancho," returned Don Quixote, "it shall be as thou wilt, for thy plan does not seem to me a bad one, and three days hence thou wilt depart, for I wish thee to observe in the meantime what I do and say for her sake, that thou mayest be able to tell it."

"But what more have I to see besides what I have seen?" said Sancho.

"Much thou knowest about it!" said Don Quixote. "I have now got to tear up my garments, to scatter about my armor, knock my head against these rocks, and more of the same sort of thing, which thou must witness."

"For the love of God," said Sancho, "be careful, your worship, how you give yourself those knocks on the head. I should think, if indeed knocks on the head seem necessary to you, and this business cannot be done without them, you might be content—as the whole thing is feigned, and counterfeit—you might be content, I say, with giving them to yourself in the water, or against something soft, like cotton; and leave it all to me; for I'll tell my lady that your worship knocked your head against a point of rock harder than a diamond."

"I thank thee for thy good intentions, friend Sancho," answered Don Quixote, "but my knocks on the head must be real, solid, and valid, without anything fanciful about them, and it will be needful to leave me some lint to dress my wounds."

"It was bad losing the ass," replied Sancho, "for with him lint and all were lost; but I beg of your worship to reckon as past the three days you allowed me for seeing the mad things you do, for I take them as seen already and pronounced upon, and I will tell wonderful stories to my lady; so write the letter and send me off at once."

"But how shall we manage to write the letter?" said he of the Rueful Countenance.

"And the ass-colt order too," added Sancho.

"All shall be included," said Don Quixote; "and as there is no paper, it

86

would be well done to write it on the leaves of trees, as the ancients did, or on tablets of wax; though that would be as hard to find just now as paper. But it has just occurred to me how it may be conveniently and even more than conveniently written, and that is in the notebook that belonged to Cardenio, and thou wilt take care to have it copied on paper, in a good hand, at the first village thou comest to where there is a schoolmaster, or if not, any sacristan will copy it; but see thou give it not to any notary to copy, for they write a law hand that Satan could not make out."

"But what is to be done about the signature?" said Sancho.

"The letters of Amadis were never signed," said Don Quixote.

"That is all very well," said Sancho, "but the order must be signed, and if it is copied they will say the signature is false, and I shall be left without ass-colts."

"The order shall go signed in the same book," said Don Quixote, "and on seeing it my niece will make no difficulty about obeying it; as to the love letter thou canst put by way of signature, '*Yours till death, the Knight of the Rueful Countenance.*' And it will be no great matter if it is in some other person's hand, for as well as I recollect Dulcinea can neither read nor write, nor in the whole course of her life has she seen handwriting or letter of mine, for my love and hers have been always platonic, not going beyond a modest look, and even that so seldom that I can safely swear I have not seen her four times in all. And perhaps even of those four times she has not once perceived that I was looking at her: such is the retirement and seclusion in which her father Lorenzo Corchuelo and her mother Aldonza Nogales have brought her up."

"So, so!" said Sancho. "Lorenzo Corchuelo's daughter is the lady Dulcinea del Toboso, otherwise called Aldonza Lorenzo?"

"She it is," said Don Quixote, "and she it is that is worthy to be lady of the whole universe."

"I know her well," said Sancho, "and let me tell you she can fling a crowbar as well as the lustiest lad in all the town. Giver of all good! but she is a brave lass, and a right and stout one, and fit to be helpmate to any knight-errant that is or is to be, who may make her his lady. What sting she has and what a voice! I can tell you one day she posted herself on the top of the belfry of the village to call some laborers of theirs that were in a plowed field of her father's, and though they were better than half a league off they heard her as well as if they were at the foot of the tower; and the best of her is that she is not a bit prudish, for she has plenty of affability, and jokes with every-

87

body, and has a grin and a jest for everything. But I must own the truth to your worship, Señor Don Quixote; until now I have been under a great mistake, for I believed truly that the lady Dulcinea must be some princess your worship was in love with, or some person great enough to deserve the rich presents you have sent her, such as the Biscayan and the galley slaves."

"I have told thee many times, Sancho," said Don Quixote, "that thou art a mighty great chatterer, and that with a blunt wit thou art always striving at sharpness. Thinkest thou that the Amarillises, the Sylvias, and all the rest of them, that the books, the ballads, the barbers' shops, the theatres are full of, were really and truly ladies of flesh and blood? Nothing of the kind; the poets only invent them for the most part to furnish a subject for their verses, and that they may pass for lovers, or for men valiant enough to be so; and so it suffices me to think and believe that the good Aldonza Lorenzo is fair and virtuous; and I, for my part, reckon her the most exalted princess in the world. For thou shouldst know, Sancho, if thou dost not know, that two things alone beyond all others are incentives to love, and these are great beauty and a good name, and these two things are to be found in Dulcinea in the highest degree, for in beauty no one equals her and in good name few approach her; and to put the whole thing in a nutshell, I persuade myself that all I say is as I say, neither more nor less, and I picture her in my imagination as I would have her to be, as well in beauty as in condition."

"I say that your worship is entirely right," said Sancho, "and that I am an ass. But I know not how the name of ass came into my mouth, for a rope is not to be mentioned in the house of him who has been hanged; but now for the letter, and then, God be with you, I am off."

Don Quixote took out the notebook, and, retiring to one side, very deliberately began to write the letter, and when he had finished it he called to Sancho, saying he wished to read it to him, so that he might commit it to memory, in case of losing it on the road; for with evil fortune like his anything might be apprehended. To which Sancho replied, "Write it two or three times there in the book and give it to me, and I will carry it very carefully, because to expect me to keep it in my memory is all nonsense, for I have such a bad one that I often forget my own name; but for all that repeat it to me, as I shall like to hear it, for surely it will run as if it was in print."

"Listen," said Don Quixote, "this is what it says:

"Sovereign and exalted Lady: The pierced by the point of absence, the wounded to the heart's core, sends thee, sweetest Dulcinea del Toboso, the health that he himself enjoys not. If thy beauty despises me, if thy worth is not for me, if thy scorn is my affliction, though I be sufficiently long-suffering, hardly shall I endure this anxiety, which, besides being oppressive, is protracted. My good squire Sancho will relate to thee in full, fair ingrate, dear enemy, the condition to which I am reduced on thy account: if it be thy pleasure to give me relief, I am thine; if not, do as may be pleasing to thee; for by ending my life I shall satisfy thy cruelty and my desire.

"Thine till death,

"The Knight of the Rueful Countenance."

"By the life of my father," said Sancho, when he heard the letter, "it is the loftiest thing I ever heard. And how well you fit in 'The Knight of the Rueful Countenance' into the signature. I declare your worship is indeed the very devil, and there is nothing you don't know."

"Everything is needed for the calling I follow," said Don Quixote.

"Now then," said Sancho, "let your worship put the order for the three ass-colts on the other side, and sign it very plainly, that they may recognize it at first sight."

"With all my heart," said Don Quixote, and as he had written it he read it to this effect:

"Mistress Niece: By this first of ass-colts please pay to Sancho Panza, my squire, three of the five I left at home in your charge: said three ass-colts to be paid and delivered for the same number received here in hand, which upon this and upon his receipt shall be duly paid. Done in the heart of the Sierra Morena, the twenty-seventh of August of this present year."

"That will do," said Sancho. "Now let your worship sign it."

"There is no need to sign it," said Don Quixote, "but merely to put my flourish, which is the same as a signature, and enough for three asses, or even three hundred."

"I can trust your worship," returned Sancho; "let me go and saddle Rocinante, and be ready to give me your blessing, for I mean to go at once without seeing the fooleries your worship is going to do; I'll say I saw you do so many that she will not want any more. It will be a saving of time for my return, which will be with the news your worship desires and deserves. But apart from all this, what has your worship to eat until I come back? Will you sally out on the road like Cardenio to force it from the shepherds?"

"Let not that anxiety trouble thee," replied Don Quixote, "for even if I had it I should not eat anything but the herbs and the fruits which this meadow and these trees may yield me; the beauty of this business of mine lies in not eating, and in performing other mortifications."

"Do you know what I am afraid of?" said Sancho upon this; "that I shall not be able to find my way back to this spot where I am leaving you, it is such an out-of-the-way place."

"Observe the landmarks well," said Don Quixote, "for I will try not to go far from this neighborhood, and I will even take care to mount the highest of these rocks to see if I can discover thee returning; however, not to miss me and lose thyself, the best plan will be to cut some branches of the broom that is so abundant about here, and as thou goest to lay them at intervals until thou hast come out upon the plain; these will serve thee, as marks and signs for finding me on thy return."

"So I will," said Sancho Panza, and having cut some, he asked his master's blessing, and not without many tears on both sides, took his leave of him, and mounting Rocinante, of whom Don Quixote charged him earnestly to have as much care as of his own person, he set out for the plain, strewing at intervals the branches of broom as his master had recommended him; and so he went his way, though Don Quixote still entreated him to see him do were it only a couple of mad acts. He had not gone a hundred paces, however, when he returned and said:

"I must say, señor, your worship said quite right, that in order to be able to swear without a weight on my conscience that I had seen you do mad things, it would be well for me to see if it were only one; though in your worship's remaining here I have seen a very great one."

"Did I not tell thee so?" said Don Quixote. "Wait, Sancho, and I will do them in the saying of a credo," and pulling off his breeches in all haste he stripped himself to his skin and his shirt, and then, without more ado, he cut a couple of gambados in the air, and a couple of somersaults, heels over head, making such a display that, not to let him see it a second time, Sancho turned Rocinante's head, and felt easy, and satisfied in his mind that he could swear he had left his master mad.

CHAPTER 18

The Curate's Plan

COMING OUT upon the high road, Sancho made for El Toboso, and the next day reached the inn where the mishap of the blanket had befallen him. As soon as he recognized it he felt as if he were once more flying through the air, and he could not bring himself to enter it though it was an hour when he might well have done so, for it was dinnertime, and he longed to taste something hot as it had been all cold fare with him for many days past. This craving drove him to draw near to the inn, still undecided whether to go in or not, and as he was hesitating there came out two persons who at once recognized him, and said one to the other:

"Señor curate, is not he on the horse there Sancho Panza who, our adventurer's housekeeper told us, went off with her master as squire?"

"So it is," said the curate, "and that is our friend Don Quixote's horse"; and if they knew him so well it was because they were the curate and the barber of his own village, the same who had carried out the scrutiny and sentence upon the books; and as soon as they recognized Sancho Panza and Rocinante, being anxious to hear of Don Quixote, they approached, and calling him by his name the curate said, "Friend Sancho Panza, where is your master?"

Sancho recognized them at once, and determined to keep secret the place and circumstances where and under which he had left his master, so he replied that his master was engaged in a certain quarter on a certain matter of great importance to him which he could not disclose.

"Nay, nay," said the barber, "if you don't tell us where he is, Sancho Panza,

91

we will suspect as we suspect already, that you have murdered and robbed him, for here you are mounted on his horse; in fact, you must produce the master of the hack, or else take the consequences."

"There is no need of threats with me," said Sancho, "for I am not a man to rob or murder anybody; let his own fate, or God who made him, kill each one; my master is engaged very much to his taste doing penance in the midst of these mountains"; and then, offhand and without stopping, he told them how he had left him, and how he was carrying a letter to the lady Dulcinea del Toboso, the daughter of Lorenzo Corchuelo, with whom he was over head and ears in love. They were both amazed at what Sancho Panza told them; for though they were aware of Don Quixote's madness and the nature of it, each time they heard of it they were filled with fresh wonder. They then asked Sancho Panza to show them the letter he was carrying to the lady Dulcinea del Toboso. He said it was written in a notebook, and that his master's directions were that he should have it copied on paper at the first village he came to. On this the curate said if he showed it to him, he himself would make a fair copy of it. Sancho put his hand into his bosom in search of the notebook but could not find it, nor, if he had been searching until now, could he have found it, for Don Quixote had kept it, and had never given it to him, nor had he himself thought of asking for it. When Sancho discovered he could not find the book his face grew deadly pale, and in great haste he again felt his body all over, and seeing plainly it was not to be found, without more ado he gave himself half a dozen cuffs on the face and nose till they were bathed in blood.

Seeing this, the curate and the barber asked him what had happened that he gave himself such rough treatment.

"What should happen?" replied Sancho, "but to have lost from one hand to the other, in a moment, three ass-colts, each of them like a castle?"

"How is that?" said the barber.

"I have lost the notebook," said Sancho, "that contained the letter to Dulcinea, and an order signed by my master in which he directed his niece to give me three ass-colts out of four or five he had at home"; and he then told them about the loss of Dapple.

The curate consoled him, telling him that when his master was found he would get him to renew the order, and make a fresh draft on paper, as was usual and customary; for those made in notebooks were never accepted or honored.

Sancho comforted himself with this. Then he told them more about his master, but he never said a word about the blanketing that had befallen himself in that inn, into which he refused to enter.

"You speak like a man of sense," said the curate, "and you are acting like a good Christian; but what must now be done is to take steps to coax your master out of that useless penance you say he is performing; and we had best turn into this inn to consider what plan to adopt, and also to dine, for it is now time."

Sancho said they might go in, but that he would wait there outside, and that he would tell them afterwards the reason why he was unwilling, and why it did not suit him to enter it; but he begged them to bring him out something to eat, and to let it be hot, and also to bring barley for Rocinante. They left him outside and went in, and presently the barber brought him out something to eat. By and by, after they had between them carefully thought over what they should do to carry out their object, the curate hit upon an idea very well adapted to humor Don Quixote, and effect their purpose; and his notion, which he explained to the barber, was that he himself should assume the disguise of a wandering damsel, while the other should try as best he could to pass for a squire, and that they should thus proceed to where Don Quixote was, and he, pretending to be an aggrieved and distressed damsel, should ask a favor of him, which as a valiant knight-errant he could not refuse to grant; and the favor he meant to ask him was that he should accompany her whither she would conduct him, in order to redress a wrong which a wicked knight had done her, while at the same time she should entreat him not to require her to remove her mask, nor ask her any question touching her circumstances until he had righted her with the wicked knight. And he had no doubt that Don Quixote would comply with any request made in these terms, and that in this way they might remove him and take him to his own village, where they would endeavor to find out if his extraordinary madness admitted of any kind of remedy.

The curate's plan did not seem a bad one to the barber, but on the contrary so good that they immediately set about putting it in execution. They begged a petticoat and hood of the landlady, leaving her in pledge a new cassock of the curate's; and the barber made a beard out of a gray-brown or red ox-tail in which the landlord used to stick his comb. The landlady asked them what they wanted these things for, and the curate told her in a few words about the madness of Don Quixote, and how this disguise was intended to get him away from the mountain where he then was. The landlord and landlady immediately came to the conclusion that the madman was their guest, the master of the blanketed squire, and they told the curate all that had passed between him and them, not omitting what Sancho had been so silent about.

They then took leave of all, and set out under the guidance of Sancho Panza, who went along telling them of the encounter with the madman they met in the Sierra, saying nothing, however, about the finding of the valise and its contents; for with all his simplicity the lad was a trifle covetous.

The next day they reached the place where Sancho had laid the broom branches as marks to direct him to where he had left his master, and recognizing the trail he told them that here was the entrance, and that they would do well to dress themselves, if that was required to deliver his master; for they had already told him that going in this guise and dressing in this way were of the highest importance in order to rescue his master from the pernicious life he had adopted; and they charged him strictly not to tell his master who they were, or that he knew them, and should he ask, as ask he would, if he had given the letter to Dulcinea, to say that he had, and that, as she did not know how to read, she had given an answer by word of mouth, saying that she commanded him, on pain of her displeasure, to come and see her at once. He said, too, that it would be as well for him to go on before them to find him, and give him his lady's answer; for that perhaps might be enough to bring him away from the place without putting them to all this trouble. They approved of what Sancho proposed, and resolved to wait for him until he brought back word of having found his master.

CHAPTER 19

Cardenio Ends His Story

SANCHO PUSHED on into the glens of the Sierra, leaving them in one through which there flowed a little gentle rivulet, and where the rocks and trees afforded a cool and grateful shade. It was an August day with all the heat of one, and the hour was three in the afternoon, all which made the spot the more inviting and tempted them to wait there for Sancho's return, which they did. They were reposing, then, in the shade, when a voice unaccompanied by the notes of any instrument, but sweet and pleasing in its tone, reached their ears, at which they were not a little astonished, as the place did not seem to them likely quarters for one who sang so well.

The song ended with a deep sigh, and the listeners determined to find out who the unhappy being could be whose voice was as rare as his sighs were piteous, and they had not proceeded far when on turning the corner of a rock they discovered a man of the same aspect and appearance as Sancho had described to them when he told them the story of Cardenio. He, showing no astonishment when he saw them, stood still with his head bent down upon his breast like one in deep thought, without raising his eyes to look at them after the first glance when they suddenly came upon him. The curate, who was aware of his misfortune and recognized him by the description, approached him and in a few sensible words urged him to quit a life of such misery, lest he should end it there, which would be the greatest of all misfortunes. Cardenio was then in his right mind, so he replied to them thus:

"I see plainly, sirs, whoever you may be, that Heaven sends me, though I

95

deserve it not, those who seek to draw me away from this to some better retreat. If it be, sirs, that you are here with the same design as others have come with, before you proceed with your wise arguments, I entreat you to hear the story of my countless misfortunes, for perhaps when you have heard it you will spare yourselves the trouble you would take in offering consolation to grief that is beyond the reach of it."

As they, both of them, desired nothing more than to hear from his own lips the cause of his suffering, they entreated him to tell it; and thereupon the unhappy gentleman began his sad story in nearly the same words and manner in which he had related it to Don Quixote and the goatherd a few days before. Coming to the incident of a note which Don Fernando had found in the volume of "Amadis of Gaul," Cardenio said, "By this letter I was induced to demand Luscinda for my wife, and this letter it was that suggested to Don Fernando his design of ruining me before mine could be carried into effect. I told Don Fernando that all Luscinda's father was waiting for was that mine should ask her of him, which I did not dare to suggest to him, fearing that he would not consent to do so; not because he did not know perfectly well the rank, goodness, virtue, and beauty of Luscinda, and that she had qualities that would do honor to any family in Spain, but because I was aware that he did not wish me to marry so soon, before seeing what the Duke Ricardo would do for me. To all this Don Fernando answered that he would take it upon himself to speak to my father, and persuade him to speak to Luscinda's father. O covetous Judas. Who could have thought that Don Fernando, a highborn gentleman, intelligent, bound to me by gratitude for my services, one who could win the object of his love wherever he might set his affections, could have become so cruel as to rob me of my one ewe lamb that was not even yet in my possession?

"To proceed, then: Don Fernando finding my presence an obstacle to the execution of his treacherous and wicked design, resolved to send me to his elder brother under the pretext of asking money from him to pay for six horses which, purposely, and with the sole object of sending me away that he might the better carry out his infernal scheme, he had purchased the very day he offered to speak to my father, and the price of which he now desired me to fetch. Could I have anticipated this treachery? Nay; so far from that, I offered with the greatest pleasure to go at once, in my satisfaction at the good bargain that had been made. That night I spoke with Luscinda, and told her what had been agreed upon with Don Fernando, and how I had strong hopes of our fair and reasonable wishes being realized. She, as unsuspicious as I was of the treachery of Don Fernando, bade me try to return speedily, as she believed the fulfillment of our desires would be delayed only so long as my father put off speaking to hers.

"I reached the place whither I had been sent, gave the letter to Don Fernando's brother, and was kindly received but not promptly dismissed, for he desired me to wait, very much against my will, eight days in some place where the duke his father was not likely to see me, as his brother wrote that the money was to be sent without his knowledge.

"The command was one that exposed me to the temptation of disobeying it, as it seemed to me impossible to endure life for so many days separated from Luscinda, nevertheless as a dutiful servant I obeyed.

Four days later there came a man in quest of me with a letter which he gave me, and which by the address I perceived to be from Luscinda, as the writing was hers. I opened it with fear and trepidation, persuaded that it must be something serious that had impelled her to write to me when at a distance, as she seldom did so when I was near. Before reading it I asked the man who it was that had given it to him, and how long he had been upon the road; he told me that as he happened to be passing through one of the streets of the city at the hour of noon, a very beautiful lady called to him from a window, and with tears in her eyes said to him hurriedly, 'Brother, if you are, as you seem to be, a Christian, for the love of God I entreat you to have this letter dispatched without a moment's delay to the place and person named in the address, all which is well known, and by this you will render a great service to our Lord; and that you may be at no inconvenience in doing so, take what is in this handkerchief'; and said he, 'with this she threw me a handkerchief out of the window in which were tied up a hundred reals and this gold ring which I bring here together with the letter I have given you. And then without waiting for any answer she left the window, though not before she saw me take the letter and the handkerchief, and I had by signs let her know that I would do as she bade me; and so, seeing myself so well paid for the trouble I would have in bringing it to you, and knowing by the address that it was to you it was sent (for, señor, I know you very well), and also unable to resist that beautiful lady's tears, I resolved to trust no one else, but to come myself and give it to you, and in sixteen hours from the time when it was given me I have made the journey, which, as you know, is eighteen leagues.'

97

"All the while the good-natured courier was telling me this, I hung upon his words, my legs trembling under me so that I could scarcely stand. However, I opened the letter and read these words:

" 'The promise Don Fernando gave you to urge your father to speak to mine, he has fulfilled much more to his own satisfaction than to your advantage. I have to tell you, señor, that he has demanded me for a wife, and my father, led away by what he considers Don Fernando's superiority over you, has favored his suit so cordially that in two days hence the betrothal is to take place with such secrecy and so privately that the only witnesses are to be the Heavens above and a few of the household. Picture to yourself the state I am in; judge if it be urgent for you to come; the issue of the affair will show you whether I love you or not. God grant this may come to your hand before mine shall be forced to link itself with his who keeps so ill the faith that he has pledged.'

"Such, in brief, were the words of the letter, words that made me set out at once without waiting any longer for reply or money. I reached home the same day, by the hour which served for speaking with Luscinda, and fortune was pleased to be for once so kind that I found Luscinda at the grating that was the witness of our loves.

"As soon as Luscinda saw me she said, 'Cardenio, I am in my bridal dress, and the treacherous Don Fernando and my covetous father are waiting for me in the hall with the other witnesses, who shall be the witnesses of my death before they witness my betrothal. Be not distressed, my friend, but contrive to be present at this sacrifice, and if that cannot be prevented by my words, I have a dagger concealed which will prevent more deliberate violence, putting an end to my life and giving thee a first proof of the love I have borne and bear thee.' I replied to her distractedly and hastily, in fear lest I should not have time to reply, 'May thy words be verified by thy deeds, lady; and if thou hast a dagger to save thy honor, I have a sword to defend thee or kill myself if fortune be against us.'

"I think she could not have heard all these words, for I perceived that they called her away in haste, as the bridegroom was waiting. Reflecting how important it was that I should be present at what might take place on the occasion, I nerved myself as best I could and went in, for I well knew all the entrances and outlets; and besides, with the confusion that in secret pervaded the house no one took notice of me, so, without being seen, I found an opportunity of placing myself in the recess formed by a window of the hall itself, and concealed by the ends and borders of two tapestries, from between which I could, without being seen, see all that took place in the room.

"The bridegroom entered the hall in his usual dress, without ornament of any kind; as groomsman he had with him a cousin of Luscinda's and except the servants of the house there was no one else in the chamber. Soon afterwards Luscinda came out from an antechamber, attended by her mother and two of her damsels, arrayed and adorned as became her rank and beauty, and in full festival and ceremonial attire.

"All being assembled in the hall, the priest of the parish came in and as he took the pair by the hand to perform the requisite ceremony, at the words, 'Will you, Señora Luscinda, take Señor Don Fernando, here present, for your lawful husband?' I thrust my head and neck out from between the tapestries, and with eager ears and throbbing heart set myself to listen to Luscinda's answer, awaiting in her reply the sentence of death or the grant of life.

"The priest stood waiting for the answer of Luscinda, who for a long time withheld it; and just as I thought she was taking out the dagger to save her honor, or struggling for words to make some declaration of the truth on my behalf, I heard her say in a faint and feeble voice, 'I will.' Don Fernando said the same, and giving her the ring they stood linked by a knot that could never be loosed. The bridegroom then approached to embrace his bride; and she, pressing her hand upon her heart, fell fainting in her mother's arms. It only remains now for me to tell you the state I was in when in that consent that I heard I saw all my hopes mocked, the words and promises of Luscinda proved falsehoods, and the recovery of the prize I had that instant lost rendered impossible forever.

"They were all thrown into confusion by Luscinda's fainting, and as her mother was unlacing her to give her air a sealed paper was discovered in her bosom which Don Fernando seized at once and began to read by the light of one of the torches. As soon as he had read it he seated himself in a chair, leaning his cheek on his hand in the attitude of one deep in thought, without taking any part in the efforts that were being made to recover his bride from her fainting fit.

"Seeing all the household in confusion, I ventured to come out regardless whether I were seen or not, and determined, if I were, to do some frenzied deed that would prove to all the world the righteous indignation of my breast in the punishment of the treacherous Don Fernando, and even in that of the fickle fainting traitress. But my fate, doubtless reserving me for greater sorrows,

99

if such there be, so ordered it that just then I had enough and to spare of that reason which has since been wanting to me; and so, without seeking to take vengeance on my greatest enemies (which might have been easily taken, as all thought of me was so far from their minds), I resolved to take it upon myself, and on myself to inflict the pain they deserved, perhaps with even greater severity than I should have dealt out to them had I then slain them. In a word, I quitted the house and rode out of the city, and when I found myself alone in the open country, screened by the darkness of the night, and tempted by the stillness to give vent to my grief without apprehension or fear of being heard or seen, then I broke silence and lifted up my voice in maledictions upon Luscinda and Don Fernando, as if I could thus avenge the wrong they had done me.

"I journeyed onward for the remainder of the night, and by daybreak I reached one of the passes of these mountains, among which I wandered for three days more without taking any path or road, until I came to some meadows lying on I know not which side of the mountains, and there I inquired of some herdsmen in what direction the most rugged part of the range lay. They told me that it was in this quarter, and I at once directed my course hither, intending to end my life here; but as I was making my way among these crags, my mule dropped dead through fatigue and hunger. I was left on foot, worn out, famishing, without anyone to help me or any thought of seeking help: and so thus I lay stretched on the ground, how long I know not, after which I rose up free from hunger, and found beside me some goatherds, who no doubt were the persons who had relieved me in my need, for they told me how they had found me, and how I had been uttering ravings that showed plainly I had lost my reason; and since then I am conscious that I am not always in full possession of it, but at times so deranged and crazed that I do a thousand mad things.

"Thus do I pass the wretched life that remains to me, until it be Heaven's will to bring it to a close, or so to order my memory that I no longer recollect the beauty and treachery of Luscinda, or the wrong done me by Don Fernando."

CHAPTER 20

The Coming of Dorothea

C ARDENIO BROUGHT to a close his long story, so full of love and misfortune; but just as the curate was about to address some words of comfort to him, he was stopped by a voice that reached his ear, saying in melancholy tones:

"O God! is it possible I have found a place that may serve as a secret grave for the weary load of this body that I support so unwillingly? For there is no one to look to for counsel in doubt, comfort in sorrow, or relief in distress!"

All this was heard distinctly by the curate and those with him, and as it seemed to them to be uttered close by, as indeed it was, they got up to look for the speaker, and before they had gone twenty paces they discovered behind a rock, seated at the foot of an ash tree, a youth in the dress of a peasant, whose face they were unable at the moment to see as he was leaning forward, bathing his feet in the brook that flowed past. They approached so silently that he did not perceive them, being fully occupied in bathing his feet, which were so fair that they looked like two pieces of shining crystal brought forth among the other stones of the brook. The whiteness and beauty of these feet struck them with surprise, for they did not seem to have been made to crush clods or to follow the plow and the oxen as their owner's dress suggested. The youth had on a loose double-skirted dark brown jacket bound tight to his body with a white cloth; he wore besides breeches and gaiters of brown cloth, and on his head a brown montera; and he had the gaiters turned up as far as the middle of the leg, which verily seemed to be of pure alabaster. As soon as he had done bathing his beautiful feet, he wiped them with a towel he took from under the montera, on taking off which he raised his face, and those who were watching him had an opportunity of seeing exquisite beauty.

The youth then took off the montera, and shaking his head from side to side there broke loose and spread out a mass of hair that the beams of the sun might have envied; by this they knew that what had seemed a peasant was a lovely woman, nay the most beautiful their eyes had ever beheld. In their anxiety to learn who she was, they resolved to show themselves, and at the stir they made in getting upon their feet the fair damsel raised her head, and parting her hair from before her eyes with both hands, she looked to see who had made the noise, and the instant she perceived them she started to her feet, and without waiting to put on her shoes or gather up her hair, hastily snatched up a bundle as though of clothes that she had beside her, and endeavored to take flight; but before she had gone six paces she fell to the ground, her delicate feet being unable to bear the roughness of the stones; seeing which, they hastened towards her, and the curate addressing her first said:

"Stay, señora, whoever you may be, for we whom you see here only desire to be of service to you; you have no need to attempt a flight so heedless, for neither can your feet bear it, nor we allow it."

Taken by surprise and bewildered, she made no reply to these words. They, however, came towards her, and the curate taking her hand went on to say:

"What your dress would hide, señora, is made known to us by your hair; a clear proof that it can be no trifling cause that has disguised your beauty in a garb so unworthy of it, and sent it into solitudes like these where we have had the good fortune to find you, if not to relieve your distress, at least to offer you comfort. And so, señora, or señor, or whatever you prefer to be, dismiss the fears that our appearance has caused you and make us acquainted with your good or evil fortunes."

While the curate was speaking, the disguised damsel stood as if spellbound, looking at them without opening her lips or uttering a word. But on the curate addressing some further words to the same effect to her, sighing deeply she broke silence and said:

"That my honor may not be left a matter of doubt in your minds, now that you have discovered me to be a woman, and see that I am young, alone, and in this dress, things that taken together or separately would be enough

102

to destroy any good name, I feel bound to tell what I would willingly keep secret if I could."

She seated herself on a stone with the three placed beside her, and, after an effort to restrain some tears that came to her eyes, in a clear and steady voice began her story thus:

"In this Andalusia there is a town from which a duke takes a title which makes him one of those that are called Grandees of Spain. This nobleman has two sons, the elder heir to his dignity and apparently to his good qualities; the younger heir to I know not what, unless it be treachery. My parents are this lord's vassals, lowly in origin, but so wealthy that by their wealth and free-handed way of life they are coming by degrees to be considered gentlefolk by birth, and even by position; though the wealth and nobility they thought most of was having me for their daughter.

"I was the mirror in which they beheld themselves, the staff of their old age, and the object in which, with submission to Heaven, all their wishes centered, and mine were in accordance with theirs, for I knew their worth; and as I was mistress of their hearts, so was I also of their possessions.

"While I was leading this busy life, in a retirement that might compare with that of a monastery, the eyes of love, or idleness, more properly speaking, discovered me, with the help of the assiduity of Don Fernando; for that is the name of the younger son of the duke I told you of."

The moment the speaker mentioned the name of Don Fernando, Cardenio changed color and broke into a sweat, with such signs of emotion that the curate and the barber, who observed it, feared that one of the mad fits which they heard attacked him sometimes was coming upon him; but Cardenio showed no further agitation and remained quiet, regarding the peasant girl with fixed attention, for he began to suspect who she was. She, however, without noticing the excitement of Cardenio, continuing her story, went on to say:

"And they had hardly discovered me, when, as he owned afterwards, he was smitten with a violent love for me, as the manner in which it displayed itself plainly showed. Don Fernando bribed all the household, he gave and offered gifts and presents to my parents; the love letters that used to come to my hand, no one knew how, were innumerable, containing more promises and oaths than there were letters in them; all which not only did not soften me, but hardened my heart against him, as if he had been my

mortal enemy. Not that the highbred bearing of Don Fernando was dis-
agreeable to me, or that I found his importunities wearisome; for it gave me
a certain sort of satisfaction to find myself so sought and prized by a
gentleman of such distinction, and I was not displeased at seeing my praises
in his letters (for however ugly we women may be, it seems to me that it
always pleases us to hear ourselves called beautiful); but that my own sense
of right was opposed to all this. My parents, who now very plainly perceived Don Fernando's purpose, told me they trusted and confided their
honor and good name to my virtue alone, and bade me consider the
disparity between Don Fernando and myself, from which I might conclude
that his intentions, whatever he might say to the contrary, had for their
aim his own pleasure rather than my advantage. Their sound advice
strengthened my resolution, and I never gave Don Fernando a word in reply
that could hold out to him any hope of success, however remote.

"At length he learned that my parents were contemplating marriage
for me in order to put an end to his hopes, and this intelligence or suspicion
made him act as you shall hear. One night, as I was in my chamber with
no other companion than a damsel who waited on me, with the doors locked,
I found him standing before me, a vision that so astounded me that it deprived
my eyes of sight, and my tongue of speech. I had no power to utter a cry,
nor, I think, did he give me time to utter one, as he immediately approached
me, and taking me in his arms (for, overwhelmed as I was, I was powerless
to help myself), he began to make such professions to me that I know not
how falsehood could have had the power of dressing them up to seem so
like truth; and the traitor contrived that his tears should vouch for his words,
and his sighs for his sincerity.

"I began in some degree to recover myself, and I said to him with more
courage than I thought I could have possessed, 'I am your vassal, señor,
but I am not your slave; I have my self-respect as much as you, a lord and
gentleman: with me your violence will be to no purpose, your wealth will
have no weight, your words will have no power to deceive me, nor your
sighs or tears to soften me: were I to see any of the things I speak of in him
whom my parents gave me as a husband, his will should be mine, and mine
should be bounded by his; and my honor being preserved, I would willingly
yield him what you, señor, would now obtain by force; and this I say lest
you should suppose that any but my lawful husband shall ever win anything
of me.' 'If that,' said this disloyal gentleman, 'be the only scruple you feel,

fairest Dorothea, see here I give you my hand to be yours, and let Heaven, from which nothing is hid, and this image of Our Lady you have here, be witnesses of this pledge.' "

When Cardenio heard her name, he showed fresh agitation and felt convinced of the truth of his former suspicion, but he was unwilling to interrupt the story, and wished to hear the end of what he already all but knew.

"Don Fernando," Dorothea continued, "taking an image that stood in the chamber, placed it as a witness of our betrothal, and with the most binding words and extravagant oaths gave me his promise to become my husband. At the same time I argued the matter in my own mind, saying to myself, 'I may as well avail myself of the honor that chance offers me, for even though his inclination for me should not outlast the attainment of his wishes, I shall be, after all, his wife before God. And if I strive to repel him by scorn, I can see that, fair means failing, he is in a mood to use force, and I shall be left dishonored and without any means of proving my innocence to those who cannot know how innocently I have come to be in this position; for what arguments would persuade my parents that this gentleman entered my chamber without my consent?'

"All these questions and answers passed through my mind in a moment; but the oaths of Don Fernando, the witnesses he appealed to, the tears he shed, and lastly the charms of his person and his highbred grace, which, accompanied by such signs of genuine love, might well have conquered a heart even more free and coy than mine—these were the things that more than all began to influence me and lead me unawares to my ruin. I called my waiting-maid to me, that there might be a witness on earth besides those in Heaven, and again Don Fernando renewed and repeated his oaths, and pressed me closer in his arms, from which he had never allowed me to escape; and so I was left by my maid, and he became a traitor.

"The day which followed the night of my misfortune did not come so quickly, I imagine, as Don Fernando wished, for when desire has attained its object, the greatest pleasure is to fly from the scene of pleasure. I say so because Don Fernando made all haste to leave me, and by the adroitness of my maid, who was indeed the one who had admitted him, gained the street before daybreak; but on taking leave of me he told me, though not with as much earnestness and fervor as when he came, that I might rest assured of his faith and of the sanctity and sincerity of his oaths; and to confirm his words he drew a rich ring off his finger and placed it upon mine. He then took his departure and I was left, I know not whether sorrowful or happy; all I can say is, I was left agitated and troubled in mind and almost bewildered by what had taken place, for as yet I was unable to make up my mind whether what had befallen me was for good or evil.

He came no more, nor for more than a month could I catch a glimpse of him in the street or in church, while I wearied myself with watching for one; although I knew he was in the town, and almost every day went out hunting, a pastime he was very fond of. I remember well how sad and dreary those days and hours were to me; I remember well how I began to doubt as they went by, and to lose confidence in the faith of Don Fernando; and I remember, too, how I was forced to put a constraint on my tears and on the expression of my countenance, not to give my parents cause to ask me why I was so melancholy. But all this was suddenly brought to an end, for the time came when my patience gave way and the secret of my heart became known abroad. The reason was, that a few days later it was reported in the town that Don Fernando had been married in a neighboring city to a maiden of rare beauty, the daughter of parents of distinguished position. It was said, too, that her name was Luscinda, and that at the betrothal some strange things had happened."

Cardenio heard the name of Luscinda, but he only shrugged his shoulders, bit his lips, bent his brows, and before long two streams of tears escaped from his eyes. Dorothea, however, did not interrupt her story, but went on in these words:

"This sad intelligence reached my ears, and, instead of being struck with a chill, with such wrath and fury did my heart burn that I scarcely restrained myself from rushing out into the streets, proclaiming openly the perfidy and treachery of which I was the victim; but this transport of rage was for the time checked by a resolution I formed, to be carried out the same night, and that was to assume this dress, which I got from a servant of my father's, to whom I confided the whole of my misfortune, and whom I entreated to accompany me to the city where I heard my enemy was. I packed up in a linen pillowcase a woman's dress, and some jewels and money to provide for emergencies, and in the silence of the night, without letting my treacherous maid know, I sallied forth from the house, accompanied by my servant and abundant anxieties, and on foot set out for the city. I reached my destination in two days and a half, and on entering the city inquired for the house of Luscinda's parents. The first person I asked gave me more in reply than I sought to know; he showed me the house, and told me all that had occurred at the betrothal of the daughter of the family, an affair of such notoriety in the city that it was the talk of every knot of idlers in the street. He said that on the night of Don Fernando's betrothal with Luscinda, as soon as she had consented to be his bride by saying, 'Yes,' she was taken with a sudden fainting fit, and that on the bridegroom approaching to unlace the bosom of her dress to give her air, he found a paper in her own handwriting, in which she declared that she could not be Don Fernando's bride, because she was already Cardenio's, who, according to the man's account, was a gentleman of distinction of the same city; and if she had accepted Don Fernando, it was only in obedience to her parents. In short, he said, the words of the paper made it clear she meant to kill herself on the completion of the bethrothal, and gave her reasons for putting an end to herself; all of which was confirmed, it was said, by a dagger they found somewhere in her clothes. On seeing this, Don Fernando, persuaded that Luscinda had slighted and trifled with him, assailed her before she had recovered from her swoon, and tried to stab her with the dagger that had been found, and would have succeeded had not her parents and those who were present prevented him. It was said, moreover, that Don Fernando went away at once, and that Luscinda did not recover from her prostration until the next day, when she told her parents how she was really the bride of that Cardenio I have mentioned. I learned besides that Cardenio, according to report, had been present at the betrothal; and that upon seeing her betrothed contrary to his expectation, he had quitted the city in despair, leaving behind him a letter declaring the wrong Luscinda had done him, and his intention of going where no one should ever see him again. All this was a matter of notoriety in the city, and everyone spoke of it; especially when it became known that Luscinda was missing from her father's house and from the city, for she was not to be found anywhere, to the distraction of her parents, who knew not what steps to take to recover her.

"While I was in the city, uncertain what to do, as I could not find Don Fernando, I heard notice given by the public crier offering a great reward to anyone who should find me, and giving the particulars of my age and of the very dress I wore. The instant I heard the notice I quitted the city with my servant, who now began to show signs of wavering in his fidelity to me, and the same night, for fear of discovery, we entered the most thickly wooded part of these mountains. But, as is commonly said, one evil calls up another and the end of one misfortune is apt to be the beginning of one still greater, and so it proved in my case; for my worthy servant, until then so faithful and trusty, when he found me in this lonely spot, moved more by his own villainy than by my beauty, sought to take advantage of the opportunity which these solitudes seemed to present him. But just Heaven, that seldom fails to aid good intentions, so aided mine that with my slight strength and with little exertion I pushed him over a precipice, where I left him, whether dead or alive I know not; and then, with greater speed than seemed possible in my terror and fatigue, I made my way into the mountains, without any thought or purpose save that of hiding myself among them, and escaping my father and those dispatched in search of me by his orders. It is now I know not how many months since with this object I came here, where I met a herdsman who engaged me as his servant at a place in the heart of this Sierra, and all this time I have been serving him as herd, striving to keep always afield to hide these locks which have now unexpectedly betrayed me. But all my care and pains were unavailing, for my master made the discovery that I was not a man, and I thought it a lesser evil to leave him and again conceal myself among these crags, than make trial of my strength and argument with him. So, as I say, once more I went into hiding to seek for some place where I might implore Heaven to have pity on my misery, and grant me help and strength to escape from it, or let me die among the solitudes, leaving no trace of an unhappy being who, by no fault of hers, has furnished matter for scandal at home and abroad."

CHAPTER 21

Don Quixote Is Tricked

WITH THESE WORDS Dorothea became silent, and the color that overspread her face showed plainly the pain and shame she was suffering at heart. The curate was just about to offer her some consolation and advice when Cardenio forestalled him, saying, "So then, señora, you are the fair Dorothea, the only daughter of the rich Clenardo?" Dorothea was astonished at hearing her father's name, and at the miserable appearance of him who mentioned it, for it has been already said how wretchedly clad Cardenio was; so she said to him:

"And who may you be, brother, who seem to know my father's name so well? For so far, if I remember rightly, I have not mentioned it in the whole story of my misfortunes."

"I am that unhappy being, señora," replied Cardenio, "whom, as you have said, Luscinda declared to be her husband; I am the unfortunate Cardenio, whom the wrongdoing of him who has brought you to your present condition has reduced to the state you see me in, bare, ragged, bereft of all human comfort, and what is worse, of reason. I betook myself to these solitudes, resolved to end here the life I hated as if it were my mortal enemy. But fate would not rid me of it, contenting itself with robbing me of my reason, perhaps to preserve me for the good fortune I have had in meeting you; for if that which you have just told us be true, as I believe it to be, it may be that Heaven has yet in store for both of us a happier termination to our misfortunes than we look for; because seeing that Luscinda cannot marry Don Fernando, being mine, as she has herself so openly declared, and that

Don Fernando cannot marry her as he is yours, we may reasonably hope that Heaven will restore to us what is ours, as it is still in existence and not yet alienated or destroyed. I entreat you, señora, to form new resolutions in your better mind, as I mean to do in mine, preparing yourself to look forward to happier fortunes; for I swear to you by the faith of a gentleman and a Christian not to desert you until I see you in possession of Don Fernando, and if I cannot by words induce him to recognize his obligation to you, in that case to avail myself of the right which my rank as a gentleman gives me, and with just cause challenge him on account of the injury he has done you."

Cardenio's words completed the astonishment of Dorothea, not knowing how to return thanks for such an offer. The curate replied for both, commended the sound reasoning of Cardenio, and urged them to come with him to his village, where they might furnish themselves with what they needed, and take measures to discover Don Fernando, or restore Dorothea to her parents, or do what seemed to them most advisable. Cardenio and Dorothea thanked him, and accepted the kind offer he made them; and the barber said some kindly words also, and also explained to them in a few words the object that had brought them there, and the strange nature of Don Quixote's madness, and how they were waiting for his squire, who had gone in search of him.

At this moment they heard a shout, and recognized it as coming from Sancho Panza, who, not finding them where he had left them, was calling aloud to them. They went to meet him, and in answer to their inquiries about Don Quixote, he told them how he had found him stripped to his shirt, lank, yellow, half dead with hunger, and sighing for his lady Dulcinea; and although he had told him that she commanded him to quit that place and come to El Toboso, where she was expecting him, he had answered that he was determined not to appear in the presence of her beauty until he had done deeds to make him worthy of her favor. The curate told him not to be uneasy, for they would fetch him away in spite of himself. He then told Cardenio and Dorothea what they had proposed to do to cure Don Quixote, or at any rate take him home; upon which Dorothea said that she could play the distressed damsel better than the barber; especially as she had there the dress in which to do it.

Dorothea then took out of her pillowcase a complete petticoat of some rich stuff, and a green mantle of some other fine material, and a necklace and other ornaments out of a little box, and with these in an instant she so arrayed herself that she looked like a great and rich lady. All this, and more, she said, she had taken from home in case of need, but that until then she had had no occasion to make use of it. They were all highly delighted with her grace, air, and beauty, and declared Don Fernando to be a man of very little taste when he rejected such charms. But the one who admired her most was Sancho Panza, for it seemed to him (what indeed was true) that in all the days of his life he had never seen such a lovely creature; and he asked the curate with great eagerness who this beautiful lady was, and what she wanted in these out-of-the-way quarters.

"She is called the Princess Micomicona," said the curate, "for as her kingdom is Micomicon, it is clear that must be her name."

By this time Dorothea had seated herself upon the curate's mule, and the barber had fitted the ox-tail beard to his face, and they now told Sancho to conduct them to where Don Quixote was, warning him not to say that he knew either the curate or the barber. Neither the curate nor Cardenio, however, thought fit to go with them; Cardenio lest he should remind Don Quixote of the quarrel he had with him, and the curate as there was no necessity for his presence just yet, so they allowed the others to go on before them, while they themselves followed slowly on foot. The curate did not forget to instruct Dorothea how to act, but she said they might make their minds easy, as everything would be done exactly as the books of chivalry required and described.

They had gone about three-quarters of a league when they discovered Don Quixote in a wilderness of rocks, by this time clothed, but without his armor; and as soon as Dorothea saw him and was told by Sancho that that was Don Quixote, she whipped her palfrey, the well-bearded barber following her, and on coming up to him her squire sprang from his mule and came forward to receive her in his arms, and she dismounting with great ease of manner advanced to kneel before the feet of Don Quixote; and though he strove to raise her up she without rising addressed him in this fashion:

"From this spot I will not rise, O valiant knight, until your goodness and courtesy grant me a boon, which will redound to the honor and renown of your person and render a service to the most disconsolate and afflicted damsel the sun has seen; and if the might of your strong arm corresponds to the repute of your immortal fame, you are bound to aid the helpless being who, led by the savor of your renowned name, hath come from far distant lands to seek your aid in her misfortunes."

111

"I will not answer a word, beauteous lady," replied Don Quixote, "nor will I listen to anything further concerning you, until you rise from the earth."

"I will not rise, señor," answered the afflicted damsel, "unless of your courtesy the boon I ask is first granted me."

"I grant and accord it," said Don Quixote, "provided without detriment or prejudice to my king, my country, or her who holds the key of my heart and freedom, it may be complied with."

"It will not be to the detriment or prejudice of any of them, my worthy lord," said the damsel.

"Let your great beauty rise, for I grant the boon which you would ask of me," said Don Quixote.

"Then what I ask," said the damsel, "is that your magnanimous person accompany me at once whither I will conduct you, and that you promise not to engage in any other quest until you have avenged me of a traitor who, against all human and divine law, has usurped my kingdom."

"I repeat that I grant it," replied Don Quixote; "and so, lady, you may from this day forth lay aside the melancholy that distresses you, and let your failing hopes gather new life and strength, for with the help of God and of my arm you will soon see yourself restored to your kingdom."

The distressed damsel strove with much pertinacity to kiss his hands; but Don Quixote, who was in all things a polished and courteous knight, would by no means allow it, but made her rise and embraced her with great politeness, and ordered Sancho to look to Rocinante's girths, and to arm him without a moment's delay. Sancho took down the armor, which was hung up on a tree like a trophy, and having seen to the girths armed his master in a trice, who as soon as he found himself in his armor exclaimed:

"Let us be gone in the name of God to bring aid to this great lady."

The barber was all this time on his knees at great pains to hide his laughter and not let his beard fall, for had it fallen maybe their fine scheme would have come to nothing; but now seeing the boon granted, and the promptitude with which Don Quixote prepared to set out in compliance with it, he rose and took his lady's hand, and between them they placed her upon the mule. Don Quixote then mounted Rocinante, and the barber settled himself on his beast, Sancho being left to go on foot, which made him feel anew the loss of his Dapple.

Cardenio and the curate were watching all this from among some bushes, not knowing how to join company with the others; but the curate soon hit

"I grant the boon and accord it," said Don Quixote.

upon a way of effecting their purpose, and with a pair of scissors he had in a case he quickly cut off Cardenio's beard, and putting on him a gray jerkin of his own he gave him a black cloak, leaving himself in his breeches and doublet, while Cardenio's appearance was so different from what it had been that he would not have known himself had he seen himself in a mirror. Having effected this, although the others had gone on ahead while they were disguising themselves, they easily came out on the high road before them, for the brambles and awkward places they encountered did not allow those on horseback to go as fast as those on foot. They then posted themselves on the level ground at the outlet of the Sierra, and as soon as Don Quixote and his companions emerged from it the curate began to examine him very deliberately, as though he were striving to recognize him, and after having stared at him for some time he hastened towards him with open arms exclaiming, "A happy meeting with the mirror of chivalry, my worthy compatriot Don Quixote of La Mancha!"

Don Quixote, astonished at the stranger's words, looked at him attentively, and at length recognized him, very much surprised to see him there, and made great efforts to dismount. This, however, the curate would not allow, on which Don Quixote said, "Permit me, señor curate, for it is not fitting that I should be on horseback and so reverend a person as your worship on foot."

"On no account will I allow it," said the curate; "your mightiness must remain on horseback, for it is on horseback you achieve the greatest deeds and adventures that have been beheld in our age."

"Nor even for that will I consent," answered Don Quixote, "and I know it will be the good pleasure of my lady the princess, out of love for me, to order her squire to give up the saddle of his mule to your worship, and he can sit behind if the beast will bear it."

"It will, I am sure," said the princess, "and I am sure, too, that I need not order my squire, for he is too courteous and considerate to allow a Churchman to go on foot when he might be mounted."

"That he is," said the barber, and at once alighting, he offered his saddle to the curate, who accepted it without much entreaty; but unfortunately as the barber was mounting behind, the mule lifted its hind hoofs and let fly a couple of kicks in the air, which so took Master Nicholas by surprise that he came to the ground, giving so little heed to his beard that it fell off, and all he could do when he found himself without it was to cover his face hastily with both his hands and moan that his teeth were knocked out.

Don Quixote when he saw all that bundle of beard detached, without jaws or blood, from the face of the fallen squire, exclaimed:

"By the living God, but this is a great miracle! It has knocked off and plucked away the beard from his face as if it had been shaved off designedly."

The curate, seeing the danger of discovery that threatened his scheme, at once pounced upon the beard and hastened with it to where Master Nicholas lay, still uttering moans, and drawing his head to his breast had it on in an instant, muttering over him some words which he said were a certain special charm for sticking on beards, as they would see; and as soon as he had it fixed he left him, and the squire appeared well bearded and whole as before, whereat Don Quixote was beyond measure astonished, and begged the curate to teach him that charm, as he was persuaded that it must be good for more than beards.

"And so it is," said the curate, and he promised to teach it to him on the first opportunity.

Three then being mounted, that is to say, Don Quixote, the princess, and the curate, and three on foot, Cardenio, the barber, and Sancho Panza, Don Quixote said to the damsel:

"Let your highness, lady, lead on whithersoever is most pleasing to you." But before she could answer, the curate said:

"Towards what kingdom would your ladyship direct our course? Is it perchance towards that of Micomicon? It must be, or else I know little about kingdoms."

She, being ready on all points, understood that she was to answer "Yes," so she said, "Yes, señor, my way lies towards that kingdom."

"In that case," said the curate, "we must pass right through my village."

"I would ask the señor curate to tell me," said Don Quixote, "what it is that has brought him into these parts, alone, unattended, and so lightly clad that I am filled with amazement."

"I will answer that briefly," replied the curate; "you must know then, Señor Don Quixote, that Master Nicholas, our friend and barber, and I were going to Seville; and passing by this place yesterday we were attacked by four footpads, who stripped us even to our beards. The story goes in the neighborhood that those who attacked us belong to a number of galley slaves who, they say, were set free almost on the very same spot by a man of such valor that, in spite of the commissary and the guards, he released the whole of them; and beyond all doubt he must have been out of his senses, or he must be as great a scoundrel as they, or some man without a heart or conscience to let the wolf loose among the sheep, the fox among the hens, the fly among the honey. He has defrauded justice, and opposed his king and lawful master, for he opposed his just commands; he has, I say, robbed the galleys of their feet, stirred up the Holy Brotherhood which for many years past has been quiet, and, lastly, has done a deed by which his soul may be lost without any gain to his body." Sancho had told the curate and the barber of the adventure of the galley slaves, which, so much to his glory, his master had achieved, and hence the curate in alluding to it made the most of it to see what would be said or done by Don Quixote, who changed color at every word, not daring to say that it was he who had been the liberator of those worthy people. "These, then," said the curate, "were they who robbed us; and God in his mercy pardon him who would not let them go to the punishment they deserved."

CHAPTER 22

Dapple's Return

THE CURATE had hardly ceased speaking, when Sancho said, "In faith, then, señor curate, he who did that deed was my master; and it was not for want of my telling him beforehand and warning him to mind what he was about, and that it was a sin to set them at liberty, as they were all on the march there because they were special scoundrels."

"Blockhead!" said Don Quixote at this, "it is no concern of knights-errant to inquire whether any oppressed persons that they may meet on the high roads suffer as they do because of their faults or because of their misfortunes. It only concerns them to aid them as persons in need of help, having regard to their sufferings and not to their rascalities."

Dorothea, who was shrewd and sprightly, and by this time thoroughly understood Don Quixote's crazy turn, and that all except Sancho Panza were making game of him, said to him, on observing his irritation, "Sir Knight, calm yourself, for if the curate had known that the galley slaves had been set free by that unconquered arm he would have stopped his mouth thrice over, or even bitten his tongue three times before he would have said a word that tended towards disrespect of your worship."

"That I swear heartily," said the curate, "and I would have even plucked off a mustache."

While this was going on they saw coming along the road they were following a man mounted on an ass, who when he came close seemed to be a gypsy; but Sancho Panza, whose eyes and heart were there wherever he saw

116

asses, no sooner beheld the man than he knew him to be Gines de Pasamonte; for it was, in fact, Dapple that carried Pasamonte, who to escape recognition and to sell the ass had disguised himself as a gypsy, being able to speak the gypsy language. Sancho saw him and recognized him, and the instant he did so he shouted to him, "Ginesillo, you thief, give up my treasure, quit my ass, be off, rip, get thee gone, thief, and give up what is not thine."

There was no necessity for so many words or objurgations, for at the first one Gines jumped down, and at a trot like racing speed made off and got clear of them all. Sancho hastened to his Dapple, and embracing him, he said, "How hast thou fared, my blessing, Dapple of my eyes, my comrade?" all the while kissing him and caressing him as if he were a human being. The ass held his peace, and let himself be kissed and caressed by Sancho without answering a single word. They all came up and congratulated him on having found Dapple, Don Quixote especially, who told him that notwithstanding this he would not cancel the order for the three ass-colts, for which Sancho thanked him.

While the two went along conversing in this fashion, Master Nicholas called out to them to wait a while, as they wanted to halt and drink at a little spring there was there. Cardenio had now put on the clothes which Dorothea was wearing when they found her, and though they were not very good, they were far better than those he put off. They dismounted together by the side of the spring, and with what the curate had provided himself with at the inn they appeased, though not very well, the keen appetite they all of them brought with them.

While they were so employed there happened to come by a youth passing on his way, who stopping to examine the party at the spring, the next moment ran to Don Quixote and clasping him round the legs, began to weep freely, saying, "O señor, do you not know me? Look at me well; I am that lad Andres that your worship released from the oak tree where I was tied."

Don Quixote recognized him, and taking his hand he turned to those present and said: "That your worships may see how important it is to have knights-errant to redress the wrongs and injuries done by tyrannical and wicked men in this world, I may tell you that some days ago passing through a wood, I heard cries and piteous complaints as of a person in pain and distress; I immediately hastened, impelled by my bounden duty, to the quarter whence the plaintive accents seemed to me to proceed, and I found tied to an oak this lad who now stands before you, which in my heart I rejoice at, for his testimony will not permit me to depart from the truth in any particular. He was, I say, tied to an oak, naked from the waist up, and a clown, whom I afterwards found to be his master, was scarifying him by lashes with the reins of his mare. As soon as I saw him I asked the reason of so cruel a flagellation. The boor replied that he was flogging him because he was his servant and because of carelessness that proceeded rather from dishonesty than stupidity; on which this boy said, 'Señor, he flogs me only because I ask for my wages.' The master made I know not what speeches and explanations, which, though I listened to them, I did not accept. In short, I compelled the clown to unbind him, and to swear he would take him with him, and pay him real by real. Is not all this true, Andres my son? Didst thou not mark with what authority I commanded him, and with what humility he promised to do all I enjoined, specified, and required of him? Answer without hesitation; tell these gentlemen what took place, that they may see that it is as great an advantage as I say to have knights-errant abroad."

"All that your worship has said is quite true," answered the lad; "but the end of the business turned out just the opposite of what your worship supposes."

"How! the opposite?" said Don Quixote. "Did not the clown pay thee then?"

"Not only did he not pay me," replied the lad, "but as soon as your worship had passed out of the wood and we were alone, he tied me up again to the same oak and gave me a fresh flogging, that left me like a flayed Saint Bartholomew; and every stroke he gave me he followed up with some jest or gibe about having made a fool of your worship, and but for the pain I was suffering I should have laughed at the things he said. In short he left me in such a condition that I have been until now in a hospital getting cured of the injuries which that rascally clown inflicted on me then; for all which your worship is to blame; for if you had gone your own way and not come where there was no call for you, nor meddled in other people's affairs, my master would have been content with giving me one or two dozen lashes, and would have then loosed me and paid me what he owed me; but when your worship abused him so out of measure, and gave him so many hard words, his anger was kindled; and as he could not get revenge himself on you, as soon as he saw you had left him the storm burst upon me."

"The mischief," said Don Quixote, "lay in my going away; for I should not have gone until I had seen thee paid; because I ought to have known well by long experience that there is no clown who will keep his word if he finds it will not suit him to keep it; but thou rememberest, Andres, that I swore if he did not pay thee I would seek him, and find him."

"That is true," said Andres; "but it was of no use."

"Thou shalt see now whether it is of use or not," said Don Quixote; and so saying, he got up hastily and bade Sancho bridle Rocinante, who was browsing while they were eating. Dorothea asked him what he meant to do. He replied that he meant to go in search of this clown and chastise him for such iniquitous conduct, and see Andres paid to the last maravedi. To which she replied that he must remember that in accordance with his promise he could not engage in any enterprise until he had concluded hers; and that as he knew this better than anyone, he should restrain his ardor until his return from her kingdom.

"That is true," said Don Quixote, "and Andres must have patience until my return as you say, señora; but I once more swear not to stop until I have seen him avenged."

"I have no faith in those oaths," said Andres. "I would rather have now something to help me to get to Seville than all the revenges in the world; if you have here anything to eat that I can take with me, give it me, and God be with your worship and all knights-errant; and may their errands turn out as well for themselves as they have for me."

Sancho took out from his store a piece of bread and another of cheese, and giving them to the lad he said, "Here, take this, brother Andres, for we have all of us a share in your misfortune."

"Why, what share have you got?"

"This share of bread and cheese I am giving you," answered Sancho, "and God knows whether I shall feel the want of it myself or not; for I would have you know, friend, that we squires to knights-errant have to bear a great deal of hunger and hard fortune, and even other things more easily felt than told."

Andres seized his bread and cheese, and seeing that nobody gave him anything more, bent his head, and said before leaving, "For the love of God, sir knight-errant, if you ever meet me again, though you may see them cutting me to pieces, give me no aid, but leave me to my misfortune, which will not be so great but that a greater will come to me by being helped by your worship, on whom, and on all the knights-errant that have ever been born, God send his curse."

Don Quixote was getting up to chastise him, but he took to his heels at such a pace that no one attempted to follow him; and mightily chapfallen was Don Quixote at Andres' story, and the others had to take great care to restrain their laughter so as not to put him entirely out of countenance.

CHAPTER 23

Battle with the Wineskins

THEIR DAINTY REPAST being finished, they saddled at once, and without any adventure worth mentioning they reached next day the inn, the object of Sancho Panza's fear and dread; but though he would have rather not entered it, there was no help for it. The landlady, the landlord, their daughter, and Maritornes, when they saw Don Quixote and Sancho coming, went out to welcome them with signs of hearty satisfaction, which Don Quixote received with dignity and gravity, and bade them make up a better bed for him than the last time: to which the landlady replied that if he paid better than he did the last time she would give him one fit for a prince. Don Quixote said he would, so they made up a tolerable one for him in the same garret as before; and he lay down at once, being sorely shaken and in want of sleep.

All the people of the inn were struck with astonishment at the beauty of Dorothea, and at the comely figure of the shepherd Cardenio. The curate made them get ready such fare as there was in the inn, and the landlord, in hope of better payment, served them up a tolerably good dinner. All this time Don Quixote was asleep, and they thought it best not to waken him, as sleeping would now do him more good than eating.

While at dinner, the company consisting of the landlord, his wife, their daughter, Maritornes, and all the travelers, they discussed the strange craze of Don Quixote and the manner in which he had been found; and the landlady, looking round to see if Sancho was there, when she saw he was not, she gave them the whole story of his blanketing, which they received with no little amusement.

At this moment, Sancho Panza himself burst forth in wild excitement from the garret where Don Quixote was lying, shouting, "Run, sirs! quick; and help my master, who is in the thick of the toughest and stiffest battle I ever laid eyes on. By the living God he has given the giant, the enemy of my lady the Princess Micomicona, such a slash that he has sliced his head clean off as if it were a turnip."

"What are you talking about, brother?" said the curate. "Are you in your senses, Sancho?"

Here they heard a loud noise in the chamber, and Don Quixote shouting out, "Stand, thief, brigand, villain; now I have got thee, and thy scimitar shall not avail thee!" And then it seemed as though he were slashing vigorously at the wall.

"Don't stop to listen," said Sancho, "but go in and part them or help my master: though there is no need of that now, for no doubt the giant is dead by this time and giving account to God of his past wicked life; for I saw the blood flowing on the ground, and the head cut off and fallen on one side, and it is as big as a large wineskin."

"May I die," said the landlord at this, "if Don Quixote or Don Devil has not been slashing some of the skins of red wine that stand full at his bed's head, and the spilled wine must be what this good fellow takes for blood"; and so saying he went into the room and the rest after him, and there they found Don Quixote in the strangest costume in the world. He was in his shirt, which was not long enough in front to cover his thighs completely and was six fingers shorter behind; his legs were very long and lean, covered with hair, and anything but clean; on his head he had a little greasy red cap that belonged to the host, round his left arm he had rolled the blanket of the bed, to which Sancho, for reasons best known to himself, owed a grudge, and in his right hand he held his unsheathed sword, with which he was slashing about on all sides, uttering exclamations as if he were actually fighting some giant: and the best of it was his eyes were not open, for he was fast asleep, and dreaming that he was doing battle with the giant. For his imagination was so wrought upon by the adventure he was going to accomplish, that it made him dream he had already reached the kingdom of Micomicon, and was engaged in combat with his enemy; and believing he was laying on the giant, he had given so many sword cuts to the skins that the whole room was full of wine. On seeing

"Stand, thief, brigand, villain!"

this the landlord was so enraged that he fell on Don Quixote, and with his clenched fist began to pummel him in such a way, that if Cardenio and the curate had not dragged him off, he would have brought the war of the giant to an end. But in spite of all the poor gentleman never woke until the barber brought a great pot of cold water from the well and flung it with one dash all over his body, on which Don Quixote woke up, but not so completely as to understand what was the matter. Dorothea, seeing how slight his attire was, would not go in to witness the battle between her champion and her opponent. As for Sancho, he went searching all over the floor for the head of the giant, and not finding it he said, "This head is not to be seen anywhere about, though I saw it cut off with my own eyes and the blood running from the body as if from a fountain."

"What blood and fountains are you talking about, enemy of God and his saints?" said the landlord. "Don't you see, you thief, that the blood and the fountain are only these skins here that have been stabbed and the red wine swimming all over the room?—and I wish I saw the soul of him that stabbed them swimming in hell."

"I know nothing about that," said Sancho; "all I know is it will be my bad luck that through not finding this head my county will melt away like salt in water"; for Sancho awake was worse than his master asleep, so much had his master's promises addled his wits.

The landlord was beside himself at the coolness of the squire and the mischievous doings of the master, and swore it should not be like the last time when they went without paying; and that their privileges of chivalry should not hold good this time to let one or other of them off without paying, even to the cost of the plugs that would have to be put to the damaged wineskins. The curate was holding Don Quixote's hands, who, fancying he had now ended the adventure and was in the presence of the Princess Micomicona, knelt before the curate and said, "Exalted and beauteous lady, your highness may live from this day forth fearless of any harm this base being could do you; and I too from this day forth am released from the promise I gave you, since by the help of God on high and by the favor of her by whom I live and breathe, I have fulfilled it so successfully."

"Did not I say so?" said Sancho on hearing this.

Who could have helped laughing at the absurdities of the pair, master and man? And laugh they did, all except the landlord, who cursed; but at length the barber, Cardenio, and the curate contrived with no small trouble to get

Don Quixote on the bed, and he fell asleep with every appearance of excessive weariness. They left him to sleep, and came out to the gate of the inn to console Sancho Panza on not having found the head of the giant; but much more work had they to appease the landlord, who was furious at the sudden death of his wineskins; and said the landlady half scolding, half crying, "At an evil moment and in an unlucky hour he came into my house, this knight-errant—would that I had never set eyes on him, for dear he has cost me."

Just at that instant the landlord, standing at the gate, exclaimed, "Here comes a fine troop of guests! If they stop here we may rejoice."

"What are they?" asked Cardenio.

"Four men," said the landlord, "with lances and bucklers, and all with black veils, and with them is a woman in white, also veiled, and two attendants on foot."

"Are they very near?" asked the curate.

"So near," answered the landlord, "that here they come."

Hearing this, Dorothea covered her face, and Cardenio retreated into Don Quixote's room, and they hardly had time to do so before the whole party the host had described entered the inn.

CHAPTER 24

Lovers' Meeting

THE FOUR that were on horseback, who were of highbred appearance and bearing, dismounted, and came forward to take down the woman who rode on the sidesaddle, and one of them taking her in his arms placed her in a chair that stood at the entrance of the room where Cardenio had hidden himself. All this time neither she nor they had removed their veils or spoken a word, only on sitting down on the chair the woman gave a deep sigh and let her arms fall like one who was ill and weak. The attendants on foot then led the horses away to the stable. Observing this, the curate, curious to know who these people in such a dress and preserving such silence were, went to where the servants were standing and put the question to one of them, who answered him.

"Faith, sir, I cannot tell you who they are. I only know they seem to be people of distinction, particularly he who advanced to take the lady you saw in his arms; and I say so because all the rest show him respect, and nothing is done except what he directs and orders."

"And the lady, who is she?" asked the curate.

"That I cannot tell you either," said the servant, "for I have not seen her face all the way: I have indeed heard her sigh many times and utter such groans that she seems to be giving up the ghost every time; but it is no wonder if we do not know more than we have told you, as my comrade and I have only been in their company two days, for having met us on the road they persuaded us to accompany them to Andalusia, promising to pay us well."

"And have you heard any of them called by his name?" asked the curate.

125

"No, indeed," replied the servant; "they all preserve a marvelous silence on the road, for not a sound is to be heard among them except the poor lady's sighs and sobs, which make us pity her; and we feel sure that wherever it is she is going, it is against her will, and as far as one can judge from her dress she is a nun or, what is more likely, about to become one; and perhaps it is because taking the vows is not of her own free will, that she is so unhappy as she seems to me."

"That may well be," said the curate, and leaving them he returned to where Dorothea was, who, hearing the veiled lady sigh, moved by natural compassion drew near to her and said, "What are you suffering from, señora? If it be anything that women are accustomed and know how to relieve, I offer you my services with all my heart."

To this the unhappy lady made no reply; and though Dorothea repeated her offers more earnestly she still kept silence, until the gentleman with the veil, who, the servant said, was obeyed by the rest, approached and said to Dorothea, "Do not give yourself the trouble, señora, of making any offers to that woman, for it is her way to give no thanks for anything that is done for her; and do not try to make her answer unless you want to hear some lie from her lips."

"I have never told a lie," was the immediate reply of her who had been silent until now; "on the contrary, it is because I am truthful and so ignorant of lying devices that I am now in this miserable condition; and this I call you yourself to witness, for it is my unstained truth that has made you false and a liar."

Cardenio heard these words distinctly, being quite close to the speaker, for there was only the door of Don Quixote's room between them, and the instant he did so, uttering a loud exclamation he cried, "Good God! What is this I hear? What voice is this that has reached my ears?" Startled at the voice, the lady turned her head; and not seeing the speaker she stood up and attempted to enter the room; observing which the gentleman held her back, preventing her from moving a step. In her agitation and sudden movement the silk with which she had covered her face fell off and disclosed a countenance of marvelous beauty, but pale and terrified; for she kept turning her eyes, everywhere she could direct her gaze, with an eagerness that made her look as if she had lost her senses, and so marked that it excited the pity of Dorothea and all who beheld her, though they knew not what caused it.

The gentleman grasped her firmly by the shoulders, and being so fully occupied with holding her back, he was unable to put a hand to his veil which was falling off, as it did at length entirely, and Dorothea, who was holding the lady in her arms, raising her eyes saw that he who likewise held her was her husband, Don Fernando. The instant she recognized him, with a prolonged plaintive cry drawn from the depths of her heart, she fell backwards fainting, and but for the barber being close by to catch her in his arms, she would have fallen completely to the ground. The curate at once hastened to uncover her face and throw water on it, and as he did so Don Fernando, for he it was who held the other in his arms, recognized her and stood as if death-stricken by the sight; not, however, relaxing his grasp of Luscinda, for it was she who was struggling to release herself from his hold, having recognized Cardenio by his voice, as he had recognized her. Cardenio also heard Dorothea's cry as she fell fainting, and imagining that it came from his Luscinda burst forth in terror from the room, and the first thing he saw was Don Fernando with Luscinda in his arms. Don Fernando, too, knew Cardenio at once; and all three, Luscinda, Cardenio, and Dorothea, stood in silent amazement scarcely knowing what had happened to them.

They gazed at one another without speaking. The first to break silence was Luscinda, who thus addressed Don Fernando: "Leave me, Señor Don Fernando, for the sake of what you owe to yourself; if no other reason will induce you, leave me to cling to the wall of which I am the ivy, to the support from which neither your importunities, nor your threats, nor your promises, nor your gifts have been able to detach me. See how Heaven, by ways strange and hidden from our sight, has brought me face to face with my true husband; and well you know by dear-bought experience that death alone will be able to efface him from my memory. May this plain declaration, then, lead you, as you can do nothing else, to turn your love into rage, your affection into resentment, and so to take my life; for if I yield it up in the presence of my beloved husband I count it well bestowed; it may be by my death he will be convinced that I kept my faith to him to the last moment of life."

Meanwhile Dorothea had come to herself, and had heard Luscinda's words, by which she guessed who she was; but seeing that Don Fernando did not yet release her or reply to her, summoning up her resolution as well as she could she rose and with a flood of tears addressed him thus:

"If, my lord, the beams of that sun that thou holdest eclipsed in thine arms did not dazzle and rob thine eyes of sight thou wouldst have seen by this time that I, so long as thou wilt have it so, am the unhappy and unfortunate Doro-

127

thea. I am that lowly peasant girl whom thou in thy goodness or for thy pleasure wouldst raise high enough to call herself thine. Bethink thee, my lord, the unsurpassable affection I bear thee may compensate for the beauty and noble birth for which thou wouldst desert me. Thou canst not be the fair Luscinda's because thou art mine, nor can she be thine because she is Cardenio's; and it will be easier, remember, to bend thy will to love one who adores thee, than to lead one to love thee who abhors thee now. Do not by deserting me let my shame become the talk of the gossips in the streets; make not the old age of my parents miserable; for the loyal services they as faithful vassals have ever rendered thine are not deserving of such a return. Reflect that there is little or no nobility in the world that has not traveled the same road, and, moreover, that true nobility consists in virtue, and if thou art wanting in that, refusing me what in justice thou owest me, then even I have higher claims to nobility than thine. To make an end, señor, these are my last words to thee: whether thou wilt, or wilt not, I am thy wife; witness thy words, which must not and ought not to be false."

All this and more the injured Dorothea delivered with such earnest feeling and such tears that all present, even those who came with Don Fernando, were constrained to join her in them. Don Fernando listened to her without replying, until, ceasing to speak, she gave way to such sobs that it must have been a heart of brass that was not softened by the sight of so great sorrow. Luscinda stood regarding her with no less compassion for her sufferings than admiration for her intelligence and beauty, and would have gone to her to say some words of comfort to her, but was prevented by Don Fernando's grasp which held her fast. He, overwhelmed with confusion and astonishment, after regarding Dorothea for some moments with a fixed gaze, opened his arms, and, releasing Luscinda, exclaimed: ·

"Thou hast conquered, fair Dorothea, thou hast conquered, for it is impossible to have the heart to deny the united force of so many truths."

Luscinda in her feebleness was on the point of falling to the ground when Don Fernando released her, but Cardenio, who stood near, having retreated behind Don Fernando to escape recognition, casting fear aside and regardless of what might happen, ran forward to support her, and said as he clasped her in his arms, "If Heaven in its compassion is willing to let thee rest at last, mistress of my heart, true, constant, and fair, nowhere canst thou rest more safely than in these arms that now receive thee, and received thee before when fortune permitted me to call thee mine."

At these words Luscinda looked up at Cardenio, satisfying herself by her eyes that it was he, and hardly knowing what she did, flung her arms around his neck and pressing her face close to his, said, "Yes, my dear lord, you are the true master of this your slave, even though adverse fate interpose again, and fresh dangers threaten this life that hangs on yours."

A strange sight was this for Don Fernando and those that stood around, filled with surprise at an incident so unlooked for. Dorothea fancied that Don Fernando changed color and looked as though he meant to take vengeance on Cardenio, for she observed him put his hand to his sword; and the instant the idea struck her, with wonderful quickness she clasped him round the knees, and holding him so as to prevent his moving, she said, while her tears continued to flow, "What is it thou wouldst do, my only refuge, in this unforeseen event? For God's sake I entreat of thee, allow these two lovers to live in peace and quiet without any interference from thee so long as Heaven permits them; and in so doing thou wilt prove the generosity of thy noble spirit, and the world shall see that with thee reason has more influence than passion."

All the time Dorothea was speaking, Cardenio, though he held Luscinda in his arms, never took his eyes off Don Fernando, determined, if he saw him make any hostile movement, to try and defend himself and resist as best he could all who might assail him, though it should cost him his life. But now Don Fernando's friends, as well as the curate and the barber, who had been present all the while, not forgetting the worthy Sancho Panza, ran forward and gathered round Don Fernando, entreating him to have regard for the tears of Dorothea, and not suffer her reasonable hopes to be disappointed, since, as they firmly believed, what she said was but the truth.

They added to these such other forcible arguments that Don Fernando's manly heart, being after all nourished by noble blood, was touched, and yielded to the truth which, even had he wished it, he could not gainsay; and he showed his submission, and acceptance of the good advice that had been offered to him, by stooping down and embracing Dorothea, saying to her, "Rise, dear lady, it is not right that what I hold in my heart should be kneeling at my feet; and if until now I have shown no sign of what I own, it may have been by Heaven's decree in order that, seeing the constancy with which you love me, I may learn to value you as you deserve. What I entreat of you is that you reproach me not with my transgression and grievous wrongdoing; for the same cause and force that drove me to make you mine impelled me to struggle against being yours; and to prove this, turn and look at the eyes of the now happy Luscinda, and you will see in them an excuse for all my errors:

and as she has found and gained the object of her desires, and I have found in you what satisfies all my wishes, may she live in peace and contentment as many happy years with her Cardenio, as on my knees I pray Heaven to allow me to live with my Dorothea"; and with these words he once more embraced her and pressed his face to hers with so much tenderness that he had to take great heed to keep his tears from completing the proof of his love and repentance in the sight of all. Not so Luscinda, and Cardenio, and almost all the others, for they shed so many tears, some in their own happiness, some at that of the others, that one would have supposed a heavy calamity had fallen upon them all. Even Sancho Panza was weeping; though afterwards he said he only wept because he saw that Dorothea was not as he fancied the queen Micomicona, of whom he had expected great favors.

Their wonder as well as their weeping lasted some time, and then Don Fernando recounted what had befallen him in the city after he had found in Luscinda's bosom the paper in which she declared that she was Cardenio's wife, and never could be his. He said he meant to kill her, and would have done so had he not been prevented by her parents, and that he quitted the house full of rage and shame, and resolved to avenge himself when a more convenient opportunity should offer. The next day he learned that Luscinda had disappeared from her father's house, and that no one could tell whither she had gone. Finally, at the end of some months he ascertained that she was in a convent and meant to remain there all the rest of her life, if she were not to share it with Cardenio; and as soon as he had learned this, taking these three gentlemen as his companions, he arrived at the place where she was, but avoided speaking to her, fearing that if it were known he was there stricter precautions would be taken in the convent; and watching a time when the porter's lodge was open he left two to guard the gate, and he and the other entered the convent in quest of Luscinda, whom they found in the cloisters in conversation with one of the nuns, and carrying her off without giving her time to resist, they reached a place with her where they provided themselves with what they required for taking her away; all which they were able to do in complete safety, as the convent was in the country at a considerable distance from the city. He added that when Luscinda found herself in his power she lost all consciousness, and after returning to herself did nothing but weep and sigh without speaking a word; and thus in silence and tears they reached that inn, which for him was reaching heaven where all the mischances of earth are over and at an end.

CHAPTER 25

Maritornes' Prank

To all this Sancho listened with no little sorrow at heart to see how his hopes of dignity were fading away and vanishing in smoke, and how the fair Princess Micomicona had turned into Dorothea, and the giant into Don Fernando, while his master was sleeping tranquilly, totally unconscious of all that had come to pass. So with a long face he went in to his master, who had just awakened, and said to him:

"Sir Rueful Countenance, your worship may as well sleep on as much as you like, without troubling yourself about killing any giant or restoring her kingdom to the princess; for that is all over and settled now."

"I should think it was," replied Don Quixote, "for I have had the most prodigious and stupendous battle with the giant that I ever remember having had all the days of my life; and with one backstroke—swish!—I brought his head tumbling to the ground, and so much blood gushed forth from him that it ran in rivulets over the earth like water."

"Like red wine, your worship had better say," replied Sancho; "for I would have you know, if you don't know it, that the dead giant is a hacked wineskin, and the blood four-and-twenty gallons of red wine that it had in its belly; and the devil take it all."

"What art thou talking about, fool?" said Don Quixote; "art thou in thy senses?"

"Let your worship get up," said Sancho, "and you will see the nice business you have made of it, and what we have to pay; and you will see the queen

131

turned into a private lady called Dorothea, and other things that will astonish you, if you understand them."

"I shall not be surprised at anything of the kind," returned Don Quixote; "for if thou dost remember the last time we were here I told thee that everything that happened here was a matter of enchantment, and it would be no wonder if it were the same now."

"I could believe all that," replied Sancho, "if my blanketing was the same sort of thing also; only it wasn't, but real and genuine; for I saw the landlord, who is here today, holding one end of the blanket and jerking me up to the skies very neatly and smartly, and with as much laughter as strength; and when it comes to be a case of knowing people, I hold for my part, simple and sinner as I am, that there is no enchantment about it at all, but a great deal of bruising and bad luck."

"Well, well, God will give a remedy," said Don Quixote; "hand me my clothes and let me go out, for I want to see these transformations and things thou speakest of."

Sancho fetched him his clothes; and while he was dressing, the curate gave Don Fernando and the others present an account of Don Quixote's madness and of the stratagem they had made use of to withdraw him from that Peña Pobre where he fancied himself stationed because of his lady's scorn. He described to them also nearly all the adventures that Sancho had mentioned, at which they marveled and laughed not a little, thinking it, as all did, the strangest form of madness a crazy intellect could be capable of. But now, the curate said, that the lady Dorothea's good fortune prevented her from proceeding with their purpose, it would be necessary to devise or discover some other way of getting him home.

Cardenio proposed to carry out the scheme they had begun, and suggested that Luscinda would act and support Dorothea's part sufficiently well.

"No," said Don Fernando, "that must not be, for I want Dorothea to follow out this idea of hers; and if the worthy gentleman's village is not very far off, I shall be happy if I can do anything for his relief."

"It is but a few days' journey from here," said the curate.

"Even if it were more," said Don Fernando, "I would gladly travel so far for the sake of doing so good a work."

At this moment Don Quixote came out in full panoply, with Mambrino's helmet, all dented as it was, on his head, his buckler on his arm, and leaning on his staff or pike. The strange figure he presented filled Don Fernando and the rest with amazement as they contemplated his lean yellow face half a league long, his armor of all sorts, and the solemnity of his deportment. They stood silent waiting to see what he would say, and he, fixing his eyes on the fair Dorothea, addressed her with great gravity and composure:

"I am informed, fair lady, by my squire here, that your greatness has been annihilated and your being abolished, since, from a queen and lady of high degree as you used to be, you have been turned into a private maiden. If your father has brought about this metamorphosis in your person for the reason I have mentioned, you ought not to attach any importance to it; for there is no peril on earth through which my sword will not force a way, and with it, before many days are over, I will bring your enemy's head to the ground and place on yours the crown of your kingdom."

Don Quixote said no more, and waited for the reply of the princess, who aware of Don Fernando's determination to carry on the deception until Don Quixote had been conveyed to his home, with great ease of manner and gravity made answer, "Whoever told you, valiant Knight of the Rueful Countenance, that I had undergone any change or transformation did not tell you the truth, for I am the same as I was yesterday. It is true that certain strokes of good fortune, that have given me more than I could have hoped for, have made some alteration in me; but I have not therefore ceased to be what I was before, or to entertain the same desire I have had all through of availing myself of the might of your valiant and invincible arm. And so, señor, let your goodness reinstate the father that begot me in your good opinion, and be assured that he was a wise and prudent man, since by his craft he found out such a sure and easy way of remedying my misfortune; for I believe, señor, that had it not been for you I should never have lit upon the good fortune I now possess; and in this I am saying what is perfectly true; as most of these gentlemen who are present can fully testify. All that remains is to set out on our journey tomorrow, for today we could not make much way; and for the rest of the happy result I am looking forward to, I trust to God and the valor of your heart."

So said the sprightly Dorothea, and on hearing her Don Quixote turned to Sancho, and said to him, with an angry air, "I declare now, little Sancho, thou art the greatest little villain in Spain. Say, thief and vagabond, hast thou not just now told me that this princess had been turned into a maiden called Dorothea?"

"Let your worship be calm, señor," returned Sancho, "for it may well be that I have been mistaken as to the change of the lady princess Micomicona;

133

but as to the giant's head, or at least as to the piercing of the wineskins, and the blood being red wine, I make no mistake; because the wounded skins are there at the head of your worship's bed, and the wine has made a lake of the room. For the rest, I am heartily glad that her ladyship the queen is as she was, for it concerns me as much as anyone."

"I tell thee again, Sancho, thou art a fool," said Don Quixote.

"Let us say no more about it," said Don Fernando, "and as her ladyship the princess proposes to set out tomorrow because it is too late today, so be it, and we will pass the night in pleasant conversation, and tomorrow we will all accompany Señor Don Quixote; for we wish to witness the valiant achievements he is about to perform in the course of this mighty enterprise which he has undertaken."

"It is I who shall wait upon and accompany you," said Don Quixote; "and I am much gratified by the favor that is bestowed upon me, and the good opinion entertained of me, which I shall strive to justify or it shall cost me my life."

Many were the compliments and expressions of politeness that passed between Don Quixote and Don Fernando. In short, everybody was well pleased, and as now the hour was growing late, they resolved to retire to rest for the remainder of the night. Don Quixote offered to mount guard over the castle lest they should be attacked by some giant or other malevolent scoundrel, covetous of the great treasure of beauty the castle contained. Those who understood him returned him thanks for this service. Sancho Panza alone was fuming at the lateness of the hour for retiring to rest; and he of all was the one that made himself most comfortable, as he stretched himself on the trappings of his ass.

The ladies, then, having retired to their chamber, and the others having disposed themselves with as little discomfort as they could, Don Quixote sallied out of the inn to act as sentinel of the castle as he had promised.

Deep silence reigned all through the inn. The only persons not asleep were the landlady's daughter and her servant Maritornes, who, knowing Don Quixote was outside the inn mounting guard in armor and on horseback, resolved, the pair of them, to play some trick upon him, or at any rate to amuse themselves for a while by listening to his nonsense. As it so happened there was not a window in the whole inn that looked outwards except a hole in the wall of a straw-loft through which they used to throw out the straw. At this hole the two damsels posted themselves, and observed Don Quixote on his horse, leaning on his pike and from time to time sending forth such deep and doleful sighs, that he seemed to pluck up his soul by the roots with each of them; and they could hear him, too, saying in a soft, tender, loving tone, "O my lady Dulcinea del Toboso, perfection of all beauty, what is thy grace doing now? Art thou, perchance, mindful of thy enslaved knight who of his own free will hath exposed himself to so great perils, and all to serve thee?"

Don Quixote had got so far in his pathetic speech when the landlady's daughter began to signal to him, saying, "Señor, come over here, please."

At these signals and voice Don Quixote turned his head and saw by the light of the moon, which then was in its full splendor, that someone was calling to him from the hole in the wall, which seemed to him to be a window, and what is more, with a gilt grating, as rich castles, such as he believed the inn to be, ought to have; and it immediately suggested itself to his imagination that the fair damsel, the daughter of the lady of the castle, overcome by love for him, was endeavoring to win his affections; and with this idea, not to show himself discourteous or ungrateful, he turned Rocinante's head and approached the hole, and as he perceived the two damsels he said:

"I pity you, beauteous lady, that you should have directed your thoughts of love to a quarter from whence it is impossible that such a return can be made to you as is due to your great merit and gentle birth, for which you must not blame this unhappy knight-errant whom love renders incapable of submission to any other than her whom, the first moment his eyes beheld her, he made absolute mistress of his soul. If, of the love you bear me, you should find that there is anything else in my power wherein I can gratify you, demand it of me; for I swear to grant it this instant, though it be the very beams of the sun shut up in a vial."

"My mistress wants nothing of that sort, sir knight," said Maritornes at this.

"What then, discreet dame, is it that your mistress wants?" replied Don Quixote.

"Only one of your fair hands," said Maritornes, "to enable her to vent over it the great passion which has brought her to this loophole, so much to the risk of her honor."

Maritornes felt sure that Don Quixote would present the hand she had asked, and making up her mind what to do, she got down from the hole and went into the stable, where she took the halter of Sancho Panza's ass, and in all haste returned to the hole, just as Don Quixote had planted himself standing on Rocinante's saddle in order to reach the grated window where he supposed the lovelorn damsel to be; and giving her his hand, he said, "Lady, take this hand, or rather this scourge of the evil-doers of the earth. I present it to you, not that you may kiss it, but that you may infer what must be the strength of the arm that has such a hand."

"That we shall see presently," said Maritornes, and making a running knot on the halter, she passed it over his wrist and coming down from the hole tied the other end very firmly to the bolt of the door of the straw-loft.

Don Quixote, feeling the roughness of the rope on his wrist, exclaimed, "Your grace seems to be grating rather than caressing my hand; treat it not so harshly, for it is not to blame for the offense my resolution has given you, nor is it just to wreak all your vengeance on so small a part; remember that one who loves so well should not revenge herself so cruelly."

But there was nobody now to listen to these words of Don Quixote's, for as soon as Maritornes had tied him she and the other made off, ready to die with laughing, leaving him fastened in such a way that it was impossible for him to release himself.

He was, as has been said, standing on Rocinante, with his arm passed through the hole and his wrist tied to the bolt of the door, and in mighty fear and dread of being left hanging by the arm if Rocinante were to stir one side or the other; so he did not dare to make the least movement, although from the patience and imperturbable disposition of Rocinante, he had good reason to expect that he would stand without budging for a whole century. Finding himself fast, then, and that the ladies had retired, he began to fancy that all this was done by enchantment. Nevertheless he pulled his arm to see if he could release himself, but it had been made so fast that all his efforts were in vain. It is true he pulled it gently lest Rocinante should move, but try as he might to seat himself in the saddle, he had nothing for it but to stand upright or pull his hand off. Then it was he wished for the sword of Amadis, against which no enchantment whatever had any power; then he cursed his ill fortune; then he magnified the loss the world would sustain by his absence while he remained there enchanted, for that he believed he was beyond all doubt; then he once more took to thinking of his beloved Dulcinea del Toboso; then he called to his worthy squire Sancho Panza, who, buried in sleep and stretched upon the pack-saddle of his ass, was, at that moment, oblivious. At last, morning found him in such a state of desperation and perplexity that he was bellowing like a bull, for he had no hope that day would bring any relief to his suffering, which he believed would last forever, inasmuch as he was enchanted;

"Your grace seems to be grating rather than caressing my hand."

and of this he was convinced by seeing that Rocinante never stirred, much or little, and he felt persuaded that he and his horse were to remain in this state, without eating or drinking or sleeping, until the malign influence of the stars was overpast, or until some other more sage enchanter should disenchant him.

But he was very much deceived in this conclusion, for daylight had hardly begun to appear when there came up to the inn four men on horseback, well equipped, with firelocks across their saddle-bows. They called out and knocked loudly at the gate of the inn, which was still shut; on seeing which, Don Quixote, even there where he was, did not forget to act as sentinel, and said in an imperious tone, "Knights, or squires, or whatever ye be, ye have no right to knock at the gates of this castle; for it is plain enough that they who are within are either asleep, or else are not in the habit of throwing open the fortress until the sun's rays are spread over the whole surface of the earth. Withdraw to a distance, and wait till it is broad daylight, and then we shall see whether it will be proper or not to open to you."

"What the devil fortress or castle is this," said one, "to make us stand on such ceremony? If you are the innkeeper bid them open to us; we are travelers who only want to feed our horses and go on, for we are in haste."

"Do you think, gentlemen, that I look like an innkeeper?" said Don Quixote.

"I don't know what you look like," replied the other; "but I know that you are talking nonsense when you call this inn a castle."

"A castle it is," returned Don Quixote, "nay, more, one of the best in this whole province, and it has within it people who have had the scepter in the hand and the crown on the head."

"It would be better if it were the other way," said the traveler, "the scepter on the head and the crown in the hand; but if so, maybe there is within some company of players, with whom it is a common thing to have those crowns and scepters you speak of; for in such a small inn as this, and where such silence is kept, I do not believe any people entitled to crowns and scepters can have taken up their quarters."

"You know but little of the world," returned Don Quixote, "since you are ignorant of what commonly occurs in knight-errantry."

But the comrades of the spokesman, growing weary of the dialogue with Don Quixote, renewed their knocks with great vehemence, so much so that the host, and not only he but everybody in the inn, awoke, and he got up to ask who knocked. It happened at this moment that one of the horses of the four who were seeking admittance went to smell Rocinante, who melancholy, dejected, and with drooping ears stood motionless, supporting his sorely stretched master; and as he was, after all, flesh, though he looked as if he were made of wood, he could not help giving way and in return smelling the one who had come to offer him attentions. But he had hardly moved at all when Don Quixote lost his footing; and slipping off the saddle, he would have come to the ground, but for being suspended by the arm, which caused him such agony that he believed either his wrist would be cut through or his arm torn off.

CHAPTER 26

Journey in an Ox Cart

So loud were the shouts of Don Quixote that the landlord, opening the gate of the inn in all haste, came out in dismay, and ran to see who was uttering such cries, and those who were outside joined him. Maritornes, who had been by this time roused up by the same outcry, suspecting what it was, ran to the loft and, without anyone seeing her, untied the halter by which Don Quixote was suspended, and down he came to the ground in the sight of the landlord and the travelers, who approaching asked him what was the matter with him that he shouted so. He without replying a word took the rope off his wrist, and rising to his feet leaped upon Rocinante, braced his buckler on his arm, put his lance in rest, and making a considerable circuit of the plain came back at a half-gallop exclaiming:

"Whoever shall say that I have been enchanted with just cause, provided my lady the Princess Micomicona grants me permission to do so, I give him the lie, challenge him and defy him to single combat."

The newly arrived travelers were amazed at the words of Don Quixote; but the landlord removed their surprise by telling them who he was, and not to mind him as he was out of his senses. Don Quixote, when he saw that not one of the four travelers took any notice of him or replied to his challenge, was furious and ready to die with indignation and wrath; and if he could have found in the ordinances of chivalry that it was lawful for a knight-errant to undertake or engage in another enterprise, when he had plighted his word and faith not to involve himself in any until he had made an end of the one to which he was pledged, he would have attacked the whole of them, and would have made them return an answer in spite of themselves. But considering that it would not become him, nor be right, to begin any new emprise until he had established Micomicona in her kingdom, he was constrained to hold his peace.

To the illustrious company it seemed time to depart. They devised a plan so that, without giving Dorothea and Don Fernando the trouble of going back with Don Quixote to his village under pretense of restoring Queen Micomicona, the curate and the barber might carry him away with them as they proposed, and the curate be able to take his madness in hand at home; and in pursuance of their plan they arranged with the owner of an ox cart who happened to be passing that way to carry him after this fashion. They constructed a kind of cage with wooden bars, large enough to hold Don Quixote comfortably; and then Don Fernando and his companions, together with the landlord, by the directions and advice of the curate, covered their faces and disguised themselves, some in one way, some in another, so as to appear to Don Quixote quite different from the persons he had seen in the castle. This done, in profound silence they entered the room where he was now asleep, taking his rest after the past frays, and advancing to where he was sleeping tranquilly, not dreaming of anything of the kind happening, they seized him firmly and bound him fast hand and foot, so that, when he awoke startled, he was unable to move, and could only marvel and wonder at the strange figures he saw before him; upon which he at once gave way to the idea which his crazed fancy invariably conjured up before him, and took it into his head that all these shapes were phantoms of the enchanted castle, and that he himself was unquestionably enchanted as he could neither move nor help himself; precisely what the curate, the concocter of the scheme, expected would happen.

Of all that were there Sancho was the only one who was at once in his senses and in his own proper character, and he, though he was within very little of sharing his master's infirmity, did not fail to perceive who all these disguised figures were; but he did not dare to open his lips until he saw what came of this assault and capture of his master; nor did the latter utter a word, waiting to see the upshot of his mishap; which was that, bringing in the cage, they shut him up in it and nailed the bars so firmly that they could not be easily burst open. They then took him on their shoulders, and passed out of the room.

When Don Quixote saw himself caged and hoisted on the cart, he said, "Many grave histories of knights-errant have I read; but never yet have I read, seen, or heard of their carrying off enchanted knights-errant in this fashion. What thinkest thou of the matter, Sancho my son?"

"I don't know what to think," answered Sancho, "not being as well read as your worship in errant writings; but for all that I venture to say and swear that these apparitions that are about us are not quite catholic."

Don Fernando and Cardenio, apprehensive of Sancho's making a complete discovery of their scheme, towards which he had already gone some way, resolved to hasten their departure, and calling the landlord aside, they directed him to saddle Rocinante and put the pack-saddle on Sancho's ass, which he did with great alacrity. Cardenio hung the buckler on one side of the bow of Rocinante's saddle and the basin on the other, and by signs commanded Sancho to mount his ass and take Rocinante's bridle. But before the cart was put in motion, out came the landlady and her daughter and Maritornes to bid Don Quixote farewell, pretending to weep with grief at his misfortune; and to them Don Quixote said:

"Weep not, good ladies, for all these mishaps are the lot of those who follow the profession I profess; and if these reverses did not befall me I should not esteem myself a famous knight-errant; for such things never happen to knights of little renown and fame, because nobody in the world thinks about them. Forgive me, fair ladies, if, through inadvertence, I have in aught offended you; for the favors that ye have bestowed upon me in this castle shall be held in memory by me, that I may requite them as they deserve."

While this was passing between the ladies of the castle and Don Quixote, the curate and the barber bade farewell to Don Fernando and his companions, and in particular to Dorothea and Luscinda. They all embraced one another, and promised to let each other know how things went with them, and Don Fernando directed the curate where to write to him, to tell him what became of Don Quixote, assuring him that there was nothing that could give him more pleasure than to hear of it, and that he too, on his part, would send him word of everything he thought he would like to know, about his marriage and Luscinda's return to her home. The curate promised to comply with his request carefully, and they embraced once more, and renewed their promises.

The curate then mounted and his friend the barber did the same, both masked, so as not to be recognized by Don Quixote, and set out following in the rear of the cart. The order of march was this: first went the cart with

141

the owner leading it; Then followed Sancho Panza on his ass, leading Rocinante by the bridle; and behind came the curate and the barber on their mighty mules, with faces covered, as aforesaid, and a grave and serious air, measuring their pace to suit the slow steps of the oxen. Don Quixote was seated in the cage, with his hands tied and his feet stretched out, leaning against the bars as silent and as patient as if he were a stone statue and not a man of flesh. Thus slowly they made, it might be, two leagues, until they reached a valley which the carter thought a convenient place for resting and feeding his oxen, and he said so to the curate, but the barber was of opinion that they ought to push on a little farther, as at the other side of a hill which appeared close by he knew there was a valley that had more grass and much better than the one where they proposed to halt; and his advice was taken and they continued their journey.

Just at that moment the curate, looking back, saw coming on behind them six or seven mounted men, well equipped, who soon overtook them, for they were traveling, not at the sluggish, deliberate pace of oxen, but like men who rode canons' mules, and in haste to take their noontide rest as soon as possible at an inn which was in sight not a league off. The quick travelers came up with the slow, and courteous salutations were exchanged; and one of the newcomers, who was, in fact, a canon of Toledo and master of the others who accompanied him, observing the regular order of the procession, the cart, Sancho, Rocinante, the curate and the barber, and above all Don Quixote caged and confined, could not help asking what was the meaning of carrying the man in that fashion.

Don Quixote overheard the conversation and said, "Haply, gentlemen, you are versed in matters of errant chivalry? Because if you are I will tell you my misfortunes; if not, there is no good in my giving myself the trouble of relating them"; but here the curate and the barber, seeing that the travelers were engaged in conversation with Don Quixote, came forward, in order to answer in such a way as to save their stratagem from being discovered.

The canon, replying to Don Quixote, said, "In truth, brother, I do know about books of chivalry. So if that be all, you may safely tell me what you please."

"Then, señor," replied Don Quixote, "if that be so, I would have you know that I am held enchanted in this cage by the envy and fraud of wicked enchanters; for virtue is more persecuted by the wicked than loved by the good. I am a knight-errant."

"What Señor Don Quixote of La Mancha says," observed the curate, "is the truth; for he goes enchanted in this cart, not from any fault or sins of his, but because of the malevolence of those to whom virtue is odious and valor hateful. This, señor, is the Knight of the Rueful Countenance, if you have ever heard him named, whose valiant achievements and mighty deeds shall be written on imperishable marble."

At this point Sancho Panza, who had drawn near to hear the conversation, said, in order to make everything plain, "Well, sirs, you may like or dislike what I am going to say, but the fact of the matter is, my master, Don Quixote, is just as much enchanted as my mother. He is in his full senses, he eats and he drinks, and if that's the case, what do they mean by wanting me to believe that he is enchanted? For I have heard many a one say that enchanted people neither eat, nor sleep, nor talk; and my master, if you don't stop him, will talk more than thirty lawyers." Then turning to the curate he exclaimed, "Ah, señor curate, señor curate! Do you think I don't know you? Do you think I don't guess and see the drift of these new enchantments? Well then, I can tell you I know you, for all your face is covered, and I can tell you I am up to you, however you may hide your tricks. After all, where envy reigns virtue cannot live, and where there is niggardliness there can be no liberality. Ill betide the devil! If it had not been for your worship, my master would be married to the Princess Micomicona this minute, and I should be a count at least; for no less was to be expected, as well from the goodness of my master, him of the Rueful Countenance, as from the greatness of my services. But I see now how true it is what they say in these parts, that the wheel of fortune turns faster than a mill-wheel, and that those who were up yesterday are down today. I am sorry for my wife and children, for when they might fairly and reasonably expect to see their father return to them a governor or viceroy of some island or kingdom, they will see him come back a horse-boy. I have said all this, señor curate, only to urge you to lay to your conscience your ill-treatment of my master; and have a care that God does not call you to account in another life for making a prisoner of him in this way, and charge against you all the succors and good deeds that my lord Don Quixote leaves undone while he is shut up."

"So you are of the same fraternity as your master, too, Sancho?" exclaimed the barber. "By God, I begin to see that you will have to keep him company in the cage, and be enchanted like him for having caught some of his humor and chivalry. It was an evil hour when you let yourself be persuaded by his promises, and that island you long so much for found its way into your head."

"If I long for an island," returned Sancho, "other people long for worse. Each of us is the son of his own works; and being a man I may come to be pope, not to say governor of an island, especially as my master may win so many that he will not know whom to give them to. And as to the enchantment of my master, God knows the truth; leave it as it is; it only makes it worse to stir it."

The barber did not care to answer Sancho lest by his plain speaking he should disclose what the curate and he himself were trying so hard to conceal; and under the same apprehension the curate had asked the canon to ride on a little in advance, so that he might tell him the mystery of this man in the cage, and other things that would amuse him. The canon agreed, and going on ahead with his servants, listened with attention to the account of the character, life, madness, and ways of Don Quixote, given him by the curate, who described to him briefly the beginning and origin of his craze, and told him the whole story of his adventures up to his being confined in the cage, together with the plan they had of taking him home to try if by any means they could discover a cure for his madness. The canon and his servants were surprised anew when they heard Don Quixote's strange story, and when it was finished he said, "To tell the truth, señor curate, I for my part consider what they call books of chivalry to be mischievous to the State; and though, led by idle and false taste, I have read the beginnings of almost all that have been printed, I never could manage to read any one of them from beginning to end. And though it may be the chief object of such books to amuse, I do not know how they can succeed, when they are so full of such monstrous nonsense. When they want to give us a picture of a battle, after having told us that there are a million combatants on the side of the enemy, let the hero of the book be opposed to them, and we have perforce to believe, whether we like it or not, that the said knight wins the victory by the single might of his strong arm."

The canon and the curate had proceeded thus far with their conversation, when the barber, coming forward, joined them, and said to the curate, "This is the spot, señor curate, that I said was a good one for fresh and plentiful pasture for the oxen, while we take our noontide rest."

"And so it seems," returned the curate, and he told the canon what he proposed to do, on which he too made up his mind to halt with them, at-

Sancho approached the cage in which Don Quixote had been placed.

tracted by the aspect of the fair valley that lay before their eyes; and also to learn more particulars about the doings of Don Quixote. The canon ordered some of his servants to go on to the inn, which was not far distant, and fetch from it what eatables there might be for the whole party, as he meant to rest for the afternoon where he was; to which one of his servants replied that the sumpter mule, which by this time ought to have reached the inn, carried provisions enough to make it unnecessary to get anything from the inn except barley.

"In that case," said the canon, "take all the beasts there, and bring the sumpter mule back."

While this was going on, Sancho, perceiving that he could speak to his master without having the curate and the barber, of whom he had his suspicions, present all the time, approached the cage in which Don Quixote, was placed, and said, "Señor, to ease my conscience I want to tell you the state of the case as to your enchantment, and that is that these two here, with their faces covered, are the curate of our village and the barber; and I suspect they have hit upon this plan of carrying you off in this fashion, out of pure envy because your worship surpasses them in doing famous deeds; and if this be the truth it follows that you are not enchanted, but hoodwinked and made a fool of."

CHAPTER 27

The Enchanted Homecoming

SANCHO," said Don Quixote, "I have already told thee there are many sorts of enchantments, and it may be that in the course of time they have been changed, one for another, and that now it may be the way with enchanted people to do all that I do, though they did not do so before; so it is vain to argue or draw inferences against the usage of the time. I feel that I am enchanted, and that is enough to ease my conscience; for it would weigh heavily on it if I thought that I was not enchanted, and that in a cowardly way I allowed myself to lie in this cage, defrauding multitudes of the succor I might afford to those in need and distress, who at this very moment may be in sore want of my aid and protection."

"Still for all that," replied Sancho, "I say that for your greater and fuller satisfaction, it would be well if your worship were to try to get out of this prison and see if you could once more mount your good Rocinante, who seems to be enchanted too, he is so melancholy and dejected; and then we might try our chance in looking for adventures again; and if we have no luck there will be time enough to go back to the cage; in which, on the faith of a good and loyal squire, I promise to shut myself up along with your worship, if so be you are so unfortunate, or I so stupid, as not to be able to carry out my plan."

"I am content to do as thou sayest, brother Sancho," said Don Quixote, "and when thou seest an opportunity for effecting my release I will obey thee absolutely; but thou wilt see, Sancho, how mistaken thou art in thy conception of my misfortune."

The knight-errant and the ill-errant squire kept up their conversation till they reached the place where the curate, the canon, and the barber, who had already dismounted, were waiting for them. The carter at once unyoked the oxen and left them to roam at large about the pleasant green spot, the freshness of which seemed to invite, not enchanted people like Don Quixote, but wide-awake, sensible folk like his squire, who begged the curate to allow his master to leave the cage for a little. The curate said he would very gladly comply with his request, only that he feared his master, finding himself at liberty, would take to his old courses and make off where nobody could ever find him again.

"I will answer for his not running away," said Sancho.

"And I also," said the canon, "especially if he gives me his word as a knight not to leave us without our consent."

Don Quixote, who was listening to all this, said, "I give it—moreover one who is enchanted as I am cannot do as he likes with himself; for he who had enchanted him could prevent his moving from one place for three ages, and if he attempted to escape would bring him back flying."

The canon took his hands, tied together as they both were, and on his word and promise they unbound him, and rejoiced beyond measure he was to find himself out of the cage. The first thing he did was to stretch himself all over, and then he went to where Rocinante was standing and giving him a couple of slaps on the haunches said, "I still trust in God, O flower of steeds, that we shall soon see ourselves, both of us, as we wish to be, thou with thy master on thy back, and I mounted upon thee, following the calling for which God sent me into the world."

The canon gazed at him, wondering at the extraordinary nature of his madness, and that in all his remarks and replies he should show such excellent sense, and only lose his stirrups when the subject of chivalry was broached. And so, moved by compassion, he said to him, as they all sat on the green grass awaiting the arrival of the provisions:

"Is it possible, gentle sir, that the idle reading of books of chivalry can have had such an effect on your worship as to upset your reason so that you fancy yourself enchanted, and the like, all as far from the truth as falsehood itself is? How can there be any human understanding that can persuade itself there ever was all that infinity of Amadises in the world, or all that multitude of famous knights, in a word, all that nonsense the books of chivalry contain?"

To which Don Quixote returned, "I know not what more there is to be

147

said. I only guide myself by the example set me by the great Amadis of Gaul."

By this time the canon's servants, who had gone to the inn to fetch the sumpter mule, had returned, and making a carpet and the green grass of the meadow serve as a table, they seated themselves in the shade of some trees and made their repast there. As they were eating they suddenly heard a loud noise and the sound of a bell that seemed to come from among some thick bushes that were close by, and the same instant they observed a beautiful goat, spotted all over black, white, and brown, spring out of the thicket with a goatherd after it, calling to it and uttering the usual cries to make it stop or turn back to the fold. The fugitive goat, frightened, ran towards the company as if seeking their protection and then stood still, and the goatherd coming up seized it by the horns and began to talk to it as if it were possessed of reason and understanding: "Ah wanderer, wanderer, Spotty, Spotty; how have you gone limping all this time? What wolves have frightened you, my daughter? Won't you tell me what is the matter, my beauty? A plague on your humors and the humors of those you take after! Come back, come back, my darling; and if you will not be so happy, at any rate you will be safe in the fold with your companions; for if you who ought to lead them, go wandering astray, what will become of them?"

The goatherd's talk amused all who heard it, but especially the canon, who said to him, "As you live, brother, take it easy, and be not in such a hurry to drive this goat back to the fold; for, being a female, as you say, she will follow her natural instinct in spite of all you can do to prevent it. Take this morsel and drink a sup, and that will soothe your irritation, and in the meantime the goat will rest herself." And so saying, he handed him the loins of a cold rabbit on a fork.

The goatherd took it with thanks, and drank and calmed himself, and then said, "I should be sorry if your worships were to take me for a simpleton for having spoken so seriously as I did to this animal; but the truth is there is a certain mystery in the words I used. I am a clown, but not so much of one but that I know how to behave to men and to beasts."

"That I can well believe," said the curate, "for I know already by experience that the woods breed men of learning, and shepherds' huts harbor philosophers."

The goatherd, noticing Don Quixote's sorry appearance and looks, was filled with wonder, and asked the barber, who was next him, "Señor, who is this man who makes such a strange figure?"

"Who should it be," said the barber, "but the famous Don Quixote of La Mancha, the undoer of injustice, the righter of wrongs, the protector of damsels, the terror of giants, and the winner of battles?"

"That," said the goatherd, "sounds like what one reads in the books of the knights-errant, who did all that you say this man does; though it is my belief that either you are joking, or else this gentleman has empty lodgings in his head."

"You are a scoundrel," said Don Quixote, "and it is you who are empty and a fool!" And passing from words to deeds, he caught up a loaf that was near him and sent it full in the goatherd's face, with such force that he flattened his nose; but the goatherd, who did not understand jokes, and found himself roughly handled in such good earnest, paying no respect to carpet, tablecloth, or diners, sprang upon Don Quixote, and seizing him by the throat with both hands would no doubt have throttled him, had not Sancho Panza that instant come to the rescue, and grasping him by the shoulders flung him down on the table, smashing plates, breaking glasses, and up-setting and scattering everything on it. Don Quixote, finding himself free, strove to get on top of the goatherd, who, with his face covered with blood, and soundly kicked by Sancho, was on all fours feeling about for one of the table knives to take a bloody revenge with. The canon and the curate, how-ever, prevented him, but the goatherd so contrived it that he got Don Quixote under him, and rained down upon him such a shower of fisticuffs that the poor knight's face streamed with blood as freely as his own. The canon and the curate were bursting with laughter. Sancho alone was frantic, for he could not free himself from the grasp of one of the canon's servants, who kept him from going to his master's assistance.

At last, while they were all, with the exception of the two bruisers who were mauling each other, in high glee and enjoyment, they heard a trumpet sound a note so doleful that it made them all look in the direction whence the sound seemed to come. But the one that was most excited by hearing it was Don Quixote, who though sorely against his will, was under the goatherd, and something more than pretty well pummeled. "Brother devil," he said, "I ask thee to agree to a truce for but one hour, for the solemn note of yonder trumpet that falls on our ears seems to me to summon me to

149

some new adventure." The goatherd, who was by this time tired of pummeling and being pummeled, released him at once, and Don Quixote rising to his feet and turning his eyes to the quarter where the sound had been heard, suddenly saw coming down the slope of a hill several men clad in white like penitents.

The fact was that the clouds had that year withheld their moisture from the earth, and in all the villages of the district they were organizing processions, imploring God to open the hands of his mercy and send the rain; and to this end the people of a village that was hard by were going in procession to a holy hermitage there was on one side of that valley. Don Quixote, when he saw the strange garb of the penitents, without reflecting how often he had seen it before, took it into his head that this was a case of adventure, and that it fell to him alone as a knight-errant to engage in it; and he was all the more confirmed in this notion, by the idea that an image draped in black they had with them was some illustrious lady that these villains and discourteous thieves were carrying off by force. As soon as this occurred to him he ran with all speed to Rocinante, who was grazing at large, and taking the bridle and the buckler from the saddle-bow, he had him bridled in an instant, and calling to Sancho for his sword he mounted Rocinante, braced his buckler on his arm, and in a loud voice exclaimed to those who stood by, "Now, noble company, ye shall see how important it is that there should be knights in the world professing the order of knight-errantry; now, I say, ye shall see, by the deliverance of that worthy lady who is borne captive there, whether knights-errant deserve to be held in estimation," and so saying he brought his legs to bear on Rocinante—for he had no spurs— and at a full canter set off to encounter the penitents, though the curate, the canon, and the barber ran to prevent him. But it was out of their power, nor did he even stop for the shouts of Sancho calling after him, "Where are you going, Señor Don Quixote? What devils have possessed you? That is a procession of penitents, and the lady they are carrying on that stand there is the blessed image of the immaculate Virgin. Take care what you are doing, señor, for this time it may be safely said you don't know what you are about." Sancho labored in vain, for his master was so bent on coming to quarters with these sheeted figures and releasing the lady in black that he did not hear a word; and even had he heard, he would not have turned back if the king had ordered him. He came up with the procession and reined in Rocinante, who was already anxious enough to slacken speed a little, and in a

Sancho Panza came to the rescue.

hoarse, excited voice he exclaimed, "You who hide your faces, perhaps because you are not good subjects, pay attention and listen to what I am about to say to you." The first to halt were those who were carrying the image, and one of the four ecclesiastics who were chanting the Litany, struck by the strange figure of Don Quixote, the leanness of Rocinante, and the other ludicrous peculiarities he observed, said in reply to him, "Brother, if you have anything to say to us say it quickly, for we cannot stop to hear anything, unless indeed it is short enough to be said in two words."

"I will say it in one," replied Don Quixote, "and it is this; that at once, this very instant, ye release that fair lady whose tears and sad aspect show plainly that ye are carrying her off against her will, and that ye have committed some scandalous outrage against her; and I, who was born into the world to redress all such like wrongs, will not permit you to advance another step until you have restored to her the liberty she pines for and deserves."

From these words all the hearers concluded that he must be a madman, and began to laugh heartily, and their laughter acted like gunpowder on Don Quixote's fury, for drawing his sword without another word he made a rush at the stand. One of those who supported it, leaving the burden to his comrades, advanced to meet him, flourishing a forked stick that he had for propping up the stand when resting, and with this he caught a mighty cut Don Quixote made at him that severed it in two; but with the portion that remained in his hand he dealt such a whack on the shoulder of Don Quixote's sword arm that poor Don Quixote came to the ground in a sad plight.

Sancho Panza, who was coming on close behind, puffing and blowing, seeing him fall, cried out to his assailant not to strike him again, for he was a poor enchanted knight, who had never harmed anyone all the days of his life; but what checked the clown was, not Sancho's shouting, but seeing that Don Quixote did not stir hand or foot; and so, fancying he had killed him, he hastily hitched up his tunic under his girdle and took to his heels across the country like a deer.

By this time all Don Quixote's companions had come up to where he lay; but the processionists seeing them come running, apprehended mischief, and clustering round the image, awaited the attack, resolved to defend themselves and even to take the offensive against their asailants if they could. Fortune, however, arranged the matter better than they expected, for all Sancho did was to fling himself on his master's body, raising over him the most doleful and laughable lamentation that ever was heard, for he believed he was dead.

The curate was known to another curate who walked in the procession, and their recognition of one another set at rest the apprehensions of both parties; the first then told the other in two words who Don Quixote was, and he and the whole troop of penitents went to see if the poor gentleman was dead, and heard Sancho Panza saying, with tears in his eyes, "O flower of chivalry, that with one blow of a stick hast ended the course of thy well-spent life! O pride of thy race, honor and glory of all La Mancha, nay, of all the world!"

At the cries and moans of Sancho, Don Quixote came to himself, and the first word he said was, "He who lives separated from you, sweetest Dulcinea, has greater miseries to endure than these. Aid me, friend Sancho, to mount the enchanted cart, for I am not in a condition to press the saddle of Rocinante, as this shoulder is all knocked to pieces."

"That I will do with all my heart, señor," said Sancho; "and let us return to our village with these gentlemen, who seek your good, and there we will prepare for making another sally, which may turn out more profitable and creditable to us."

"Thou art right, Sancho," returned Don Quixote; "it will be wise to let the malign influence of the stars which now prevails pass off."

The canon, the curate, and the barber told him he would act very wisely in doing as he said; and so they placed Don Quixote in the cart as before. The procession once more formed itself in order and proceeded on its road; the goatherd took his leave of the party. The canon begged the curate to let him know how Don Quixote did, whether he was cured of his madness or still suffered from it, and then begged leave to continue his journey; in short, they all separated and went their ways, leaving to themselves the curate and the barber, Don Quixote, Sancho Panza and his ass, and the good Rocinante, who regarded everything with as great resignation as his master. The carter yoked his oxen and made Don Quixote comfortable on a truss of hay, and at his usual deliberate pace took the road the curate directed, and at the end of six days they reached Don Quixote's village, and entered it about the middle of the day, which it so happened was a Sunday, and the people were all in the plaza, through which Don Quixote's cart passed. They all flocked to see what was in the cart, and when they recognized their townsman they were filled with amazement, and a boy ran off to bring the news to his housekeeper and his niece that their master and uncle had come back all lean and yellow and stretched on a truss of hay on an ox cart. It was piteous to hear the cries the two good ladies raised, how they beat their breasts and poured out fresh maledictions on those accursed books of chivalry; all which was renewed when they saw Don Quixote coming in at the gate.

At the news of Don Quixote's arrival Sancho Panza's wife came running, for she by this time knew that her husband had gone away with him as his squire, and on seeing Sancho, the first thing she asked him was if the ass was well. Sancho replied that he was, better than his master was.

"Thanks be to God," said she, "for being so good to me; but now tell me, my friend, what have you made by your squirings? What gown have you brought me back? What shoes for your children?"

"I bring nothing of that sort, wife," said Sancho; "though I bring other things of more consequence and value."

"I am very glad of that," returned his wife; "show me these things of more value and consequence, my friend; for I want to see them to cheer my heart that has been so sad and heavy all these ages that you have been away."

"I will show them to you at home, wife," said Sancho; "be content for the present; for if it please God that we should again go on our travels in search of adventures, you will soon see me a count, or governor of an island, and that not one of those everyday ones, but the best that is to be had."

"Heaven grant it, husband," said she, "for indeed we have need of it. But tell me, what's this about islands, for I don't understand it?"

"Honey is not for the mouth of the ass," returned Sancho; "all in good time thou shalt see, wife—nay, thou wilt be surprised to hear thyself called 'your ladyship' by all thy vassals."

"What are you talking about, Sancho, with your ladyships, islands, and vassals?" returned Teresa Panza—for so Sancho's wife was called.

"Don't be in such a hurry to know all this, Teresa," said Sancho; "it is enough that I am telling you the truth, so shut your mouth. But I may tell you this much by the way, that there is nothing in the world more delightful than to be a person of consideration, squire to a knight-errant, and a seeker of adventures. To be sure most of those one finds do not end as pleasantly as one could wish, for out of a hundred, ninety-nine will turn out cross and contrary. I know it by experience, for out of some I came blanketed, and out of others belabored. Still, for all that, it is a fine thing to be on the lookout for what may happen, crossing mountains, searching woods, climbing rocks, visiting castles, putting up at inns, all at free quarters."

While this conversation passed between Sancho Panza and his wife, Don

Quixote's housekeeper and niece took him in and undressed him and laid him in his old bed. He eyed them askance, and could not make out where he was. The curate charged his niece to be very careful to make her uncle comfortable and to keep a watch over him lest he should make his escape from them again, telling her what they had been obliged to do to bring him home. On this the pair once more lifted up their voices and renewed their maledictions upon the books of chivalry, and implored heaven to plunge the authors of such lies and nonsense into the midst of the bottomless pit.

They were, in short, kept in anxiety and dread lest their uncle and master should give them the slip the moment he found himself somewhat better.

And as they feared so it fell out.

DON QUIXOTE

PART II

CHAPTER 1

Don Quixote at Home

THE CURATE AND THE BARBER remained nearly a month without seeing Don Quixote lest they should bring back to his recollection what had taken place. They did not, however, omit to visit his niece and housekeeper, and charge them to be careful to treat him with attention, and give him things to eat such as were good for the heart and the brain, whence, it was plain to see, all his misfortune proceeded. The niece and housekeeper replied that they did so, and meant to do so with all possible care, for they could perceive that their master was now and then beginning to show signs of being in his right mind. This gave great satisfaction to the curate and the barber, for they concluded they had taken the right course in carrying him off enchanted on the ox cart. So they resolved to pay him a visit and test the improvement in his condition, and they agreed not to touch upon any point connected with knight-errantry so as not to run the risk of reopening wounds which were still so tender.

They came to see him consequently, and found him sitting up in bed in a green baize waistcoat and a red Toledo cap, and so withered and dried up that he looked as if he had been turned into a mummy. They were very cordially received by him; they asked him after his health, and he talked to them about himself very naturally and in very well-chosen language. In the course of their conversation they fell to discussing systems of government, correcting this abuse and condemning that, reforming one practice and abolishing another; and so completely did they remodel the State that they seemed to have thrust it into a furnace and taken out something quite different from what they had put in; and on all the subjects they dealt with, Don Quixote spoke with such good sense that the pair of examiners were fully convinced that he was quite recovered and in his full senses.

The niece and housekeeper were present at the conversation and could not find words enough to express their thanks to God at seeing their master so clear in his mind. The curate, however, changing his original plan, which was to avoid touching upon matters of chivalry, resolved to test Don Quixote's recovery thoroughly, and see whether it were genuine or not; and so, from one subject to another, he came at last to talk of the news that had come from the capital, and, among other things, he said it was considered certain that the Turk was coming down with a powerful fleet, and that no one knew what his purpose was, or when the great storm would burst; and that his Majesty had made provision for the security of the coasts of Naples and Sicily and the island of Malta.

To this Don Quixote replied, "His Majesty has acted like a prudent warrior in providing for the safety of his realms in time, so that the enemy may not find him unprepared; but if my advice were taken I would recommend him to adopt a measure which at present, no doubt, his Majesty is very far from thinking of."

The barber asked Don Quixote what would be his advice as to the measures that he said ought to be adopted; for perhaps it might prove to be one that would have to be added to the list of the many impertinent suggestions that people were in the habit of offering to princes.

"Mine, master shaver," said Don Quixote, "will not be impertinent, but, on the contrary, pertinent."

"I don't mean that," said the barber, "but that experience has shown that most of the expedients which are proposed to his Majesty are either impossible or absurd."

"Mine, however," replied Don Quixote, "is neither impossible nor absurd, but the easiest, the most reasonable that could suggest itself to any projector's mind."

"You take a long time to tell it, Señor Don Quixote," said the curate.

"I don't choose to tell it here, now," said Don Quixote, "and have it reach the ears of the lords of the council tomorrow morning, and some other carry off the thanks and rewards of my trouble."

"For my part," said the barber, "I give my word here and before God that I will not repeat what your worship says."

"I know the oath is a good one," said Don Quixote, "because I know the barber to be an honest fellow."

"Even if he were not," said the curate, "I will go bail and answer for him that in this matter he will be as silent as a dummy, under pain of paying any penalty that may be pronounced."

"And who will be security for you, señor curate?" said Don Quixote.

"My profession," replied the curate, "which is to keep secrets."

"Ods body!" said Don Quixote at this. "What more has his Majesty to do but to command, by public proclamation, all the knights-errant that are scattered over Spain to assemble on a fixed day in the capital; for even if no more than half a dozen come, there may be one among them who alone will suffice to destroy the entire might of the Turk. If only the famous Don Belianis were alive now, or Amadis of Gaul! If any of these were alive today, and were to come face to face with the Turk, by my faith, I would not give much for the Turk's chance. But God will have regard for his people, and will provide someone, who, if not so valiant as the knights-errant of yore, at least will not be inferior to them in spirit; but God knows what I mean, and I say no more."

"Alas!" exclaimed the niece at this, "may I die if my uncle does not want to turn knight-errant again"; to which Don Quixote replied, "A knight-errant I shall die, and let the Turk come down or go up when he likes, and in as strong force as he can, once more I say, God knows what I mean."

Hereupon the curate observed, "I would gladly be relieved of a doubt, arising from what Don Quixote has said, that worries and works my conscience."

"The señor curate has leave for more than that," returned Don Quixote, "so he may declare his doubt, for it is not pleasant to have a doubt on one's conscience."

"Well then, with that permission," said the curate, "I say my doubt is that, all I can do, I cannot persuade myself that the whole pack of knights-errant such as you, Señor Don Quixote, have mentioned, were really and truly persons of flesh and blood, that ever lived in the world; on the contrary, I suspect it to be all fiction, fable, and falsehood, and dreams told by men awakened from sleep, or rather still half asleep."

"That is another mistake," replied Don Quixote, "into which many have fallen who do not believe that there ever were such knights in the world, and I have often, with different people and on different occasions, tried to expose this almost universal error to the light of truth. Sometimes I have not been successful in my purpose, sometimes I have, supporting it upon the shoulders of the truth; which truth is so clear that I can almost say I have with my own eyes seen Amadis of Gaul, who was a man of lofty stature, fair complexion, with a handsome though black beard, of a countenance between gentle and stern in expression, sparing of words, slow to anger, and quick to put it away from him; and as I have depicted Amadis, so I could, I think, describe all the knights-errant that are in all the histories in the world."

"Strange," the curate began, but at this moment they heard the house-keeper and the niece, who had previously withdrawn from the conversation, exclaiming aloud in the courtyard, and at the noise they all ran out.

The niece and the housekeeper were exclaiming to Sancho, who was striving to force his way in to see Don Quixote while they held the door against him, "What does the vagabond want in this house? Be off to your own, brother, for it is you, and no one else, that delude my master, and lead him astray, and take him tramping about the country."

To which Sancho replied, "Devil's own housekeeper! It is I who am deluded, and led astray, and taken tramping about the country, and not thy master! He has carried me all over the world, and you are mightily mistaken. He enticed me away from home by a trick, promising me an island, which I am still waiting for."

"May evil islands choke thee, thou detestable Sancho," said the niece. "What are islands? Is it something to eat, glutton and gormandizer that thou art?"

"It is not something to eat," replied Sancho, "but something to govern and rule, and better than four cities or four judgeships at court."

"For all that," said the housekeeper, "you don't enter here, you bag of mischief and sack of knavery; go govern your house and dig your seed-patch, and give over looking for islands or shylands."

The curate and the barber listened with great amusement to the words of the three; but Don Quixote called to Sancho and made the other two hold their tongues and let him come in. Sancho entered, and the curate and the barber took their leave of Don Quixote, of whose recovery they now despaired when they saw how wedded he was to his crazy ideas, and how saturated with the nonsense of his unlucky chivalry; and said the curate to the barber, "You will see, friend, that when we are least thinking of it, our gentleman will be off once more for another flight."

"I have no doubt of it," returned the barber; "but I do not wonder so much at the madness of the knight as at the simplicity of the squire, who has such a firm belief in all that about the island."

"God help them," said curate; "and let us be on the lookout to see what comes of all these absurdities of the knight and squire, for it seems as if they had both been cast in the same mold, and the madness of the master without the simplicity of the man would not be worth a farthing."

"That is true," said the barber, "and I should like very much to know what the pair are talking about at this moment."

"I promise you," said the curate, "the niece or the housekeeper will tell us by and by, for they are not the ones to forget to listen."

Meanwhile Don Quixote shut himself up in his room with Sancho, and when they were alone he said to him, "It grieves me greatly, Sancho, that thou sayest I took thee out of thy cottage, when thou knowest I did not remain in my house. We sallied forth together, we took the road together, we wandered abroad together; we have had the same fortune and the same luck; if they blanketed thee once, they belabored me a hundred times, and that is the only advantage I have of thee."

"That was only reasonable," replied Sancho, "for, by what your worship says, misfortunes belong more properly to knights-errant than to their squires."

"Thou art mistaken, Sancho," said Don Quixote, "according to the maxim *quando caput dolet*, etc."

"I don't understand any language but my own," said Sancho.

"I mean to say," said Don Quixote, "that when the head suffers all the members suffer; and so, being thy lord and master, I am thy head, and thou a part of me as thou art my servant; and therefore any evil that affects me should give thee pain, and what affects thee give pain to me."

"It should be so," said Sancho, "but when I was blanketed as a member, my head was on the other side of the wall, looking on while I was flying through the air, and did not feel any pain whatever; and if the members are obliged to feel the suffering of the head, it should be obliged to feel their sufferings."

"Let us put that aside for the present," said Don Quixote, "for we shall have opportunities enough for considering the point. Tell me, Sancho my friend, what do they say about me in the village here? What do the common people think of me? What do the hidalgos? What do the caballeros? What do they say of my valor; of my achievements; of my courtesy? How do they treat the task I have undertaken in reviving and restoring to the world the now forgotten order of chivalry? In short, Sancho, I would have thee tell me all that has come to thine ears on this subject."

"That I will do with all my heart, master," replied Sancho. "If your worship wants to know all about the calumnies they bring against you, I will fetch you one this instant who can tell you the whole of them without missing an atom; for last night Samson, the son of Bartholomew Carrasco, who has been studying at Salamanca, came home after having been made a Bachelor of Arts, and when I went to welcome him, he told me that your worship's history is already abroad in books, with the title of THE INGENIOUS GENTLEMAN DON QUIXOTE OF LA MANCHA; and he says they mention me in it by my own name of Sancho Panza, and the lady Dulcinea del Toboso too, and various things that happened to us when we were alone; so that I crossed myself in my wonder how the historian who wrote them down could have known them."

"I promise thee, Sancho," said Don Quixote, "the author of our history will be some sage enchanter; for to such nothing that they choose to write about is hidden."

"Very likely," replied Sancho. "Well, if your worship wishes me to fetch the bachelor I will go for him in a twinkling."

"Thou wilt do me a great pleasure, my friend," said Don Quixote, "for what thou hast told me has amazed me, and I shall not eat a morsel that will agree with me until I have heard all about it."

"Then I am off for him," said Sancho; and leaving his master he went in quest of the bachelor, with whom he returned in a short time.

CHAPTER 2

Knight and Bachelor

THE BACHELOR, though he was called Samson, was of no great bodily size, but he was a very great wag; he was of a sallow complexion, but very sharp-witted, somewhere about four-and-twenty years of age, with a round face, a flat nose, and a large mouth, all indications of a mischievous disposition and a love of fun and jokes; and of this he gave a sample as soon as he saw Don Quixote, by falling on his knees before him and saying, "Let me kiss your mightiness's hand, Señor Don Quixote of La Mancha, for your worship is one of the most famous knights-errant that have ever been, or will be, all the world over. A blessing on Cide Hamete Benengeli, the Moor, who has written the history of your great deeds."

Don Quixote made him rise, and said, "So, then, it is true that there is a history of me, and that it was a Moor and a sage who wrote it?"

"So true is it, señor," said Samson, "that my belief is there are more than twelve thousand volumes of the said history in print this very day, and I am persuaded there will not be a country or language in which there will not be a translation of it."

"One of the things," observed Don Quixote, "that ought to give most pleasure to a virtuous and eminent man is to find himself in his lifetime in print, familiar in people's mouths with a good name; I say with a good name, for if it be the opposite, then there is no death to be compared to it."

"If it goes by good name and fame," said the bachelor, "your worship alone bears away the palm from all the knights-errant; for the Moor in

163

his own language, and the Christian in his, have taken care to set before us your gallantry, your high courage in encountering dangers, your fortitude in adversity, your patience under misfortunes as well as wounds, the purity of the love of your worship and my lady Doña Dulcinea del Toboso—"

"Tell me, señor bachelor," said Sancho at this point, "does the adventure with the Yanguesans come in, when our good Rocinante went hankering after mares?"

"The sage has left nothing in the ink-bottle," replied Samson; "he tells all and sets down everything, even to the capers that worthy Sancho cut in the blanket."

"I cut no capers in the blanket," returned Sancho; "in the air I did, and more of them than I liked."

"There is no human history in the world, I suppose," said Don Quixote, "that has not its ups and downs, but more than others, such as deal with chivalry, for they can never be entirely made up of prosperous adventures."

"That is true," said Samson; "but it is one thing to write as a poet, another to write as a historian; the poet may describe or sing things, not as they were, but as they ought to have been; but the historian has to write them down, not as they ought to have been, but as they were, without adding anything to the truth or taking anything from it."

"To write in any other way," Don Quixote agreed, "would not be to write truth, but falsehood. In fact," he said, "the conclusion I arrive at, señor bachelor, is that to write histories, or books of any kind, there is need of great judgment and a ripe understanding. To give expression to humor, and write in a strain of graceful pleasantry, is the gift of great geniuses. The cleverest character in comedy is the clown, for he who would make people take him for a fool, must not be one. History is in a measure a sacred thing, for it should be true, and where the truth is, there God is."

"Your worship," said Sancho, "there's a sinking of the stomach come over me, and my old woman is waiting for me; after dinner I'll come back." And without another word or waiting for a reply he made off home.

Don Quixote begged the bachelor to stay and sup with him. The bachelor accepted the invitation and remained, and a couple of young pigeons were added to the ordinary fare. At dinner they talked chivalry, Samson falling in with his host's humor. The banquet came to an end, and they took their afternoon sleep. Sancho returned later and their conversation was resumed.

"The sage has left nothing in the ink bottle," replied Samson.

Samson, returning to the late subject of conversation, said, "Some say that the author forgot to state in the book what Sancho did with those hundred crowns that he found in the valise in the Sierra Morena."

To which Sancho answered, "I spent them for my own good, and my wife's, and my children's, and it is they that have made my wife bear so patiently all my wanderings on highways and byways, in the service of my master, Don Quixote; for if after all this time I had come back to the house without a rap and without the ass, it would have been a poor lookout for me. And if my master would take my advice, we would be *now* afield, redressing outrages and righting wrongs, as is the use and custom of good knights-errant."

Sancho had hardly uttered these words when the neighing of Rocinante fell upon their ears, which neighing Don Quixote accepted as a happy omen, and he resolved to make another sally in three or four days from that time. Announcing his intention to the bachelor, he asked his advice as to the quarter in which he ought to commence his expedition, and the bachelor replied that in his opinion he ought to go to the city of Saragossa, where there were to be certain solemn joustings at the festival of St. George, at which he might win renown above all the knights of Aragon. He commended his gallant resolution, but admonished him to proceed with greater caution in encountering dangers, because his life did not belong to him, but to all those who had need of him to protect and aid them in their misfortunes.

"That's what I abominate, Señor Samson," said Sancho here; "my master will attack a hundred armed men as a greedy boy would half a dozen melons. Body of the world, señor bachelor! There is a time to attack and a time to retreat. Moreover, I have heard it said that the mean of valor lies between the extremes of cowardice and rashness. But I warn my master that if he is to take me with him it must be on the condition that he is to do all the fighting, and that I am not to be called upon to do anything except what concerns keeping him clean and comfortable. I don't set up to be a fighting man, Señor Samson, but only the best and most loyal squire that ever served knight-errant; and if my master Don Quixote, in consideration of my many faithful services, is pleased to give me some island of the many his worship says one may stumble on in these parts, I will take it as a great favor."

"Brother Sancho," said Samson, "put your trust in God and in Señor Don Quixote, for he will give you a kingdom, not to say an island."

"God grant it," said Don Quixote. "We shall see; and I seem to see it already."

He then begged the bachelor, if he were a poet, to do him the favor of composing some verses for him conveying the farewell he meant to take of his lady Dulcinea del Toboso, and to see that a letter of her name was placed at the beginning of each line, so that, at the end of the verses, "Dulcinea del Toboso" might be read by putting together the first letters.

"For," said Don Quixote, "unless the name stands there plain, no woman would believe the verses were made for her."

They agreed upon this, and that the departure should take place in three days from that time. Don Quixote charged the bachelor to keep it a secret, especially from the curate and Master Nicholas, and from his niece and the housekeeper, lest they should prevent the execution of his praiseworthy and valiant purpose. Samson promised all, and then took his leave, charging Don Quixote to inform him of his good or evil fortunes whenever he had an opportunity; and thus they bade each other farewell, and Sancho went away to make the necessary preparations for their expedition.

CHAPTER 3

On to El Toboso

S ANCHO CAME HOME in such glee and spirits that his wife noticed his happiness a bowshot off, so much so that it made her ask him, "What have you got, Sancho friend, that you are so glad?"

"Hark ye, Teresa," replied Sancho, "I am glad because I have made up my mind to go back to the service of my master Don Quixote, who means to go out a third time to seek for adventures; and I am going with him again with the thought that I may find another hundred crowns like those we have spent; though it makes me sad to have to leave thee and the children. But mind, Theresa, you must look to Dapple carefully for the next three days, so that he may be fit to take arms. Double his feed, and see to the pack-saddle and other harness, for it is not to a wedding we are bound."

"I know well enough, husband," said Teresa, "that squires-errant don't eat their bread for nothing, and so I will be always praying to our Lord to deliver you speedily from all that hard fortune."

"I can tell you, wife," said Sancho, "if I did not expect to see myself governor of an island before long, I would drop down dead on the spot."

"Nay, then, husband," said Teresa; "let the devil take all the governments in the world; you have lived until now without a government, and when it is God's will you will go to your grave without a government. The best sauce in the world is hunger, and as the poor are never without that, they always eat with a relish. But mind, Sancho, if by good luck you *should* find yourself with some government, don't forget me and your children. Remember that Sanchico is now full fifteen; and I say if you are bent upon having a government, take your son Sancho with you, and teach him from this time on how to hold a government; for sons ought to inherit and learn the trades of their fathers."

"As soon as I have the government," said Sancho, "I will send for him by post, and I will send thee money; and do thou dress him so as to hide what he is and make him look what he is to be."

"You send the money," said Teresa, "and I'll dress him up for you as fine as you please."

While Sancho Panza and his wife held their conversation, Don Quixote's niece and housekeeper were not idle, for by a thousand signs they began to perceive that their uncle and master meant to give them the slip the third time, and once more betake himself to his, for them, ill-errant chivalry.

And when there came a knocking at the door, and Sancho Panza said that it was he, the housekeeper ran to hide herself so as not to see him; in such abhorrence did she hold him. The niece let him in, and his master Don Quixote came forward to receive him with open arms, and the pair shut themselves up in his room, where they were soon in earnest conversation.

By the advice and with the approval of the great Samson, who was now their oracle, they had arranged that their departure should take place three days thence, by which time they could have all that was requisite for the journey ready. Samson's intention in persuading them to sally forth once more was all by the advice of the curate and barber, with whom he had previously discussed the subject. Finally, then, during those three days, Don Quixote and Sancho provided themselves with what they considered necessary, and Sancho having pacified his wife, and Don Quixote his niece and housekeeper, at nightfall, unseen by anyone except the bachelor, who thought fit to accompany them half a league out of the village, they set out for El Toboso, Don Quixote on his good Rocinante and Sancho on his old Dapple, his saddlebags furnished with certain matters in the way of victuals, and his purse with money that Don Quixote gave him to meet emergencies. Samson embraced him, and entreated him to let him hear of his good or evil fortunes, so that he might rejoice over the former or condole with him over the latter, as the laws of friendship required. Don Quixote promised him he would do so, and Samson returned to the village, and the other two took the road for the great city of El Toboso.

CHAPTER 4

Sancho Solves His Problem

THE MOMENT Samson took his departure, Rocinante began to neigh, and Dapple to sigh, which, by both knight and squire, was accepted as a good sign and a very happy omen.

Said Don Quixote, "Sancho, my friend, night is drawing on upon us as we go, and more darkly than will allow us to reach El Toboso by daylight; for there I am resolved to go before I engage in another adventure, and there I shall obtain the blessing of the peerless Dulcinea, with which blessing I feel assured that I shall bring to a happy termination every perilous adventure; for nothing in life makes knights-errant more valorous than finding themselves favored by their ladies."

"So I believe," replied Sancho; "but I think it will be difficult for your worship to speak with her or see her, at any rate where you will be able to receive her blessing; unless, indeed, she throws it over the wall of the yard where I saw her the time before, when I took her the letter that told of the follies and mad things your worship was doing in the heart of Sierra Morena."

"Didst thou take that for a yard wall, Sancho," said Don Quixote, "where thou sawest that never sufficiently extolled grace and beauty? It must have been the gallery, corridor, or portico of some rich and royal palace."

"It might have been all that," returned Sancho, "but to me it looked like a wall, unless I am short of memory."

"At all events, let us go there, Sancho," said Don Quixote; "for, so that I see her, it is the same to me whether it be over a wall, or at a window, or through the chink of a door."

They passed that night without anything worth mention happening to them, whereat Don Quixote was not a little dejected; but at length the next day, at daybreak, they saw the great city of El Toboso, at the sight of which Don Quixote's spirits rose and Sancho's fell, for he did not know Dulcinea's house, nor in all his life had he ever seen her, any more than his master; so that they were both uneasy, the one to see her, the other at not having seen her, and Sancho was at a loss to know what he was to do when his master sent him to El Toboso. In the end, Don Quixote made up his mind to enter the city at night, and they waited until the time came among some oak trees that were near El Toboso.

'Twas at the very midnight hour—more or less—when Don Quixote and Sancho quitted the wood and entered El Toboso. The town was in deep silence, for all the inhabitants were asleep. The night was darkish, though Sancho would have been glad had it been quite dark, so as to find in the darkness an excuse for his blundering. All over the place nothing was to be heard except the barking of the dogs, which deafened the ears of Don Quixote and troubled the heart of Sancho. Now and then an ass brayed, pigs grunted, cats mewed, and the various noises they made seemed louder in the silence of the night; all of which the enamored knight took to be of evil omen; nevertheless he said to Sancho, "Sancho, my son, lead on to the palace of Dulcinea, it may be that we shall find her awake."

"Body of the sun! what palace am I to lead to," said Sancho, "when what I saw her highness in was only a very little house?"

"Most likely she had then withdrawn into some small apartment of her palace," said Don Quixote, "to amuse herself with damsels, as great ladies and princesses are accustomed to do."

"Señor," said Sancho, "if your worship will have it in spite of me that the house of my lady Dulcinea is a palace, is this an hour, think you, to find the door open; and will it be right for us to go knocking till they hear us and open the door; making a disturbance and confusion all though the household?"

"Let us first of all find out the palace for certain," replied Don Quixote, "and then I will tell thee, Sancho, what we had best do; but look, Sancho, for either I see badly, or that dark mass that one sees from here should be Dulcinea's palace."

"Then let your worship lead the way," said Sancho, "perhaps it may be so;

though I see it with my eyes and touch it with my hands, I'll believe it as much as I believe it is daylight now."

Don Quixote took the lead, and having gone a matter of two hundred paces he came upon the mass that produced the shade, and then he perceived that the building in question was no palace, but the chief church of the town, and said he, "It's the church we have lit upon, Sancho."

"So I see," said Sancho, "and God grant we may not light upon our graves; it is no good sign to find oneself wandering in a graveyard at this time of night; and that, after my telling your worship, if I don't mistake, that the house of this lady will be in an alley without an outlet."

"The curse of God on thee for a blockhead!" said Don Quixote; "where hast thou ever heard of castles and royal palaces being built in alleys without an outlet?"

"Señor," replied Sancho, "every country has a way of its own; perhaps here in El Toboso it is the way to build palaces and grand buildings in alleys; so I entreat your worship to let me search about among these streets or alleys before me, and perhaps, in some corner or other, I may stumble on this palace—and I wish I saw the dogs eating it for leading us such a dance."

"Speak respectfully of what belongs to my lady, Sancho," said Don Quixote.

"I'll hold my tongue," said Sancho, "but how am I to take it patiently when your worship wants me, with only once seeing the house of our mistress, to know it always, and find it in the middle of the night, when your worship can't find it, who must have seen it thousands of times?"

"Thou wilt drive me to desperation, Sancho," said Don Quixote. "Look here, heretic, have I not told thee a thousand times that I have never once in my life seen the peerless Dulcinea or crossed the threshold of her palace, and that I am enamored solely by hearsay and by the great reputation she bears for beauty and discretion?"

"I hear it now," returned Sancho; "and I may tell you that if you have not seen her, no more have I."

"That cannot be," said Don Quixote, "for, at any rate, thou saidst, on bringing back the answer to the letter I sent by thee, that thou sawest her."

"Don't mind that, señor," said Sancho; "I must tell you that my seeing

171

her and the answer I brought you back were by hearsay too, for I can no more tell who the lady Dulcinea is than I can hit the sky."

"Sancho, Sancho," said Don Quixote, "there are times for jests and times when jests are out of place; if I tell thee that I have neither seen nor spoken to the lady of my heart, it is no reason why thou shouldst say thou hast not spoken to her or seen her, when the contrary is the case, as thou well knowest."

Sancho, seeing his master somewhat dissatisfied, said to him, "Señor, daylight will be here before long, and it will not do for us to let the sun find us in the street; it will be better for us to quit the city, and for your worship to hide in some forest in the neighborhood, and I will come back in the daytime, and I won't leave a nook or corner of the whole village that I won't search for the house, castle, or palace, of my lady."

"Sancho," said Don Quixote, "I thank thee for the advice thou hast given me, and take it most gladly. Come, my son, let us go look for some place where I may hide."

Sancho was in a fever to get his master out of the town, lest he should discover the falsehood of the reply he had brought to him in the Sierra Morena on behalf of Dulcinea; so he hastened their departure, which they took at once, and two miles out of the village they found a forest or thicket wherein Don Quixote concealed himself.

"Go, my son," said Don Quixote, "and be not dazed when thou findest thyself exposed to the light of that sun of beauty thou art going to seek."

"I will go and return quickly," said Sancho; "cheer up that little heart of yours, master mine, for at the present moment you seem to have got one no bigger than a hazel nut; remember what they say, that a stout heart breaks bad luck."

With this, Sancho wheeled about and gave Dapple the stick, and Don Quixote remained behind, seated on his horse, resting in his stirrups and leaning on the end of his lance, filled with sad and troubled forebodings; and there we will leave him, and accompany Sancho, who went off no less serious and troubled than he left his master; so much so, that as soon as he had got out of the thicket, and looking round saw that Don Quixote was not within sight, he dismounted from his ass, and seating himself at the foot of a tree began to commune with himself, saying, "Now, brother Sancho, let us know where your worship is going. Are you going to look for some ass that has been lost? Not at all. Then what are you going to look for? I am going to look for a princess, that's all. And where do you expect to find her, Sancho? Where? Why, in the great city of El Toboso. That's all very well, but do you know her house, Sancho? And have you ever seen her by any chance? Neither I nor my master ever saw her. And does it strike you that it would be just and right if the El Toboso people, finding out that you were here with the intention of going to tamper with their princesses and trouble their ladies, were to come and cudgel your ribs, and not leave a whole bone in you? The devil, the devil and nobody else, has mixed me up in this business!"

Such was the soliloquy Sancho held with himself, and all the conclusion he could come to was to say to himself again, "Well, there's remedy for everything except death, under whose yoke we have all to pass, whether we like it or not, when life's finished. I have seen by a thousand signs that this master of mine is a madman fit to be tied, and for that matter, I too, am not behind him; for I'm a greater fool than he is when I follow him and serve him. Well then, if he be mad, as he is, it will not be very hard to make him believe that some country girl, the first I come across here, is the lady Dulcinea; and if he does not believe it, I'll swear it; and if he should swear, I'll swear again; and if he persists I'll persist still more. Maybe, by holding out in this way, I may put a stop to his sending me on messages of this kind another time; or maybe he will think, as I suspect he will, that one of those wicked enchanters, who he says have a spite against him, has changed her form for the sake of doing him an ill turn and injuring him."

With this reflection Sancho made his mind easy, counting the business as good as settled, and stayed there till the afternoon so as to make Don Quixote think he had time enough to go to El Toboso and return; and things turned out so luckily for him that as he got up to mount Dapple, he spied, coming from El Toboso towards the spot where he stood, three peasant girls on three colts.

The instant Sancho saw the peasant girls, he returned full speed to seek his master, and found him sighing and uttering a thousand passionate lamentations. When Don Quixote saw him he exclaimed, "What news, Sancho, my friend? Am I to mark this day with a white stone or a black?"

"Good news," replied Sancho. "So good that your worship has only to spur Rocinante and get out into the open field to see the lady Dulcinea del Toboso, who, with two others, damsels of hers, is coming to see your worship."

"Holy God! What art thou saying, Sancho, my friend?" exclaimed Don Quixote. "Take care thou art not deceiving me, or seeking by false joy to cheer my real sadness."

"What could I get by deceiving your worship," returned Sancho, "especially when it will so soon be shown whether I tell the truth or not? Come, señor, push on, and you will see the princess our mistress coming, robed and adorned—in fact, like what she is. Her damsels and she are all one glow of gold, all bunches of pearls, all diamonds, all rubies, all cloth of brocade; with their hair loose on their shoulders like so many sunbeams playing with the wind; and moreover, they come mounted on three piebald cackneys, the finest sight you ever saw."

"Hackneys, you mean, Sancho," said Don Quixote.

"There is not much difference between cackneys and hackneys," said Sancho; "but no matter what they come on, there they are, the finest ladies one could wish for, especially my lady the princess Dulcinea, who staggers one's senses."

"Let us go, Sancho, my son," said Don Quixote, "and in guerdon of this news, as unexpected as it is good, I bestow upon thee the best spoil I shall win in the first adventure I may have; or if that does not satisfy thee, I promise thee the foals I shall have this year from my three mares."

"I'll take the foals," said Sancho, "for it is not quite certain that the spoils of the first adventure will be good ones."

By this time they had cleared the wood, and saw the three village lasses close at hand. Don Quixote looked all along the road to El Toboso, and as he could see nobody except the three peasant girls, he was completely puzzled, and asked Sancho if it was outside the city he had left them.

"How outside the city?" returned Sancho. "Are your worship's eyes in the back of your head, that you can't see that they are these who are coming here, shining like the very sun at noonday?"

"I see nothing, Sancho," said Don Quixote, "but three country girls on three jackasses."

"Now, may God deliver me from the devil!" said Sancho, "and can it be that your worship takes three hackneys—or whatever they're called—as white as the driven snow, for jackasses?"

"Well, I can only say, Sancho, my friend," said Don Quixote, "that it is as plain they are jackasses—or jennyasses—as that I am Don Quixote, and thou Sancho Panza: at any rate, they seem to me to be so."

174

"Hush, señor," said Sancho, "don't talk that way, but open your eyes, and come and pay your respects to the lady of your thoughts, who is close upon us now"; and with these words he advanced to receive the three village lasses, and dismounting from Dapple, caught hold of one of the asses of the three country girls by the halter, and dropping on both knees on the ground, he said, "Queen and princess and duchess of beauty, may it please your haughtiness to receive into your favor your captive knight who stands there quite stupefied at finding himself in your magnificent presence. I am Sancho Panza, his squire, and he the vagabond knight Don Quixote of La Mancha, otherwise called 'The Knight of the Rueful Countenance.'"

Don Quixote had by this time placed himself on his knees beside Sancho, and, with eyes starting out of his head and a puzzled gaze, was regarding her whom Sancho called queen and lady; and as he could see nothing in her except a village lass, and not a very well-favored one, for she was platter-faced and snub-nosed, he was perplexed and bewildered, and did not venture to open his lips. The country girls, at the same time, were astonished to see these two men, so different in appearance, on their knees, preventing their companion from going on. She, however, who had been stopped, breaking silence, said angrily and testily, "Get out of the way, bad luck to you, and let us pass, for we are in a hurry."

To which Sancho returned, "Oh, princess, is not your magnanimous heart softened by seeing the pillar and prop of knight-errantry on his knees before your sublimated presence?"

On hearing this, one of the others exclaimed, "Woa then! See how the lordlings come to make game of the village girls now. Go your own way, and let us go ours, and it will be better for you."

"Get up, Sancho," said Don Quixote at this. "I see that fortune, 'with evil done to me unsated still,' has taken possession of all the roads by which any comfort may reach 'this wretched soul.' And thou, O highest perfection of excellence that can be desired, though the malign enchanter that persecutes me has transformed thy unparagoned beauty and changed thy features into those of a poor peasant girl, refuse not to look upon me with tenderness and love."

"Hey-day! My grandfather!" cried the girl. "Much I care for your love-making! Get out of the way and let us pass, and we'll thank you."

Sancho stood aside to let her go, very well pleased to have got so well out of the hobble he was in. The instant the village lass who had done duty for

Dulcinea found herself free, prodding her "cackney" with a spike she had at the end of a stick, she set off at full speed across the field. The she-ass, however, feeling the point more acutely than usual, began cutting such capers that it flung the lady Dulcinea to the ground; seeing which, Don Quixote ran to raise her up, and Sancho to fix and girth the pack-saddle, which also had slipped under the ass's belly. The pack-saddle being secured, as Don Quixote was about to lift up his enchanted mistress in his arms and put her upon her beast, the lady, getting up from the ground, saved him the trouble, for, going back a little, she took a short run, and putting both hands on the croup of the ass she dropped into the saddle more lightly than a falcon, and sat astride like a man. As soon as the others saw Dulcinea mounted, they pushed on after her, and sped away without looking back, for more than half a league.

Don Quixote followed them with his eyes, and when they were no longer in sight, he turned to Sancho and said, "How now, Sancho? thou seest how I am hated by enchanters! And see to what a length the malice and spite they bear me go, when they seek to deprive me of the happiness it would give me to see my lady in her own proper form! Once more I say, and will say a thousand times, I am the most unfortunate of men."

Sancho, the rogue, had enough to do to hide his laughter, at hearing the simplicity of the master he had so nicely befooled. At length, after a good deal more conversation had passed between them, they remounted their beasts, and followed the road to Saragossa, which they expected to reach in time to take part in a certain grand festival which is held every year in that illustrious city; but before they got there many strange things happened to them.

CHAPTER 5

The "Cortes of Death"

DEJECTED BEYOND MEASURE, Don Quixote pursued his journey, turning over in his mind the cruel trick the enchanters had played him in changing his lady Dulcinea into the vile shape of the village lass, nor could he think of any way of restoring her to her original form; and these reflections so absorbed him, that without being aware of it he let go Rocinante's bridle, and he, perceiving the liberty that was granted him, stopped at every step to crop the fresh grass with which the plain abounded.

Sancho recalled him from his reverie. "Melancholy, señor," said he, "was made, not for beasts, but for men; but if men give way to it overmuch they turn to beasts; control yourself, your worship; be yourself again; gather up Rocinante's reins; cheer up, rouse yourself and show that gallant spirit that knights-errant ought to have. The devil fly away with all the Dulcineas in the world; for the well-being of a single knight-errant is of more consequence than all the enchantments on earth."

"Hush, Sancho," said Don Quixote in a faint voice, "utter no blasphemies against that enchanted lady; for I alone am to blame for her misfortune; her calamity has come of the hatred the wicked bear me."

"So say I," returned Sancho; "his heart 'twould rend in twain, I vow, who saw her once, to see her now."

"Thou mayest well say that, Sancho," replied Don Quixote, "as thou sawest her in the full perfection of her beauty. But perhaps the enchantment does not go so far as to deprive conquered and presented giants and knights of the power of recognizing Dulcinea; we will try by experiment with one

177

or two of the first I vanquish and send to her, whether they see her or not, by commanding them to return and give me an account of what happened to them in this respect."

"I declare, I think what your worship has proposed is excellent," said Sancho, "and that by this plan we shall find out if it be that it is only from your worship she is hidden. But so long as the lady Dulcinea is well and happy, we on our part will make the best of it, and get on as well as we can, seeking our adventures, and leaving Time to take his own course; for he is the best physician for these and greater ailments."

Don Quixote was about to reply to Sancho Panza, but he was prevented by a cart crossing the road full of the most diverse and strange personages and figures that could be imagined. He who led the mules and acted as carter was a hideous demon; the cart was open to the sky, and the first figure that presented itself to Don Quixote's eyes was that of Death itself with a human face; next to it was an angel with large painted wings, and at one side an emperor, with a crown, to all appearance of gold, on his head. At the feet of Death was the god called Cupid, without his bandage, but with his bow, quiver, and arrows; there was also a knight in full armor, except that he had no helmet, but only a hat decked with plumes of divers colors; and along with these there were others with a variety of costumes and faces. All this, unexpectedly encountered, took Don Quixote somewhat aback, and struck terror into the heart of Sancho; but the next instant Don Quixote was glad of it, believing that some new perilous adventure was presenting itself to him, and under this impression, and with a spirit prepared to face any danger, he planted himself in front of the cart, and in a loud and menacing tone, exclaimed, "Carter, or coachman, or devil, or whatever thou art, tell me at once who thou art, whither thou art going, and who these folk are thou carriest in thy wagon, which looks more like Charon's boat than an ordinary cart."

To which the devil, stopping the cart, answered quietly, "Señor, we are players of Angulo el Malo's company; we have been acting the play of 'The Cortes of Death' this morning in a village behind that hill, and we have to act it this afternoon in that village which you can see from this; and as it is so near, and to save the trouble of undressing and dressing again, we go in the costumes in which we perform. That lad there appears as Death, that other as an angel, that woman, the manager's wife, plays the queen, this one the soldier, that the emperor, and I the devil; and I am one of the principal characters of the play, for in this company I take the leading parts. If you want to know anything more about us, ask me and I will answer with the utmost exactitude, for as I am a devil I am up to everything."

"By the faith of a knight-errant," replied Don Quixote, "when I saw this cart I fancied some great adventure was presenting itself to me; but I declare one must touch with the hand what appears to the eye, if illusions are to be avoided. God speed you, good people; keep your festival, and remember, if you demand of me anything wherein I can render you a service, I will do it gladly, for from a child I was fond of the play, and in my youth a keen lover of the actor's art."

While they were talking, fate so willed it that one of the company in a mummers' dress with a great number of bells, and armed with three blown ox-bladders at the end of a stick, joined them, and this merry-andrew approaching Don Quixote, began flourshing his stick and banging the ground with the bladders and cutting capers with great jingling of the bells, which so startled Rocinante that, in spite of Don Quixote's efforts to hold him in, taking the bit between his teeth he set off across the plain with greater speed than the bones of his anatomy ever gave any promise of.

Sancho, who thought his master was in danger of being thrown, jumped off Dapple, and ran in all haste to help him; but by the time he reached him he was already on the ground, and beside him was Rocinante, who had come down with his master, the usual end and upshot of Rocinante's vivacity and high spirits. But the moment Sancho quitted his beast to go and help Don Quixote, the dancing devil with the bladders jumped up on Dapple, and beating him with them, more by the fright and the noise than by the pain of the blows, made him fly across the fields towards the village where they were going to hold their festival. Sancho witnessed Dapple's career and his master's fall, and did not know which of the two cases of need he should attend to first; but in the end, like a good squire and good servant, he let his love for his master prevail over his affection for his ass. He came to where Don Quixote lay in a far sorrier plight than he liked, and having helped him to mount Rocinante, he said to him, "Señor the devil has carried off my Dapple."

"What devil?" asked Don Quixote.

"The one with the bladders," said Sancho.

"Then I will recover him," said Don Quixote, "even if he be shut up with him in the deepest and darkest dungeons of hell."

179

"You need not take the trouble, señor," said Sancho; "keep cool, for as I now see, the devil has let Dapple go and he is coming back to his old quarters." And so it turned out, for, having come down with Dapple, in imitation of Don Quixote and Rocinante, the devil made off on foot to the town, and the ass came back to his master.

"For all that," said Don Quixote, "it will be well to visit the discourtesy of that devil upon some of those in the cart, even if it were the emperor himself."

"Don't think of it, your worship," returned Sancho; "take my advice and never meddle with actors, for they are a favored class; I myself have known an actor taken up for two murders, and yet come off scot-free."

"Still, for all that," said Don Quixote, "the player devil must not go off boasting, even if the whole human race favors him."

So saying, he made for the cart, which was now very near the town, shouting out as he went, "Stay! halt! ye merry, jovial crew! I want to teach you how to treat asses and animals that serve the squires of knights-errant for steeds."

So loud were the shouts of Don Quixote, that those in the cart heard and understood them, and, guessing by the words what the speaker's intention was, Death in an instant jumped out of the cart, and the emperor, the devil carter and the angel after him, nor did the queen or the god Cupid stay behind; and all armed themselves with stones and formed in line, prepared to receive Don Quixote on the points of their pebbles.

Don Quixote, when he saw them drawn up in such a gallant array with uplifted arms ready for a mighty discharge of stones, checked Rocinante and began to consider in what way he could attack them with the least danger to himself. As he halted, Sancho came up, and seeing him disposed to attack this well-ordered squadron, said to him, "It would be the height of madness to attempt such an enterprise; remember that it is rashness, and not valor, for a single man to attack an army that has Death in it; and if this reflection will not make you keep quiet, perhaps it will to know for certain that among all these, though they look like kings, princes, and emperors, there is not a single knight-errant."

"Now indeed thou hast hit the point, Sancho," said Don Quixote, "which may and should turn me from the resolution I had already formed. I cannot and must not draw sword, as I have many a time before told thee, against anyone who is not a dubbed knight; it is for thee, Sancho, if thou wilt, to take vengeance for the wrong done to thy Dapple; and I will help thee from here by shouts and salutary counsels."

"There is no occasion to take vengeance on anyone, señor," replied Sancho; "for it is not the part of good Christians to revenge wrongs; and besides, I will arrange it with my ass to leave his grievance to my good will and pleasure, and that is to live in peace as long as heaven grants me life."

"Well," said Don Quixote, "if that be thy determination, good Sancho, sensible Sancho, let us leave these phantoms alone and turn to the pursuit of worthier adventures; for, from what I see of this country, we cannot fail to find plenty of marvelous ones in it."

He at once wheeled about, Sancho ran to take possession of his Dapple, Death and his flying squadron returned to their cart and pursued their journey, and thus the dread adventure of the cart of Death ended happily, thanks to the advice Sancho gave his master.

The night succeeding the day of the encounter with Death, Don Quixote and his squire passed under some tall shady trees, and Don Quixote at Sancho's persuasion ate a little from the store carried by Dapple, and over their supper Sancho said to his master, "Señor, what a fool I should have looked if I had chosen for my reward the spoils of the first adventure your worship achieved, instead of the foals of the three mares. After all, 'a sparrow in the hand is better than a vulture on the wing.'"

"At the same time, Sancho," replied Don Quixote, "if thou hadst let me attack them as I wanted, at the very least the emperor's gold crown and Cupid's painted wings would have fallen to thee as spoils, for I should have taken them by force and given them into thy hands."

"The scepters and crowns of those play-actor emperors," said Sancho, "were never yet pure gold, but only brass foil or tin."

"That is true," said Don Quixote, "for it would not be right that the accessories of the drama should be real, instead of being mere fictions and semblances, like the drama itself; which places before us at every step a mirror in which we may see vividly displayed what goes on in human life. Come, tell me, hast thou not seen a play acted in which one plays the villain, another the knave, this one the merchant, that the soldier, one the sharp-witted fool, another the foolish lover; and when the play is over, and they have put off the dresses they wore in it, all the actors become equal."

"Yes, I have seen that," said Sancho.

"Well then," said Don Quixote, "the same thing happens in the comedy

181

and life of this world, where some play emperors, others popes, and, in short, all the characters that can be brought into a play; but when it is over, that is to say when life ends, death strips them all of the garments that distinguish one from the other, and all are equal in the grave."

In conversation of this kind they passed a good part of the night, but Sancho felt a desire to let down the curtains of his eyes, as he used to say when he wanted to go to sleep; and stripping Dapple he left him at liberty to graze his fill. He did not remove Rocinante's saddle, as his master's express orders were, that so long as they were in the field or not sleeping under a roof Rocinante was not to be stripped—the ancient usage established and observed by knights-errant being to take off the bridle and hang it on the saddle-bow, but to remove the saddle from the horse—never! Sancho acted accordingly, and gave him the same liberty he had given Dapple, between whom and Rocinante there was a friendship unequaled. The two beasts would scratch one another when they were together and when they were tired or full, Rocinante would lay his neck across Dapple's, stretching half a yard or more on the other side, and the pair would stand thus, gazing thoughtfully on the ground, for three days, or at least so long as they were left alone, or hunger did not drive them to go and look for food. How firm the friendship must have been between these two peaceful animals, shaming men, who preserve friendships with one another so badly!

CHAPTER 6

A New Adventure

Sancho at last fell asleep at the foot of a cork tree, while Don Quixote dozed at that of a sturdy oak; but a short time only had elapsed when a noise he heard behind him awoke him, and rising up startled, he listened and looked in the direction the noise came from, and perceived two men on horseback, one of whom, letting himself drop from the saddle, said to the other, "Dismount, my friend, and take the bridles off the horses, for, so far as I can see, this place will furnish grass for them, and the solitude and silence my lovesick thoughts have need of." As he said this he stretched himself upon the ground, and as he flung himself down, the armor in which he was clad rattled, whereby Don Quixote perceived that he must be a knight-errant; and going over to Sancho, who was asleep, he shook him by the arm and with no small difficulty brought him back to his senses, and said in a low voice to him, "Brother Sancho, we have got an adventure."

"God send us a good one," said Sancho; "and where may the adventure be?"

"Where, Sancho?" replied Don Quixote. "Turn thine eyes and look, and thou wilt see stretched there a knight-errant, who, it strikes me, is not over and above happy, for I saw him fling himself off his horse and throw himself on the ground with a certain air of dejection, and his armor rattled as he fell."

"Well," said Sancho, "how does your worship make out that to be an adventure?"

"I do not mean to say," returned Don Quixote, "that it is a complete adventure, but that it is the beginning of one, for it is in this way adventures

183

begin. But listen, for it seems he is tuning a lute or guitar, and he must be getting ready to sing something."

"Faith, you are right," said Sancho, "and no doubt he is some enamored knight."

"There is no knight-errant that is not," sad Don Quixote; "but let us listen to him, for out of the abundance of the heart the mouth speaketh."

Sancho was about to reply to his master, but the Knight of the Grove's voice, which was neither very bad nor very good, stopped him, and listening attentively the pair heard him sing a love song.

With an "Ah me!" that seemed to be drawn from the inmost recesses of his heart, the Knight of the Grove brought his lay to an end, and shortly afterwards exclaimed in a piteous voice, "O fairest and most ungrateful woman on earth! What! can it be, most serene Casildea de Vandalia, that thou wilt suffer this thy captive knight to waste away and perish? It is not enough that I have compelled all the knights of Navarre, all the knights of La Mancha, to confess thee the most beautiful in the world?"

"Not so," said Don Quixote at this, "for I am of La Mancha, and I have never confessed anything of the sort. But let us listen, perhaps he will tell us more about himself."

"That he will," returned Sancho, "for he seems in a mood to bewail himself for a month at a stretch."

But this was not the case, for the Knight of the Grove, hearing voices near him, instead of continuing his lamentation, stood up and exclaimed in a distinct but courteous tone, "Who goes there? What are you? Do you belong to the number of the happy or of the miserable?"

"Of the miserable," answered Don Quixote.

"Then come to me," said he of the Grove, "and rest assured that it is to woe itself and affliction itself you come."

Don Quixote, finding himself answered in such a soft and courteous manner, went over to him, and so did Sancho.

The doleful knight took Don Quixote by the arm, saying, "Sit down here, sir knight; for I see that you are one, and of those that profess knight-errantry."

To which Don Quixote made answer, "A knight I am of the profession you mention, and I feel for the misfortunes of others. From what you have just now sung I gather that yours spring from love, I mean from the love you bear that fair ingrate you named in your lament."

"Look and thou wilt see stretched there a knight-errant."

In the meantime, they had seated themselves together on the hard ground peaceably and sociably, just as if, as soon as day broke, they were not going to break one another's heads.

"Are you, sir knight, in love perchance?" asked he of the Grove of Don Quixote.

"By mischance I am," replied Don Quixote; "though the ills arising from well-bestowed affections should be esteemed favors rather than misfortunes."

"That is true," returned he of the Grove, "if scorn did not unsettle our reason and understanding."

"I was never scorned by my lady," said Don Quixote.

"Certainly not," said Sancho, who stood close by, "for our lady is as a lamb, and softer than a roll of butter."

"Is this your squire?" asked he of the Grove.

"He is," said Don Quixote.

"I never yet saw a squire," said he of the Grove, "who ventured to speak when his master was speaking."

"By my faith then," said Sancho, "I have spoken, and am fit to speak, in the presence of one as much, or even—but never mind—it only makes it worse to stir it."

The squire of the Grove took Sancho by the arm, saying to him, "Let us two go where we can talk in squire style as much as we please, and leave these gentlemen our masters to fight it out over the story of their loves; and, depend upon it, daybreak will find them at it without having made an end of it."

"So be it by all means," said Sancho; "and I will tell your worship who I am, that you may see whether I am to be reckoned among the number of the most talkative squires."

With this the two squires withdrew to one side, and between them there passed a conversation as droll as that which passed between their masters was serious.

The squire of the Grove said to Sancho, "A hard life it is we lead and live, señor, we that are squires to knights-errant; verily, we eat our bread in the sweat of our faces, which is one of the curses God laid on our first parents."

"It may be said, too," added Sancho, "that we eat it in the chill of our bodies; for who gets more heat and cold than the miserable squires of knight-errantry? Even so it would not be so bad if we had something to eat, for woes are lighter if there's bread; but sometimes we go a day or two without breaking our fast."

"All that," said he of the Grove, "may be endured and put up with when we have hopes of reward; for, unless the knight-errant he serves is excessively unlucky, after a few turns the squire will at least find himself rewarded with a fine government of some island or fair county."

"I," said Sancho, "have already told my master that I shall be content with the government of some island, and he is so noble and generous that he has promised it to me ever so many times."

"Well, then, you are wrong there," said he of the Grove; "for those island governments are not all satisfactory; some are awkward, some are poor, and some are dull. In truth, sir squire, I have made up my mind to have done with these drunken vagaries of these knights, and go back to my village, and bring up my children; for I have three, like three Oriental pearls."

"I have two," said Sancho, "that might be presented before the Pope himself, especially a girl who is as tall as a lance, and as fresh as an April morning, and as strong as a porter. And to see them again I pray God to deliver me from this perilous calling of squire into which I have fallen a second time, decoyed and beguiled by a purse with a hundred ducats that I found one day in the heart of the Sierra Morena; and the devil is always putting a bag full of doubloons before my eyes; and so long as I think of this I make light of all the hardships I endure with this simpleton of a master of mine, who, I well know, is more of a madman than a knight."

"If you come to talk of that sort," said he of the Grove, "there is not a greater one in the world than my master, for in order that another knight may recover the senses he has lost, he makes a madman of himself and goes looking for what, when found, may, for all I know, fly in his own face."

"And is he in love perchance?" asked Sancho.

"He is," said he of the Grove, "with one Casildea de Vandalia, the cruelest lady the whole world could produce; but that cruelty is not the only foot he limps on, for he has greater schemes in his head, as will be seen before many hours are over."

"There's no road so smooth but it has some hole or hindrance in it," said Sancho. "Madness will have more followers and hangers-on than sound sense; but if there be any truth in the common saying, that to have companions in trouble gives some relief, I may take consolation from you, inasmuch as you serve a master as crazy as my own."

"Crazy but valiant," replied he of the Grove, "and more roguish than crazy or valiant."

186

"Mine is not that," said Sancho; "I mean he has nothing of the rogue in him; on the contrary, he has no thought of doing harm to anyone, only good to all, nor has he any malice whatever in him; a child might persuade him that it is night at noonday; and for this simplicity I love him as the core of my heart, and I can't bring myself to leave him, let him do ever such foolish things."

"For all that, brother and señor," said he of the Grove, "if the blind lead the blind, both are in danger of falling into the pit. It seems to me," he added, "that with all this talk of ours our tongues are sticking to the roofs of our mouths; but I have a pretty good loosener hanging from the saddle-bow of my horse." And getting up he came back the next minute with a large bota of wine and a pasty half a yard across.

Sancho, looking at it, said, "And do you carry this with you, señor?"

"Why, what are you thinking about?" said the other. "Do you take me for some paltry squire? I carry a better larder on my horse's croup than a general takes with him when he goes on a march."

Sancho ate without requiring to be pressed, and said he, "You are a proper trusty squire, one of the right sort, sumptuous and grand, not like me, unlucky beggar, that have nothing more in my saddlebags than a scrap of cheese, so hard that one might brain a giant with it, and, to keep it company, a few dozen beans and as many more filberts and walnuts; thanks to the austerity of my master, and the idea he has that knights-errant must not sustain themselves on anything except dried fruits and the herbs of the field."

"By my faith, brother," said he of the Grove, "my stomach is not made for thistles, or wild pears, or roots of the woods; let our masters do as they like, with their chivalry notions; I carry my prog-basket and this bota hanging to the saddle-bow, whatever they may say." And so saying he thrust it into Sancho's hands, who raising it aloft pointed to his mouth, gazed at the stars for a quarter of an hour; and when he had done drinking let his head fall on one side, and giving a deep sigh, exclaimed, "Ah!"

The end of it was that the two squires talked so much and drank so much that sleep had to tie their tongues and moderate their thirst, for to quench it was impossible; and so the pair of them fell asleep clinging to the now nearly empty bota and with half-chewed morsels in their mouths; and there we will leave them for the present, to relate what passed between the Knight of the Grove and him of the Rueful Countenance.

CHAPTER 7

The Knight of the Mirrors

Among the many things that passed between Don Quixote and the Knight of the Grove, he of the Grove said to Don Quixote, "In fine, sir knight, I would have you know that my destiny led me to fall in love with the peerless Casildea de Vandalia. This same Casildea, then, that I speak of, returned my honorable passion and gentle aspirations by compelling me, as his stepmother did Hercules, to engage in many perils of various sorts, at the end of each promising me that, with the end of the next, the object of my hopes should be attained; but my labors have gone on increasing link by link until they are past counting. Last of all she has commanded me to go through all the provinces of Spain and compel all the knights-errant wandering therein to confess that she surpasses all women alive today in beauty, and that I am the most valiant knight on earth; in support of which claim I have already traveled over the greater part of Spain, and have there vanquished several knights who have dared to contradict me; but what I most pride myself upon is having vanquished in single combat that so famous knight Don Quixote of La Mancha, and made him confess that my Casildea is more beautiful than his Dulcinea. Thus the innumerable achievements of the said Don Quixote are now set down to my account and have become mine."

Don Quixote was amazed when he heard the Knight of the Grove, and was a thousand times on the point of telling him he lied; but he restrained himself as well as he could, in order to force him to confess the lie with his own lips; so he said to him quietly, "As to what you say, sir knight, about having vanquished most of the knights of Spain, or even of the whole world, I say nothing; but that you have vanquished Don Quixote of La Mancha I consider doubtful; it may have been some other that resembled him, although there are few like him."

"How! not vanquished?" said he of the Grove; "by the heaven that is above us I fought Don Quixote and overcame him and made him yield; and he is a man of tall stature, gaunt features, long, lank limbs, with hair turning gray, an aquiline nose rather hooked, and large black drooping mustaches; he does battle under the name of 'The Countenance,' and he has for squire a peasant called Sancho Panza; he rules the reins of a famous steed called Rocinante; and lastly, he has for the mistress of his will a certain Dulcinea del Toboso. If all these tokens are not enough to vindicate the truth of what I say, here is my sword, that will compel incredulity itself to give credence to it."

"Calm yourself, sir knight," said Don Quixote, "and give ear to what I am about to say to you. I would have you know that this Don Quixote you speak of is the greatest friend I have in the world; so much so that I may say I regard him in the same light as my own person; and from the precise and clear indications you have given I cannot but think that he must be the very one you have vanquished. On the other hand, I see with my eyes and feel with my hands that it is impossible it can have been the same; unless indeed it be that, as he has many enemies who are enchanters, and one in particular who is always persecuting him, some one of these may have taken his shape in order to allow himself to be vanquished, so as to defraud him of the fame that his exalted achievements as a knight have earned for him throughout the known world. And in confirmation of this, I must tell you, too, that it is but ten hours since these said enchanters his enemies transformed the shape and person of the fair Dulcinea del Toboso into a mean village lass, and in the same way they must have transformed Don Quixote; and if all this does not suffice to convince you of the truth of what I say, here is Don Quixote himself, who will maintain it by arms, on foot or on horseback or in any way you please."

And so saying he stood up and laid his hand on his sword, waiting to see what the Knight of the Grove would do, who in an equally calm voice said in reply, "Pledges don't distress a good payer; he who has succeeded in vanquishing you once when transformed, Sir Don Quixote, may fairly hope to subdue you in your own proper shape; but as it is not becoming for knights to perform their feats of arms in the dark, like highwaymen and bullies, let us wait till daylight, that the sun may behold our deeds; and the conditions of our combat shall be that the vanquished shall be at the victor's disposal, to do all that he may enjoin, provided the injunction be such as shall be becoming a knight."

"I am more than satisfied with these conditions," replied Don Quixote; and so saying, they betook themselves to where their squires lay, and found them snoring, and in the same posture they were in when sleep fell upon them. They roused them up, and bade them get the horses ready, as at sunrise they were to engage in a bloody and arduous single combat; at which intelligence Sancho was aghast, trembling for the safety of his master because of the mighty deeds he had heard the squire of the Grove ascribe to his; but without a word the two squires went in quest of their mounts; for by this time the three horses and the ass had smelled one another out, and were all together.

On the way, he of the Grove said to Sancho, "You must know, brother, that it is the custom with the fighting men of Andalusia, when they are seconds in any quarrel, not to stand idle with folded arms while their principals fight; I say so to remind you that while our masters are fighting, we, too, have to fight, and knock one another to shivers."

"That custom, sir squire," replied Sancho, "may hold good among those bullies and fighting men you talk of, but certainly not among the squires of knights-errant; at least, I have never heard my master speak of any custom of the sort, and he knows all the laws of knight-errantry by heart. Anyway, I have no sword, for I never carried one in my life."

"I know a good remedy for that," said he of the Grove; "I have here two linen bags of the same size; you shall taken one, and I the other, and we will fight at bag blows with equal arms."

"If that's the way, so be it with all my heart," said Sancho, "for that sort of battle will serve to knock the dust out of us instead of hurting us."

"That will not do," said the other, "for we must put into the bags, to keep the wind from blowing them away, half a dozen nice smooth pebbles, all of the same weight."

"Body of my father!" said Sancho. "Even if they are filled with floss silk, I can tell you, señor, I am not going to fight; let our masters fight, that's their lookout, and let us drink and live; for time will take care to ease us of our lives."

"Still," returned he of the Grove, "we must fight, if it be only for half an hour."

"By no means," said Sancho; "I am not going to be so discourteous or so ungrateful as to have any quarrel with one I have eaten and drunk with; besides, who could bring himself to fight in cold blood, without anger or provocation?"

"I can remedy that entirely," said he of the Grove, "and in this way: before we begin the battle, I will come up to your worship fair and softly, and give you three or four buffets, with which I shall stretch you at my feet and rouse your anger, though it were sleeping sounder than a dormouse."

"To match that plan," said Sancho, "I have another that is not a whit behind it; I will take a cudgel, and before your worship comes near enough to waken my anger I will send yours so sound to sleep with whacks, that it won't waken unless it be in the other world."

"Very good," said he of the Grove; "God will send the dawn and we shall be all right."

And now gay-plumaged birds of all sorts began to warble in the trees, and with their varied and gladsome notes seemed to welcome and salute the fresh morn that was beginning to show the beauty of her countenance at the gates and balconies of the east. But hardly had the light of day made it possible to see and distinguish things, when the first object that presented itself to the eyes of Sancho Panza was the squire of the Grove's nose, which was so big that it almost overshadowed his whole body. It was of enormous size, hooked in the middle, covered with warts, and of a mulberry color like an eggplant; it hung down two fingers' length below his mouth, and the size, the color, the warts, and the bend of it, made his face so hideous that Sancho, as he looked at him, began to tremble hand and foot like a child in convulsions, and he vowed in his heart to let himself be given two hundred buffets, sooner than be provoked to fight that monster. Don Quixote examined his adversary, and found that he already had his helmet on and the visor lowered, so that he could not see his face; he observed, however, that he was a sturdily built man, but not very tall in stature. Over his armor he wore a surcoat of what seemed to be the finest cloth of gold, all bespangled with glittering mirrors like little moons, which gave him an extremely gallant and splendid appearance; above his helmet fluttered a great quantity of plumes, and his lance, which was leaning against a tree, was very long and stout, and had a steel point more than a palm in length.

Don Quixote observed all, and took note of all, and from what he saw he concluded that the said knight must be a man of great strength, but he did not for all that give way to fear, like Sancho Panza; on the contrary, with a composed air, he said to the Knight of the Mirrors, "If, sir knight, your great eagerness to fight has not banished your courtesy, by it I would entreat you to raise your visor a little, in order that I may see if the comeliness of your countenance corresponds with that of your equipment."

"Whether you come victorious or vanquished out of this emprise, sir knight," replied he of the Mirrors, "you will have more than enough time to see me; and if now I do not comply with your request, it is because it seems to me I should do a serious wrong to the fair Casildea de Vandalia in wasting time while I stopped to raise my visor before compelling you to confess what you are already aware I maintain."

"Well then," said Don Quixote, "while we are mounting you can at least tell me if I am that Don Quixote whom you said you vanquished."

"To that we answer you," said he of the Mirrors, "that you are as like the very knight I vanquished as one egg is like another, but as you say enchanters persecute you, I will not venture to say positively whether you are the said person or not."

"That," said Don Quixote, "is enough to convince me that you are under a deception; however, entirely to relieve you of it, let our horses be brought, and in less time than it would take you to raise your visor, if God, my lady, and my arm stand me in good stead, I shall see your face, and you shall see that I am not the vanquished Don Quixote you take me to be."

With this, they mounted, and Don Quixote wheeled Rocinante round in order to take a proper distance to charge back upon his adversary, and he of the Mirrors did the same; but Don Quixote had not moved away twenty paces when he heard himself called by the other, and, each returning halfway, he of the Mirrors said to him, "Remember, sir knight, that the terms of our combat are, that the vanquished shall be at the victor's disposal."

"I am aware of it already," said Don Quixote, "provided what is imposed upon the vanquished be things that do not transgress the limits of chivalry."

"That is understood," replied he of the Mirrors.

At this moment the extraordinary nose of the squire presented itself to Don Quixote's view, and he was no less amazed than Sancho at the sight; insomuch that he set him down as a monster of some kind, or a human being of some new species or unearthly breed. Sancho, seeing his master retiring to run his course, did not like to be left alone with the nosy man, fearing that with one flap of that nose on his own the battle would be all over for him and he would be left stretched on the ground, either by the blow or with fright; so he ran after his master, holding on to Rocinante's stirrup-leather, and when it seemed to him time to turn about, he said, "I implore of your worship, señor, before you turn to charge, to help me up into this cork tree, from which I will be able to witness the gallant encounter your worship is going to have with this knight, more to my taste and better than from the ground."

"It seems to me rather, Sancho," said Don Quixote, "that thou wouldst mount a scaffold in order to see the bulls without danger."

"To tell the truth," returned Sancho, "the monstrous nose of that squire has filled me with terror, and I dare not stay near him."

"It is," said Don Quixote, "such a one that were I not what I am it would terrify me too; so, come, I will help thee up where thou wilt."

While Don Quixote waited for Sancho to mount into the cork tree he of the Mirrors took as much ground as he considered requisite, and, supposing Don Quixote to have done the same, without waiting for any sound of trumpet or other signal to direct them, he wheeled his horse, which was not more agile or better-looking than Rocinante, and at his top speed, which was an easy trot, he proceeded to charge his enemy; seeing him, however, engaged in putting Sancho up, he drew rein, and halted in mid career, for which his horse was very grateful, as he was already unable to go.

Don Quixote, fancying that his foe was coming down upon him flying, drove his spurs vigorously into Rocinante's lean flanks and made him scud along in such style that history tells us that on this occasion only was he known to make something like running, for on all others it was a simple trot with him; and with this unparalleled fury he bore down where he of the Mirrors stood digging his spurs into his horse, without being able to make him stir a finger's length from the spot where he had come to a standstill in his course.

At this lucky moment and crisis, Don Quixote came upon his adversary, in trouble with his horse, and embarrassed with his lance, which he either could not manage, or had no time to lay in rest. Don Quixote, however, paid no attention to these difficulties, and in perfect safety to himself and without any risk, encountered him of the Mirrors with such force that he brought him to the ground in spite of himself over the haunches of his horse, and with so heavy a fall that he lay to all appearance dead, not stirring hand or foot. The instant Sancho saw him fall he slid down from the cork tree, and made all haste to where his master was, who, dismounting from Rocinante, went and stood over him of the Mirrors. Unlacing his helmet to see if he was dead, and to give him air if he should happen to be alive, he saw with astonishment, the very face of the bachelor Samson Carrasco! As soon as he saw it he called out in a loud voice, "Make haste here, Sancho, and behold what thou art to see but not to believe; quick, my son, and learn what magic can do, and wizards and enchanters are capable of."

Sancho came up, and when he saw the countenance of the bachelor Carrasco, he fell to crossing himself a thousand times, and blessing himself as many more. All this time the prostrate knight showed no signs of life, and Sancho said to Don Quixote, "It is my opinion, señor, that in any case your worship should take and thrust your sword into the mouth of this one here that looks like the bachelor Samson Carrasco; perhaps in him you will kill one of your enemies, the enchanters."

"Thy advice is not bad," said Don Quixote, "for of enemies the fewer the better"; and he was drawing his sword to carry into effect Sancho's counsel and suggestion, when the squire of the Mirrors came up, now without the nose which had made him so hideous, and cried out in a loud voice, "Mind what you are about, Señor Don Quixote; that is your friend, the bachelor Samson Carrasco, you have at your feet, and I am his squire."

"And the nose?" said Sancho, seeing him without the hideous feature he had before; to which he replied, "I have it here in my pocket," and putting his hand into his right pocket, he pulled out a masquerade nose of varnished pasteboard of the make already described; and Sancho, examining him more and more closely, exclaimed aloud in a voice of amazement, "Holy Mary be good to me! Isn't it Tom Cecial, my neighbor?"

"Why, to be sure I am!" returned the now unnosed squire. "Tom Cecial I am, friend Sancho Panza; and I'll tell you presently the means and tricks and falsehoods by which I have been brought here; but in the meantime, beg and entreat of your master not to wound or slay the Knight of the Mirrors whom he has at his feet; because, beyond all dispute, it is the rash and ill-advised bachelor Samson Carrasco, our fellow townsman."

At this moment he of the Mirrors came to himself, and Don Quixote perceiving it, held the naked point of his sword over his face, and said to him, "You are a dead man, knight, unless you confess that the peerless Dulcinea del Toboso excels your Casildea de Vandalia in beauty; and in addition to this you must promise, if you should survive this encounter and fall, to go to the city of El Toboso and present yourself before her on my behalf, that she deal with you according to her good pleasure."

"I confess," said the fallen knight, "that the dirty tattered shoe of the lady Dulcinea del Toboso is better than the ill-combed though clean beard of Casildea; and I promise to go and present myself to her."

"You must also confess and believe," added Don Quixote, "that the knight you vanquished was not and could not be Don Quixote of La Mancha, but someone else in his likeness, just as I confess and believe that you, though you seem to be the bachelor Samson Carrasco, are not so, but some other resembling him, whom my enemies have here put before me in his shape, in order that I may moderate the vehemence of my wrath, and make a gentle use of the glory of my victory."

"I confess everything to be as you believe it," replied the crippled knight; "let me rise, I entreat you; if, indeed, the shock of my fall will allow me, for it has left me in a sorry plight enough."

Don Quixote helped him to rise, with the assistance of his squire Tom Cecial; from whom Sancho never took his eyes, and to whom he put questions, the replies to which furnished clear proof that he was really and truly the Tom Cecial he said; but the impression made on Sancho's mind by what his master said about the enchanters having changed the face of the Knight of the Mirrors into that of the bachelor Samson Carrasco, would not permit him to believe what he saw with his eyes. In fine, both master and man remained under the delusion. Dolefully, he of the Mirrors and his squire parted from Don Quixote and Sancho, to go look for some village where he could plaster and strap his ribs. Don Quixote and Sancho resumed their journey to Saragossa.

CHAPTER 8

Don Quixote and Don Diego

D ON QUIXOTE went off elated, and vainglorious in the highest
degree at having won a victory over such a valiant knight
as he fancied him of the Mirrors to be, and one from whose
knightly word he expected to learn whether the enchantment of his lady still
continued. But Don Quixote was of one mind, he of the Mirrors of another,
for he just then had no thought of anything but finding some village where
he could plaster himself, as has been said already.

When the bachelor Samson Carrasco recommended Don Quixote to re-
sume his knight-errantry which he had laid aside, it was in consequence of
having been previously in conclave with the curate and the barber on the
means to be adopted to induce Don Quixote to stay at home in peace and quiet
without worrying himself with his ill-starred adventures; at which consultation
it was decided by the unanimous vote of all, and on the special advice of
Carrasco, that Don Quixote should be allowed to go, as it seemed impossible
to restrain him, and that Samson should sally forth to meet him as a knight-
errant, and do battle with him, for there would be no difficulty about a cause,
and vanquish him, that being looked upon as an easy matter; and that it
should be agreed and settled that the vanquished was to be at the mercy of
the victor. Then, Don Quixote being vanquished, the bachelor knight was
to command him to return to his village and his house, and not quit it for
two years, or until he received further orders from him; all which it was clear
Don Quixote would unhesitatingly obey, rather than fail to observe the laws
of chivalry; and during the period of his seclusion he might perhaps forget

196

his folly, or there might be an opportunity of discovering some remedy for his madness. Carrasco undertook the task, and Tom Cecial, a neighbor of Sancho Panza's, a lively, feather-headed fellow, offered himself as his squire. Carrasco armed himself in the fashion described, and Tom Cecial, that he might not be known by his neighbor when they met, fitted on over his own natural nose the false one that has been mentioned; and so they followed the same route Don Quixote took, and almost came up with him in time to be present at the adventure of the cart of Death and finally encountered them in the grove; and had it not been for the extraordinary fancies of Don Quixote, and his conviction that the bachelor was not the bachelor, señor bachelor would have been incapacitated forever from taking his degree of curate, all through not finding nests where he thought to find birds.

Tom Cecial, seeing how ill they had succeeded, and what a sorry end their expedition had come to, said to the bachelor, "Sure enough, Señor Samson Carrasco, we are served right; it is easy enough to plan and set about an enterprise, but it is often a difficult matter to come well out of it. Don Quixote a madman, and we sane; he goes off laughing, safe, and sound, and you are left sore and sorry! I'd like to know now which is the madder, he who is so because he cannot help it, or he who is so of his own choice?"

To which Samson replied, "The difference between the two sorts of madmen is, that he who is so will he nil he, will be one always, while he who is so of his own accord can leave off being one whenever he likes."

"In that case," said Tom Cecial, "I was a madman of my own accord when I volunteered to become your squire, and, of my own accord, I'll leave off being one and go home."

"That's your affair," returned Samson, "but to suppose that I am going home until I have given Don Quixote a thrashing is absurd; and it is not any wish that he may recover his senses that will make me hunt him out now, but a wish for the sore pain I am in with my ribs won't let me entertain more charitable thoughts."

Thus discoursing, the pair proceeded until they reached a town where it was their good luck to find a bone-setter, with whose help the unfortunate Samson was cured. Tom Cecial left him and went home, while he stayed behind meditating vengeance.

Don Quixote pursued his journey, going along entirely absorbed in his fancies, when Sancho said to him, "Isn't it odd, señor, that I have still before my eyes that monstrous enormous nose of my neighbor, Tom Cecial?"

"And dost thou, then, believe, Sancho," said Don Quixote, "that the Knight of the Mirrors was the bachelor Carrasco, and his squire Tom Cecial, thy friend?"

"I don't know what to say to that," replied Sancho; "all I know is that the tokens he gave me about my own house, wife and children, nobody else but himself could have given me; and the face, once the nose was off, was the very face of Tom Cecial, as I have seen it many a time in my town and next door to my own house; and the sound of the voice was just the same."

"Let us reason the matter, Sancho," said Don Quixote. "Come now, by what process of thinking can it be supposed that the bachelor Samson Carrasco would come as a knight-errant, in arms offensive and defensive, to fight with me? Have I ever been by any chance his enemy? Have I ever given him any occasion to owe me a grudge? Am I his rival, or does he profess arms, that he should envy the fame I have acquired in them?"

"God knows what's the truth of it all," said Sancho; and knowing as he did that the transformation of Dulcinea had been a device and imposition of his own, his master's illusions were not satisfactory to him; but he did not like to reply lest he should say something that might disclose his trickery.

As they were engaged in this conversation they were overtaken by a man who was following the same road behind them, mounted on a very handsome flea-bitten mare, and dressed in a gaban of fine green cloth, with tawny velvet facings, and a cap of the same velvet. The trappings of the mare were of mulberry color and green. He carried a Moorish cutlass hanging from a broad green-and-gold baldric; the buskins were of the same make as the baldric; the spurs were lacquered green, and so brightly polished that, matching as they did the rest of his apparel, they looked better than if they had been of pure gold.

When the traveler came up with them he saluted them courteously, and spurring his mare was passing them without stopping, but Don Quixote called out to him, "Gallant sir, if so be your worship is going our road, and has no occasion for speed, it would be a pleasure to me if we were to join company."

"In truth," replied he on the mare, "I would not pass you so hastily but for fear that your horse might turn restive in the company of my mare."

"You may safely hold in your mare, señor," said Sancho in reply to this, "for our horse is the most virtuous and well-behaved horse in the world."

The traveler drew rein, amazed at the trim and features of Don Quixote, who rode without his helmet, which Sancho carried like a valise in front of

Don Quixote and Don Diego

Dapple's pack-saddle; and if the man in green examined Don Quixote closely, still more closely did Don Quixote examine the man in green, who struck him as being a man of intelligence. In appearance he was about fifty years of age, with but few gray hairs, an aquiline cast of features, and an expression between grave and gay; and his dress and accouterments showed him to be a man of good condition. What he in green thought of Don Quixote of La Mancha was that a man of that sort and shape he had never yet seen; he marveled at the length of his hair, his lofty stature, lankness and sallowness of his countenance, his armor, his bearing and his gravity—a figure and picture such as had not been seen in those regions for many a long day.

Don Quixote saw very plainly the attention with which the traveler was regarding him, and courteous as he was and ready to please everybody, before the other could ask him any question he anticipated him by saying, "The appearance I present to your worship being so out of the common, I should not be surprised if it filled you with wonder; but you will cease to wonder when I tell you that I am one of those knights who, as people say, go seeking adventures. I have left my home, I have mortgaged my estate, I have given up my comforts, and committed myself to the arms of Fortune, to bear me whithersoever she may please. My desire was to bring to life again knight-errantry, now dead, and for some time past, stumbling here, falling there, now coming down headlong, now raising myself up again, I have carried out a great portion of my design. Because of my many valiant achievements, I have been already found worthy to make my way in print to well nigh all, or most, of the nations of the earth. Thirty thousand volumes of my history have been printed, and it is on the road to be printed thirty thousand thousands of times, if heaven does not put a stop to it. In short, I may tell you I am Don Quixote of La Mancha, otherwise called 'The Knight of the Rueful Countenance.'"

With these words Don Quixote held his peace, and, from the time he took to answer, the man in green seemed to be at a loss for a reply; after a long pause, however, he said to him, "You were right when you saw curiosity in my amazement, sir knight; but you have not succeeded in removing the astonishment I feel at seeing you. What! is it possible that there are knights-errant in the world in these days, and histories of real chivalry printed? I cannot realize the fact that there can be anyone on earth nowadays who aids widows, or protects maidens, or defends wives, or succors orphans; nor should I believe it had I not seen it in your worship with my own eyes. Blessed be heaven! for

199

by means of this history of your noble and genuine chivalrous deeds, which you say has been printed, the countless stories of fictitious knights-errant with which the world is filled, will have been driven into oblivion."

"There is a good deal to be said on that point," said Don Quixote, "as to whether the histories of the knights-errant are fiction or not."

"Why, is there anyone who doubts that those histories are false?" said the man in green.

"I doubt it," said Don Quixote, "but never mind that just now; if our journey lasts long enough, I trust in God I shall show your worship that you do wrong."

From this last observation of Don Quixote's, the traveler began to have a suspicion that he was some crazy being, and was waiting him to confirm it by something further; but before they could turn to any new subject Don Quixote begged him to tell him who he was, since he himself had rendered account of his station and life. To this, he in the green gaban replied, "I, Sir Knight of the Rueful Countenance, am a gentleman by birth, native of the village where, please God, we are going to dine today; I am more than fairly well off, and my name is Don Diego de Miranda. I pass my life with my wife, children, and friends; my pursuits are hunting and fishing, but I keep neither hawks nor greyhounds, nothing but a tame partridge or a bold ferret or two; I have six dozen or so of books, some in our mother tongue, some Latin, some of them history, others devotional; those of chivalry have not as yet crossed the threshold of my door; I am more given to turning over the profane than the devotional, so long as they are books of honest entertainment that charm by their style and attract and interest by the invention they display, though of these there are very few in Spain. Sometimes I dine with my neighbors and friends, and often invite them; my entertainments are neat and well served without stint of anything. I have no taste for tattle, nor do I allow tattling in my presence; I pry not into my neighbors' lives, nor have I lynx-eyes for what others do. I hear mass every day; I share my substance with the poor. I strive to make peace between those whom I know to be at variance; I am the devoted servant of Our Lady, and my trust is ever in the infinite mercy of God our Lord."

Sancho listened with the greatest attention to the account of the gentleman's life and occupation; and thinking it a good and a holy life, and that he who led it ought to work miracles, he threw himself off Dapple, and running in haste seized his right stirrup and kissed his foot again and again with a devout heart and almost with tears.

Seeing this the gentleman asked him, "What are you about, brother? What are these kisses for?"

"Let me kiss," said Sancho, "for I think your worship is the first saint in the saddle I ever saw all the days of my life."

"I am no saint," replied the gentleman, "but a great sinner; but you are, brother, for you must be a good fellow, as your simplicity shows."

Sancho went back and regained his pack-saddle, having extracted a laugh from his master's profound melancholy, and excited fresh amazement in Don Diego. Don Quixote then asked him how many children he had, and observed that one of the things wherein the ancient philosophers, who were without the true knowledge of God, placed the greatest good was in the gifts of nature, in those of fortune, in having many friends, and many and good children.

"I, Señor Don Quixote," answered the gentleman, "have one son, without whom, perhaps, I should count myself happier than I am, not because he is a bad son, but because he is not so good as I could wish. He is eighteen years of age; he has been for six at Salamanca studying Latin and Greek, and when I wished him to turn to the study of other sciences I found him so wrapped up in that of poetry (if that can be called a science) that there is no getting him to take kindly to the law, which I wished him to study, or to theology, the queen of them all. I would like him to be an honor to his family, as we live in days when our kings liberally reward learning that is virtuous and worthy. But he spends the whole day in settling whether Homer expressed himself correctly or not in such and such a line of the Iliad, whether such and such lines of Virgil are to be understood in this way or in that; in short, all his talk is of the works of these poets, and those of Horace, Persius, Juvenal, and Tibullus; for of the moderns in our own language he makes no great account; but with all his seeming indifference to Spanish poetry, just now his thoughts are absorbed in making a gloss on four lines that have been sent him from Salamanca, which I suspect are for some poetical tournament."

To all this Don Quixote said in reply, "Children, señor, be they good or bad, are to be loved as we love the souls that give us life. It is for the parents to guide them from infancy in the ways of virtue, propriety, and worthy

Christian conduct, so that when grown up they may be the staff of their parents' old age, and the glory of their posterity; and to force them to study this or that science I do not think wise, though it may be no harm to persuade them; and when it is the student's good fortune that heaven has given him parents who provide him with support, it would be my advice to them to let him pursue whatever science they may see him most inclined to; and though that of poetry is less useful than pleasurable, it is not one of those that bring discredit upon the possessor. Poetry, gentle sir, is, as I take it, like a tender young maiden of supreme beauty, to adorn whom is the task of several other maidens, who are all the rest of the sciences; and she must avail herself of the help of all, and all derive their luster from her. She is the product of an Alchemy of such virtue that he who is able to practice it, will turn her into pure gold of inestimable worth. She must not be touched by the buffoons, nor by the ignorant vulgar, incapable of comprehending or appreciating her hidden treasures. And do not suppose, señor, that I apply the term vulgar here merely to plebeians and the lower orders; for everyone who is ignorant, be he lord or prince, may and should be included among the vulgar. He, then, who shall embrace and cultivate poetry under the conditions I have named, shall become famous, and his name honored throughout all the civilized nations of the earth. According to a true belief, a poet is born one; and following the bent that heaven has bestowed upon him, without the aid of study or art, he produces things that show how truly he spoke who said, '*Est Deus in nobis*,' etc. At the same time, I say that the poet by nature who calls in art to his aid will be a far better poet, and will surpass him who tries to be one relying upon his knowledge of art alone. The reason is, that art does not surpass nature, but only brings it to perfection; and thus, nature combined with art, and art with nature, will produce a perfect poet. To bring my argument to a close, I would say then, gentle sir, let your son go on as his star leads him, for being so studious as he seems to be, and having already successfully surmounted the first step of the sciences, which is that of the languages, with their help he will by his own exertions reach the summit of polite literature."

He of the green gaban was filled with astonishment at Don Quixote's argument, so much so that he began to abandon the notion about his being crazy. But in the middle of the discourse, it being not very much to his taste, Sancho had turned aside out of the road to beg a little milk from some shepherds, who were milking their ewes hard by; and just as the gentle-man, highly pleased, was about to renew the conversation, Don Quixote, raising his head, perceived a cart covered with royal flags coming along the road they were traveling; and persuaded that this must be some new ad-venture, he called aloud to Sancho to come and bring him his helmet. Sancho, hearing himself called, quitted the shepherds, and, prodding Dapple vigor-ously, came up to his master, to whom there fell a terrific and desperate adventure.

CHAPTER 9

The Challenge of the Lions

WHEN DON QUIXOTE CALLED OUT to Sancho to bring him his helmet, Sancho was buying some curds the shepherds agreed to sell him, and flurried by the great haste his master was in did not know what to do with them or what to carry them in; so, not to lose them, for he had already paid for them, he thought it best to throw them into his master's helmet, and acting on this bright idea he went to see what his master wanted with him. He, as he approached, exclaimed to him:

"Give me that helmet, my friend, for either I know little of adventures, or what I observe yonder is one that will, and does, call upon me to arm myself."

He of the green gaban, on hearing this, looked in all directions, but could perceive nothing, except a cart coming towards them with two or three small flags, which led him to conclude it must be carrying treasure of the King's, and he said so to Don Quixote. He, however, would not believe him, being always convinced that all that happened to him must be adventures and still more adventures; so he replied to the gentleman, "He who is prepared has his battle half fought; nothing is lost by my preparing myself, for I know by experience that I have enemies, visible and invisible, and I know not when, or where, or at what moment, or in what shapes they will attack me"; and turning to Sancho he called for his helmet; and Sancho, as he had no time to take out the curds, had to give it just as it was. Don Quixote took it, and without perceiving what was in it thrust it down in hot haste upon his head; but as the curds were pressed and squeezed the whey began to run all over his face and beard, whereat he was so startled that he cried out to Sancho:

"Sancho, what's this? I think my head is softening, or my brains are melting, or I am sweating from head to foot! If I am sweating it is not indeed from fear. I am convinced beyond a doubt that the adventure which is about to befall me is a terrible one. Give me something to wipe myself with, if thou hast it, for this profuse sweat is blinding me."

Sancho held his tongue, and gave him a cloth, and gave thanks to God at the same time that his master had not found out what was the matter. Don Quixote then wiped himself, and took off his helmet to see what it was that made his head feel so cool, and seeing all that white mash inside his helmet he put it to his nose, and as soon as he had smelled it he exclaimed:

"By the life of my lady Dulcinea del Toboso, but it is curds thou hast put here, thou treacherous, impudent, ill-mannered squire!"

To which, with great composure and pretended innocence, Sancho replied, "If they are curds let me have them, your worship, and I'll eat them; but let the devil eat them, for it must have been he who put them there. For I trust to my master's good sense to see that I have got no curds or milk, or anything of the sort; and that if I had, it is in my stomach I would put it and not in the helmet."

"Maybe so," said Don Quixote. All this the gentleman was observing, and with astonishment, more especially when, after having wiped himself clean, his head, face, beard, and helmet, Don Quixote put it on, and settling himself firmly in his stirrups, easing his sword in the scabbard, and grasping his lance, he cried, "Now, come who will, here am I, ready to try conclusions with Satan himself in person!"

By this time the cart with the flags had come up, unattended by anyone except the carter on a mule, and a man sitting in front. Don Quixote planted himself before it and said, "Whither are you going, brothers? What cart is this? What have you got in it? What flags are those?"

To this the carter replied, "The cart is mine; what is in it is a pair of wild caged lions, which the governor of Oran is sending to court as a present to his Majesty; and the flags are our lord the King's, to show that what is here is his property."

"And are the lions large?" asked Don Quixote.

"So large," replied the man who sat at the door of the cart, "that larger, or as large, have never crossed from Africa to Spain; I am the keeper, and

205

I have brought over others, but never any like these. They are male and female; the male is in that first cage and the female in the one behind, and they are hungry now, for they have eaten nothing today, so let your worship stand aside, for we must make haste to the place where we are to feed them."

Hereupon, smiling slightly, Don Quixote exclaimed, "Lion whelps to me! To me whelps of lions, and at such a time! Then, by God! those gentlemen who send them here shall see if I am a man to be frightened by lions. Get down, my good fellow, and as you are the keeper open the cages, and turn me out those beasts, and in the midst of this plain I will let them know who Don Quixote of La Mancha is, in spite of the enchanters who send them to me."

"So, so," said the gentleman to himself at this; "our worthy knight has shown of what sort he is; the curds, no doubt, have softened his skull and brought his brains to a head."

At this instant Sancho came up to him, saying, "Señor, for God's sake do somthing to keep my master, Don Quixote, from tackling these lions; for if he does they'll tear us all to pieces here."

"Is your master then so mad," asked the gentleman, "that you believe he will engage such fierce animals?"

"He is not mad," said Sancho, "but he is venturesome."

"I will prevent it," said the gentleman; and going over to Don Quixote, who was insisting upon the keeper's opening the cages, he said to him, "Sir knight, knights-errant should attempt adventures which encourage the hope of a successful issue, not those which entirely withhold it; for valor that trenches upon temerity savors rather of madness than of courage; moreover, these lions do not come to oppose you, nor do they dream of such a thing; they are going as presents to his Majesty, and it will not be right to stop them or delay their journey."

"Gentle sir," replied Don Quixote, "you go and mind your tame partridge and your bold ferret, and leave everyone to manage his own business. This is mine, and I know whether these gentlemen the lions come to me or not." Then turning to the keeper, he exclaimed, "By all that's good, sir scoundrel, if you don't open the cages this very instant, I'll pin you to the cart with this lance."

The carter, seeing the determination of this apparition in armor, said to him, "Please your worship, for charity's sake, señor, let me unyoke the mules and place myself in safety along with them before the lions are turned out; for if they kill them on me I am ruined for life, for all I possess is this cart and mules."

"O man of little faith," replied Don Quixote, "get down and unyoke; you will soon see that you are exerting yourself for nothing, and that you might have spared yourself the trouble."

The carter got down and with all speed unyoked the mules, and the keeper called out at the top of his voice, "I call all here to witness that against my will and under compulsion I open the cages and let the lions loose, and that I warn this gentleman that he will be accountable for all the harm and mischief which these beasts may do, and for my salary and dues as well. You, gentlemen, place yourselves in safety before I open, for I know they will do me no harm."

Once more the gentleman strove to persuade Don Quixote not to do such a mad thing, as it was tempting God to engage in such a piece of folly. To this, Don Quixote replied that he knew what he was about. The gentleman in return entreated him to reflect, for he knew he was under a delusion.

"Well, señor," answered Don Quixote, "if you do not like to be a spectator of this tragedy, as in your opinion it will be, spur your flea-bitten mare, and place yourself in safety."

Hearing this, Sancho with tears in his eyes entreated him to give up the enterprise. "Look ye, señor," said Sancho, "there's no enchantment here, nor anything of the sort, for between the bars and chinks of the cage I have seen the paw of a real lion."

"Retire, Sancho, and leave me," replied Don Quixote, "and if I die here thou knowest our old compact; thou wilt repair to Dulcinea—I say no more." To these he added some further words, renewing his commands to the keeper and repeating his warning to the gentleman to spur his mare, Sancho his Dapple, and the carter his mules, all striving to get away from the cart as far as they could before the lions broke loose. Sancho was weeping over his master's death, for this time he firmly believed it was in store for him from the claws of the lions; and he cursed his fate and called it an unlucky hour when he thought of taking service with him again; but with all his tears and lamentations he did not forget to thrash Dapple so as to put a good space between himself and the cart. The keeper, seeing that the fugitives were now some distance off, once more entreated and warned him as before; but he replied that he heard him, and that he need not trouble himself with any further warnings or entreaties, as they would be fruitless, and bade him make haste.

While the keeper was opening the first cage, Don Quixote was considering whether it would not be well to do battle on foot, instead of on horseback, and finally resolved to fight on foot, fearing that Rocinante might take fright at the sight of the lions. He therefore sprang off his horse, flung his lance aside, braced his buckler on his arm, and drawing his sword, advanced slowly with marvelous intrepidity and resolute courage, to plant himself in front of the cart, commending himself with all his heart to God and to his lady Dulcinea.

The keeper, seeing that Don Quixote had taken up his position, and that it was impossible for him to avoid letting out the male without incurring the enmity of the fiery and daring knight, flung open the doors of the first cage, containing, as has been said, the lion, which was now seen to be of enormous size, and grim and hideous mien. The first thing he did was to turn round in the cage in which he lay, and protrude his claws, and stretch himself thoroughly; he next opened his mouth, and yawned very leisurely, and with near two palms length of tongue that he had thrust forth, he licked the dust out of his eyes and washed his face. Having done this, he put his head out of the cage and looked all round with eyes like glowing coals, a spectacle and demeanor to strike terror into temerity itself. Don Quixote merely observed him steadily, longing for him to leap from the cart and come to close quarters with him, when he hoped to hew him in pieces.

So far did his unparalleled madness go; but the noble lion, more courteous than arrogant, not troubling himself about silly bravado, after having looked all round, as has been said, turned about and presented his hindquarters to Don Quixote, and very coolly and tranquilly lay down again in the cage. Seeing this, Don Quixote ordered the keeper to take a stick to him and provoke him to make him come out.

"That I won't," said the keeper, "for if I anger him, the first he'll tear in pieces will be myself. Be satisfied, sir knight, with what you have done, which leaves nothing more to be said on the score of courage, and do not seek to tempt fortune a second time. The lion has the door open; he is free to come out or not to come out; but as he has not come out so far, he will not come out today. Your worship's great courage has been fully manifested already; no brave champion, so it strikes me, is bound to do more than

The lion turned about and presented his hindquarters to Don Quixote.

challenge his enemy and wait for him on the field; if his adversary does not come, on him lies the disgrace, and he who waits for him carries off the crown of victory."

"That is true," said Don Quixote. "Close the door, my friend, and let me have, in the best form thou canst, what thou hast seen me do, by way of certificate; to wit, that thou didst open for the lion, that I waited for him, that he did not come out, that I still waited for him, and that still he did not come out, and lay down again. I am not bound to do more; enchantments avaunt, and God uphold the right, the truth, and true chivalry! Close the door as I bade thee, while I make signals to the fugitives that have left us, that they may learn this exploit from thy lips."

The keeper obeyed, and Don Quixote proceeded to recall the others, who still continued to fly, looking back at every step, all in a body, the gentleman bringing up the rear. Sancho, however, exclaimed, "May I die, if my master has not overcome the wild beasts, for he is calling to us."

They all stopped, and perceived that it was Don Quixote who was making signals, and shaking off their fears to some extent, they approached slowly until they were near enough to hear distinctly Don Quixote's voice calling to them. They returned at length to the cart, and as they came up, Don Quixote said to the carter, "Put your mules to once more, brother, and continue your journey; and do thou, Sancho, give him two gold crowns for himself and the keeper, to compensate for the delay they have incurred through me."

"That will I give with all my heart," said Sancho; "but what has become of the lions? Are they dead or alive?"

The keeper, then, in full detail, and bit by bit, described the end of the contest, exalting to the best of his power and ability the valor of Don Quixote, at the sight of whom the lion quailed, and would not and dared not come out of the cage, although he had held the door open ever so long.

"What dost thou think of this, Sancho?" said Don Quixote. "Are there any enchantments that can prevail against true valor? The enchanters may be able to rob me of good fortune, but of fortitude and courage they cannot."

Sancho paid the crowns, the carter put to, the keeper kissed Don Quixote's hands for the bounty bestowed upon him, and promised to give an account of the valiant exploit to the King himself, as soon as he saw him at court.

"Then," said Don Quixote, "if his Majesty should happen to ask who performed it, you must say THE KNIGHT OF THE LIONS; for it is my desire that into this the name I have hitherto borne of Knight of the Rueful Countenance be from this time forward changed; and in this I follow the ancient usage of knights-errant, who changed their names when they pleased, or when it suited their purpose."

The cart went its way, and Don Quixote, Sancho, and he of the green gaban went theirs. All this time, Don Diego de Miranda had not spoken a word, being entirely taken up with observing and noting all that Don Quixote did and said, and the opinion he formed was that he was a man of brains gone mad, and a madman on the verge of rationality.

Don Quixote roused him by saying, "No doubt, Señor Don Diego de Miranda, you set me down in your mind as a fool and a madman, and it would be no wonder if you did, for my deeds do not argue anything else. But for all that, I would have you take notice that I am neither so mad nor so foolish as I must have seemed to you. A gallant knight shows to advantage bringing his lance to bear adroitly upon a fierce bull under the eyes of his sovereign, in the midst of a spacious plaza; a knight shows to advantage arrayed in glittering armor, pacing the lists before the ladies in some joyous tournament. To greater advantage, I maintain, does the knight-errant show bringing aid to some widow in some lonely waste, than the court knight dallying with some city damsel. All knights have their own special parts to play. I, then, as it has fallen to my lot to be a member of knight-errantry, cannot avoid attempting all that to me seems to come within the sphere of my duties; thus it was my bounden duty to attack those lions that I just now attacked, although I knew it to be the height of rashness; for I know well what valor is, that it is a virtue that occupies a place between two vicious extremes, cowardice and temerity; but it will be a lesser evil for him who is valiant to rise till he reaches the point of rashness, than to sink until he reaches the point of cowardice."

"Señor Don Quixote," said Don Diego, "everything you have said and done is proved correct by the test of reason itself. But now let us make haste, and reach my village, where you shall take rest after your late exertions, for if they have not been of the body they have been of the spirit, and these sometimes tend to produce bodily fatigue."

"I take the invitation as a great favor and honor, Señor Don Diego," replied Don Quixote; and pressing forward at a better pace than before, at about two in the afternoon they reached the village and house of Don Diego.

CHAPTER 10

The Gentleman in Green

DON QUIXOTE found Don Diego de Miranda's house built in village style, with his arms in rough stone over the street door; in the patio was the storeroom, and at the entrance the cellar, with plenty of wine-jars standing round, which, coming from El Toboso, brought back to his memory his enchanted and transformed Dulcinea; and with a sigh, and not thinking of what he was saying, or in whose presence he was, he exclaimed, "O ye Tobosan jars, how ye bring back to my memory the sweet object of my bitter regrets!"

The student poet, Don Diego's son, who had come out with his mother to receive him, heard this exclamation, and both mother and son were filled with amazement at the extraordinary figure he presented. He, however, dismounting from Rocinante, advanced with great politeness to ask permission to kiss the lady's hand, while Don Diego said, "Señora, pray receive with your wonted kindness Señor Don Quixote of La Mancha, whom you see before you, a knight-errant, and the bravest and wisest in the world."

The lady, whose name was Doña Christina, received him with every sign of good will and great courtesy, and Don Quixote placed himself at her service with an abundance of well-chosen and polished phrases. Almost the same civilities were exchanged between him and the student, who listening to Don Quixote, took him to be a sensible, clear-headed person.

They led Don Quixote into a room, and Sancho removed his armor, leaving him in loose Walloon breeches and chamois-leather doublet, all stained with

211

the rust of his armor; his collar was a falling one of scholastic cut, without starch or lace, his buskins buff-colored, and his shoes polished. He wore his good sword, and over all he threw a long cloak of good gray cloth. But first of all, with five or six buckets of water he washed his head and face, and still the water remained whey-colored, thanks to Sancho's greediness and purchase of those unlucky curds that turned his master so white. Thus arrayed, and with an easy, sprightly, and gallant air, Don Quixote passed out into another room, where the student was waiting to entertain him while the table was being laid; for on the arrival of so distinguished a guest, Doña Christina was anxious to show that she knew how and was able to give a becoming reception to those who came to her house.

While Don Quixote was taking off his armor, Don Lorenzo, for so Don Diego's son was called, took the opportunity to say to his father, "What are we to make of this gentleman you have brought home to us, sir? For his name, his appearance, and your describing him as a knight-errant have completely puzzled my mother and me."

"I don't know what to say, my son," replied Don Diego; "all I can tell thee is that I have seen him act the acts of the greatest madman in the world, and heard him make observations so sensible that they efface and undo all he does. Do thou talk to him and feel the pulse of his wits, and as thou art shrewd, form the most reasonable conclusion thou canst as to his wisdom or folly; though, to tell the truth, I am more inclined to take him to be mad than sane."

With this Don Lorenzo went away to entertain Don Quixote as has been said, and in the course of the conversation that passed between them Don Quixote said to Don Lorenzo, "Your father, Señor Don Diego de Miranda, has told me of the rare abilities and subtle intellect you possess, and, above all, that you are a great poet."

"A poet, it may be," replied Don Lorenzo, "but a great one, by no means. It is true that I am somewhat given to poetry and to reading good poets, but not so much so as to justify the title of 'great' which my father gives me."

"I do not dislike that modesty," said Don Quixote; "for there is no poet who is not conceited and does not think he is the best poet in the world."

"There is no rule without an exception," said Don Lorenzo. "There may be some who are poets and yet do not think they are."

"Very few," said Don Quixote; "but tell me, what verses are those which you have now in hand, and which your father tells me keep you somewhat restless and absorbed? If they are for a poetical tournament, contrive to carry off the second prize; for the first always goes by favor or personal standing, the second by simple justice; and so the third comes to be the second, and the first, reckoning in this way, will be third; but, for all that, the title of first is a great distinction."

"So far," said Don Lorenzo to himself, "I should not take you to be a madman; but let us go on." So he said to him, "Your worship has apparently attended the schools; what sciences have you studied?"

"That of knight-errantry," said Don Quixote, "which is as good as that of poetry, and even a finger or two above it."

"I do not know what science that is," said Don Lorenzo, "and until now I have never heard of it."

"It is a science," said Don Quixote, "that comprehends in itself all or most of the sciences in the world, for he who professes it must be a jurist, and must know the rules of justice, so as to give to each one what belongs to him and is due to him. He must be a theologian, so as to be able to give a clear and distinctive reason for the Christian faith he professes. He must be a physician, and above all a herbalist, so as in wastes and solitudes to know the herbs that have the property of healing wounds, for a knight-errant must not go looking for someone to cure him at every step. He must be an astronomer, so as to know by the stars how many hours of the night have passed, and what clime and quarter of the world he is in. He must know mathematics, for at every turn some occasion for them will present itself to him; and, to come down to minor particulars, he must, I say, be able to swim. He must know how to shoe a horse, and repair his saddle and bridle; and, to return to higher matters, he must be faithful to God and to his lady; he must be pure in thought, decorous in words, generous in works, valiant in deeds, patient in suffering, compassionate towards the needy, and, lastly, an upholder of the truth though its defense should cost him his life. Of all these qualities, great and small, is a true knight-errant made up; judge then, Señor Don Lorenzo, whether it be a contemptible science which the knight who studies and professes it has to learn, and whether it may not compare with the very loftiest that are taught in the schools."

"If that be so," replied Don Lorenzo, "this science, I protest, surpasses all."

"How, if that be so?" said Don Quixote.

"What I mean to say," said Don Lorenzo, "is, that I doubt whether there are now, or ever were, any knights-errant, and adorned with such virtues."

"Many a time," replied Don Quixote, "have I said what I now say once more, that the majority of the world are of opinion that there never were any knights-errant in it. I will not now stop to disabuse you of the error you share with the multitude. All I shall do is to pray to heaven to deliver you from it, and show you how beneficial and necessary knights-errant were in days of yore, and how useful they would be in these days were they but in vogue; but now, for the sins of the people, sloth and indolence, gluttony and luxury are triumphant."

"Our guest has broken out on our hands," said Don Lorenzo to himself at this point; "but, for all that, he is a glorious madman, and I should be a dull blockhead to doubt it."

Here, being summoned to dinner, they brought their colloquy to a close. Don Diego asked his son what he had been able to make out as to the wits of their guest. To which he replied, "All the doctors and clever scribes in the world will not make sense of the scrawl of his madness; he is a madman full of lucid intervals."

They went into dinner, and the repast was such as Don Diego said on the road he was in the habit of giving to his guests, neat, plentiful, and tasty; but what pleased Don Quixote most was the marvelous silence that reigned throughout the house, for it was like a Carthusian monastery.

When the cloth had been removed, grace said, and their hands washed, Don Quixote earnestly pressed Don Lorenzo to repeat to him his verses for the poetical tournament, to which he replied, "Not to be like those poets who, when they are asked to recite their verses, refuse, and when they are not asked for them cannot be restrained. I will repeat my verse, for which I do not expect any prize, having composed it merely as an exercise of ingenuity."

When Don Lorenzo had finished reciting his verse, Don Quixote stood up, and in a loud voice, almost a shout, exclaimed as he grasped Don Lorenzo's right hand in his, "By the highest heavens, O noble youth, but you are the best poet on earth, and deserve to be crowned with laurel. Heaven grant that the judges who rob you of the first prize—that Phœbus may pierce them with his arrows, and the Muses never cross the thresholds of their doors!"

Is there any need to say that Don Lorenzo enjoyed hearing himself praised by Don Quixote, albeit he looked upon him as a madman? O power of flattery, how far-reaching art thou, and how wide are the bounds of thy pleasant jurisdiction!

For four days was Don Quixote most sumptuously entertained in Don Diego's house, at the end of which time he asked his permission to depart, telling him he thanked him for the kindness and hospitality he had received in his house, but that, as it did not become knights-errant to give themselves up for long to idleness and luxury, he was anxious to fulfill the duties of his calling in seeking adventures, of which he was informed there was an abundance in that neighborhood, where he hoped to employ his time until the day came round for the jousts at Saragossa, for that was his proper destination; and that, first of all, he meant to enter the cave of Montesinos, of which so many marvelous things were reported all through the country.

Don Diego and his son commended his laudable resolution, and bade him furnish himself with all he wanted from their house and belongings.

The day of his departure came at length, as welcome to Don Quixote as it was sad and sorrowful to Sancho Panza, who was very well satisfied with the abundance of Don Diego's house, and objected to returning to the starvation of the woods and wilds. However, he filled and packed his saddlebags with what he considered needful. On taking leave, Don Quixote said to Don Lorenzo, "I know not whether I have told you already, but if you wish to spare yourself fatigue and toil in reaching the inaccessible summit of the temple of fame, you have nothing to do but to turn aside out of the somewhat narrow path of poetry and take the still narrower one of knight-errantry, wide enough, however, to make you an emperor in the twinkling of an eye."

In this speech Don Quixote wound up the evidence of his madness, but still better in what he added when he said, "God knows, I would gladly take Don Lorenzo with me to teach him how to spare the humble, and trample the proud underfoot, virtues that are part and parcel of the profession I belong to; but since his tender age does not allow of it, nor his praiseworthy pursuits permit it, I will simply content myself with impressing it upon your worship that you will become famous as a poet if you are guided by the opinion of others rather than by your own; because no fathers or mothers ever think their own children ill-favored, and this sort of deception prevails still more strongly in the case of the children of the brain."

Both father and son were amazed afresh at the strange medley Don Quixote talked, at one moment sense, at another nonsense, and at the

215

pertinacity and persistence he displayed in going through thick and thin in quest of his unlucky adventures, which he made the end and aim of his desires. There was a renewal of offers of service and civilities, and then, with the gracious permission of the lady of the castle, they took their departure, Don Quixote on Rocinante, and Sancho on Dapple.

CHAPTER 11

In the Cave of Montesinos

D ON QUIXOTE had gone but a short distance beyond Don Diego's village when he fell in with a couple of curates mounted on asses. As they traveled the road together, Don Quixote begged them to find him a guide to show him the way to the cave of Montesinos, as he had a great desire to enter it and see with his own eyes if the wonderful tales that were told of it were true.

One of the curates said he would conduct him to a cousin of his own, a famous scholar, and one very much given to reading books of chivalry, who would have great pleasure in taking him to the very mouth of the cave, and would show him the lakes of Ruidera. And he assured Don Quixote he would find him entertaining, for he was a youth who could write books good enough to be printed and dedicated to princes.

They reached a hamlet on the road to the famous cave, where the cousin lived, and he readily agreed to act as their guide. Sancho restocked his saddlebags, along with those of the cousin; and so commending themselves to God and bidding farewell to the two curates, they set out.

On the way Don Quixote asked the cousin of what sort his pursuits and studies were, to which he replied that his pursuits and studies were making books for the press, all of great utility and no less entertainment to the nation. One was called "The Book of Liveries," in which he described seven hundred and three liveries, with their colors, mottoes, and ciphers.

"Another book I have," he said, "I call 'The Supplement to Polydore Vergil,' which treats of the invention of things and I establish and elucidate

217

elegantly some things of great importance which Polydore omitted to mention. He forgot to tell us who was the first man in the world that had a cold in his head, and who was the first to try salivation for the French disease, but I give it accurately set forth, and quote more than five-and-twenty authors in proof of it, so you may perceive I have labored to good purpose and that the book will be of service to the whole world."

Sancho, who had been very attentive to the cousin's words, said to him, "Tell me, señor—and God give you luck in printing your books—can you tell me (for of course you know, as you know everything) who was the first man that scratched his head? For to my thinking it must have been our father Adam."

"So it must," replied the cousin; "for there is no doubt but Adam had a head and hair; and being the first man in the world he would have scratched himself sometimes."

"So I think," said Sancho; "but now tell me, who was the first tumbler in the world?"

"Really, brother," answered the cousin, "I could not at this moment say positively without having investigated it. I will look it up when I go back to where I have my books, and will satisfy you the next time we meet."

"Look here, señor," said Sancho, "don't give yourself any trouble about it, for I have just this minute hit upon what I asked you. The first tumbler in the world, you must know, was Lucifer, when they cast or pitched him out of heaven; for he came tumbling into the bottomless pit."

"You are right, friend," said the cousin; and said Don Quixote, "Sancho, that question and answer are not thine own; thou hast heard them from someone else."

"Hold your peace, señor," said Sancho. "Faith, if I take to asking questions and answering, I'll go on from this till tomorrow morning. Nay! to ask foolish things and answer nonsense I needn't go looking for help from my neighbors."

"Thou hast said more than thou art aware of, Sancho," said Don Quixote; "for there are some who weary themslves out in learning and proving things that, after they are known and proved, are not worth a farthing to the understanding or memory."

In this and other pleasant conversation the day went by, and that night they put up at a small hamlet whence it was not more than two leagues to the cave of Montesinos, so the cousin told Don Quixote, adding, that if he was bent upon entering it, it would be requisite for him to provide himself with ropes, so that he might be tied and lowered into its depths. Don Quixote said that even if it reached to the bottomless pit he meant to see where it went to; so they bought about a hundred fathoms of rope, and next day at two in the afternoon they arrived at the cave.

On coming within sight of it the cousin, Sancho, and Don Quixote dismounted, and the first two immediately tied the latter very firmly with the ropes, and as they were girding and swathing him Sancho said to him, "Mind what you are about, master mine; don't go burying yourself alive, or putting yourself where you'll be like a bottle put to cool in a well; it's no affair or business of your worship's to become the explorer of this, which must be worse than a Moorish dungeon."

"Tie me and hold thy peace," said Don Quixote, "for an emprise like this, friend Sancho, was reserved for me."

When Sancho had finished the tying (which was not over the armor but only over the doublet) Don Quixote observed, "It was careless of us not to have provided ourselves with a small cattle-bell to be tied on the rope close to me, the sound of which would show that I was still descending and alive; but as that is out of the question now, in God's hand be it to guide me"; and forthwith he fell on his knees and in a low voice offered up a prayer to heaven, and then exclaimed aloud, "O peerless Dulcinea del Toboso, refuse me not thy favor and protection now that I stand in such need of them. I am about to precipitate, to sink, to plunge myself into the abyss that is here before me, only to let the world know that while thou dost favor me there is no impossibility I will not attempt and accomplish." With these words, the cousin and Sancho giving him rope, he lowered himself into the depths of the dread cavern; and as he entered it Sancho sent his blessing after him, saying, "God guide thee and send thee back safe, sound, and unhurt to the light of this world thou art leaving to bury thyself in the darkness thou art seeking there"; and the cousin offered up almost the same prayers and supplications.

Don Quixote kept calling to them to give him rope and more rope, and they gave it out little by little, and by the time the calls, which came out of the cave as out of a pipe, ceased to be heard they had let down the hundred fathoms of rope. They were inclined to pull Don Quixote up again, as they could give him no more rope; however, they waited about half an hour, at the end of which time they began to gather in the rope again with great ease and without feeling any weight, which made them fancy Don Quixote was remaining below; and persuaded that it was so, Sancho wept bitterly, and hauled away in great haste in order to settle the question. When, however, they had come to, as it seemed, rather more than eighty fathoms they felt a weight, at which they were greatly delighted; and at last, at ten fathoms more, they saw Don Quixote distinctly, and Sancho called out to him, saying, "Welcome back, señor, for we had begun to think you were going to stop there to found a family." But Don Quixote answered not a word, and drawing him out entirely they perceived he had his eyes shut and every appearance of being fast asleep.

They stretched him on the ground and untied him, but still he did not awake; however, they shook and pulled him about, so that after some time he came to himself, stretching himself just as if he were waking up from a deep and sound sleep, and looking about him he said, "God forgive you, friends; ye have taken me away from the sweetest and most delightful existence and spectacle that ever human being enjoyed or beheld."

The cousin and Sancho Panza begged him to explain himself, and tell them what he had seen in that hell down there.

"Hell do you call it?" said Don Quixote. "Call it by no such name, for it does not deserve it, as ye shall soon see."

He then begged them to give him something to eat, as he was very hungry. They put the stores of the saddlebags into requisition, and all three sitting down, they made a luncheon and a supper of it all in one; and then Don Quixote of La Mancha said, "Let no one rise, and attend to me, my sons, both of you."

It was about four in the afternoon when the sun, veiled in clouds, with subdued light and tempered beams, enabled Don Quixote to relate, without heat or inconvenience, what he had seen in the cave of Montesinos to his two illustrious hearers, and he began as follows:

"A matter of some twelve or fourteen times a man's height down in this pit, on the right-hand side, there is a recess or space, roomy enough to contain a large cart with its mules. A little light reaches it through some chinks or crevices, communicating with it and open to the surface of the earth. This recess or space I perceived so I resolved to enter it and rest myself for a while. I seated myself considering what I was to do to lower myself to the bottom, having no one to hold me up; and as I was thus deep in thought and perplexity, suddenly and without provocation a profound sleep fell upon me, and when I least expected it, I know not how, I awoke and found myself in the midst of the most beautiful, delightful meadow that nature could produce or the most lively human imagination conceive. I opened my eyes, I rubbed them, and found I was not asleep but thoroughly awake. Nevertheless, I felt my head to satisfy myself whether it was I myself who was there or some empty delusive phantom; but touch, feeling, the collected thoughts that passed through my mind, all convinced me that I was the same then and there that I am this moment. Next there presented itself to my sight a stately royal palace or castle, with walls that seemed built of clear transparent crystal; and through two great doors that opened wide therein, I saw coming forth and advancing towards me a venerable old man. He approached me, and the first thing he did was to embrace me closely, and then he said to me, 'For a long time now, O valiant knight Don Quixote of La Mancha, we who are here enchanted in these solitudes have been hoping to see thee, that thou mayest make known to the world what is shut up and concealed in this deep cave, called the cave of Montesinos, which thou hast entered, an achievement reserved for thy invincible heart and stupendous courage alone to attempt. Come with me, illustrious sir, and I will show thee the marvels hidden within this transparent castle, whereof I am the alcaide and perpetual warden; for I am Montesinos himself, from whom the cave takes its name.' "

"I wonder," said Sancho, "that your worship did not get upon the old fellow and bruise every bone of him with kicks, and pluck his beard until you didn't leave a hair in it."

"Nay, Sancho, my friend," said Don Quixote, "it would not have been right in me to do that, for we are all bound to pay respect to the aged, even though they be not knights, but especially to those who are, and who are enchanted; I only know I gave him as good as he brought in the many other questions and answers we exchanged."

"I cannot understand, Señor Don Quixote," remarked the cousin here, "how it is that your worship, in such a short space of time as you have been below there, could have said and answered so much."

"How long is it since I went down?" asked Don Quixote.

"Little better than an hour," replied Sancho.

"That cannot be," returned Don Quixote, "because night overtook me while I was there, and day came, and it was night again and day again three times; so that, by my reckoning, I have been three days in those remote regions beyond our ken."

"My master must be right," replied Sancho; "for as everything that has happened to him is by enchantment, maybe what seems to us an hour would seem three days and nights there."

"That's it," said Don Quixote.

"And did your worship eat anything all that time, señor?" asked the cousin.

"I never touched a morsel," answered Don Quixote, "nor did I feel hunger, or think of it."

"And do the enchanted eat?" said the cousin.

"Never," said Don Quixote.

"And do the enchanted sleep, now, señor?" asked Sancho.

"Certainly not," replied Don Quixote; "at least, during those three days I was with them not one of them closed an eye, nor did I either."

"Forgive me, señor," said Sancho, "if I say that of all this you have told us now, may God take me—I was just going to say the devil—if I believe a single particle."

"What!" said the cousin. "Has Señor Don Quixote, then, been lying?"

"I don't believe my master lies," said Sancho.

"If not, what dost thou believe?" asked Don Quixote.

"I believe," replied Sancho, "that that enchanter down there stuffed your imagination or your mind with all this rigmarole you have been treating us to."

"All that might be, Sancho," replied Don Quixote, "but it is not so, everything I saw with my own eyes, and touched with my own hands. But what will you say when I tell you now how, among the countless other marvelous things Montesinos showed me, he showed me three country girls who went skipping and capering like goats over the pleasant fields there, and the instant I beheld them I knew one to be the peerless Dulcinea del Toboso, and the other two those same country girls that were with her and that we spoke to on the road from El Toboso!"

When Sancho Panza heard his master say this he was ready to die with laughter; for, as he knew the real truth about the pretended enchantment of Dulcinea, in which he himself had been the enchanter and concocter of all the evidence, he made up his mind at last that, beyond all doubt, his master was stark mad.

"I recognized her," Don Quixote went on, "by her wearing the same garments she wore when thou didst point her out to me. I spoke to her, but she did not utter a word in reply; on the contrary, she turned her back on

222

me and took to flight, at such a pace that crossbow bolt could not have over-taken her."

"O blessed God!" exclaimed Sancho aloud at this, "is it possible that such things can be in the world, and that enchanters and enchantments can have such power in it as to have changed my master's right senses into a craze so full of absurdity! O señor, señor, for God's sake, consider yourself, have a care for your honor, and give no credit to this silly stuff that has left you scant and short of wits."

"Thou talkest in this way because thou lovest me, Sancho," said Don Quixote; "and not being experienced in the things of the world, everything that has some difficulty about it seems to thee impossible; but we will travel on, and I will tell thee some of the things I saw down there which will make thee believe what I have related now, the truth of which admits of neither reply nor question."

CHAPTER 12

The Amazing Ape

JUST AS NIGHT was falling, they reached an inn; and it was not without satisfaction that Sancho perceived his master took it for a real inn, and not a castle as usual. They entered, and Sancho and the cousin proceeded to see to their beasts.

At this moment there came in the gate of the inn a man entirely clad in chamois leather, hose, breeches, and doublet, who said in a loud voice, "Señor host, have you room? Here's the divining ape and the show of the Release of Melisendra just coming."

"Ods body!" said the landlord, "why, it's Master Pedro! We're in for a grand night!" I forgot to mention that the said Master Pedro had his left eye and nearly half his cheek covered with a patch of black taffeta, showing that something ailed all that side. "Your worship is welcome, Master Pedro," continued the landlord, "but where are the ape and the show, for I don't see them?" "They are close at hand," said he in the chamois leather, "but I came on first to know if there was any room." "I'd make the Duke of Alva himself clear out to make room for Master Pedro," said the landlord. "Bring in the ape and the show; there's company in the inn tonight that will pay to see that and the cleverness of the ape." "So be it by all means," said the man with the patch. "I'll go back and hurry on the cart with the ape and the show"; and with this he went out of the inn.

Don Quixote at once asked the landlord what this Master Pedro was, and what was the show and what was the ape he had with him; to which the landlord replied, "This is a famous puppet-showman. He has also

224

with him an ape with the most extraordinary gift ever seen in an ape or imagined in a human being; for if you ask him anything, he listens attentively to the question, and then jumps on his master's shoulder, and pressing close to his ear tells him the answer which Master Pedro then delivers. He says a great deal more about things past than about things to come; and though he does not always hit the truth in every case, most times he is not far wrong, so that he makes us fancy he has got the devil in him. He gets two reals for every question if the ape answers; I mean if his master answers for him after he has whispered into his ear; and so it is believed that this same Master Pedro is very rich. He is a 'gallant man' as they say in Italy, and good company, and leads the finest life in the world; talks more than six, drinks more than a dozen, and all by his tongue, and his ape, and his show."

Master Pedro now came back, and in a cart followed the show and the ape—a big one, but not vicious-looking. As soon as Don Quixote saw him, he asked him, "Can you tell me, sir fortuneteller, what fish do we catch, and how will it be with us? See, here are my two reals," and he bade Sancho give them to Master Pedro; but he answered for the ape and said, "Señor, this animal does not give any answer or information touching things that are to come; of things past he knows something, and more or less of things present."

"Gad," said Sancho, "I would not give a farthing to be told what's past with me, for who knows that better than I do myself? And to pay for being told what I know would be mighty foolish. But as you know things present, here are my two reals, and tell me, most excellent sir ape, what is my wife Teresa Panza doing now, and what is she diverting herself with?"

Master Pedro refused to take the money, saying, "I will not receive payment in advance or until the service has been first rendered"; and then with his right hand he gave a couple of slaps on his left shoulder, and with one spring the ape perched himself upon it, and putting his mouth to his master's ear began chattering his teeth rapidly; and having kept this up as long as one would be saying a credo, with another spring he brought himself to the ground, and the same instant Master Pedro ran in great haste and fell upon his knees before Don Quixote, and embracing his legs exclaimed, "These legs do I embrace as I would embrace the two pillars of Hercules, O illustrious reviver of knight-errantry, so long consigned to oblivion! O never yet duly extolled knight, Don Quixote of La Mancha, courage of the faint-hearted, prop of the tottering, arm of the fallen, staff and counsel of all who are unfortunate!"

Don Quixote was thunderstruck, Sancho astounded, the cousin staggered, the landlord in perplexity, and, in short, everyone amazed at the words of the puppet-showman, who went on to say, "And thou, worthy Sancho Panza, the best squire and squire to the best knight in the world! Be of good cheer, for thy good wife Teresa is well, and she is at this moment hackling a pound of flax; and more by token she has at her left hand a jug with a broken spout that holds a good drop of wine, with which she solaces herself at her work."

"That I can well believe," said Sancho. "My Teresa is one of those that won't let themselves want for anything, though their heirs may have to pay for it."

"Now I declare," said Don Quixote, "he who reads much and travels much sees and knows a great deal. I say so because what amount of persuasion could have persuaded me that there are apes in the world that can divine as I have seen now with my own eyes? For I am that very Don Quixote of La Mancha this worthy animal refers to, though he has gone rather too far in my praise."

Master Pedro, who had by this time risen from Don Quixote's feet, said, "I have already said that this little beast gives no answer as to the future; but if he did, to oblige Señor Don Quixote, here present, I would give up all the profits in the world. And now, because I have promised it, and to afford him pleasure, I will set up my show and offer entertainment to all who are in the inn, without any charge whatever." As soon as he heard this, the landlord, delighted beyond measure, pointed out a place where the show might be fixed, which was done at once.

Don Quixote was not very well satisfied with the divinations of the ape, as he did not think it proper that an ape should divine anything, either past or future; so while Master Pedro was arranging the show, he retired with Sancho into a corner of the stable, where, without being overheard by anyone, he said to him, "Look here, Sancho, I have been seriously thinking over this ape's extraordinary gift, and have come to the conclusion that beyond doubt this Master Pedro, his master, has a pact with the devil."

"Nevertheless," said Sancho, "I would be glad if your worship would make Master Pedro ask his ape whether what happened to your worship in the cave of Montesinos is true; for, begging your worship's pardon, I, for my part, take it to have been all flam and lies, or at any rate something you dreamt."

"That may be," replied Don Quixote; "however, I will do what you suggest; though I have my own scruples about it."

At this point Master Pedro came up in quest of Don Quixote, to tell him the show was now ready and to come and see it, for it was worth seeing. Don Quixote explained his wish, and begged him to ask his ape at once to tell him whether certain things which had happened to him in the cave of Montesinos were dreams or realities, for to him they appeared to partake of both. Upon this Master Pedro, without answering, went back to fetch the ape, and, having placed it in front of Don Quixote and Sancho, said: "See here, señor ape, this gentleman wishes to know whether certain things which happened to him in the cave of Montesinos were false or true."

On his making the usual sign the ape mounted on his left shoulder and seemed to whisper in his ear, and Master Pedro said at once, "The ape says that the things you saw or that happened to you in that cave are, part of them false, part true; and that he only knows this and no more as regards this question; but if your worship wishes to know more, on Friday next he will answer all that may be asked him, for his gift is at present exhausted, and will not return to him till Friday, as he has said."

"Did I not say, señor," said Sancho, "that I could not bring myself to believe that all your worship said about the adventures in the cave was true, or even the half of it?"

"The course of events will tell, Sancho," replied Don Quixote. "Time, that discloses all things, leaves nothing that it does not drag into the light of day, though it be buried in the bosom of the earth. But enough of that for the present; let us go and see Master Pedro's show, for I am sure there must be something novel in it."

Don Quixote and Sancho went to where the show was already put up and uncovered, set all around with lighted wax tapers which made it look splendid and bright. When they came to it Master Pedro ensconced himself inside it, for it was he who had to work the puppets, and a boy, a servant of his, posted himself outside to act as showman and explain the mysteries of the exhibition, having a wand in his hand to point to the figures as they came out. And so, all who were in the inn being arranged in front of the show, some of them standing, and Don Quixote, Sancho, the page, and cousin, accommodated with the best places, the puppet show began.

All who were watching the show were hanging on the lips of the interpreter of its wonders, when drums and trumpets were heard to sound inside it and cannon to go off. The noise was soon over, and then the boy lifted up his voice and said, "This true story which is here represented to your worships is taken word for word from the French chronicles and from the Spanish ballads that are in everybody's mouth. Its subject is the release by Señor Don Gaiferos of his wife Melisendra, when a captive in Spain at the hands of the Moors in the city of Sansueña."

The boy went on: "See what a numerous and glittering crowd of horsemen issues from the city in pursuit of the two faithful lovers, what a blowing of trumpets there is, what sounding of horns, what beating of drums and tabors; I fear me they will overtake them and bring them back tied to the tail of their own horse, which would be a dreadful sight."

Don Quixote, seeing such a swarm of Moors and hearing such a din, thought it would be right to aid the fugitives, and standing up he exclaimed in a loud voice, "Never, while I live, will I permit foul play to be practiced in my presence on such a famous knight and fearless lover as Don Gaiferos. Halt! ill-born rabble, follow him not nor pursue him, or ye will have to reckon with me in battle!" and suiting the action to the word, he drew his sword, and with one bound placed himself close to the show, and with unexampled rapidity and fury began to shower down blows on the puppet troop of Moors, knocking over some, decapitating others, maiming this one and demolishing that; and among many more he delivered one downstroke which, if Master Pedro had not ducked, made himself small, and got out of the way, would have sliced off his head as easily as if it had been made of almond-paste. Master Pedro kept shouting, "Hold hard! Señor Don Quixote! Can't you see they're not real Moors you're knocking down and killing and destroying, but only little pasteboard figures! Look—sinner that I am!—how you're wrecking and ruining all that I'm worth!" But in spite of this, Don Quixote did not leave off discharging a continuous rain of cuts, slashes, downstrokes, and backstrokes, and at length, in less than the space of two credos, he brought the whole show to the ground, with all its fittings and figures shivered and knocked to pieces, King Marsilio badly wounded, and the Emperor Charlemagne with his crown and head split in two. The whole audience was thrown into confusion, the ape fled to the roof of the inn, the cousin was frightened, and even Sancho Panza himself was in mighty fear, for, as he swore after the storm was over, he had never seen his master in such a furious passion.

The complete destruction of the show being thus accomplished, Don

The ape mounted on his left shoulder and seemed to whisper in his ear.

Quixote became a little calmer, and said, "I wish I had here before me now all those who do not or will not believe how useful knights-errant are in the world; just think, if I had not been here present, what would have become of the brave Don Gaiferos and the fair Melisendra! Depend upon it, by this time those dogs would have overtaken them and inflicted some outrage upon them. So, then, long live knight-errantry beyond everything living on earth this day!"

"Let it live, and welcome," said Master Pedro at this in a feeble voice, "and let me die, for not half an hour, nay, barely a minute ago, I saw myself lord of kings and emperors, with my stables filled with countless horses, and my trunks and bags with gay dresses unnumbered; and now I find myself ruined and laid low, destitute and a beggar, and above all without my ape, for, by my faith, my teeth will have to sweat for it before I have caught him; and all through the reckless fury of sir knight here, who, they say, protects the fatherless, and rights wrongs, and does other charitable deeds; but whose generous intentions have been found wanting in my case only, blessed and praised be the highest heavens! Verily, knight of the rueful figure he must be, to have disfigured mine."

Sancho Panza was touched by Master Pedro's words, and said to him, "Don't weep and lament, Master Pedro; you break my heart; let me tell you my master, Don Quixote, is so scrupulous a Christian that, if he can make out that he has done you any wrong, he will own it, and be willing to pay for it and make it good, and something over and above."

"Only let Señor Don Quixote pay me for some part of the work he has destroyed," said Master Pedro, "and I would be content, and his worship would ease his conscience, for he cannot be saved who keeps what is another's against the owner's will, and makes no restitution."

"That is true," said Don Quixote, "but at present I am not aware that I have got anything of yours, Master Pedro."

"What!" returned Master Pedro; "and these relics lying here on the bare hard ground—what scattered and shattered them but the invincible strength of that mighty arm? And whose were they but mine? And what did I get my living by but by them?"

"Now am I fully convinced," said Don Quixote, "of what I had many a time before believed; that the enchanters who persecute me do nothing more than put figures like these before my eyes, and then change and turn them into what they please. In truth and earnest, I assure you gentlemen who now hear me, that to me everything that has taken place here seemed to take place literally. That was why my anger was roused; and to be faithful to my calling as a knight-errant I sought to give aid and protection to those who fled, and with this good intention I did what you have seen. If the result has been opposite of what I intended, it is no fault of mine, but of those wicked beings that persecute me; but, for all that, I am willing to condemn myself in costs for this error of mine, though it did not proceed from malice; let Master Pedro see what he wants for the spoiled figures, for I agree to pay it at once in good and current money of Castile."

Master Pedro made him a bow, saying, "I expected no less of the valiant Don Quixote of La Mancha. Master landlord here and the great Sancho Panza shall be the arbitrators and appraisers between your worship and me of what these dilapidated figures are worth or may be worth."

The landlord and Sancho consented, and then Master Pedro picked up from the ground King Masilio of Saragossa with his head off, and said, "Here you see how impossible it is to restore this king to his former state, so I think, saving your better judgments, that for his death, decease, and demise, four reals and a half may be given me."

"Proceed," said Don Quixote.

"Well then, for this cleavage from top to bottom," continued Master Pedro, taking up the split Emperor Charlemagne, "it would not be much if I were to ask five reals and a quarter."

"It's not little," said Sancho.

"Nor is it much," said the landlord. "Make it even, and say five reals."

"Let him have the whole five and a quarter," said Don Quixote, "for the sum total of this notable disaster does not stand on a quarter more or less; and make an end of it quickly, Master Pedro, for it's getting on to supper-time, and I have some hints of hunger."

"For this figure," said Master Pedro, "that is without a nose, and wants an eye, and is the fair Melisendra, I ask, and I am reasonable in my charge, two reals and twelve maravedis."

"The very devil must be in it," said Don Quixote, "if Melisendra and her husband are not by this time at least on the French border, for the horse they rode on seemed to me to fly rather than gallop; so you needn't try to sell me the cat for the hare, showing me here a noseless Melisendra when she is now, maybe, enjoying herself at her ease with her husband in France."

Master Pedro, perceiving that Don Quixote was beginning to wander,

230

and return to his original fancy, was not disposed to let him escape, so he said to him, "This cannot be Melisendra, but must be one of the damsels that waited on her; so if I'm given sixty maravedis for her, I'll be content and sufficiently paid."

And so he went on, putting values on more smashed figures, which, after the two arbitrators had adjusted them to the satisfaction of both parties, came to forty reals and three-quarters; and over and above this sum, which Sancho at once disbursed, Master Pedro asked for two reals for his trouble in catching the ape.

"Let him have them, Sancho," said Don Quixote; "not to catch the ape, but to get drunk; and two hundred would I give this minute for the good news, to anyone who could tell me positively, that the lady Doña Melisendra and Señor Don Gaiferos were now in France and with their own people."

"No one could tell us that better than my ape," said Master Pedro, "but there's no devil that could catch him now; I suspect, however, that affection and hunger will drive him to come looking for me tonight; but tomorrow will soon be here and we shall see."

In short, the puppet-show storm passed off, and all supped in peace and good fellowship at Don Quixote's expense, for he was the height of generosity. Soon after daybreak the cousin came to bid Don Quixote fare-well, as he was returning home. Master Pedro did not care to engage in any more palaver with Don Quixote, whom he knew right well; so he rose before the sun, and having got together the remains of his show and caught his ape, he too went off to seek his adventures. The landlord, who did not know Don Quixote, was as much astonished at his mad freaks as at his generosity. To conclude, Sancho, by his master's orders, paid him very liberally, and taking leave of him they quitted the inn at about eight in the morning and took to the road.

CHAPTER 13

The Enchanted Bark

B Y STAGES, a few days after quitting the inn, Don Quixote and
Sancho reached the river Ebro, and the sight of it was a great
delight to Don Quixote as he gazed upon the charms of its
banks, the clearness of its stream, the gentleness of its current and the
abundance of its crystal waters.

As they were thus proceeding, then, they discovered a small boat, without
oars or any other gear, that lay at the water's edge tied to the stem of a tree
growing on the bank. Don Quixote looked all round, and seeing nobody, at
once, without more ado, dismounted from Rocinante and bade Sancho
get down from Dapple and tie both beasts securely to the trunk of a poplar
or willow that stood there. Sancho asked him the reason of this sudden
dismounting and tying. Don Quixote made answer, "Thou must know,
Sancho, that this bark is plainly, and without the possibility of any alternative,
calling me to enter it, and in it go to give aid to some knight or other person
of distinction in need of it, who is no doubt in some sore strait."

"As that's the case," said Sancho, "and your worship chooses to give in
to these—I don't know if I may call them absurdities—at every turn, there's
nothing for it but to obey. But I warn your worship that it is my opinion
this bark is no enchanted one, but belongs to some of the fishermen of the
river, for they catch the best shad in the world here."

As Sancho said this, he tied the beasts, leaving them to the care and
protection of the enchanters with sorrow enough in his heart. Don Quixote
bade him not be uneasy about deserting the animals, "for he who would

232

carry themselves over such longinquous roads and regions would take care
to feed them."

"I don't understand that logiquous," said Sancho, "nor have I ever heard
the word all the days of my life."

"Longinquous," replied Don Quixote, "means far off; but it is no wonder
thou dost not understand it, for thou art not bound to know Latin, like
some who pretend to know it and don't."

"Now they are tied," said Sancho; "what are we to do next?"

"What?" said Don Quixote, "cross ourselves and weigh anchor; I mean,
embark and cut the moorings by which the bark is held"; and the bark
began to drift away slowly from the bank. But when Sancho saw himself
somewhere about two yards out in the river, he began to tremble and give
himself up for lost; but nothing distressed him more than hearing Dapple
bray and seeing Rocinante struggling to get loose, and said he to his master,
"Dapple is braying in grief at our leaving him, and Rocinante is trying to
escape and plunge in after us. O dear friends, peace be with you, and may
this madness that is taking us away from you, turned into sober sense,
bring us back to you." And with this he fell weeping so bitterly that Don
Quixote said to him, sharply and angrily, "What art thou afraid
of, cowardly creature? What art thou weeping at, heart of butter-paste?
Who pursues or molests thee, thou soul of a tame mouse? What dost thou
want, unsatisfied in the very heart of abundance? Art thou, perchance,
tramping barefoot over the Riphæan mountains, instead of being seated
on a bench like an archduke on the tranquil stream of this pleasant river,
from which in a short space we shall come out upon the broad sea? But we
must have already emerged and gone seven hundred or eight hundred leagues."

"I don't believe a bit of it," said Sancho, "for I can see with my own eyes
that we have not moved five yards away from the bank, or shifted two yards
from where the animals stand, for there are Rocinante and Dapple in the
very same place where we left them; and watching a point, as I do now,
I swear by all that's good, we are not moving at the pace of an ant."

The boat was quietly gliding in midstream, not moved by any occult
intelligence or invisible enchanter, but simply by the current, just there smooth
and gentle.

They now came in sight of some large water mills that stood in the middle
of the river, and the instant Don Quixote saw them he cried out, "Seest thou
there, my friend? There stands the castle or fortress, where there is, no

doubt, some knight in durance, or ill-used queen, in whose aid I am brought hither."

"What the devil city, fortress, or castle is your worship talking about, señor?" said Sancho; "don't you see that those are mills that stand in the river to grind corn?"

"Hold thy peace, Sancho," said Don Quixote; "though they look like mills they are not so; I have already told thee that enchantments transform things and change their proper shapes."

By this time, the boat, having reached the middle of the stream, began to move less slowly than hitherto. The millers belonging to the mills, when they saw the boat coming down the river, and on the point of being sucked in by the draft of the wheels, ran out in haste, several of them, with long poles to stop it, and being all mealy, with faces and garments covered with flour, they presented a sinister appearance. They raised loud shouts, crying, "Devils of men, where are you going? Are you mad? Do you want to drown yourselves, or dash yourselves to pieces among these wheels?"

"Did I not tell thee, Sancho," said Don Quixote at this, "that we had reached the place where I am to show what the might of my arm can do? See what ruffians and villains come out against me; see what monsters oppose me; see what hideous countenances come to frighten us! You shall soon see, scoundrels!" And then standing up in the boat he began in a loud voice to hurl threats at the millers, exclaiming, "Ill-conditioned and worse-counseled rabble, restore to liberty and freedom the person ye hold in durance in this your fortress or prison, high or low or of whatever rank or quality he be, for I am Don Quixote of La Mancha, otherwise called the Knight of the Lions, for whom, by the disposition of heaven above, it is reserved to give a happy issue to this adventure!" And so saying he drew his sword and began making passes in the air at the millers, who, hearing but not understanding all this nonsense, strove to stop the boat, which was now getting into the rushing channel of the wheels. Sancho fell upon his knees devoutly appealing to heaven to deliver him from such imminent peril; which it did by the activity and quickness of the millers, who, pushing against the boat with their poles, stopped it, not however, without upsetting and throwing Don Quixote and Sancho into the water; and lucky it was for Don Quixote that he could swim like a goose, though the weight of his armor carried him twice to the bottom; and had it not been for the millers, who plunged in and hoisted them both out, it would have been Troy town with the pair of them. As soon as, more drenched than thirsty, they were landed, Sancho went down on his knees and with clasped hands and eyes raised to heaven, prayed a long and fervent prayer to God to deliver him evermore from the rash projects of his master. The fishermen, the owners of the boat, which the mill-wheels had knocked to pieces, now came up, and seeing it smashed they proceeded to strip Sancho and to demand payment for it from Don Quixote; but he with great calmness, just as if nothing had happened to him, told the millers and fishermen that he would pay for the bark most cheerfully, on condition that they delivered up to him, free and unhurt, the person or persons that were in durance in that castle of theirs.

"What persons or what castle art thou talking of, madman? Art thou for carrying off the people who come to grind corn in these mills?"

"That's enough," said Don Quixote to himself. "It would be preaching in the desert to attempt by entreaties to induce this rabble to do any virtuous action. In this adventure two mighty enchanters must have encountered one another, and one frustrates what the other attempts; one provided the bark for me, and the other upset me; God help us, this world is all machinations and schemes at cross purposes one with the other. I can do no more." And then turning towards the mills he said aloud, "Friends, whoe'er ye be that are immured in that prison, forgive me that, to my misfortune and yours, I cannot deliver you from your misery; this adventure is doubtless reserved and destined for some other knight."

So saying he settled with the fishermen, and paid fifty reals for the boat, which Sancho handed to them very much against the grain, saying, "With a couple more bark businesses like this we shall have sunk our whole capital."

The fishermen and the millers stood staring in amazement at the two figures, so very different to all appearance from ordinary men, and were wholly unable to make out the drift of the observations and questions Don Quixote addressed to them; and coming to the conclusion that they were madmen, they left them and betook themselves, the millers to their mills, and the fishermen to their huts. Don Quixote and Sancho returned to their beasts, and so ended the adventure of the enchanted bark.

CHAPTER 14

The Duke and the Duchess

THEY REACHED THEIR BEASTS in low spirits and bad humor enough, knight and squire, Sancho particularly, for with him what touched the stock of money touched his heart. In fine, without exchanging a word, they mounted and quitted the famous river, Don Quixote absorbed in thoughts of his love, Sancho in thinking of his advancement, which just then, it seemed to him, he was very far from securing; and he began to cast about for an opportunity of retiring from his master's service and going home some day, without entering into any explanations or taking any farewell of him. Fortune, however, ordered matters after a fashion very much the opposite of what he contemplated.

It so happened that the next day toward sunset, on coming out of a wood, Don Quixote cast his eyes over a green meadow, and at the far end of it observed some people, and as he drew nearer saw that it was a hawking party. Coming closer, he distinguished among them a lady of graceful mien, on a pure white palfrey or hackney caparisoned with green trappings and a silver-mounted sidesaddle. The lady was also in green, and so richly and splendidly dressed that splendor itself seemed personified in her. On her left hand she bore a hawk, a proof to Don Quixote's mind that she must be some great lady and the mistress of the whole hunting party, which was the fact; so he said to Sancho, "Run, Sancho, my son, and say to that lady on the palfrey with the hawk that I, the Knight of the Lions, kiss the hands of her exalted beauty, and if her excellence will grant me leave I will go and kiss them in person and place myself at her service for aught that may be in my power and her highness may command."

Sancho went off at top speed, forcing Dapple out of his regular pace, and came to where the fair huntress was standing, and dismounting knelt before her and said, "Fair lady, that knight that you see there, the Knight of the Lions by name, is my master, and I am a squire of his, and at home they call me Sancho Panza. This same Knight of the Lions, who was called not long since the Knight of the Rueful Countenance, sends by me to say may it please your highness to give him leave that, with your permission, approbation, and consent, he may come and carry out his wishes, which are, as he says and I believe, to serve your exalted loftiness and beauty."

"You have indeed, worthy squire," said the lady, "delivered your message with all the formalities such messages require; rise up, for it is not right that the squire of a knight so great as he of the Rueful Countenance, of whom we have heard a great deal here, should remain on his knees; rise, my friend, and bid your master welcome to the services of myself and the duke my husband, in a country house we have here."

Sancho got up, charmed as much by the beauty of the good lady as by her highbred air and her courtesy, but, above all, by what she had said about having heard of his master, the Knight of the Rueful Countenance.

"Tell me, brother squire," asked the duchess, "this master of yours, is he not one of whom there is a history extant in print, called 'The Ingenious Gentleman, Don Quixote of La Mancha,' who has for the lady of his heart a certain Dulcinea del Toboso?"

"He is the same, señora," replied Sancho, "and that squire of his who figures, or ought to figure, in the said history under the name of Sancho Panza, is myself, unless they have changed me in the cradle, I mean in the press."

"I am rejoiced at all this," said the duchess; "go, brother Panza, and tell your master that he is welcome to my estate, and that nothing could happen to me that could give me greater pleasure."

Sancho returned to his master mightily pleased with this gratifying answer, and told him all the great lady had said to him. Don Quixote drew himself up briskly in his saddle, fixed himself in his stirrups, settled his visor, gave Rocinante the spur, and with an easy bearing advanced to kiss the hands of the duchess, who, having sent to summon the duke her

237

husband, told him, while Don Quixote was approaching, all about the message.

Don Quixote now came up with his visor raised, and as he seemed about to dismount Sancho made haste to go and hold his stirrup for him; but in getting down off Dapple he was so unlucky as to hitch his foot in one of the ropes of the pack-saddle in such a way that he was unable to free it, and was left hanging by it with his face and breast on the ground. Don Quixote, who was not used to dismount without having the stirrup held, fancying that Sancho had by this time come to hold it for him, threw himself off with a lurch and brought Rocinante's saddle after him, which was no doubt badly girthed, and saddle and he both came to the ground; not without discomfiture to him and abundant curses muttered between his teeth against the unlucky Sancho, who had his foot still in the shackles. The duke ordered his huntsmen to go to the help of knight and squire, and they raised Don Quixote, sorely shaken by his fall; and he, limping, advanced as best he could to kneel before the noble pair. This, however, the duke would by no means permit. On the contrary, dismounting from his horse, he went and embraced Don Quixote, saying, "I am grieved, Sir Knight of the Rueful Countenance, that your first experience on my ground should have been such an unfortunate one as we have seen; but the carelessness of squires is often the cause of worse accidents."

"That which has happened to me in meeting you, mighty prince," replied Don Quixote, "cannot be unfortunate, even if my fall had not stopped short of the depths of the bottomless pit. My squire, God's curse upon him, is better at unloosing his tongue in talking impertinence than in tightening the girths of a saddle to keep it steady; but however I may be, fallen or raised up, on foot or on horseback, I shall always be at your service and that of my lady the duchess, your worthy consort, worthy queen of beauty and paramount princess of courtesy."

"Gently, Señor Don Quixote of La Mancha," said the duke. "Where my lady Doña Dulcinea del Toboso is, it is not right that other beauties should be praised."

Sancho, by this time released from his entanglement, was standing by, and before his master could answer he said, "There is no denying, and it must be maintained, that my lady Dulcinea del Toboso is very beautiful; but the hare jumps up where one least expects it; and I have heard say that what we call nature is like a potter that makes vessels of clay, and he who makes one fair vessel can as well make two, or three, or a hundred; I say so because, by my faith, my lady the duchess is in no way behind my mistress the lady Dulcinea del Toboso."

Don Quixote turned to the duchess and said, "Your highness may conceive that never had knight-errant in this world a more talkative or a droller squire than I have, and he will prove the truth of what I say, if your highness is pleased to accept of my services for a few days."

To which the duchess made answer, "That worthy Sancho is droll I consider a very good thing, because it is a sign that he is shrewd; for drollery and sprightliness, Señor Don Quixote, as you very well know, do not take up their abode with dull wits; and as good Sancho is droll and sprightly I here set him down as shrewd."

"And talkative," added Don Quixote.

"So much the better," said the duke, "for many droll things cannot be said in few words; but not to lose time in talking, come, great Knight of the Rueful Countenance—"

"Of the Lions, your highness must say," said Sancho, "for there is no Rueful Countenance now."

"He of the Lions be it," continued the duke. "I say, let Sir Knight of the Lions come to a castle of mine close by, where he shall be given that reception which is due to so exalted a personage, and which the duchess and I are wont to give to all knights-errant who come there."

By this time Sancho had fixed and girthed Rocinante's saddle, and Don Quixote having got on his back and the duke mounted a fine horse, they placed the duchess in the middle and set out for the castle. The duchess desired Sancho to come to her side, for she found infinite enjoyment in listening to his shrewd remarks. Sancho required no pressing, but pushed himself in between them and the duke, who thought it rare good fortune to receive such a knight-errant and such a homely squire in their castle.

Supreme was the satisfaction that Sancho felt at seeing himself, as it seemed, an established favorite with the duchess, for he looked forward to finding in her castle what he had found in Don Diego's house. He was always fond of good living, and always seized by the forelock any opportunity of feasting himself whenever it presented itself.

Before they reached the country house or castle, the duke went on in advance and instructed all his servants how they were to treat Don Quixote. As they entered a spacious court two fair damsels came forward and threw over Don Quixote's shoulders a large mantle of the finest scarlet cloth, and at the same instant all the galleries of the court were lined with the men-servants and women-servants of the household, crying, "Welcome, flower and cream of knight-errantry!" while all or most of them flung pellets filled with scented water over Don Quixote and the duke and duchess; at all which Don Quixote was greatly astonished, and this was the first time that he thoroughly felt and believed himself to be a knight-errant in reality and not merely in fancy, now that he saw himself treated in the same way as he had read of such knights being treated in days of yore.

Sancho, deserting Dapple, hung on to the duchess and entered the castle, but feeling some twinges of conscience at having left the ass alone, he approached a respectable duenna who had come out with the rest to receive the duchess, and in a low voice he said to her, "Señora Gonzalez, or however your grace may be called—"

"I am called Doña Rodriguez de Grijalba," replied the duenna. "What is your will, brother?" To which Sancho made answer, "I should be glad if your worship would do me the favor to go out to the castle gate, where you will find a gray ass of mine; make them, if you please, put him in the stable, or put him there yourself, for the poor little beast is rather easily frightened, and cannot bear being alone at all."

"If the master is as wise as the man," said the duenna, "we have got a fine bargain. Be off with you, brother, and bad luck to you and him who brought you here; go, look after your ass, for we, the duennas of this house, are not used to work of that sort, and you'll get nothing from me but a fig."

"At any rate, it will be a very ripe one," said Sancho.

"Son of a dog," said the duenna, all aglow with anger, "whether I'm old or not, it's with God I have to reckon, not with you, you garlic-stuffed scoundrel!" and she said it so loud that the duchess heard it, and turning round and seeing the duenna in such a state of excitement, and her eyes flaming so, asked whom she was wrangling with.

"With this good fellow here," said the duenna, "who has particularly requested me to go and put an ass of his that is at the castle gate into the stable; and what is more he called me old."

"That," said the duchess, "I should have considered the greatest affront that could be offered me." And addressing Sancho, she said to him, "You must know, friend Sancho, that Doña Rodriguez is very youthful, and that she

The duchess desired Sancho to come to her side.

wears that hood more for authority and custom's sake than because of her years."

"May all the rest of mine be unlucky," said Sancho, "if I meant it that way. I only spoke because the affection I have for my ass is so great, and I thought I could not commend him to a more kind-hearted person than the lady Doña Rodriguez."

Don Quixote, who was listening, said to him, "Is this proper conversation for the place, Sancho?"

"Señor," replied Sancho, "everyone must mention what he wants wherever he may be; I thought of Dapple here, and I spoke of him here; if I had thought of him in the stable I would have spoken there."

On which the duke observed, "Sancho is quite right, and there is no reason at all to find fault with him. Dapple shall be fed to his heart's content, and Sancho may rest easy, for he shall be treated like himself."

While this conversation, amusing to all except Don Quixote, was proceeding, they ascended the staircase and ushered Don Quixote into a chamber hung with rich cloth of gold and brocade; six damsels relieved him of his armor and waited on him like pages, all of them prepared and instructed by the duke and duchess as to what they were to do. They asked him to let himself be stripped that they might put a shirt on him, but he would not on any account, saying that modesty became knights-errant just as much as valor. However, he said they might give the shirt to Sancho; and shutting himself in with him in a room where there was a sumptuous bed, he undressed and put on the shirt; and then, finding himself alone with Sancho, he said to him, "Tell me, thou new-fledged buffoon and old booby, dost thou think it right to offend and insult a duenna so deserving of reverence and respect as that one just now? Was that a time to bethink thee of thy Dapple, or are these noble personages likely to let the beasts fare badly when they treat their owners in such elegant style? For God's sake, Sancho, restrain thyself, and don't show the thread so as to let them see what a coarse, boorish texture thou art of."

Sancho promised him with much earnestness to keep his mouth shut, and to bite off his tongue before he uttered a word that was not altogether to the purpose and well considered.

Don Quixote dressed himself, put on his baldric with his sword, threw the scarlet mantle over his shoulders, placed on his head a montera of green satin that the damsels had given him, and thus arrayed passed out into the large room, where he found the damsels drawn up in double file, the same number on each side, all with the appliances for washing the hands, which they presented to him with profuse obeisances and ceremonies. Then came twelve pages, together with the seneschal, to lead him to dinner, as his hosts were already waiting for him. They placed him in the midst of them, and with much pomp and stateliness they conducted him into another room, where there was a sumptuous table laid with but four covers. The duchess and the duke came out to the door of the room to receive him, and with them a grave ecclesiastic, one of those who rule noblemen's houses; one of those who, not being born magnates themselves, never know how to teach those who are how to behave as such.

A vast number of polite speeches were exchanged, and at length, taking Don Quixote between them, they proceeded to sit down to table. The duke pressed Don Quixote to take the head of the table, and, though he refused, the entreaties of the duke were so urgent that he had to accept it.

The ecclesiastic took his seat opposite to him, and the duke and duchess those at the sides. All this time Sancho stood by, gaping with amazement at the honor he saw shown to his master by these illustrious persons; and observing all the ceremonious pressing that had passed between the duke and Don Quixote to induce him to take his seat at the head of the table, he said, "If your worship will give me leave I will tell you a story of what happened in my village about this matter of seats."

The moment Sancho said this Don Quixote trembled, feeling sure that he was about to say something foolish. Sancho glanced at him, and guessing his thoughts, said, "Don't be afraid of my going astray, señor, or saying anything that won't be pat to the purpose; I haven't forgotten the advice your worship gave me just now about talking much or little, well or ill."

"It would be well," said Don Quixote, "if your highnesses would order them to turn out this idiot, for he will talk a heap of nonsense."

"By the life of the duke, Sancho shall not be taken away from me for a moment," said the duchess. "I am very fond of him, for I know he is very discreet."

"Discreet be the days of your holiness," said Sancho, "for the good opinion you have of my wit, though there's none in me; but the story I want to tell is this. There was an invitation given by a gentleman of my town, a very

rich one, and one of quality, for he was one of the Alamos of Medina del
Campo, and married to Doña Mencia de Quiñones, the daughter of Don
Alonso de Marañon, Knight of the Order of Santiago, that was drowned at
the Herradura—him there was that quarrel about years ago in our village,
that my master Don Quixote was mixed up in, to the best of my belief, that
Tomasillo the scapegrace, the son of Balbastro the smith, was wounded in—
Isn't all this true, master mine? As you live, say so, that these gentlefolk
may not take me for some lying chatterer."

"So far," said the ecclesiastic, "I take you to be more a chatterer than a
liar; but I don't know what I shall take you for by and by."

"Thou citest so many witnesses and proofs, Sancho," said Don Quixote,
"that I have no choice but to say thou must be telling the truth; go on,
and cut the story short, for thou art taking the way not to make an end for
two days to come."

"He is not to cut it short," said the duchess; "on the contrary, for my
gratification, he is to tell it as he knows it, though he should not finish it these
six days; and if he took so many they would be to me the pleasantest I ever
spent."

"Well then, sirs, I say," continued Sancho, "that this same gentleman,
whom I know as well as I do my own hands, for it's not a bowshot from
my house to his, invited a poor but respectable laborer—"

"Get on, brother," said the churchman. "At the rate you are going you
will not stop with your story short of the next world."

"I'll stop less than halfway, please God," said Sancho; "and so I say this
laborer, coming to the house of the gentleman I spoke of that invited him
—rest his soul, he is now dead; and more by token he died the death of an
angel, so they say; for I was not there, for just at that time I had gone to
reap at Tembleque—"

"As you live, my son," said the churchman, "make haste back from Tembleque, and finish your story without burying the gentleman, unless you want
to make more funerals."

"Well then, it so happened," said Sancho, "that as the pair of them were
going to sit down to table—and I think I can see them now plainer than
ever—"

Great was the enjoyment the duke and duchess derived from the irritation
the worthy churchman showed at the long-winded, halting way Sancho had

243

of telling his story, while Don Quixote was chafing with rage and vexation.

"So, as I was saying," continued Sancho, "as the pair of them were going to sit down to table, as I said, the laborer insisted upon the gentleman's taking the head of the table, and the gentleman insisted upon the laborer's taking it, as his orders should be obeyed in his house; but the laborer, who plumed himself on his politeness and good breeding, would not on any account, until the gentleman, out of patience, putting his hands on his shoulders, compelled him by force to sit down, saying, 'Sit down, you stupid lout, for wherever I sit will be the head to you'; and that's the story, and, troth, I think it hasn't been brought in amiss here."

Don Quixote turned all colors, which, on his sunburned face, mottled it till it looked like jasper. The duke and duchess suppressed their laughter so as not altogether to mortify Don Quixote, for they saw through Sancho's impertinence; and to change the conversation, and keep Sancho from uttering more absurdities, the duchess asked Don Quixote what news he had of the lady Dulcinea, and if he had sent her any presents of giants or miscreants lately, for he could not but have vanquished a good many.

To which Don Quixote replied, "Señora, my misfortunes, though they had a beginning, will never have an end. I have vanquished giants and I have sent her caitiffs and miscreants; but where are they to find her if she is enchanted and turned into the most ill-favored peasant wench that can be imagined?"

The ecclesiastic, when he heard them talking of giants and caitiffs and enchantments, began to suspect that this must be Don Quixote of La Mancha, whose story the duke was always reading; and he had himself often reproved him for it, telling him it was foolish to read such fooleries; and becoming convinced that his suspicion was correct, addressing the duke, he said very angrily to him, "Señor, your excellence will have to give account to God for what this good man does. This Don Quixote, or Don Simpleton, or whatever his name is, cannot, I imagine, be such a blockhead as your excellence would have him, holding out encouragement to him to go on with his vagaries and follies." Then turning to address Don Quixote he said, "And you, numskull, who put it into your head that you are a knight-errant, and vanquish giants and capture miscreants? Go your ways in a good hour, and in a good hour be it said to you. Go home and bring up your children if you have any, and attend to your business, and give over going wandering about the world, gaping and making a laughingstock of yourself to all who know you and all who don't. Where, in heaven's name, have you discovered that there are or ever were knights-errant? Where are there giants in Spain or miscreants in La Mancha, or enchanted Dulcineas, or all the rest of the silly things they tell about you?"

Don Quixote listened attentively to the reverend gentleman's words, and as soon as he perceived he had done speaking, regardless of the presence of the duke and duchess, he sprang to his feet with angry looks and an agitated countenance.

CHAPTER 15

In the Duke's Castle

THE PLACE I am in, the presence in which I stand, and the respect I have and always have had for the profession to which your worship belongs, hold and bind the hands of my just indignation," said Don Quixote. "But pious, well-meant reproof requires a different demeanor and arguments of another sort; at any rate, to have reproved me in public, and so roughly, exceeds the bounds of proper reproof, for that comes better with gentleness than with rudeness; and it is not seemly to call the sinner roundly blockhead and booby, without knowing anything of the sin that is reproved. Come, tell me, for which of the stupidities you have observed in me do you condemn and abuse me, and bid me go home and look after my house and wife and children, without knowing whether I have any? Is nothing more needed than to get a footing, by hook or by crook, in other people's houses to rule over the masters (and that, perhaps, after having been brought up in all the straitness of some seminary, and without having ever seen more of the world than may lie within twenty or thirty leagues round), to fit one to lay down the law rashly for chivalry, and pass judgment on knights-errant? Is it, haply, an idle occupation, or is the time ill spent that is spent in roaming the world in quest, not of its enjoyments, but of those arduous toils whereby the good mount upwards to the abodes of everlasting life? If gentlemen, great lords, nobles, men of high birth, were to rate me as a fool I should take it as an irreparable insult; but I care not a farthing if clerks who have never entered upon or trod the paths of chivalry should think me foolish. Knight I am, and knight I will die, if such be the pleasure of the Most

High. Some take the broad road of overweening ambition; others that of mean and servile flattery; others that of deceitful hypocrisy, and some that of true religion; but I, led by my star, follow the narrow path of knight-errantry, and in pursuit of that calling I despise wealth, but not honor. I have redressed injuries, righted wrongs, punished insolences, vanquished giants, and crushed monsters. My intentions are always directed to worthy ends, to do good to all and evil to none; and if he who means this, does this, and makes this his practice deserves to be called a fool, it is for your highnesses to say, O most excellent duke and duchess."

"Good, by God!" cried Sancho. "Say no more in your own defense, master mine, for there's nothing more in the world to be said, thought, or insisted on. And besides, when this gentleman denies, as he has, that there are or ever have been any knights-errant in the world, is it any wonder if he knows nothing of what he has been talking about?"

"Perhaps, brother," said the ecclesiastic, "you are that Sancho Panza that is mentioned, to whom your master has promised an island?"

"Yes, I am," said Sancho, "and what's more, I am one who deserves it as much as anyone; I am one of the sort—'Attach thyself to the good, and thou wilt be one of them,' and of those, 'Not with whom thou art bred, but with whom thou art fed,' and of those, 'Who leans against a good tree, a good shade covers him'; I have leaned upon a good master, and I have been for months going about with him, and please God I shall be just such another; long life to him and long life to me, for neither will he be in any want of empires to rule, or I of islands to govern."

"No, Sancho my friend, certainly not," said the duke, "for in the name of Señor Don Quixote I confer upon you the government of one of no small importance that I have at my disposal."

"Go down on thy knees, Sancho," said Don Quixote, "and kiss the feet of his excellence for the favor he has bestowed upon thee."

Sancho obeyed, and on seeing this the ecclesiastic stood up from table completely out of temper, exclaiming, "By the gown I wear, I am almost inclined to say that your excellence is as great a fool as these sinners. No wonder they are mad, when people who are in their senses sanction their madness! I leave your excellence with them. For so long as they are in the house, I will remain in my own, and spare myself the trouble of reproving what I cannot remedy." And without uttering another word, or eating another morsel, he went off, the entreaties of the duke and duchess being entirely unavailing to stop him;

not that the duke said much to him, for he could not, because of the laughter his uncalled-for anger provoked.

When he had done laughing, he said to Don Quixote, "You have replied on your own behalf so stoutly, Sir Knight of the Lions, that there is no occasion to seek further satisfaction for this, which, though it may look like an offense, is not so at all, for ecclesiastics can give no offense, as you very well know."

"That is true," said Don Quixote, "and the reason is, that he who is not liable to offense cannot give offense to anyone. Ecclesiastics, as they cannot defend themselves, though they may receive offense cannot be insulted, because between the offense and the insult there is, as your excellence very well knows, this difference: the insult comes from one who is capable of offering it, and does so, and maintains it; the offense may come from any quarter without carrying insult."

Don Quixote finally grew calm, and dinner came to an end.

The seneschal went away to dinner and took Sancho along with him, while the duke and duchess and Don Quixote remained at table discussing a great variety of things, but all bearing on the calling of arms and knight-errantry.

The duchess begged Don Quixote, as he seemed to have a retentive memory, to describe and portray to her the beauty and features of the lady Dulcinea del Toboso, for, judging by what fame trumpeted abroad of her beauty, she felt sure she must be the fairest creature in the world, nay, in all La Mancha.

Don Quixote sighed on hearing the duchess's request, and said, "I would do so certainly, had she not been blurred to my mind's eye by the misfortune that fell upon her a short time since, one of such a nature that I am more ready to weep over it than to describe it. For your highnesses must know that, going a few days back to kiss her hands and receive her benediction, approbation, and permission for this third sally, I found her altogether a different being from the one I sought; I found her enchanted and changed from a princess into a peasant, from fair to foul, from an angel into a devil, from fragrant to pestiferous, from refined to clownish, from a dignified lady into a jumping tomboy, and, in a word, from Dulcinea del Toboso into a coarse Sayago wench."

"God bless me!" said the duke aloud at this. "Who can have done the world such an injury?"

"Who?" replied Don Quixote; "who could it be but some malignant enchanter of the many that persecute me out of envy—that accursed race born into the world to obscure and bring to naught the achievements of the good, and glorify and exalt the deeds of the wicked?"

"There is no denying it," said the duchess; "but still, if we are to believe the history of Don Quixote that has come out here lately with general applause, it is to be inferred from it, if I mistake not, that you never saw the lady Dulcinea, and that the said lady is nothing in the world but an imaginary lady, one that you yourself begot and gave birth to in your brain, and adorned with whatever charms and perfections you chose."

"There is a good deal to be said on that point," said Don Quixote. "God knows whether there be any Dulcinea or not in the world, or whether she is imaginary or not imaginary; these are things the proof of which must not be pushed to extreme lengths."

"I protest, Señor Don Quixote," said the duchess, "that in all you say, you go most cautiously. Henceforth I will believe myself, and I will take care that everyone in my house believes, even my lord the duke if needs be, that there is a Dulcinea in El Toboso, and that she is living today, and that she is beautiful and nobly born and deserves to have such a knight as Señor Don Quixote in her service."

CHAPTER 16

How to Disenchant Dulcinea

GREAT WAS the pleasure the duke and duchess took in the conversation of Don Quixote and Sancho Panza; and between them they plotted and arranged to play a joke on Don Quixote that was to be a rare one and entirely in knight-errantry style. They took as their basis of action what Don Quixote had told them about the cave of Montesinos, in order to play him a famous one. But what the duchess marveled at above all was that Sancho's simplicity could be so great as to make him believe as absolute truth that Dulcinea had been enchanted, when it was he himself who had been the enchanter and trickster in the business. Having, therefore, instructed their servants in everything they were to do, six days afterwards they took him out to hunt, with as great a retinue of huntsmen and beaters as a crowned king.

They presented Don Quixote with a hunting suit, and Sancho with another of the finest green cloth; but Don Quixote declined to put his on, saying that he must soon return to the hard pursuit of arms, and could not carry wardrobes or stores with him. Sancho, however, took what they gave him, meaning to sell it the first opportunity.

The appointed day having arrived, Don Quixote armed himself, and Sancho arrayed himself, and mounted on his Dapple (for he would not give him up though they offered him a horse), he placed himself in the midst of the troop of huntsmen. The duchess came out splendidly attired, and Don Quixote, in pure courtesy and politeness, held the rein of her palfrey, though the duke wanted not to allow him; and at last they reached a wood that lay between two high mountains, where, after occupying various posts, ambushes, and paths, and distributing the party in different positions, the hunt began with great noise, shouting, and hallooing, so that, between the baying of the hounds and the blowing of the horns, they could not hear one another.

The duchess dismounted, and with a sharp boar-spear in her hand posted herself where she knew the wild boars were in the habit of passing. The duke and Don Quixote likewise dismounted and placed themselves one at each side of her. Sancho took up a position in the rear of all without dismounting from Dapple, whom he dared not desert lest some mischief should befall him.

Scarcely had they taken their stand in a line with several of their servants, when they saw a huge boar, closely pressed by the hounds and followed by the huntsmen, making towards them, grinding his teeth and tusks, and scattering foam from his mouth. As soon as he saw him Don Quixote, bracing his shield on his arm, and drawing his sword, advanced to meet him; the duke with boar-spear did the same; but the duchess would have gone in front of them all had not the duke prevented her. Sancho alone, deserting Dapple at the sight of the mighty beast, took to his heels as hard as he could and strove in vain to mount a tall oak. As he was clinging to a branch, however, halfway up in his struggle to reach the top, the bough, such was his ill-luck and hard fate, gave way, and caught in his fall by a broken limb of the oak, he hung suspended in the air unable to reach the ground. Finding himself in this position, and that the green coat was beginning to tear, and reflecting that if the fierce animal came that way he might be able to get at him, he began to utter such cries, and call for help so earnestly, that all who heard him and did not see him felt sure he must be in the teeth of some wild beast.

In the end the tusked boar fell pierced by the blades of the many spears they held in front of him; and Don Quixote, turning round at the cries of Sancho, for he knew by them that it was he, saw him hanging from the oak head downwards, with Dapple, who did not forsake him in his distress, close beside him. Don Quixote went over and unhooked Sancho, who, as soon as he found himself on the ground, looked at the rent in his hunting coat and was grieved to the heart, for he thought he had got a patrimonial estate in that suit.

Meanwhile they had slung the mighty boar across the back of a mule, and having covered it with sprigs of rosemary and branches of myrtle, they bore it away as the spoils of victory to some large field tents which had been pitched in the middle of the wood, where they found the tables laid and dinner served, in such grand and sumptuous style that it was easy to see the rank and magnificence of those who had provided it. Sancho, as he showed the rents in his torn suit to the duchess, observed, "If we had been hunting hares, or after small birds, my coat would have been safe from being in the plight it's in; I don't know what pleasure one can find in lying in wait for an animal that may take your life with his tusk if he gets at you. And I would not have kings and princes expose themselves to such dangers for the sake of a pleasure which, to my mind, ought not to be one, as it consists in killing an animal that has done no harm whatever."

"Quite the contrary, Sancho. You are wrong there," said the duke; "for hunting is more suitable and requisite for kings and princes than for anybody else. The chase is the emblem of war; it has stratagems, wiles, and crafty devices for overcoming the enemy in safety; in it extreme cold and intolerable heat have to be borne, indolence and sleep are despised, the bodily powers are invigorated, the limbs of him who engages in it are made supple, and, in a word, it is a pursuit which may be followed without injury to anyone and with enjoyment to many; and the best of it is, it is not for everybody, as field sports of other sorts are, except hawking, which also is only for kings and great lords. Reconsider your opinion therefore, Sancho, and when you are governor take to hunting, and you will find the good of it."

"Nay," said Sancho, "the good governor should have a broken leg and keep at home. It would be a nice thing if, after people had been at the trouble of coming to look for him on business, the governor were to be away in the forest enjoying himself; the government would go on badly in that fashion. By my faith, señor, hunting and amusements are more fit for idlers than for governors; for these huntings don't suit my condition or agree with my conscience."

"God grant it may turn out so," said the duke, "because it's a long step from saying to doing."

"Be that as it may," said Sancho, " 'pledges don't distress a good payer,' and 'he whom God helps does better than he who gets up early.' I mean to say that if God gives me help and I do my duty honestly, no doubt I'll govern better than a gerfalcon. Nay, let them only put a finger in my mouth, and they'll see whether I can bite or not."

"The curse of God and all his saints upon thee, thou accursed Sancho!" exclaimed Don Quixote. "When will the day come—as I have often said to thee—when I shall hear thee make one single coherent, rational remark without proverbs? Pray, your highnesses, leave this fool alone, for he will grind

252

your souls between, not to say two, but two thousand proverbs, dragged in as much in season, and as much to the purpose as—may God grant as much health to him, or to me if I want to listen to them!"

"Sancho Panza's proverbs," said the duchess, "are not less to be esteemed for the conciseness of the maxims. For my own part, I can say they give me more pleasure than others that may be more seasonably introduced."

In pleasant conversation of this sort they passed out of the tent into the wood, and the day was spent in visiting some of the posts and hiding-places, and then night closed in, not, however, as brilliantly or tranquilly as might have been expected at the season, for it was then midsummer; but bringing with it a kind of haze that greatly aided the project of the duke and duchess. And thus, as night began to fall, and a little after twilight set in, suddenly the whole wood on all four sides seemed to be on fire, and shortly after, here, there, on all sides, a vast number of trumpets and other military instruments were heard, as if several troops of cavalry were passing through the wood. The blaze of the fire and the noise of the warlike instruments almost blinded the eyes and deafened the ears of those that stood by, and indeed of all who were in the wood; trumpets and clarions brayed, drums beat, fifes played, so unceasingly and so fast that he could not have had any senses who did not lose them with the confused din of so many instruments. The duke was astounded, the duchess amazed, Don Quixote wondering, Sancho Panza trembling, and indeed, even they who were aware of the cause were frightened. In their fear, silence fell upon them, and a postilion, in the guise of a demon, passed in front of them, blowing, in lieu of a bugle, a hugh hollow horn that gave out a horrible hoarse note.

"Ho there! Brother courier," cried the duke, "who are you? Where are you going? What troops are these that seem to be passing through the wood?"

To which the courier replied in a harsh, discordant voice, "I am the devil; I am in search of Don Quixote of La Mancha; those who are coming this way are six troops of enchanters, who are bringing on a triumphal car the peerless Dulcinea del Toboso; she comes under enchantment, together with the gallant Frenchman Montesinos, to give instructions to Don Quixote as to how she, the said lady, may be disenchanted."

"If you were the devil, as you say and as your appearance indicates," said the duke, "you would have known the said knight Don Quixote of La Mancha, for you have him here before you."

"By God and upon my conscience," said the devil, "I never observed it, for my mind is occupied with so many different things that I was forgetting the main thing I came about."

"This demon must be an honest fellow and a good Christian," said Sancho; "for if he wasn't he wouldn't swear by God and his conscience; I feel sure now there must be good souls even in hell itself."

Without dismounting, the demon then turned to Don Quixote and said, "The unfortunate but valiant knight Montesinos sends me to thee, the Knight of the Lions (would that I saw thee in their claws), bidding me tell thee to wait for him wherever I may find thee, as he brings with him her whom they call Dulcinea del Toboso, that he may show thee what is needful in order to disenchant her; and as I came for no more I need stay no longer; demons of my sort be with thee, and good angels with these gentles"; and so saying he blew his huge horn, turned about and went off without waiting for a reply from anyone.

They all felt fresh wonder, but particularly Sancho and Don Quixote; Sancho to see how, in defiance of the truth, they would have it that Dulcinea was enchanted; Don Quixote because he could not feel sure whether what had happened to him in the cave of Montesinos was true or not; and as he was deep in these cogitations the duke said to him, "Do you mean to wait, Señor Don Quixote?"

"Why not?" replied he. "Here will I wait, fearless and firm, though all hell should come to attack me."

Night now closed in more completely, and many lights began to flit through the wood, just as those fiery exhalations from the earth, that look like shooting stars to our eyes, flit through the heavens; a frightful noise, too, was heard, like that made by the solid wheels the ox carts usually have, by the harsh, ceaseless creaking of which, they say, the bears and wolves are put to flight. In addition to all this commotion, there came a further disturbance to increase the tumult, for now it seemed as if in truth, on all four sides of the wood, four encounters or battles were going on at the same time; in one quarter resounded the dull noise of a terrible cannonade, in another numberless muskets were being discharged, the shouts of the combatants sounded almost close at hand.

In a word, the bugles, the horns, the clarions, the trumpets, the drums, the cannon, the musketry, and above all the tremendous noise of the carts, all made up together a din so confused and terrific that Don Quixote had need to summon up all his courage to brave it; but Sancho's gave way, and he fell fainting on the skirt of the duchess's robe, who let him lie there and promptly bade them throw water in his face. This was done, and he came to himself by the time one of the carts with the creaking wheels reached the spot. It was drawn by four plodding oxen all covered wth black housings; on each horn they had fixed a large lighted wax taper, and on the top of the cart was constructed a raised seat, on which sat a venerable old man with a beard whiter than the very snow, and so long that it fell below his waist. He was dressed in a long robe of black buckram; for as the cart was thickly set with a multitude of candles it was easy to make out everything that was on it. Leading it were two hideous demons, also clad in buckram, with countenances so frightful that Sancho, having once seen them, shut his eyes so as not to see them again. As soon as the cart came opposite the spot the old man rose from his lofty seat, and standing up said in a loud voice, "I am the sage Lirgandeo," and without another word the cart then passed on. Behind it came another of the same form, with another aged man enthroned, who, stopping the cart, said in a voice no less solemn than that of the first, "I am the sage Alquife, the great friend of Urganda the Unknown," and passed on. Then another cart came by at the same pace, but the occupant of the throne was not old like the others, but a man stalwart and robust, and of a forbidding countenance, who as he came up said in a voice far hoarser and more devilish, "I am the enchanter Archelaus, the mortal enemy of Amadis of Gaul and all his kindred," and then passed on. Having gone a short distance the three carts halted and the monotonous noise of their wheels ceased, and soon after they heard another, not noise, but sound of sweet, harmonious music, of which Sancho was very glad, taking it to be a good sign; and said he to the duchess, from whom he did not stir a step, for a single instant, "Señora, where there's music there can't be mischief."

"Nor where there are lights and it is bright," said the duchess.

"That remains to be seen," said Don Quixote, who was listening to all.

They saw advancing towards them, to the sound of this pleasing music, what they call a triumphal car, drawn by six gray mules with white linen housings, on each of which was mounted a penitent, robed also in white, with a large lighted wax taper in his hand. The car was, perhaps, three times as large as the former ones, and in front and on the sides stood twelve more penitents, all as white as snow and all with lighted tapers, a spectacle to excite fear as well as wonder; and on a raised throne was seated a nymph draped in a multitude of silver-tissue veils with an embroidery of countless gold spangles glitter-

255

ing all over them, that made her appear, if not richly, at least brilliantly, apparelled. She had her face covered with thin transparent sendal, the texture of which did not prevent the fair features of a maiden from being distinguished, while the numerous lights made it possible to judge of her beauty and of her years, which seemed to be not less than seventeen but not to have yet reached twenty. Beside her was a figure in a robe of state, as they call it, reaching to the feet, while the head was covered with a black veil. But the instant the car was opposite the duke and duchess and Don Quixote the music of the clarions ceased, and then that of the lutes and harps on the car. And the figure in the robe rose up, and flinging it apart and removing the veil from its face, disclosed to their eyes the shape of Death itself, fleshless and hideous, at which sight Don Quixote felt uneasy, Sancho frightened, and the duke and duchess displayed a certain trepidation. Having risen to its feet, this living death, in a sleepy voice and with a tongue hardly awake, held forth as follows:

> "I am that Merlin who the legends say
> The devil had for father, and the lie
> Hath gathered credence with the lapse of time.
> Of magic prince, of Zoroastric lore
> Monarch and treasurer, with jealous eye
> I view the efforts of the age to hide
> The gallant deeds of doughty errant knights,
> Who are, and ever have been, dear to me.
>
> "Enchanters and magicians and their kind
> Are mostly hard of heart; not so am I;
> For mine is tender, soft, compassionate,
> And its delight is doing good to all.
> In the dim caverns of the gloomy Dis,
> Where, tracing mystic lines and characters,
> My soul abideth now, there came to me
> The sorrow-laden plaint of her, the fair,
> The peerless Dulcinea del Toboso.
> I knew of her enchantment and her fate,
> From high-born dame to peasant wench transformed;
> And touched with pity, first I turned the leaves
> Of countless volumes of my devilish craft,

256

And then, in this grim grisly skeleton
Myself encasing, hither have I come
To show where lies the fitting remedy
To give relief in such a piteous case.

"O thou, the pride and pink of all that wear
The adamantine steel! O shining light,
O beacon, polestar, path and guide of all
Who, scorning slumber and the lazy down,
Adopt the toilsome life of bloodstained arms!
To thee, great hero who all praise transcends,
La Mancha's luster and Iberia's star,
Don Quixote, wise as grave, to thee I say—
For peerless Dulcinea del Toboso
Her pristine form and beauty to regain,
'Tis needful that thy esquire Sancho shall,
On his own sturdy buttocks bared to heaven,
Three thousand and three hundred lashes lay,
And that they smart and sting and hurt him well.
Thus have the authors of her woe resolved.
And this is, gentles, wherefore I have come."

"By all that's good," exclaimed Sancho at this, "I'll just as soon give myself three stabs with a dagger as three, not to say three thousand, lashes. The devil take such a way of disenchanting! I don't see what my backside has got to do with enchantments. By God, if Señor Merlin has not found out some other way of disenchanting the lady Dulcinea del Toboso, she may go to her grave enchanted."

"But I'll take you, Don Clown stuffed with garlic," said Don Quixote, "and tie you to a tree and give you, not three thousand three hundred, but six thousand six hundred lashes, and so well laid on that they won't be got rid of if you try three thousand three hundred times; don't answer me a word or I'll tear your soul out."

On hearing this Merlin said, "That will not do, for the lashes worthy Sancho has to receive must be given of his own free will and not by force, and at whatever time he please, for there is no fixed limit assigned to him; but it is permitted him, if he likes to commute by half the pain of this whipping, to let them be given by the hand of another, though it may be somewhat weighty."

"Not a hand, my own or anybody else's, weighty or weighable, shall touch me," said Sancho. "Was it I that gave birth to the lady Dulcinea del Toboso, that my backside is to pay for the sins of her eyes? My master, indeed, that's a part of her—for he's always calling her 'my life' and 'my soul,' and his stay and prop—may and ought to whip himself for her and take all the trouble required for her disenchantment. But for me to whip myself! Abernuncio!"

"Well then, the fact is, friend Sancho," said the duke, "that unless you become softer than a ripe fig, you shall not get hold of the government. It would be a nice thing for me to send my islanders a cruel governor who won't yield to the tears of afflicted damsels or to the prayers of wise, magisterial, ancient enchanters and sages. In short, Sancho, either you must be whipped by yourself, or they must whip you, or you shan't be governor."

"Señor," said Sancho, "won't two days' grace be given me in which to consider what is best for me?"

"No, certainly not," said Merlin. "Here, this minute, and on the spot, the matter must be settled; either Dulcinea will return to the cave of Montesinos and to her former condition of peasant wench, or else in her present form shall be carried to the Elysian fields, where she will remain waiting until the number of stripes is completed."

"Now then, Sancho!" said the duchess, "show courage, and gratitude for your master Don Quixote's bread that you have eaten; we are all bound to oblige and please him for his benevolent disposition and lofty chivalry. Consent to this whipping, my son; to the devil with the devil, and leave fear to milksops, for 'a stout heart breaks bad luck,' as you very well know."

To this Sancho replied with an irrelevant remark, which, addressing Merlin, he made to him, "Will your worship tell me, Señor Merlin—when that courier devil came up he gave my master a message from Señor Montesinos, charging him to wait for him here, as he was coming to arrange how the lady Doña Dulcinea del Toboso was to be disenchanted; but up to the present we have not seen Montesinos, nor anything like him."

To which Merlin made answer, "The devil, Sancho, is a blockhead and a great scoundrel; I sent him to look for your master, but not with a message from Montesinos but from myself; for Montesinos is in his cave expecting, or more properly speaking, waiting for his disenchantment; for there's the tail to be skinned yet for him; if he owes you anything, or you have any business to transact with him, I'll bring him to you and put him where you choose; but for the present make up your mind to consent to this penance, and believe me it will be very good for you, for soul as well for body—for your soul because of the charity with which you perform it, for your body because I know that you are of a sanguine habit and it will do you no harm to draw a little blood."

"There are a great many doctors in the world; even the enchanters are doctors," said Sancho. "However, as everybody tells me the same thing—though I can't see it myself—I say I am willing to give myself the three thousand three hundred lashes, provided I am to lay them on whenever I like, without any fixing of days or times; and I'll try and get out of debt as quickly as I can, that the world may enjoy the beauty of the lady Dulcinea del Toboso; as it seems, contrary to what I thought, that she is beautiful after all. It must be a condition, too, that I am not to be bound to draw blood with the scourge, and that if any of the lashes happen to be fly-flappers they are to count. Item, that, in case I should make any mistake in the reckoning, Señor Merlin, as he knows everything, is to keep count, and let me know how many are still wanting or over the number."

"There will be no need to let you know of any over," said Merlin, "because, when you reach the full number, the lady Dulcinea will at once, and that very instant, be disenchanted, and will come in her gratitude to seek out the worthy Sancho, and thank him, and even reward him for the good work. So you have no cause to be uneasy about stripes too many or too few; heaven forbid I should cheat anyone of even a hair of his head."

"Well then, in God's hands be it," said Sancho; "in the hard case I'm in I give in; I say I accept the penance on the conditions laid down."

The instant Sancho uttered these last words the music of the clarions struck up once more, and again a host of muskets were discharged, and Don Quixote hung on Sancho's neck kissing him again and again on the forehead and cheeks. The duchess and the duke expressed the greatest satisfaction, and the car began to move on.

And now bright smiling dawn came on apace; the flowers of the field, revived, raised up their heads, and the crystal waters of the brooks, murmuring over the gray and white pebbles, hastened to pay their tribute to the expectant rivers; the glad earth, the unclouded sky, the fresh breeze, the clear light, each and all showed that the day that came treading on the skirts of morning would be calm and bright. The duke and duchess, pleased with their hunt and at having carried out their plans so cleverly and successfully, returned to their castle resolved to follow up their joke; for to them there was no reality that could afford them more amusement.

CHAPTER 17

The Distressed Duenna

THE ENTIRE COMPANY betook themselves to a garden where they broke their fast, and after the cloth had been removed and they had amused themselves for a while with Sancho's rich conversation, the melancholy sound of a fife and harsh discordant drum made itself heard. All seemed somewhat put out by this dull, confused, martial harmony, especially Don Quixote, who could not keep his seat from pure disquietude. As to Sancho, it is needless to say that fear drove him to his usual refuge, the side or the skirts of the duchess; and indeed and in truth the sound they heard was a most doleful and melancholy one. While they were still in uncertainty they saw advancing towards them through the garden two men clad in mourning robes so long and flowing that they trailed upon the ground. As they marched they beat two great drums which were likewise draped in black, and beside them came the fife player, black and somber like the others. Following these came a personage of gigantic stature enveloped rather than clad in a gown of the deepest black, the skirt of which was of prodigious dimensions. With measured pace he advanced to kneel before the duke, who, with the others, awaited him standing. The duke, however, would not on any account allow him to speak until he had risen. The prodigious scarecrow obeyed, and standing up, removed the veil from his face and disclosed the most enormous, the longest, the whitest and the thickest beard that human eyes had ever beheld until that moment, and then fetching up a grave, sonorous voice from the depths of his broad, capacious chest, and fixing his eyes on the duke, he said:

260

"Most high and mighty señor, my name is Trifaldin of the White Beard; I am squire to the Countess Trifaldi, otherwise called the Distressed Duenna, on whose behalf I bear a message to your highness, which is that your magnificence will be pleased to grant her permission to come and tell you her trouble, which is one of the strangest and most wonderful that the mind could imagine; but first she desires to know if the valiant and never vanquished knight, Don Quixote of La Mancha, is in this your castle, for she has come in quest of him on foot and without breaking her fast from the kingdom of Kandy to your realms here; a thing which ought to be regarded as a miracle or set down to enchantment; she is even now at the gate of this fortress, and only waits for your permission to enter. I have spoken." And with that he coughed, and stroked down his beard with both his hands, and stood very tranquilly waiting for the response of the duke, which was to this effect: "Many days ago, worthy squire Trifaldin of the White Beard, we heard of the misfortune of my lady the Countess Trifaldi, whom the enchanters have caused to be called the Distressed Duenna. Bid her enter, O stupendous squire, and tell her that the valiant knight Don Quixote of La Mancha is here, and from his generous disposition she may safely promise herself every protection and assistance."

On hearing this Trifaldin bent the knee to the ground, and making a sign to the fifer and drummers to strike up, he turned and marched out of the garden to the same notes and at the same pace as when he entered, leaving them all amazed at his bearing and solemnity. Turning to Don Quixote, the duke said, "After all, renowned knight, the mists of malice and ignorance are unable to hide or obscure the light of valor and virtue. I say so, because your excellence has been barely six days in this castle, and already the unhappy and the afflicted come in quest of you from lands far distant and remote."

"I wish, señor duke," replied Don Quixote, "that blessed ecclesiastic, who at table the other day showed such ill-will and bitter spite against knights-errant, were here now to see with his own eyes whether knights of the sort are needed in the world. Let this duenna come and ask what she will, for I will effect her relief by the might of my arm and the dauntless resolution of my bold heart."

They heard the notes of the fife and drums once more, from which they concluded that the Distressed Duenna was making her entrance. The duchess asked the duke if it would be proper to go out to receive her, as she was a countess and a person of rank.

261

"In respect of her being a countess," said Sancho, before the duke could reply, "I am for your highnesses going out to receive her; but in respect of her being a duenna, it is my opinion you should not stir a step."

"Who bade thee meddle in this, Sancho?" said Don Quixote.

"Who, señor?" said Sancho. "I meddle for I have a right to meddle, as a squire who has learned the rules of courtesy in the school of your worship, the most courteous and best-bred knight in the whole world of courtliness."

Following the melancholy musicians there filed into the garden as many as twelve duennas, in two lines, all dressed in ample mourning robes apparently of milled serge, with hoods of fine white gauze so long that they allowed only the border of the robe to be seen. Behind them came the Countess Trifaldi, the squire Trifaldin of the White Beard leading her by the hand.

The twelve duennas and the lady came on at procession pace, their faces being covered with black veils, not transparent ones like Trifaldin's, but so close that they allowed nothing to be seen through them. As soon as the band of duennas was fully in sight, the duke, the duchess, and Don Quixote stood up, as well as all who were watching the slow-moving procession. The twelve duennas halted and formed a lane, along which the Distressed One advanced, Trifaldin still holding her hand. On seeing this the duke, the duchess, and Don Quixote went some twelve paces forward to meet her. She then, kneeling on the ground, said in a voice hoarse and rough, rather than fine and delicate, "May it please your highnesses not to offer such courtesies to this your servant, I should say to this your handmaid, for I am in such distress that I shall never be able to make a proper return, because my strange and unparalleled misfortune has carried off my wits, and I know not whither; but it must be a long way off, for the more I look for them the less I find them."

"He would be wanting in wits, señora countess," said the duke, "who did not perceive your worth by your person, for at a glance it may be seen it deserves all the cream of courtesy and flower of polite usage." And raising her up by the hand he led her to a seat beside the duchess, who likewise received her with great urbanity.

All kept still, waiting to see who would break silence, which the Distressed Duenna did in these words: "I would fain be enlightened, most mighty lord, most fair lady, and most discreet company, whether there be present in this society, circle, or company, that knight immaculatissimus, Don Quixote de la Manchissima, and his squirissimus Panza."

"The Panza is here," said Sancho, before anyone could reply, "and Don Quixotissimus too; and so, most distressedest Duenissima, you may say what you willissimus, for we are all readissimus to do you any servissimus."

On this Don Quixote rose, and addressing the Distressed Duenna, said, "If your sorrows, afflicted lady, can indulge in any hope of relief from the valor or might of any knight-errant, here are mine, which, feeble and limited though they be, shall be entirely devoted to your service. I am Don Quixote of La Mancha."

The duke and duchess, as it was they who had plotted this adventure, were ready to burst with laughter at all this, and between themselves they commended the clever acting of the Trifaldi, who, returning to her seat, said, "Queen Doña Maguncia reigned over the famous kingdom of Kandy, which lies between the great Trapobana and the Southern Sea. She was the widow of King Archipiela, and of their marriage they had issue the Princess Antonomasia, heiress of the kingdom; which Princess Antonomasia was reared and brought up under my care and direction, I being the oldest and highest in rank of her mother's duennas. Time passed, and the young Antonomasia reached the age of fourteen, and such a perfection of beauty, that nature could not raise it higher. Of this beauty, countless princes were enamored, and among them a private gentleman, who was at the court, dared to raise his thoughts to the heaven of so great beauty, trusting to his youth, his gallant bearing, his numerous accomplishments and graces, and his quickness and readiness of wit; for I may tell your highnesses, if I am not wearying you, that he played the guitar so as to make it speak, and he was, besides, a poet and a great dancer, and he could make birdcages so well that by making them alone he might have gained a livelihood, had he found himself reduced to utter poverty; and gifts and graces of this kind are enough to bring down a mountain, not to say a tender young girl. But all his gallantry, wit, and gaiety, all his graces and accomplishments, would have been of no avail, had not the impudent thief taken the precaution of gaining me over first. First, the heartless vagabond sought to win my good will and purchase my compliance, so as to get me, like a treacherous warder, to deliver up to him the keys of the fortress I had in charge. In a word, he gained an influence over my mind, and overcame my resolutions with I know not what trinkets and jewels he gave me; but it was some verses I heard him singing one night from a grating that opened on the street where he lived, that, more than anything else, made me give way and led to my fall; and if I remember rightly they ran thus:

263

> From that sweet enemy of mine
>> My bleeding heart hath had its wound;
>> And to increase the pain I'm bound
> To suffer and to make no sign.

—and other verses and burdens of the same sort, such as enchant when sung and fascinate when written.

"Had I but been the faithful duenna I should have been, his stale conceits would have never moved me. Woe is me, hapless that I am! It was not verses that conquered me, but my own simplicity; it was not music made me yield, but my own imprudence; my own great ignorance and little caution opened the way and cleared the path for Don Clavijo's advances, for that was the name of the gentleman I have referred to. But there was one hitch in this case, which was that of inequality of rank, Don Clavijo being a private gentleman, and the Princess Antonomasia, as I said, heiress to the kingdom. The entanglement remained for some time a secret, kept hidden by my cunning precautions, until Don Clavijo demanded Antonomasia as his wife before the Vicar, in virtue of an agreement to marry him made by the princess. The necessary steps were taken; the Vicar saw the agreement, and gave his decision in favor of Don Clavijo, and she was delivered over to him as his lawful wife. But the Queen Doña Maguncia, the Princess Antonomasia's mother, so took it to heart that within the space of three days we buried her."

"She died, no doubt," said Sancho.

"Of course," said Trifaldin. "They don't bury living people in Kandy, only the dead."

"Señor Squire," said Sancho, "a man in a swoon has been known to be buried before now, in the belief that he was dead; and it struck me that Queen Maguncia ought to have swooned rather than died; because with life a great many things come right."

"Let señora the Distressed One proceed, Sancho," said Don Quixote, "for I suspect she has got yet to tell us the bitter part of this so far sweet story."

"The bitter is indeed to come," said the countess. "The queen, then, being dead, we buried her; and hardly had we covered her with earth, hardly had we said our last farewells, when over the queen's grave there appeared, mounted upon a wooden horse, the giant Malambruno, Maguncia's first cousin, who besides being cruel is an enchanter; and he, to revenge the death of his cousin, punish the audacity of Don Clavijo, and in wrath at the contumacy of Antonomasia, left them both enchanted by his art on the grave itself; she being changed into an ape of brass, and he into a horrible crocodile of some unknown metal; while between the two there stands a pillar, also of metal, inscribed with the following sentence: 'These two rash lovers shall not recover their former shape until the valiant Manchegan comes to do battle with me in single combat; for the Fates reserve this unexampled adventure for his mighty valor alone.'

"This done, he drew from its sheath a huge broad scimitar, and seizing me by the hair he made as though he meant to cut my throat and shear my head clean off. I was terror-stricken, my voice stuck in my throat, and I was in the deepest distress; nevertheless I summoned up my strength as well as I could, and in a trembling and piteous voice I addressed such words to him as induced him to stay the infliction of a punishment so severe. He then caused all the duennas of the palace, those that are here present, to be brought before him; and after having dwelt upon the enormity of our offense, and denounced duennas, their characters, their evil ways and worse intrigues, laying to the charge of all what I alone was guilty of, he said he would not visit us with capital punishment, but with others of a slow nature which would be, in effect, civil death forever; and the very instant he ceased speaking we all felt the pores of our faces opening, and pricking us, as if with the points of needles. We at once put our hands up to our faces and found ourselves in the state you now see."

Here the Distressed One and the other duennas raised the veils with which they were covered, and disclosed countenances all bristling with beards, some red, some black, some white, and some grizzled, at which spectacle the duke and duchess made a show of being filled with wonder. Don Quixote and Sancho were overwhelmed with amazement, and the bystanders lost in astonishment, while the Trifaldi went on to say: "Thus did that malevolent villain Malambruno punish us, covering the tenderness and softness of our faces with these rough bristles! Would to heaven that he had swept off our heads with his enormous scimitar instead of obscuring the light of our countenances with these wool-combings that cover us!"

And as she said this she showed signs of being about to faint.

CHAPTER 18

The Flying Horse

WHEN SANCHO SAW the Distressed One faint he exclaimed: "I swear by the faith of an honest man and the shades of all my ancestors the Panzas, that never I did see or hear of, nor has my master related or conceived in his mind, such an adventure as this. A thousand devils—not to curse thee—take thee, Malambruno, for an enchanter and a giant! Couldst thou find no other sort of punishment for these sinners but bearding them? Would it not have been better—it would have been better for them—to have taken off half their noses from the middle upwards, even though they'd have snuffled when they spoke, than to have put beards on them? I'll bet they have not the means of paying anybody to shave them."

"That is the truth, señor," said one of the twelve. "We have not the money to get ourselves shaved, and if we are not relieved by Señor Don Quixote we shall be carried to our graves with beards."

"I will pluck out my own in the land of the Moors," said Don Quixote, "if I don't cure yours."

At this instant the Trifaldi recovered from her swoon and said, "The chink of that promise, valiant knight, reached my ears in the midst of my swoon, and has been the means of reviving me and bringing back my senses; and so once more I implore you, illustrious, indomitable sir, to let your gracious promises be turned into deeds."

"There shall be no delay on my part," said Don Quixote. "Bethink you, señora, of what I must do, for my heart is most eager to serve you."

"The fact is," replied the Distressed One, "it is five thousand leagues, a

266

couple more or less from this to the kingdom of Kandy, if you go by land; but if you go through the air and in a straight line, it is three thousand two hundred and twenty-seven. You must know, too, that Malambruno told me that, whenever fate provided the knight our deliverer, he himself would send him a steed far better and with less tricks than a post-horse; which said horse is guided by a peg he has in his forehead that serves for a bridle, and flies through the air with such rapidity that you would fancy the very devils were carrying him. This horse, according to ancient tradition, was made by Merlin. Malambruno stole him by his magic art, and he has him now in his possession, and makes use of him in his journeys which he constantly makes through different parts of the world; he is here today, tomorrow in France, and the next day in Potosi; and the best of it is the said horse neither eats nor sleeps nor wears out shoes, and goes at an ambling pace through the air without wings, so that he whom he has mounted upon him can carry a cup full of water in his hand without spilling a drop, so smoothly and easily does he go."

"For going smoothly and easily," said Sancho at this, "give me my Dapple, though he can't go through the air; but on the ground I'll back him against all the amblers in the world."

They all laughed, and the Distressed One continued, "And this same horse, if so be that Malambruno is disposed to put an end to our sufferings, will be here before us ere the night shall have advanced half an hour; for he announced to me that the sign he would give me whereby I might know that I had found the knight I was in quest of, would be to send me the horse wherever he might be, speedily and promptly."

"And how many is there room for on this horse?" asked Sancho.

"Two," said the Distressed One, "one in the saddle, and the other on the croup; and generally these two are knight and squire, when there is no damsel that's being carried off."

"I'd like to know, Señora Distressed One," said Sancho, "what is the name of this horse?"

"His name," said the Distressed One, "is Clavileño the Swift, which name is in accordance with his being made of wood, with the peg he has in his forehead, and with the swift pace at which he travels; and so, as far as name goes, he may compare with the famous Rocinante."

"I have nothing to say against his name," said Sancho, "but with what sort of bridle or halter is he managed?"

"I have said already," said the Trifaldi, "that it is with a peg, by turning which to one side or the other the knight who rides him makes him go as he pleases, either through the upper air, or skimming and almost sweeping the earth, or else in that middle course that is sought and followed in all well-regulated proceedings."

"I'd like to see him," said Sancho, "but to fancy I'm going to mount him, either in the saddle or on the croup, is to ask pears of the elm tree. A good joke indeed! I can hardly keep my seat upon Dapple, and on a pack-saddle softer than silk itself, and here they'd have me hold on upon haunches of plank without pad or cushion of any sort! Gad, I have no notion of bruising myself to get rid of anyone's beard; let each one shave himself as best he can; I'm not going to accompany my master on any such long journey; besides, I can't give such help to the shaving of these beards as I can to the disenchantment of my lady Dulcinea."

"Yes, you can, my friend," replied the Trifaldi, "and so much, that without you, so I understand, we shall be able to do nothing."

"In the king's name!" exclaimed Sancho, "what have squires got to do with the adventures of their masters? Are they to have the fame of such as they go through, and we the labor? Body o' me! If the historians would only say, 'Such and such a knight finished such and such an adventure, but with the help of so and so, his squire, without which it would have been impossible for him to accomplish it.' But they write curtly, "Don Paralipomenon of the Three Stars accomplished the adventure of the six monsters'; without mentioning such a person as his squire, who was there all the time, just as if there was no such being. Once more, sirs, I say my master may go alone, and much good may it do him; and I'll stay here in the company of my lady the duchess."

"For all that, you must go if it be necessary, my good Sancho," said the duchess, "for they are worthy folk who ask you; and the faces of these ladies must not remain overgrown in this way because of your idle fears; that would be a hard case indeed."

"In the king's name, once more!" said Sancho. "If this charitable work were to be done for the sake of damsels imprisoned or charity girls, a man might expose himself to some hardships; but to bear it for the sake of stripping beards off duennas! Devil take it! I'd sooner see them all bearded, from the highest to the lowest, and from the most prudish to the most affected."

"You are very hard on duennas, Sancho my friend," said the duchess. "But indeed you are wrong; there are duennas in my house that may serve as patterns of duennas; and here is my Doña Rodriguez, who will not allow me to say otherwise."

"Your excellence may say it if you like," said the Rodriguez, "for God knows the truth of everything; and whether we duennas are good or bad, bearded or smooth, we are our mothers' daughters like other women; and as God sent us into the world, he knows why he did, and on his mercy I rely, and not on anybody's beard."

"Well, Señora Rodriguez, Señora Trifaldi, and present company," said Don Quixote, "I trust in Heaven that it will look with kindly eyes upon your troubles, for Sancho will do as I bid him. Only let Clavileño come and let me find myself face to face with Malambruno, and I am certain no razor will shave you more easily than my sword shall shave Malambruno's head off his shoulders; for 'God bears with the wicked, but not forever.' "

"Ah!" exclaimed the Distressed One at this, "may all the stars of the celestial regions look down upon your greatness with benign eyes, valiant knight, that your heart may be the shield and safeguard of the abused and downtrodden race of duennas, detested by apothecaries, sneered at by squires, and made game of by pages. Ill betide the jade that in the flower of her youth would not sooner become a nun than a duenna! Unfortunate beings that we are, we duennas! Though we may be descended in the direct male line from Hector of Troy himself, our mistresses never fail to address us as 'you' if they think it makes queens of them. O giant Malambruno, though thou art an enchanter, thou art true to thy promises. Send us now the peerless Clavileño, that our misfortune may be brought to an end; for if the hot weather sets in and these beards of ours are still there, alas for our lot!"

The Trifaldi said this in such a pathetic way that she drew tears from the eyes of all and even Sancho's filled up; and he resolved in his heart to accompany his master to the uttermost ends of the earth, if so be the removal of the wool from those venerable countenances depended upon it.

When night came, it was time for the arrival of the famous horse Clavileño, the non-appearance of which was already beginning to make Don Quixote uneasy. It struck him that, as Malambruno was so long about sending it, either he himself was not the knight for whom the adventure was reserved, or else Malambruno did not dare to meet him in single combat. But lo! suddenly there came into the garden four wild-men all clad in green ivy bearing on their shoulders a great wooden horse. They placed it on its feet on the ground, and one of the wild-men said, "Let the knight who has heart for it mount this machine."

Here Sancho exclaimed, "I don't mount, for neither have I the heart nor am I a knight."

"And let the squire, if he has one," continued the wild-man, "take his seat on the croup, and let him trust the valiant Malambruno; for by no sword save his, nor by the malice of any other, shall he be assailed. It is but to turn this peg the horse has in his neck, and he will bear them through the air to where Malambruno awaits them; but lest the vast elevation of their course should make them giddy, their eyes must be covered until the horse neighs, which will be the sign of their having completed their journey."

With these words, leaving Clavileño behind them, they retired with easy dignity the way they came. As soon as the Distressed One saw the horse, almost in tears she exclaimed to Don Quixote, "Valiant knight, the promise of Malambruno has proved trustworthy. The horse has come, our beards are growing, and by every hair in them all of us implore thee to shave and shear us, as it is only mounting him with thy squire and making a happy beginning with your new journey."

"That I will, Señora Countess Trifaldi," said Don Quixote, "most gladly and with right good will, without stopping to take a cushion or put on my spurs, so as not to lose time, such is my desire to see you and all these duennas shaved clean."

"That I won't," said Sancho, "with good will or bad will, or any way at all; and if this shaving can't be done without my mounting on the croup, my master had better look out for another squire to go with him. I'm no witch to have a taste for traveling through the air. What would my islanders say when they heard their governor was going strolling about on the winds? And another thing, as it is three thousand and odd leagues from this to Kandy, if the horse tires, or the giant takes huff, we'll be half a dozen years getting back, and there won't be isle or island in the world that will know me."

"Friend Sancho," said the duke at this, "the island that I have promised you is not a moving one, or one that will run away. You know as well as I do that there is no sort of office of any importance that is not obtained by a bribe of some kind, great or small; well then, that which I look to receive for this government is that you go with your master Don Quixote, and bring this memorable adventure to a conclusion. You will always find your island on your return where you left it, and your islanders with the same eagerness they have always had to receive you as their governor, and my good will will remain the same; doubt not the truth of this, Señor Sancho, for that would be grievously wronging my disposition to serve you."

"Say no more, señor," said Sancho. "Let my master mount; bandage my eyes and commit me to God's care, and tell me if I may commend myself to our Lord or call upon the angels to protect me when we go towering up there."

To this the Trifaldi made answer, "Sancho, you may freely commend yourself to God or whom you will; for Malambruno though an enchanter is a Christian."

"Well then," said Sancho, "God and the most holy Trinity of Gaeta give me help!"

"Since the memorable adventure of the fulling mills," said Don Quixote, "I have never seen Sancho in such a fright as now. Were I as superstitious as others his abject fear would cause me some little trepidation of spirit. But come here, Sancho, for with the leave of these gentles I would say a word or two to thee in private"; and drawing Sancho aside among the trees of the garden and seizing both his hands he said, "Thou seest, brother Sancho, the long journey we have before us, and God knows when we shall return, or what leisure or opportunities this business will allow us; I wish thee therefore to retire now to thy chamber, as though thou wert going to fetch something required for the road, and in a trice give thyself if it be only five hundred lashes on account of the three thousand three hundred to which thou art bound; it will be all to the good, and to make a beginning with a thing is to have it half finished."

"By God," said Sancho, "but your worship must be out of your senses! Just as I'm about to go sitting on a bare board, your worship would have me score my backside! Indeed, your worship is not reasonable. Let us be off to shave these duennas; and on our return I promise on my word to make such haste to wipe off all that's due as will satisfy your worship; I can't say more."

"Well, I will comfort myself with that promise, my good Sancho," replied Don Quixote, "and I believe thou wilt keep it; for indeed though stupid thou art veracious."

"Let us be off, señor," said Sancho, "for I have taken the beards and tears of these ladies deeply to heart, and I sha'n't eat a bit to relish it until I have seen them restored to their former smoothness. Mount, your worship, and blindfold yourself, for if I am to go on the croup, it is plain the rider in the saddle must mount first."

"That is true," said Don Quixote, and, taking a handkerchief out of his pocket, he begged the Distressed One to bandage his eyes very carefully.

They were then blindfolded, and Don Quixote finding himself settled to his satisfaction, felt for the peg, and the instant he placed his fingers on it, all the duennas and all who stood by lifted up their voices exclaiming, "God guide thee, valiant knight! God be with thee, intrepid squire! Now, now ye go cleaving the air more swiftly than an arrow! Now ye begin to amaze and astonish all who are gazing at you from the earth! Take care not to wobble about, valiant Sancho! Mind thou fall not, for thy fall will be worse than that rash youth's who tried to steer the chariot of his father the Sun!"

As Sancho heard the voices, clinging tightly to his master and winding his arms round him, he said, "Señor, how do they make out we are going up so high, if their voices reach us here and they seem to be speaking quite close to us?"

"Don't mind that, Sancho," said Don Quixote, "for as affairs of this sort and flights like this are out of the common course of things, you can see and hear as much as you like a thousand leagues off; but don't squeeze me so tight or thou wilt upset me; and really I know not what thou hast to be uneasy or frightened at, for I can safely swear I never mounted a smoother-going steed all the days of my life; one would fancy we never stirred from one place. Banish fear, my friend, for indeed everything is going as it ought, and we have the wind astern."

"That's true," said Sancho, "for such a strong wind comes against me on this side, that it seems as if people were blowing on me with a thousand pair of bellows"; which was the case; they were puffing at him with a great pair of bellows; for the whole adventure was so well planned by the duke, the duchess, and their majordomo, that nothing was omitted to make it perfectly successful.

Don Quixote now, feeling the blast, said, "Beyond a doubt, Sancho, we must have already reached the second region of the air, where the hail and snow are generated; the thunder, the lightning, and the thunderbolts are engendered in the third region, and if we go on ascending at this rate, we shall shortly plunge into the region of fire, and I know not how to regulate this peg, so as not to mount up where we shall be burned."

And now they began to warm their faces, from a distance, with tow that could be easily set on fire and extinguished again, fixed on the end of a cane. On feeling the heat, Sancho said, "May I die if we are not already in that fire place, or very near it, for a good part of my beard has been singed, and I have a mind, señor, to uncover and see whereabouts we are."

"Do nothing of the kind," said Don Quixote. "It will not do for us to uncover ourselves, for he who has us in charge will be responsible for us; and perhaps we are gaining an altitude and mounting up to enable us to descend at one swoop on the kingdom of Kandy, as the falcon does on the heron, so

272

"Let us be off, señor," said Sancho.

as to seize it however high it may soar; and though it seems to us not half an hour since we left the garden, believe me we must have traveled a great distance."

The duke, the duchess, and all in the garden were listening to the conversation of the two heroes, and were beyond measure amused by it; and now, desirous of putting a finishing touch to this rare and well-contrived adventure, they applied a light to Clavileño's tail with some tow, and the horse, being full of squibs and crackers, immediately blew up with a prodigious noise, and brought Don Quixote and Sancho Panza to the ground half singed. By this time the bearded band of duennas, the Trifaldi and all, had vanished from the garden, and those that remained lay stretched on the ground as if in a swoon. Don Quixote and Sancho got up rather shaken, and, looking about them, were filled with amazement at finding themselves in the same garden from which they had started, and seeing such a number of people stretched on the ground. Their astonishment was increased when at one side of the garden they perceived a tall lance planted in the ground, and hanging from it by two cords of green silk a smooth white parchment on which there was the following inscription in large gold letters: "The illustrious knight Don Quixote of La Mancha has, by merely attempting it, finished and concluded the adventure of the Countess Trifaldi, otherwise called the Distressed Duenna; Malambruno is now satisfied on every point, the chins of the duennas are now smooth and clean, and King Don Clavijo and Queen Antonomasia in their original form; and when the squirely flagellation shall have been completed, the white dove find herself delivered from the pestiferous gerfalcons that persecute her, and in the arms of her beloved mate; for such is the decree of the sage Merlin, arch-enchanter of enchanters."

As soon as Don Quixote had read the inscription on the parchment he perceived clearly that it referred to the disenchantment of Dulcinea, and returning hearty thanks to heaven that he had with so little danger achieved so grand an exploit as to restore to their former complexion the countenances of those venerable duennas, he advanced towards the duke and duchess, who had not yet come to themselves, and taking the duke by the hand he said, "Be of good cheer, worthy sir, be of good cheer; it's nothing at all; the adventure is now over and without any harm done, as the inscription fixed on this post shows plainly."

The duke came to himself slowly and like one recovering consciousness after a heavy sleep, and the duchess and all who had fallen prostrate about the garden did the same, with such demonstrations of wonder and amazement that they would have almost persuaded one that what they pretended so adroitly in jest had happened to them in reality. The duke read the placard with half-shut eyes, and then ran to embrace Don Quixote with open arms, declaring him to be the best knight that had ever been seen in any age. Sancho kept looking about for the Distressed One, to see what her face was like without the beard, and if she was as fair as her elegant person promised; but they told him that, the instant Clavileño descended flaming through the air and came to the ground, the whole band of duennas with the Trifaldi vanished and that they were already shaved and without a stump left.

The duchess asked Sancho how he had fared on that long journey, to which Sancho replied, "I felt, señora, that we were flying through the region of fire, as my master told me, and I wanted to uncover my eyes for a bit; but my master, when I asked leave to uncover myself, would not let me; but as I have a little bit of curiosity about me, and a desire to know what is forbidden and kept from me, quietly and without anyone seeing me I drew aside the handkerchief covering my eyes ever so little, close to my nose, and from underneath looked towards the earth, and it seemed to me that it was altogether no bigger than a grain of mustard seed, and that the men walking on it were little bigger than hazel nuts; so you may see how high we must have got to then."

To this the duchess said, "Sancho, my friend, mind what you are saying; it seems you could not have seen the earth, but only the men walking on it; for if the earth looked to you like a grain of mustard seed, and each man like a hazel nut, one man alone would have covered the whole earth."

"That is true," said Sancho, "but for all that I got a glimpse of a bit of one side of it, and saw it all."

"Take care, Sancho," said the duchess, "with a bit of one side one does not see the whole of what one looks at."

"I don't understand that way of looking at things," said Sancho; "I only know that your ladyship will do well to bear in mind that as we were flying by enchantment so I might have seen the whole earth and all the men by enchantment whatever way I looked; and if you won't believe this, no more will you believe that, uncovering myself nearly to the eyebrows, I saw myself so close to the sky that there was not a palm and a half between me and it; and by everything that I can swear by, señora, it is mighty great! And it so happened we came by where the seven goats are. And by God and upon my soul, as in my youth I was a goatherd in my own country, as soon as I saw them I felt a longing to be among them for a little, and if I had not given

274

way to it I think I'd have burst. So I come and take, and what do I do? Without saying anything to anybody, not even to my master, softly and quietly I got down from Clavileño and amused myself with the goats—which are like violets, like flowers—for nigh three-quarters of an hour; and Clavileño never stirred or moved from one spot."

"And while the good Sancho was amusing himself with the goats," said the duke, "how did Señor Don Quixote amuse himself?"

To which Don Quixote replied, "As all these things and such like occurrences are out of the ordinary course of nature, it is no wonder that Sancho says what he does; for my own part I can only say that I did not uncover my eyes either above or below, nor did I see sky or earth or sea or shore. It is true I felt that I was passing through the region of the air, and even that I touched that of fire; but that we passed farther I cannot believe; for the region of fire being between the heaven of the moon and the last region of the air, we could not have reached that heaven where the Pleiades, the seven goats Sancho speaks of, are without being burned; and as we were not burned, either Sancho is lying or Sancho is dreaming."

"I am neither lying nor dreaming," said Sancho; "only ask me the tokens of those same goats, and you'll see by that whether I'm telling the truth or not."

"Tell us them then, Sancho," said the duchess.

"Two of them," said Sancho, "are green, two blood-red, two blue, and one a mixture of all colors."

"An odd sort of goat, that," said the duke. "In this earthly region of ours we have no such colors; I mean goats of such colors."

"That's very plain," said Sancho; "of course there must be a difference between the goats of heaven and the goats of the earth."

They did not care to ask him anything more about his journey, for they saw he was in the vein to go rambling all over the heavens giving an account of everything that went on there, without having ever stirred from the garden. Such, in short, was the end of the adventure of the Distressed Duenna, which gave the duke and duchess laughing matter not only for the time being, but for all their lives, and Sancho something to talk about for ages, if he lived so long.

But Don Quixote, coming close to his ear, said to him, "Sancho, as you would have us believe what you saw in heaven, I require you to believe me as to what I saw in the cave of Montesinos; I say no more."

275

CHAPTER 19

Sancho Panza, Governor

THE DUKE AND DUCHESS were so well pleased with the successful and droll result of the adventure of the Distressed One that they resolved to carry on the joke, seeing what a fit subject they had to deal with for making it all pass for reality. So having laid their plans and given instructions to their servants and vassals how to behave to Sancho in his government of the promised island, the next day, that following Clavileño's flight, the duke told Sancho to prepare and get ready to go and be governor, for his islanders were already looking out for him as for the showers of May.

To carry on the joke, then, the same evening they dispatched Sancho with a large following to the village that was to serve him for an island. It happened that the person who had him in charge was a majordomo of the duke's, a man of great discretion and humor—and there can be no humor without discretion—and the same who played the part of the Countess Trifaldi in the comical way that has been already described; and thus qualified, and instructed by his master and mistress as to how to deal with Sancho, he carried out their scheme admirably. Now it came to pass that as soon as Sancho saw this majordomo he seemed in his features to recognize those of the Trifaldi, and turning to his master, he said to him, "Señor, either the devil will carry me off, here on this spot, righteous and believing, or your worship will own to me that the face of this majordomo of the duke's here is the very face of the Distressed One."

Don Quixote regarded the majordomo attentively, and having done so,

276

said to Sancho, "There is no reason why the devil should carry thee off, Sancho, either righteous or believing—and what thou meanest by that I know not; the face of the Distressed One is that of the majordomo, but for all that the majordomo is not the Distressed One; for his being so would involve a mighty contradiction."

"It is no joke, señor," said Sancho, "for before this I heard him speak, and it seemed exactly as if the voice of the Trifaldi was sounding in my ears. Well, I'll hold my peace; but I'll take care to be on the lookout henceforth for any sign that may be seen to confirm or do away with this suspicion."

"Thou wilt do well, Sancho," said Don Quixote, "and thou wilt let me know all thou discoverest, and all that befalls thee in thy government."

Sancho at last set out attended by a great number of people. He was dressed in the garb of a lawyer with a gaban of tawny watered camlet over all and a montera cap of the same material, and mounted upon a mule. Behind him, in accordance with the duke's orders, followed Dapple with brand new ass-trappings and ornaments of silk, and from time to time Sancho turned round to look at his ass, so well pleased to have him with him that he would not have changed places with the emperor of Germany. On taking leave he kissed the hands of the duke and duchess and got his master's blessing, which Don Quixote gave him with tears, and he received blubbering.

As soon as Sancho had gone, Don Quixote felt his loneliness, and had it been possible for him to revoke the mandate and take away the government from him he would have done so. The duchess observed his dejection and asked him why he was melancholy; because, she said, if it was for the loss of Sancho, there were squires, duennas, and damsels in her house who would wait upon him to his full satisfaction.

"The truth is, señora," replied Don Quixote, "that I do feel the loss of Sancho; but that is not the main cause of my looking sad; and of all the offers your excellence makes me, I accept only the good will with which they are made, and as to the remainder I entreat of your excellence to permit and allow me alone to wait upon myself in my chamber."

"Indeed, Señor Don Quixote," said the duchess, "that must not be; four of my damsels, as beautiful as flowers, shall wait upon you."

"To me," said Don Quixote, "they will not be flowers, but thorns to pierce my heart. They, or anything like them, shall as soon enter my chamber as fly. If your highness wishes to gratify me still further, though I deserve it not, permit me to please myself, and wait upon myself in my own room; for I place a barrier between my inclinations and my virtue, and I do not wish to break this rule through the generosity your highness is disposed to display towards me; and, in short, I will sleep in my clothes, sooner than allow anyone to undress me."

"Say no more, Señor Don Quixote, say no more," said the duchess. "I assure you I will give orders that not even a fly, not to say a damsel, shall enter your room. I am not the one to undermine the propriety of Señor Don Quixote, for it strikes me that among his many virtues the one that is preeminent is that of modesty. Your worship may undress and dress in private and in your own way, as you please and when you please, for there will be no one to hinder you. Now, Señor Don Quixote, it is nearly suppertime, and the duke is probably waiting. Come, let us go to supper, and retire to rest early, for the journey you made yesterday from Kandy was not such a short one but that it must have caused you some fatigue."

"I feel none, señora," said Don Quixote, "for I would go so far as to swear to your excellence that in all my life I never mounted a quieter beast, or a pleasanter paced one, than Clavileño; and I don't know what would have induced Malambruno to discard a steed so swift and so gentle, and burn it so recklessly as he did."

"Probably," said the duchess, "repenting of the evil he had done to the Trifaldi and company, and others, and the crimes he must have committed as a wizard and enchanter, he resolved to make away with all the instruments of his craft; and so burned Clavileño as the chief one, and that which mainly kept him restless, wandering from land to land; and by its ashes and the trophy of the placard the valor of the great Don Quixote of La Mancha is established forever."

Don Quixote renewed his thanks to the duchess; and having supped, retired to his chamber alone, refusing to allow anyone to enter with him to wait on him, such was his fear of encountering temptations that might lead or drive him to forget his chaste fidelity to his lady Dulcinea; for he had always present to his mind the virtue of Amadis, that flower and mirror of knights-errant. He locked the door behind him, and by the light of two wax candles undressed himself, but as he was taking off his stockings—O disaster unworthy of such a personage!—there came a burst of some two dozen stitches in one of his stockings, that made it look like a window lattice. The worthy gentleman was beyond measure distressed, and at that moment he would have given an ounce of silver to have had half a drachm of green silk there; I say green silk, because the stockings were green.

However, he comforted himself on perceiving that Sancho had left behind a pair of traveling boots, which he resolved to wear the next day. At last he went to bed, out of spirits and heavy at heart, as much because he missed Sancho as because of the irreparable disaster to his stockings, the stitches of which he would have even taken up with silk of another color; which is one of the greatest signs of poverty a gentleman can show in the course of his never-failing embarrassments. He put out the candles and stretched himself on his bed, where we will leave him for the present, as the great Sancho Panza, who is about to set up his famous government, now demands our attention.

Sancho with all his attendants arrived at a village of some thousand inhabitants, and one of the largest the duke possessed. They informed him that it was called the island of Barataria. On reaching the gates of the town, which was a walled one, the municipality came forth to meet him, the bells rang out a peal, and the inhabitants showed every sign of general satisfaction. With great pomp they conducted him to the principal church to give thanks to God, and then with burlesque ceremonies they presented him with the keys of the town, and acknowledged him as perpetual governor of the island of Barataria. The costume, the beard, and the fat squat figure of the new governor astonished all those who were not in the secret, and even all who were, and they were not a few. Finally, leading him out of the church they carried him to the judgment seat and seated him on it, and the duke's majordomo said to him, "It is an ancient custom in this island, señor governor, that he who comes to take possession of this famous island is bound to answer a question which shall be put to him, and which must be a somewhat knotty and difficult one; and by his answer the people take the measure of their new governor's wit, and hail with joy or deplore his arrival accordingly."

While the majordomo was making this speech Sancho was gazing at several large letters inscribed on the wall opposite his seat, and as he could not read, he asked what that was that was painted on the wall. The answer was, "Señor, there is written and recorded the day on which your lordship took possession of this island, and the inscription says, 'This day, the so-and-so of such-and-such a month and year, Señor Don Sancho Panza took possession of this island; many years may he enjoy it.' "

"And whom do they call Don Sancho Panza?" asked Sancho.

"Your lordship," replied the majordomo; "for no other Panza but the one who is now seated in that chair has ever entered this island."

"Well then, let me tell you, brother," said Sancho, "I haven't got the 'Don,' nor has any one of my family ever had it; my name is plain Sancho Panza, and Sancho was my father's name, and Sancho was my grandfather's and they were all Panzas, without any Dons or Doñas tacked on. Let the majordomo go on with his question, and I'll give the best answer I can, whether the people deplore or not."

At this instant there came into court two old men, one carrying a cane by way of a walking stick, and the one who had no stick said, "Señor, some time ago I lent this good man ten goldcrowns in gold to gratify him and do him a service, on the condition that he was to return them to me whenever I should ask for them. A long time passed before I asked for them, for I would not put him to any greater straits to return them than he was in when I lent them to him. But thinking he was growing careless about payment I asked for them once and several times; and not only will he not give them back, but he denies that he owes them, and says I never lent him any such crowns; or if I did, that he repaid them; and I have no witnesses either of the loan, or the payment, for he never paid me. I want your worship to put him to his oath, and if he swears he returned them to me I forgive him the debt here and before God."

"What say you to this, good old man, you with the stick?" said Sancho.

To which the old man replied, "I admit, señor, that he lent them to me; but let your worship lower your staff to my oath, and I'll swear that I gave them back, and paid him really and truly."

The governor lowered the staff, and as he did so the old man who had the stick handed it to the other old man to hold for him while he swore, as if he found it in his way; and then laid his hand on the cross of the staff, saying that it was true the ten crowns that were demanded of him had been lent him; but that he had with his own hand given them back into the hand of the other, and that he, not recollecting it, was always asking for them.

Seeing this, the governor asked the creditor what answer he had to make to what his opponent said. He said that no doubt his debtor had told the truth, for he believed him to be an honest man and a good Christian, and he himself must have forgotten when and how he had given him back the crowns; and that from that time forth he would make no further demand upon him.

The debtor took his stick again, and bowing his head left the court. Observing this, and how, without another word, he made off, and observing too the resignation of the plaintiff, Sancho buried his head in his bosom and remained for a short space in deep thought, with the forefinger of his right hand on his brow and nose. Then he raised his head and bade them call back the old man with the stick, for he had already taken his departure. They brought him back, and as soon as Sancho saw him he said, "Honest man, give me that stick, for I want it."

"Willingly," said the old man. "Here it is, señor," and he put it into his hand.

Sancho took it and, handing it to the other old man, said to him, "Go, and God be with you; for now you are paid."

"I, señor!" returned the old man. "Why, is this cane worth ten goldcrowns?"

"Yes," said the governor, "or if not, I am the greatest dolt in the world; now you will see whether I have got the headpiece to govern a whole kingdom." And he ordered the cane to be broken in two, there, in the presence of all. It was done, and in the middle of it they found ten goldcrowns. All were filled with amazement, and looked upon their governor as another Solomon. They asked him how he had come to the conclusion that the ten crowns were in the cane; he replied, that observing how the old man who swore gave the stick to his opponent while he was taking the oath and swore that he had really and truly given him the crowns, and how as soon as he had done swearing he asked for the stick again, it came into his head that the sum demanded must be inside it. From this he said it might be seen that God sometimes guides those who govern in their judgments, even though they may be fools; besides he had himself heard the curate of his village mention just such another case, and he had so good a memory, that if it was not that he forgot everything he wished to remember, there would not be such a memory in all the island. To conclude, the old men went off, one crestfallen, and the other in high contentment, all who were present were astonished, and he who was recording the words, deeds, and movements of Sancho could not make up his mind whether he was to look upon him and set him down as a fool or as a man of sense.

CHAPTER 20

Sancho's Conduct

ROM THE JUSTICE court they carried Sancho to a sumptuous palace, where in a spacious chamber there was a table laid out with royal magnificence. The clarions sounded as Sancho entered the room, and four pages came forward to present him with water for his hands, which Sancho received with great dignity. The music ceased, and Sancho seated himself at the head of the table, for there was only that seat placed, and no more than one cover laid. A personage, who it appeared afterwards was a physician, placed himself standing by his side with a whalebone wand in his hand. They then lifted up a fine white cloth covering fruit and a great variety of dishes of different sorts. One who looked like a student said grace, and a page put a laced bib on Sancho, while another who played the part of head carver placed a dish of fruit before him.

But hardly had he tasted a morsel when the man with the wand touched the plate with it, and they took it away from before him with the utmost celerity. The carver, however, brought him another dish, and Sancho proceeded to try it; but before he could get at it, not to say taste it, already the wand had touched it and a page had carried it off with the same promptitude as the fruit. Sancho, seeing this, was puzzled, and looking from one to another asked if this dinner was to be eaten after the fashion of a jugglery trick.

To this he with the wand replied, "It is not to be eaten, señor governor, except as is usual and customary in other islands where there are governors. I, señor, am a physician, and I am paid a salary in this island to serve its governors as such, and I have a much greater regard for their health than

282

for my own, studying day and night and making myself acquainted with the governor's constitution, in order to be able to cure him when he falls sick. The chief thing I have to do is to attend at his dinners and suppers and allow him to eat what appears to me to be fit for him, and keep from him what I think will do him harm and be injurious to his stomach; and therefore I ordered that plate of fruit to be removed as being too moist, and that other dish I ordered to be removed as being too hot and containing many spices that stimulate thirst; for he who drinks much consumes the radical moisture wherein life consists."

"Well then," said Sancho, "that dish of roast partridges there that seems so savory will not do me any harm."

To this the physician replied, "Of those my lord the governor shall not eat so long as I live."

"Why so?" said Sancho.

"Because," replied the doctor, "our master Hippocrates, the polestar and beacon of medicine, says in one of his aphorisms that partridge is the worst of all."

"In that case," said Sancho, "let señor doctor see among the dishes that are on the table what will do me most good and least harm, and let me eat it, without tapping it with his stick; for by the life of the governor, and so may God suffer me to enjoy it, but I'm dying of hunger; and in spite of the doctor and all he may say, to deny me food is the way to take my life instead of prolonging it."

"Your worship is right, señor governor," said the physician; "and therefore your worship, I consider, should not eat of those stewed rabbits there, because it is a furry kind of food. If that veal were not roasted and served with pickles, you might try it, but it is out of the question."

Sancho on hearing this threw himself back in his chair and surveyed the doctor steadily, and in a solemn tone asked him what his name was and where he had studied.

He replied, "My name, señor governor, is Doctor Pedro Recio de Agüero. I am a native of a place called Tirteafuera, and I have the degree of doctor from the university of Osuna."

To which Sancho, glowing all over with rage, returned, "Then let Doctor Pedro Recio de Malagüero, native of Tirteafuera, graduate of Osuna, get out of my presence at once; or I swear by the sun I'll take a cudgel, and by dint of blows, beginning with him, I'll not leave a doctor in the whole island. And now give me something to eat, or else take your government; for a trade that does not feed its master is not worth two beans."

The doctor was dismayed when he saw the governor in such a passion, and he would have left the room but that the same instant a post-horn sounded in the street. The carver putting his head out of the window turned round and said, "It's a courier from my lord the duke, no doubt with some dispatch of importance."

The courier came in all sweating and flurried, and taking a paper from his bosom, placed it in the governor's hands. Sancho handed it to the majordomo and bade him read the superscription, which ran thus: *To Don Sancho Panza, Governor of the Island of Barataria, into his own hands or those of his secretary.* Sancho when he heard this said, "Which of you is my secretary?" "I am, señor," said one of those present, "for I can read and write, and am a Biscayan." "With that addition," said Sancho, "you might be secretary to the emperor himself. Open this paper and see what it says." The newborn secretary obeyed, and having read the contents said the matter was one to be discussed in private. Sancho ordered the chamber to be cleared, the majordomo and the carver only remaining; so the doctor and the others withdrew, and then the secretary read the letter, which was as follows:

It has come to my knowledge, Señor Don Sancho Panza, that certain enemies of mine and of the island are about to make a furious attack upon it some night, I know not when. It behooves you to be on the alert and keep watch, that they surprise you not. I also know by trustworthy spies that four persons have entered the town in disguise in order to take your life, because they stand in dread of your great capacity; keep your eyes open and take heed who approaches you to address you, and eat nothing that is presented to you. I will take care to send you aid if you find yourself in difficulty, but in all things you will act as may be expected of your judgment. From this place, the Sixteenth of August, at four in the morning.

> Your friend,
> THE DUKE

Sancho was astonished, and those who stood by made believe to be so too, and turning to the majordomo he said to him, "What we have got to do first, and it must be done at once, is to put Doctor Recio in the lockup; for if anyone wants to kill me it is he, and by a slow death and the worst of all, which is hunger."

"Of those my lord the governor shall not eat so long as I live."

"Likewise," said the carver, "it is my opinion your worship should not eat anything that is on this table, for the whole was a present from some nuns; and as they say, 'Behind the cross there's the devil.'"

"I don't deny it," said Sancho, "so for the present give me a piece of bread and four pounds or so of grapes; no poison can come in them; for the fact is I can't go on without eating; and if we are to be prepared for these battles that are threatening us we must be well provisioned. And you, secretary, answer my lord the duke and tell him that all his commands shall be obeyed to the letter, as he directs; and say from me to my lady the duchess that I kiss her hands. And as you are about it you may enclose a kiss of the hand to my master Don Quixote that he may see I am grateful bread; and as a good secretary and a good Biscayan you may add whatever you like and whatever will come in best; and now take away this cloth and give me something to eat, and I'll be ready to meet all the spies and assassins and enchanters that may come against me or my island."

At suppertime they gave him a beef salad with onions and some boiled calves' feet. At this he fell to with greater relish than if they had given him pheasants from Rome, veal from Sorrento, or partridges from Moron. Turning to the doctor, he said to him, "Look here, señor doctor, for the future don't trouble yourself about giving me dainty things or choice dishes to eat, for it will be only taking my stomach off its hinges; it is accustomed to goat, cow, bacon, hung beef, turnips and onions; and if by any chance it is given these palace dishes, it receives them squeamishly, and sometimes with loathing. But let nobody play pranks on me, for either we are or we are not; let us live and eat in peace and good fellowship, for when God sends the dawn, he sends it for all. I mean to govern this island without giving up a right or taking a bribe; let everyone keep his eye open, and look out for the arrow. Nay! make yourself honey and the flies eat you."

"Of a truth, señor governor," said the carver, "your worship is in the right of it in everything you have said; and I promise you in the name of all the inhabitants of this island that they will serve your worship with all zeal, affection, and good will, for the mild kind of government you have given a sample of to begin with, leaves them no ground for doing or thinking anything to your worship's disadvantage."

"That I believe," said Sancho, "and they would be great fools if they did or thought otherwise. Once more I say, see to my feeding and my Dapple's for that is the great point and what is most to the purpose; and when the hour comes let us go the rounds, for it is my intention to purge this island of all manner of uncleanness and of all idle good-for-nothing vagabonds; for I would have you know that lazy idlers are the same thing in a State as the drones in a hive, that eat up the honey the industrious bees make."

"There is so much in what your worship says, señor governor," said the majordomo, "that I am filled with wonder when I see a man like your worship, entirely without learning (for I believe you have none at all), say such things, and so full of sound maxims and sage remarks, very different from what was expected of your worship's intelligence by those who sent us or by us who came here. Every day we see something new in this world; jokes become realities, and the jokers find the tables turned upon them."

Night came, and they got ready to go the rounds, and the governor started with the majordomo, the secretary, the head-carver, the chronicler charged with recording his deeds, and alguacils and notaries enough to form a fair-sized squadron. In the midst marched Sancho with his staff, as fine a sight as one could wish to see, and but a few streets of the town had been traversed when they heard a noise as of a clashing of swords. They hastened to the spot, and found that the combatants were but two, who seeing the authorities approaching stood still, and one of them exclaimed, "Help, in the name of God and the king! Are men to be allowed to rob in the middle of this town, and rush out and attack people in the very streets?"

"Be calm, my good man," said Sancho, "and tell me what the cause of this quarrel is; for I am the governor."

Said the other combatant, "Señor governor, I will tell you in a very few words. Your worship must know that this gentleman has just now won more than a thousand reals in that gambling house opposite, and God knows how. I was there, and gave more than one doubtful point in his favor, very much against what my conscience told me. He made off with his winnings, and when I thought he was going to give me a crown or so at least by way of a present, as it is usual and customary to give men of quality of my sort who stand by to see fair or foul play, and back up swindles, and prevent quarrels, he pocketed his money and left the house. Indignant at this I followed him, and speaking him fairly and civilly asked him to give me if it were only eight reals, for he knows I am an honest man and that I have neither profession nor property, for my parents never brought me up to any or left me any. But the rogue would not give me more than four reals; so your worship may see how little shame and conscience he has. But by my faith if you had not come up I'd have made him disgorge his winnings, and he'd have learned what the range of the steelyard was."

"What say you to this?" asked Sancho. The other replied that all his antagonist said was true, and that he did not choose to give him more than four reals because he very often gave him money; and that those who expected presents ought to be civil and take what is given them with a cheerful countenance, and not make any claim against winners unless they know them for certain to be sharpers and their winnings to be unfairly won; and that there could be no better proof that he himself was an honest man than his having refused to give anything; for sharpers always pay tribute to lookers-on who know them.

"That is true," said the majordomo. "Let your worship consider what is to be done with these men."

"What is to be done," said Sancho, "is this; you, the winner, be you good, bad, or indifferent, give this assailant of yours a hundred reals at once, and you must disburse thirty more for the poor prisoners; and you who have neither profession nor property, and hang about the island in idleness, take these hundred reals now, and some time of the day tomorrow quit the island under sentence of banishment for ten years, and under pain of completing it in another life if you violate the sentence, for I'll hang you on a gibbet, or at least the hangman will by my orders. Not a word from either of you, or I'll make him feel my hand."

The one paid down the money and the other took it, and the latter quitted the island, while the other went home; and then the governor said, "Either I am not good for much, or I'll get rid of these gambling houses, for it strikes me they are very mischievous."

"This one at least," said one of the notaries, "your worship will not be able to get rid of, for a great man owns it, and what he loses every year is beyond all comparison more than what he makes by the cards. On the minor gambling houses your worship may exercise your power, and it is they that do most harm and shelter the most barefaced practices; for in the houses of lords and gentlemen of quality the notorious sharpers dare not attempt to play their tricks; and as the vice of gambling has become common, it is better that men should play in houses of repute than in some tradesman's, where they catch an unlucky fellow in the small hours of the morning and skin him alive."

"I know already, notary, that there is a good deal to be said on that point," said Sancho.

And now a tipstaff came up with a young man in his grasp, and said, "Señor governor, this youth was coming towards us, and as soon as he saw the officers of justice he turned about and ran like a deer, a sure proof that he must be some evildoer; I ran after him, and had it not been that he stumbled and fell, I should never have caught him."

"What did you run for, fellow?" said Sancho.

To which the young man replied, "Señor, it was to avoid answering all the questions officers of justice put."

"What are you by trade?"

"A weaver."

"And what do you weave?"

"Lance heads, with your worship's good leave."

"You're facetious with me! You plume yourself on being a wag? Very good; and where were you going just now?"

"To take the air, señor."

"And where does one take the air in this island?"

"Where it blows."

"Good! your answers are very much to the point; you are a smart youth; but take notice that I am the air, and that I blow upon you astern, and send you to gaol. Ho there! lay hold of him and take him off. I'll make him sleep there tonight without air."

"By God," said the young man, "your worship will make me sleep in gaol just as soon as make me king."

"Why sha'n't I make thee sleep in gaol?" said Sancho. "Have I not the power to arrest thee and release thee whenever I like?"

"All the power your worship has," said the young man, "won't be able to make me sleep in gaol."

"How? Not able!" said Sancho. "Take him away at once where he'll see his mistake with his own eyes, even if the gaoler is willing to exert his interested generosity on his behalf; for I'll lay a penalty of two thousand ducats on him if he allows him to stir a step from the prison."

"That's ridiculous," said the young man. "The fact is, all the men on earth will not make me sleep in prison."

"Tell me, you devil," said Sancho, "have you got any angel that will deliver you, and take off the irons I am going to order them to put upon you?"

"Now, señor governor," said the young man in a sprightly manner, "let us be reasonable and come to the point. Granted your worship may order me to be taken to prison, and to have irons and chains put on me, and to be shut up in a cell, and may lay heavy penalties on the gaoler if he lets me out, and that he obeys your orders; still, if I don't choose to sleep, and choose to remain awake all night without closing an eye, will your worship with all your power be able to make me sleep if I don't choose?"

"No, truly," said the secretary, "and the fellow has made his point."

"So then," said Sancho, "it would be entirely of your own choice you would keep from sleeping; not in opposition to my will?"

"No, señor," said the youth, "certainly not."

"Well then, go, and God be with you," said Sancho; "be off home to sleep, and God give you sound sleep, for I don't want to rob you of it; but for the future, let me advise you don't joke with the authorities, because you may come across someone who will bring down the joke on your own skull."

And so the night's round came to an end, and a couple of days later the government, whereby all Sancho's plans were overthrown and swept away.

CHAPTER 21

Sancho's Government Ends

To FANCY that in this life anything belonging to it will remain forever in the same state is an idle fancy; on the contrary, in it everything seems to go in a circle, I mean round and round. The spring succeeds the summer, the summer the fall, the fall the autumn, the autumn the winter, and the winter the spring, and so time rolls with never-ceasing wheel. Man's life alone, swifter than time, speeds onward to its end without any hope of renewal, save it be that other life which is endless and boundless; for there are many that by the light of nature alone, without the light of faith, have a comprehension of the fleeting nature and instability of this present life and the endless duration of that eternal life we hope for.

But we are here speaking of the rapidity with which Sancho's government came to an end, melted away, disappeared, vanished as it were in smoke and shadow. For as he lay in bed on the night of the seventh day of his government, sated, not with bread and wine, but with delivering judgments and giving opinions and making laws and proclamations, just as sleep, in spite of hunger, was beginning to close his eyelids, he heard such a noise of bell-ringing and shouting that one would have fancied the whole island was going to the bottom.

He sat up in bed and remained listening intently to try if he could make out what could be the cause of so great an uproar. Not only, however, was he unable to discover what it was, but as countless drums and trumpets now helped to swell the din of the bells and shouts, he was more puzzled than ever, and filled with fear and terror; and getting up he put on a pair of slippers because of the dampness of the floor, and without throwing a dressing gown or anything of the kind over him he rushed out of the door of his room, just in time to see approaching along a corridor a band of more than twenty persons with lighted torches and naked swords in their hands, all shouting out, "To arms, to arms, señor governor, to arms! The enemy is in the island in countless numbers, and we are lost unless your skill and valor come to our support."

Keeping up this noise, tumult, and uproar, they came to where Sancho stood dazed and bewildered by what he saw and heard, and as they approached one of them called out to him, "Arm at once, your lordship, if you would not have yourself destroyed and the whole island lost."

"What have I to do with arming?" said Sancho. "What do I know about arms or supports? Better leave all that to my master Don Quixote, who will settle it and make all safe in a trice; for I, sinner that I am, God help me, don't understand these scuffles."

"Ah, señor governor," said another, "what slackness of mettle this is! Arm yourself; here are arms for you, offensive and defensive; come out to the plaza and be our leader and captain. It falls upon you by right, for you are our governor."

"Arm me then, in God's name," said Sancho, and they at once produced two large shields they had come provided with, and placed them upon him over his shirt, without letting him put on anything else, one shield in front and the other behind, and passing his arms through openings they had made, they bound him tight with ropes, so that there he was walled and boarded up as straight as a spindle and unable to bend his knees or stir a single step. In his hand they placed a lance, on which he leaned to keep himself from falling, and as soon as they had him thus fixed they bade him march forward and lead them on and give them all courage; for with him for their guide and lamp and morning star, they were sure to bring their business to a successful issue.

"How am I to march, unlucky being that I am?" said Sancho, "when I can't stir my kneecaps, for these boards I have bound so tight to my body won't let me. What you must do is carry me in your arms, and lay me across or set me upright in some postern, and I'll hold it either with this lance or with my body."

"On, señor governor!" cried another, "it is fear more than the boards that keeps you from moving; make haste, stir yourself, for there is no time to lose; the enemy is increasing in numbers, the shouts grow louder, and the danger is pressing."

Urged by these exhortations and reproaches the poor governor made an attempt to advance, but fell to the ground with such a crash that he fancied he had broken himself all to pieces. There he lay like a tortoise enclosed in its shell; nor did the gang of jokers feel any compassion for him when they saw him down; so far from that, extinguishing their torches they began to shout afresh and to renew the calls to arms with such energy, trampling on poor Sancho, and slashing at him over the shield with their swords in such a way that, if he had not gathered himself together and made himself small and drawn in his head between the shields, it would have fared badly with the poor governor, as, squeezed into that narrow compass, he lay, sweating and sweating again, and commending himself with all his heart to God to deliver him from his present peril. Some stumbled over him, others fell upon him, and one there was who took up a position on top of him for some time, and from thence as if from a watchtower issued orders to the troops, shouting out, "Here, our side! Here the enemy is thickest! Hold the breach there! Shut that gate! Barricade those ladders! Here with your stinkpots of pitch and resin, and kettles of boiling oil! Block the streets with feather beds!" In short, in his ardor he mentioned every little thing, and every implement and engine of war by means of which an assault upon a city is warded off, while the bruised and battered Sancho, who heard and suffered all, was saying to himself, "Oh, if it would only please the Lord to let the island be lost at once, and I could see myself either dead or out of this torture!" Heaven heard his prayer, and when he least expected it he heard voices exclaiming, "Victory, victory! The enemy retreats beaten! Come, señor governor, get up, and come and enjoy the victory, and divide the spoils that have been won from the foe by the might of that invincible arm."

"Lift me up," said the wretched Sancho in a woebegone voice. They helped him to rise, and as soon as he was on his feet said, "The enemy I have beaten you may nail to my forehead; I don't want to divide the spoils of the foe, I only beg and entreat some friend, if I have one, to give me a sup of wine, for I'm parched with thirst, and wipe me dry, for I'm turning to water."

They rubbed him down, fetched him wine and unbound the shields, and he seated himself upon his bed, and with fear, agitation, and fatigue he fainted away. Those who had been concerned in the joke were now sorry they had pushed it so far; however, the anxiety his fainting away had caused them was relieved by his returning to himself. He asked what o'clock it was; they told him it was just daybreak. He said no more, and in silence began to dress himself, while all watched him, waiting to see what the haste with which he was putting on his clothes meant.

He got himself dressed at last, and then, slowly, for he was sorely bruised and could not go fast, he proceeded to the stable, followed by all who were present, and going up to Dapple embraced him and gave him a loving kiss on the forehead, and said to him, not without tears in his eyes, "Come along, comrade and friend and partner of my toils and sorrows. When I was with you and had no cares to trouble me except mending your harness and feeding your little carcase, happy were my hours, my days, and my years; but since I left you, and mounted the towers of ambition and pride, a thousand miseries, a thousand troubles, and four thousand anxieties have entered into my soul." All the while he was speaking in this strain he was fixing the pack-saddle on the ass, without a word from anyone. Then having Dapple saddled, he, with great pain and difficulty, got up on him, and addressing himself to the majordomo, the secretary, the head-carver, and Pedro Recio the doctor and several others who stood by, he said, "Make way, gentlemen, and let me go back to my old freedom; let me go look for my past life, and raise myself up from this present death. I was not born to be a governor or protect islands or cities from the enemies that choose to attack them. Plowing and digging, vinedressing and pruning, are more in my way than defending provinces or kingdoms. 'Saint Peter is very well at Rome.' Each of us is best following the trade he was born to. A reaping-hook fits my hand better than a governor's scepter, I'd rather have my fill of gazpacho than be subject to the misery of a meddling doctor who kills me with hunger, and I'd rather lie in summer under the shade of an oak, and in winter wrap myself in a double sheepskin jacket in freedom, than go to bed between holland sheets and dress in sables under the restraint of a government. God be with your worships, and tell my lord the duke that 'naked I was born, naked I find myself, I neither lose nor gain'; I mean that without a farthing I came into this government, and without a farthing I go out of it, very different from the way governors commonly leave other islands. Stand aside and let me go; I have to plaster myself, for I believe every one of my ribs is crushed, thanks to the enemies that have been trampling over me tonight."

"That is unnecessary, señor governor," said Doctor Recio, "for I will give your worship a draft against falls and bruises that will soon make you as

293

sound and strong as ever; and as for your diet I promise your worship to behave better, and let you eat plentifully of whatever you like."

"You spoke late," said Sancho. "I'd as soon turn Turk as stay any longer. Those jokes won't pass a second time. By God I'd as soon remain in this government, or take another, even if it was offered me between two plates, as fly to heaven without wings. I am of the breed of the Panzas, and they are every one of them obstinate, and if they once say 'odds,' odds it must be, no matter if it is evens, in spite of all the world. Here in this stable I leave the ant's wings that lifted me up into the air for the swifts and other birds to eat me, and let's take to level ground and our feet once more; and if they're not shod in pinked shoes of cordovan, they won't want for rough sandals of hemp. 'Every ewe to her like,' and 'let no one stretch his leg beyond the length of the sheet'; and now let me pass, for it's growing late with me."

To this the majordomo said, "Señor governor, we would let your worship go with all our hearts, though it sorely grieves us to lose you, for your wit and Christian conduct naturally make us regret you; but it is well known that every governor, before he leaves the place where he has been governing, is bound first of all to render an account. Let your worship do so for the ten days you have held the government, and then you may go and the peace of God go with you."

"No one can demand it of me," said Sancho, "but he whom my lord the duke shall appoint; I am going to meet him, and to him I will render an exact one; besides, when I go forth naked as I do, there is no other proof needed to show that I have governed like an angel."

"By God, the great Sancho is right," said Doctor Recio, "and we should let him go, for the duke will be beyond measure glad to see him."

They all agreed to this, and allowed him to go, first offering to bear him company and furnish him with all he wanted for his own comfort or for the journey. Sancho said he did not want anything more than a little barley for Dapple, and half a cheese and half a loaf for himself. They all embraced him, and he with tears embraced all of them, and left them filled with admiration not only at his remarks but at his firm and sensible resolution.

Sancho was within half a league of the duke's castle when night, somewhat dark and cloudy, overtook him. This, however, as it was summertime, did not give him much uneasiness, and he turned aside out of the road intending to wait for morning; but his ill-luck and hard fate so willed it that as he was

Going up to Dapple, he gave him a loving kiss on the forehead.

searching about for a place to make himself as comfortable as possible, he and Dapple fell into a deep dark hole that lay among some very old buildings.

As he fell he commended himself with all his heart to God, fancying he was not going to stop until he reached the depths of the bottomless pit; but it did not turn out so, for at little more than thrice a man's height Dapple touched bottom, and he found himself sitting on him without having received any hurt or damage whatever. He felt himself all over and held his breath to try whether he was quite sound or had a hole made in him anywhere, and finding himself all right and whole and in perfect health he was profuse in his thanks to God our Lord for the mercy that had been shown him, for he thought surely he had been broken into a thousand pieces.

He also felt along the sides of the pit with his hands to see if it were possible to get out of it without help, but he found they were quite smooth and afforded no hold anywhere, at which he was greatly distressed, especially when he heard how pathetically and dolefully Dapple was bemoaning himself, and no wonder he complained, nor was it from ill-temper, for in truth he was not in very good shape.

"Alas," said Sancho, "what unexpected accidents happen at every step to those who live in this miserable world! Who would have said that one who saw himself yesterday sitting on a throne, governor of an island, giving orders to his servants and his vassals, would see himself today buried in a pit without a soul to help him, or servant or vassal to come to his relief? Here must we perish with hunger, my ass and myself, if indeed we don't die first, he of his bruises and injuries, and I of grief and sorrow. At any rate I'll not be as lucky as my master Don Quixote of La Mancha, when he went down into the cave of that enchanted Montesinos, where he found people to make more of him than if he had been in his own house. There he saw fair and pleasant visions, but here I'll see, I imagine, toads and adders. Unlucky wretch that I am, what an end my follies and fancies have come to! They'll take up my bones out of this, when it is heaven's will that I'm found, picked clean, white and polished, and my good Dapple's with them, and by that, perhaps, it will be found out who we are, at least by such as have heard that Sancho Panza never separated from his ass, nor his ass from Sancho Panza."

In this strain did Sancho bewail himself, and his ass listened to him, but answered him never a word, such was the distress and anguish the poor beast found himself in. At length, after a night spent in bitter moanings and

295

lamentations, day came, and by its light Sancho perceived that it was wholly impossible to escape out of that pit without help, and he fell to bemoaning his fate and uttering loud shouts to find out if there was anyone within hearing; but all his shouting was only crying in the wilderness, for there was not a soul anywhere in the neighborhood to hear him, and then at last he gave himself up for dead. Dapple was lying on his back, and Sancho helped him to his feet, which he was scarcely able to keep; and then taking a piece of bread out of his saddlebags which had shared their fortunes in the fall, he gave it to the ass, to whom it was not unwelcome, saying to him as if he understood him, "With bread all sorrows are less."

That same morning, Don Quixote, having sallied forth to exercise himself, was putting Rocinante through his paces; and brought his feet so close to a pit that but for reining him in tightly it would have been impossible for him to avoid falling into it. He pulled him up, however, without a fall, and coming a little closer examined the hole without dismounting; but as he was looking at it he heard loud cries proceeding from it, and by listening attentively was able to make out that he who uttered them was saying, "Ho, above there! is there any Christian that hears me, or any charitable gentleman that will take pity on a sinner buried alive, on an unfortunate disgoverned governor?"

It struck Don Quixote that it was the voice of Sancho Panza he heard, whereat he was taken aback and amazed, and raising his own voice as much as he could, he cried out, "Who is below there? Who is that complaining?"

"Who should be here, or who should complain," was the answer, "but the forlorn Sancho Panza, for his sins and for his ill-luck governor of the island of Barataria, squire that was to the famous knight Don Quixote of La Mancha?"

When Don Quixote heard this his amazement was redoubled and his perturbation grew greater than ever, for it suggested itself to his mind that Sancho must be dead, and that his soul was in torment down there; and carried away by this idea he exclaimed, "I conjure thee by everything that as a Catholic Christian I can conjure thee by, tell me who thou art; and if thou art dead and a soul in torment, tell me what thou wouldst have me do for thee; for as my profession is to give aid and succor to those that need it in this world, it will also extend to aiding and succoring the distressed of the other, who cannot help themselves."

"In that case," answered the voice, "your worship who speaks to me must be my master Don Quixote of La Mancha; nay, from the tone of the voice it is plain it can be nobody else."

"Don Quixote I am," replied Don Quixote, "he whose profession it is to aid and succor the living and the dead in their necessities. Without further delay, therefore, declare thyself, and tell me who thou art."

"By all that's good," was the answer, "I swear, Señor Don Quixote of La Mancha, that I am your squire Sancho Panza, and that I have never died all my life; but that, having given up my government for reasons that would require more time to explain, I fell last night into this pit where I am now, and Dapple is witness and won't let me lie, for more by token he is here with me."

Nor was this all; one would have fancied the ass understood what Sancho said, because that moment he began to bray so loudly that the whole cave rang again.

"Famous testimony!" exclaimed Don Quixote. "I know that bray as well as if I was its mother, and thy voice too, my Sancho. Wait while I go to the duke's castle, which is close by, and I will bring someone to take thee out of this pit into which thy sins no doubt have brought thee."

"Go, your worship," said Sancho, "and come back quick, for God's sake; for I cannot bear being buried alive any longer, and I'm dying of fears."

Don Quixote left him, and hastened to the castle to tell the duke and duchess what had happened to Sancho, and they were not a little astonished at it; they could easily understand his having fallen, for the cave had been in existence there from time immemorial; but they could not imagine how he had quitted the government without their receiving any intimation of his coming. To be brief, they fetched ropes and tackle, and by dint of many hands and much labor they drew up Dapple and Sancho Panza out of the darkness into the light of day. A student who saw him remarked, "That's the way all bad governors should come out of their governments, as this sinner comes out of the depths of the pit, dead with hunger, pale, and I suppose without a farthing."

Sancho overheard him and said, "It is eight or ten days, brother growler, since I entered upon the government of the island they gave me, and all that time I never had a bellyful of victuals, no not for an hour; doctors persecuted me and enemies crushed my bones; nor had I any opportunity of taking bribes or levying taxes; and if that be the case, as it is, I don't deserve, I think, to come out in this fashion. God knows my meaning and that's enough; I say no more, though I could."

"Be not angry at what thou hearest, Sancho," said Don Quixote, "or there will never be an end of it; keep a safe conscience and let them say what they like; for trying to stop slanderers' tongues is like trying to put gates to the open plain. If a governor comes out of his government rich, they say he has been a thief; and if he comes out poor, that he has been a noodle and a blockhead."

"They'll be pretty sure this time," said Sancho, "to set me down for a fool rather than a thief."

Thus talking, and surrounded by boys and a crowd of people, they reached the castle, where in one of the corridors the duke and duchess stood waiting for them; but Sancho would not go up to see the duke until he had first put up Dapple in the stable, for he said he had passed a very bad night in his last quarters; then he went upstairs to see his lord and lady, and kneeling before them he said, "Because it was your highnesses' pleasure, not because of any desert of my own, I went to govern your island of Barataria, which 'I entered naked, and naked I find myself; I neither lose nor gain.' Whether I have governed well or ill, I have had witnesses who will say what they think fit. I have answered questions, I have decided causes, and always dying of hunger, for Doctor Pedro Recio of Tirteafuera, the island and governor doctor, would have it so. Enemies attacked us by night and put us in a great quandary, but the people of the island say they came off safe and victorious by the might of my arm; and may God give them as much health as there's truth in what they say. In short, during that time I have weighed the cares and responsibilities governing brings with it, and by my reckoning I find my shoulders can't bear them. And so, before the government threw me over I preferred to throw the government over; and yesterday morning I left the island as I found it; and though I meant to make some useful laws, I made hardly any, as I was afraid they would not be kept; for in that case it comes to the same thing to make them or not to make them. I quitted the island, as I said, without any escort except my ass; I fell into a pit, and had not heaven sent me my master Don Quixote, I'd have stayed there till the end of the world. So now my lord and lady duke and duchess, here is your governor Sancho Panza, who in the bare ten days he has held the government has come by the knowledge that he would not give anything to be governor, not to say of an island, but of the whole world; and that point being settled, I take a leap out of the government and pass into the service of my master Don Quixote; for after all, though in it I eat my bread in fear and trembling, at any rate I take my fill; and for my part, so long as I'm full, it's all alike to me whether it's with carrots or with partridges."

Here Sancho brought his long speech to an end, Don Quixote having been the whole time in dread of his uttering a host of absurdities; and when he found him leave off with so few, he thanked heaven in his heart. The duke embraced Sancho and told him he was heartily sorry he had given up the government so soon, but that he would see that he was provided with some other post on his estate less onerous and more profitable. The duchess also embraced him, and gave orders that he should be taken good care of, as it was plain to see he had been badly treated and worse bruised.

CHAPTER 22

Prisoners of Roque

D ON QUIXOTE now felt it right to quit a life of such idleness as he was leading in the castle; for he fancied that he was making himself sorely missed by remaining shut up and inactive amid the countless luxuries and enjoyments his hosts lavished upon him as a knight-errant. And so one day he asked the duke and duchess to grant him permission to take his departure. They gave it, showing at the same time that they were very sorry he was leaving them.

The day of their departure, Don Quixote, coming out, made his appearance at an early hour in full armor in the courtyard of the castle. The whole household of the castle were watching him from the corridors, and the duke and duchess, too, came out to see him. Sancho was mounted on his Dapple, with his saddlebags, valise, and provender, supremely happy because the duke's majordomo, the same that had acted the part of the Trifaldi, had given him a little purse with two hundred gold crowns to meet the necessary expenses of the road, but of this Don Quixote knew nothing as yet.

When Don Quixote reached the open country, he felt at his ease, and in fresh spirits to take up the pursuit of chivalry once more; and turning to Sancho he said, "Freedom, Sancho, is one of the most precious gifts that heaven has bestowed upon men; no treasures that the earth holds buried or the sea conceals can compare with it; for freedom, as for honor, life may and should be ventured; and on the other hand, captivity is the greatest evil that can fall to the lot of man. I say this, Sancho, because thou hast seen the good cheer, the abundance we have enjoyed in this castle we are leaving; well then, amid those dainty banquets and snow-cooled beverages I felt as though I were undergoing the straits of hunger, because I did not enjoy them with the same freedom as if they had been mine own; for the sense of being under an obligation to return benefits and favors received is a restraint that checks the independence of the spirit. Happy he, to whom heaven has given a piece of bread for which he is not bound to give thanks to any but heaven itself!"

"For all your worship says," said Sancho, "it is not becoming that there should be no thanks on our part for two hundred gold crowns that the duke's majordomo has given me in a little purse which I carry next my heart, like a warming plaster or comforter, to meet any chance calls; for we sha'n't always find castles where they'll entertain us; now and then we may light upon road-side inns where they'll cudgel us."

In conversation of this sort the knight and squire-errant pursued their journey, pushing on to reach an inn which was in sight, apparently a league off. I say an inn, because Don Quixote called it so, contrary to his usual practice of calling all inns castles. They reached it, and asked the landlord if they could put up there. He said yes, with as much comfort and as good fare as they could find in Saragossa. They dismounted, and Sancho stowed away his larder in a room of which the landlord gave him the key. He took the beasts to the stable, fed them, and came back to see what orders Don Quixote, who was seated on a bench at the door, had for him, giving special thanks to heaven that this inn had not been taken for a castle by his master. Suppertime came, and they repaired to their room, and Sancho asked the landlord what he had to give them for supper. To this the landlord replied that his mouth should be the measure; he had only to ask what he would; for that inn was provided with the birds of the air and the fowls of the earth and the fish of the sea.

"There's no need of all that," said Sancho; "if they'll roast us a couple of chickens we'll be satisfied, for my master is delicate and eats little, and I'm not over and above gluttonous."

The landlord replied he had no chickens, for the kites had stolen them.

"Well then," said Sancho, "let señor landlord tell them to roast a pullet, so that it is a tender one."

"Pullet! My father!" said the landlord. "Indeed and in truth it's only yesterday I sent over fifty to the city to sell; but saving pullets ask what you will."

"In that case," said Sancho, "you will not be without veal or kid."

"Just now," said the landlord, "there's none in the house, for it's all finished; but next week there will be enough and to spare."

301

"Much good that does us," said Sancho; "I'll lay a bet that all these short-comings are going to wind up in plenty of bacon and eggs."

"By God," said the landlord, "my guest's wits must be precious dull; I tell him I have neither pullets nor hens, and he wants me to have eggs! Talk of other dainties, if you please, and don't ask for hens again."

"Body o' me!" said Sancho, "let's settle the matter; say at once what you have got, and let us have no more words about it."

"In truth and earnest, señor guest," said the landlord, "all I have is a couple of cow-heels like calves' feet, or a couple of calves' feet like cow-heels; they are boiled with chick peas, onions, and bacon, and at this moment they are crying, 'Come eat me, come eat me.'"

"I mark them for mine on the spot," said Sancho.

The next day Don Quixote arose betimes. Sancho paid the landlord magnificently, and recommended him either to say less about the providing of his inn or to keep it better provided.

It was a fresh morning giving promise of a cool day as Don Quixote quitted the inn, first of all taking care to ascertain the most direct road to Barcelona. Nothing worthy of being recorded happened to him for six days, at the end of which, having turned aside out of the road, he was overtaken by night in a thicket of oak trees.

Master and man dismounted from their beasts, and as soon as they had settled themselves at the foot of the trees, Sancho, who had had a good noon-tide meal that day, let himself, without more ado, pass the gates of sleep. But Don Quixote, whom his thoughts, far more than hunger, kept awake, could not close an eye, and roamed in fancy to and fro through all sorts of places.

When day dawned, Sancho rose and strolled about, but as he was about to lean against a tree he felt something touch his head, and putting up his hands encountered somebody's two feet with shoes and stockings on them. He trembled with fear and made for another tree, where the very same thing happened to him, and he fell a-shouting, calling upon Don Quixote to come and protect him. Don Quixote did so, and asked him what had happened to him, and what he was afraid of. Sancho replied that all the trees were full of men's feet and legs. Don Quixote felt them, and guessed at once what it was, and said to Sancho, "Thou hast nothing to be afraid of, for these feet and legs that thou feelest belong no doubt to some outlaws that have been hanged on these trees; for the authorities in these parts are wont to hang them up by twenties and thirties when they catch them; whereby I conjecture that I must be near Barcelona"; and it was, in fact, as he supposed; with the first light they looked up and saw that the fruit hanging on those trees were out-laws' bodies.

And if the dead freebooters scared them, their hearts were no less troubled by upwards of forty living ones, who all of a sudden surrounded them, and in the Catalan tongue bade them stand and wait until their captain came up. Don Quixote was on foot with his horse unbridled and his lance leaning against a tree, and in short completely defenseless; he thought it best there-fore to fold his arms and bow his head and reserve himself for a more favorable occasion and opportunity. The robbers made haste to search Dapple, and did not leave him a single thing of all he carried in the saddlebags and in the valise; and lucky it was for Sancho that the duke's crowns and those he had brought from home were in a girdle that he wore round him. But for all that, these good folk would have stripped him, but for the arrival at that moment of their captain, who was about thirty-four years of age apparently, strongly built, above the middle height, of stern aspect and swarthy complexion. He was mounted upon a powerful horse, and had on a coat of mail, with four pistols at his waist. He saw that his squires were about to rifle Sancho Panza, but he ordered them to desist and was at once obeyed, so the girdle escaped. He won-dered to see the lance leaning against the tree, the shield on the ground, and Don Quixote in armor and dejected, with the saddest and most melancholy face that sadness itself could produce; and going up to him he said, "Be not so cast down, good man, for you have not fallen into the hands of any in-human Busiris, but into Roque Guinart's, which are more merciful than cruel."

"The cause of my dejection," returned Don Quixote, "is not that I have fallen into thy hands, O valiant Roque, whose fame is bounded by no limits on earth, but that my carelessness should have been so great that thy soldiers should have caught me unbridled, when it is my duty, according to the rule of knight-errantry which I profess, to be always on the alert and at all times my own sentinel; for let me tell thee, great Roque, had they found me on my horse, with my lance and shield, it would not have been very easy for them to reduce me to submission, for I am Don Quixote of La Mancha, he who hath filled the whole world with his achievements."

Roque Guinart at once perceived that Don Quixote's weakness was more akin to madness than to swagger; and though he had sometimes heard him spoken of, he never regarded the things attributed to him as true, nor could he persuade himself that such a humor could become dominant in the heart of man. He was extremely glad, therefore, to meet him and test at close quarters what he had heard of him at a distance; so he said to him, "Despair not, valiant knight, nor regard as an untoward fate the position in which thou findest thyself; it may be that by these slips thy crooked fortune will make itself straight; for heaven by strange circuitous ways, mysterious and incomprehensible to man, raises up the fallen and makes rich the poor."

Roque then ordered his squires to restore to Sancho everything they had stripped Dapple of, and directed them to return to the place where they had been quartered during the night, where he would rejoin them shortly.

When Roque returned, he found his squires at the place to which he had ordered them, and Don Quixote on Rocinante in the midst of them delivering a harangue to them in which he urged them to give up a mode of life so full of peril, as well to the soul as to the body; but as most of them were Gascons, rough lawless fellows, his speech did not make much impression on them. Roque on coming up asked Sancho if his men had returned and restored to him the treasures and jewels they had stripped off Dapple. Sancho said they had, but that three kerchiefs that were worth three cities were missing.

"What are you talking about, man?" said one of the bystanders. "I have got them, and they are not worth three reals."

"That is true," said Don Quixote; "but my squire values them at the rate he says, as having been given me by the person who gave them."

Roque Guinart ordered them to be restored at once; and making his men fall in line he directed all the clothing, jewelry, and money that they had taken since the last distribution to be produced; and making a hasty valuation, and reducing what could not be divided into money, he made shares for the whole band so equitably and carefully that in no case did he exceed or fall short of strict distributive justice.

When this had been done, and all left satisfied, Roque observed to Don Quixote, "If this scrupulous exactness were not observed with these fellows there would be no living with them."

Upon this Sancho remarked, "From what I have seen here, justice is such a good thing that there is no doing without it, even among the thieves themselves."

One of the squires heard this, and raising the butt end of his harquebuss would no doubt have broken Sancho's head with it had not Roque Guinart called out to him to hold his hand. Sancho was frightened out of his wits, and vowed not to open his lips so long as he was in the company of these people.

At this instant one or two of those squires who were posted as sentinels on the roads, to watch who came along them and report what passed to their chief, came up and said, "Señor, there is a great troop of people not far off coming along the road to Barcelona."

To which Roque replied, "Hast thou made out whether they are of the sort that are after us, or of the sort we are after?"

"The sort we are after," said the squire.

"Well then, away with you all," said Roque, "and bring them here to me at once without letting one of them escape."

They obeyed, and Don Quixote, Sancho, and Roque, left by themselves, waited to see what the squires brought, and while they were waiting Roque said to Don Quixote, "It must seem a strange sort of life to Señor Don Quixote, this of ours, strange adventures, strange incidents, and all full of danger; and I do not wonder that it should seem so, for in truth I must own there is no mode of life more restless or anxious than ours. What led me into it was a certain thirst for vengeance, which is strong enough to disturb the quietest hearts. I am by nature tender-hearted and kindly, but, as I said, the desire to revenge myself for a wrong that was done me so overturns all my better impulses that I keep on in this way of life in spite of what conscience tells me; and as one depth calls to another, and one sin to another sin, revenges have linked themselves together, and I have taken upon myself not only my own but those of others: it pleases God, however, that, though I see myself in this maze of entanglements, I do not lose all hope of escaping from it and reaching a safe port."

Don Quixote was amazed to hear Roque utter such excellent and just sentiments, for he did not think that among those who followed such trades as robbing, murdering, and waylaying, there could be anyone capable of a virtuous thought, and he said in reply, "Señor Roque, the beginning of health lies in knowing the disease and in the sick man's willingness to take the medicines which the physician prescribes; you are sick, you know what ails you, God, who is our physician, will administer medicines that will cure you, and cure gradually, and not of a sudden or by a miracle; besides, sinners of discernment are nearer amendment than those who are fools; and as your worship has shown good sense in your remarks, all you have to do is to keep up a good heart and trust that the weakness of your conscience will be strengthened.

305

And if you have any desire to shorten the journey and put yourself easily in the way of salvation, come with me, and I will show you how to become a knight-errant, a calling wherein so many hardships and mishaps are encountered that if they be taken as penances they will lodge you in heaven in a trice."

Roque laughed at Don Quixote's exhortation, and now the squires dispatched to make the prize came up, bringing with them two gentlemen on horseback, two pilgrims on foot, and a coach with three ladies and a child with some six servants on foot and on horseback in attendance on them, and a couple of muleteers whom the gentlemen had with them. The squires made a ring round them, both victors and vanquished maintaining profound silence, waiting for the great Roque Guinart to speak. He asked the gentlemen who they were, whither they were going, and what money they carried with them.

"Señor," replied one of them, "we are two captains of Spanish infantry; our companies are at Naples, and we are on our way to embark in four galleys which they say are at Barcelona under orders for Sicily; and we have about two or three hundred crowns, with which we are, according to our notions, rich and contented, for a soldier's poverty does not allow a more extensive hoard."

Roque asked the pilgrims the same questions he had put to the captains, and was answered that they were going to take ship for Rome, and that between them they might have about sixty reals. He asked also who was in the coach, whither they were bound and what money they had, and one of the men on horseback replied, "The persons in the coach are my lady Doña Guiomar de Quiñones, wife of the regent of the Vicaria at Naples, her little daughter, a handmaid and a duenna; we six servants are in attendance upon her, and the money amounts to six hundred crowns."

"So then," said Roque Guinart, "we have got here nine hundred crowns and sixty reals; my soldiers must number some sixty; see how much there falls to each, for I am a bad arithmetician." As soon as the robbers heard this they raised a shout of "Long life to Roque Guinart, in spite of the thieves that seek his ruin!"

The captains showed plainly the concern they felt, the regent's lady was downcast, and the pilgrims did not at all enjoy seeing their property confiscated. Roque kept them in suspense in this way for a while; but he had no desire to prolong their distress, which might be seen a bowshot off, and turning to the captains he said, "Sirs, will your worships be pleased of your courtesy to lend me sixty crowns, and her ladyship the regent's wife eighty, to satisfy this band that follows me, for 'it is by his singing the abbot gets his dinner'; and then you may at once proceed on your journey, free and unhindered, with a safeconduct which I shall give you, so that if you come across any other bands of mine that I have scattered in these parts, they may do you no harm; for I have no intention of doing injury to soldiers, or to any woman, especially one of quality."

Profuse and hearty were the expressions of gratitude with which the captains thanked Roque for his courtesy and generosity; for such they regarded his leaving them their own money. Señora Doña Guiomar de Quiñones wanted to throw herself out of the coach to kiss the feet and hands of the great Roque, but he would not suffer it on any account; so far from that, he begged her pardon for the wrong he had done her under pressure of the inexorable necessities of his unfortunate calling. The regent's lady ordered one of her servants to give the eighty crowns that had been assessed as her share at once, for the captains had already paid down their sixty. The pilgrims were about to give up the whole of their little hoard, but Roque bade them keep quiet, and turning to his men he said, "Of these crowns two fall to each man and twenty remain over; let ten be given to these pilgrims, and the other ten to this worthy squire that he may be able to speak favorably of this adventure"; and then having writing materials, with which he always went provided, brought to him, he gave them in writing a safeconduct to the leaders of his bands; and bidding them farewell let them go free and filled with admiration at his magnanimity, his generous disposition, and his unusual conduct, and inclined to regard him as an Alexander the Great rather than a notorious robber.

One of the squires observed in his mixture of Gascon and Catalan, "This captain of ours would make a better friar than highwayman; if he wants to be so generous another time, let it be with his own property and not ours."

The unlucky wight did not speak so low but that Roque overheard him, and drawing his sword almost split his head in two, saying, "That is the way I punish impudent saucy fellows." They were all taken aback, and not one of them dared to utter a word, such deference did they pay him. Roque then withdrew to one side and wrote a letter to a friend of his at Barcelona, telling him that the famous Don Quixote of La Mancha, the knight-errant of whom there was so much talk, was with him, and was, he assured him, the drollest and wisest man in the world; and that in four days from that date, that is to

307

say, on Saint John the Baptist's Day, he was going to deposit him in full armor mounted on his horse Rocinante, together with his squire Sancho on an ass, in the middle of the strand of the city; and bidding him give notice of this to his friends the Niarros, that they might divert themselves with him. He wished, he said, his enemies the Cadells could be deprived of this pleasure; but that was impossible, because the crazes and shrewd sayings of Don Quixote and the humors of his squire Sancho Panza could not help giving general pleasure to all the world. He dispatched the letter by one of his squires, who, exchanging the costume of a highwayman for that of a peasant, made his way into Barcelona and gave it to the person to whom it was directed.

CHAPTER 23

The Enchanted Head

D ON QUIXOTE passed three days and three nights with Roque,
and had he passed three hundred years he would have found
enough to observe and wonder at in his mode of life. At daybreak they were in one spot, at dinnertime in another; sometimes they fled
without knowing from whom, at other times they lay in wait, not knowing for
what. They slept standing, breaking their slumbers to shift from place to
place. There was nothing but sending out spies and scouts, posting sentinels
and blowing the matches of harquebusses, though they carried but few, for
almost all used flintlocks. Roque passed his nights in some place or other
apart from his men, that they might not know where he was, for the many
proclamations the viceroy of Barcelona had issued against his life kept him
in fear and uneasiness, and he did not venture to trust anyone, afraid that
even his own men would kill him or deliver him up to the authorities; of a
truth, a weary miserable life!

At length, by unfrequented roads, shortcuts, and secret paths, Roque, Don
Quixote, and Sancho, together with six squires, set out for Barcelona. They
reached the strand on Saint John's Eve during the night; and Roque, after
embracing Don Quixote and Sancho (to whom he presented the ten crowns
he had promised but had not until then given), left them with many expressions of good will on both sides.

Roque went back, while Don Quixote remained on horseback, just as he
was, waiting for day, and it was not long before the countenance of the fair
Aurora began to show itself, gladdening the grass and flowers, if not the ear,

though to gladden that too there came at the same moment a sound of clarions and drums, and a din of bells, and a tramp, tramp, and cries of "Clear the way there!" of some runners, that seemed to issue from the city. The dawn made way for the sun that with a face broader than a buckler began to rise slowly above the low line of the horizon; Don Quixote and Sancho gazed all round them; they beheld the sea, a sight until then unseen by them; it struck them as exceedingly spacious and broad, much more so than the lakes of Ruidera which they had seen in La Mancha. They saw the galleys along the beach, which, lowering their awnings, displayed themselves decked with streamers and pennons that trembled in the breeze and kissed and swept the water, while on board the bugles, trumpets, and clarions were sounding and filling the air far and near with melodious warlike notes. Then they began to move and execute a kind of skirmish upon the calm water, while a vast number of horsemen on fine horses and in showy liveries, issuing from the city, engaged on their side in a somewhat similar movement. The soldiers on board the galleys kept up a ceaseless fire, which they on the walls and forts of the city returned, and the heavy cannon rent the air with the tremendous noise they made, to which the gangway guns of the galleys replied. The bright sea, the smiling earth, the clear air—though at times darkened by the smoke of the guns—all seemed to fill the whole multitude with unexpected delight. Sancho could not make out how it was that those great masses that moved over the sea had so many feet.

And now the horsemen in livery came galloping up with shouts and outlandish cries and cheers to where Don Quixote stood amazed and wondering; and one of them, he to whom Roque had sent word, addressing him exclaimed, "Welcome to our city, mirror, beacon, star and cynosure of all knight-errantry in its widest extent! Welcome, I say, valiant Don Quixote of La Mancha!"

Don Quixote made no answer, nor did the horsemen wait for one, but wheeling again with all their followers, they began curvetting round Don Quixote, who, turning to Sancho, said, "These gentlemen have plainly recognized us; I will wager they have read our history."

The cavalier who had addressed Don Quixote again approached him and said, "Come with us, Señor Don Quixote, for we are all of us your servants and great friends of Roque Guinart's"; to which Don Quixote returned, "If courtesy breeds courtesy, yours, sir knight, is daughter or very nearly akin to the great Roque's; carry me where you please; I will have no will but yours, especially if you deign to employ it in your service."

"Welcome, valiant Don Quixote of La Mancha!"

The cavalier replied with words no less polite, and then, all closing in round him, they set out with him for the city, to the music of the clarions and the drums. As they were entering it, the wicked one, who is the author of all mischief, and the boys, who are wickeder than the wicked one, contrived that a couple of these audacious, irrepressible urchins should force their way through the crowd, and lifting up, one of them Dapple's tail and the other Rocinante's, insert a bunch of furze under each. The poor beasts felt the strange spurs and added to their anguish by pressing their tails tight, so much so that, cutting a multitude of capers, they flung their masters to the ground. Don Quixote, covered with shame and out of countenance, ran to pluck the plume from his poor jade's tail, while Sancho did the same for Dapple. His conductors tried to punish the audacity of the boys, but there was no possibility of doing so, for they hid themselves among the hundreds of others that were following them. Don Quixote and Sancho mounted once more, and with the same music and acclamations reached their conductor's house, which was large and stately, that of a rich gentleman.

Don Quixote's host was one Don Antonio Moreno by name, a gentleman of wealth and intelligence, and very fond of diverting himself in any fair and good-natured way; and having Don Quixote in his house he set about devising modes of making him exhibit his mad points in some harmless fashion; for jests that give pain are no jests, and no sport is worth anything if it hurts another. The first thing he did was to make Don Quixote take off his armor, and lead him, in that tight chamois suit we have already described, out on a balcony overhanging one of the chief streets of the city, in full view of the crowd and of the boys, who gazed at him as they would at a monkey. The cavaliers in livery careered before him again as though it were for him alone, and not to enliven the festival of the day, and Sancho was in high delight, for it seemed to him that, how he knew not, he had fallen upon another house like Don Diego de Miranda's, another castle like the duke's. Some of Don Antonio's friends dined with him that day, and all showed honor to Don Quixote and treated him as a knight-errant, and he becoming puffed up and exalted in consequence could not contain himself for satisfaction. Such were the drolleries of Sancho that all the servants of the house, and all who heard him, were kept hanging upon his lips. While at table Don Antonio said to him, "We hear, worthy Sancho, that you are so fond of manjar blanco and forced-meat balls, that if you have any left, you keep them in your bosom for the next day."

"No, señor, that's not true," said Sancho, "for I am more cleanly than greedy, and my master Don Quixote here knows well that we two are used to live for a week on a handful of acorns or nuts. To be sure, if it so happens that they offer me a heifer, I run with a halter; I mean, I eat what I'm given, and make use of opportunities as I find them; but whoever says that I'm an out-of-the-way eater or not cleanly, let me tell him that he is wrong; and I'd put it in a different way if I did not respect the honorable beards that are at the table."

"Indeed," said Don Quixote, "Sancho's moderation and cleanliness in eating might be inscribed and graved on plates of brass, to be kept in eternal remembrance in ages to come. It is true that when he is hungry there is a certain appearance of voracity about him, for he eats at a great pace and chews with both jaws; but cleanliness he is always mindful of; and when he was governor he learned how to eat daintily, so much so that he eats grapes, and even pomegranate pips, with a fork."

"What!" said Don Antonio, "has Sancho been a governor?"

"Ay," said Sancho, "and of an island called Barataria. I governed it to perfection for ten days; and lost my rest all the time; and learned to look down upon all the governments in the world; I got out of it by taking to flight, and fell into a pit where I gave myself up for dead, and out of which I escaped alive by a miracle."

Don Quixote then gave them a minute account of the whole affair of Sancho's government, with which he greatly amused his hearers.

On the cloth being removed, Don Antonio, taking Don Quixote by the hand, passed with him into a distant room in which there was nothing in the way of furniture except a table, apparently of jasper, resting on a pedestal of the same, upon which was set up, after the fashion of the busts of the Roman emperors, a head which seemed to be of bronze. Don Antonio traversed the whole apartment with Don Quixote and walked round the table several times, and then said, "Now, Señor Don Quixote, that I am satisfied that no one is listening to us, and that the door is shut, I will tell you of one of the rarest adventures, or more properly speaking strange things, that can be imagined, on condition that you will keep what I say to you in the remotest recesses of secrecy."

"I swear it," said Don Quixote, "and I would have you know, Señor Don Antonio, that you are addressing one who, though he has ears to hear, has no tongue to speak; so that whatever you wish to say, you may rely upon it that you have consigned it to the depths of silence."

"In reliance upon that promise," said Don Antonio, "I will astonish you with what you shall see and hear, and relieve myself of some of the vexation it gives me to have no one to whom I can confide my secrets, for they are not of a sort to be entrusted to everybody."

Don Quixote was puzzled, wondering what could be the object of such precautions; whereupon Don Antonio taking his hand passed it over the bronze head and the whole table and the pedestal of jasper on which it stood, and then said, "This head, Señor Don Quixote, has been made and fabricated by one of the greatest magicians and wizards the world ever saw. He was here in my house, and for a consideration of a thousand crowns that I gave him he constructed this head, which has the property of answering whatever questions are put to its ear. He observed the points of the compass, he studied the stars, he watched favorable moments, and at length brought it to the perfection we shall see tomorrow, for on Fridays it is mute, and this being Friday we must wait till the next day. In the interval your worship may consider what you would like to ask it; and I know by experience that in all its answers it tells the truth."

Don Quixote was amazed at the virtue and property of the head, and was inclined to disbelieve Don Antonio; but seeing what a short time he had to wait to test the matter, he did not choose to say anything except that he thanked him for having revealed to him so mighty a secret. They then quitted the room, Don Antonio locked the door, and they repaired to the chamber where the rest of the gentlemen were assembled. In the meantime Sancho had recounted to them several of the adventures and accidents that had happened his master.

That afternoon they took Don Quixote out for a stroll, not in his armor but in street costume, with a surcoat of tawny cloth upon him, that at that season would have made ice itself sweat. Orders were left with the servants to entertain Sancho so as not to let him leave the house. Don Quixote was mounted, not on Rocinante, but upon a tall mule of easy pace and handsomely caparisoned. They put the surcoat on him, and on the back, without his perceiving it, they stitched a parchment on which they wrote in large letters, "This is Don Quixote of La Mancha." As they set out upon their excursion the placard attracted the eyes of all who chanced to see him, and as they read out, "This is Don Quixote of La Mancha," Don Quixote was amazed to see how many people gazed at him, called him by his name, and recognized him, and turning to Don Antonio, who rode at his side, he observed to him, "Great are the privileges knight-errantry involves, for it makes him who professes it known and famous in every region of the earth; see, Don Antonio, even the very boys of this city know me without ever having seen me."

"True, Señor Don Quixote," returned Don Antonio; "for as fire cannot be hidden or kept secret, virtue cannot escape being recognized."

They proceeded amid the acclamations that have been described, until the press of the boys and people to read the placard grew so great that Don Antonio was forced to remove it as if he were taking off something else.

Night came and they went home, and there was a ladies' dancing party, for Don Antonio's wife, a lady of rank and gaiety, beauty and wit, had invited some friends of hers to come and do honor to her guest and amuse themselves with his strange delusions. Several of them came, they supped sumptuously, and the dance began at about ten o'clock. Among the ladies were two of a mischievous and frolicsome turn, and, though perfectly modest, somewhat free in playing tricks for harmless diversion's sake. These two were so indefatigable in taking Don Quixote out to dance that they tired him down, not only in body but in spirit. It was a sight to see the figure Don Quixote made, long, lank, lean, and yellow, his garments clinging tight to him, ungainly, and above all anything but agile. The gay ladies made secret love to him, and he on his part secretly repelled them, but finding himself hard pressed by their blandishments he lifted up his voice and exclaimed, "Leave me in peace, unwelcome overtures; avaunt, with your desires, ladies, for she who is queen of mine, the peerless Dulcinea del Toboso, suffers none but hers to lead me captive and subdue me." And so saying he sat down on the floor in the middle of the room, tired out and broken down by all this exertion in the dance.

Don Antonio directed him to be taken up bodily and carried to bed, and the first that laid hold of him was Sancho, saying as he did so, "In an evil hour you took to dancing, master mine; do you fancy all mighty men of valor are dancers, and all knights-errant given to capering? If you do, I can tell you you are mistaken; there's many a man would rather undertake to kill a giant than cut a caper."

With these and other observations Sancho set the whole ballroom laughing, and then put his master to bed, covering him up well so that he might sweat out any chill caught after his dancing.

The next day Don Antonio thought he might as well make trial of the enchanted head, and with Don Quixote, Sancho, and two others, friends of his, besides the two ladies that had tired out Don Quixote at the ball, who had remained for the night with Don Antonio's wife, he locked himself up in the chamber where the head was. He explained to them the property it possessed and entrusted the secret to them, telling them that now for the first time he was going to try the virtue of the enchanted head.

The first to approach the ear of the head was Don Antonio himself, and in a low voice but not so low as not to be audible to all, he said to it, "Head, tell me by the virtue that lies in thee what am I at this moment thinking of?"

The head, without any movement of the lips, answered in a clear and distinct voice, so as to be heard by all, "I cannot judge of thoughts."

All were thunderstruck at this, and all the more so as they saw that there was nobody anywhere near the table or in the whole room that could have answered. "How many of us are here?" asked Don Antonio once more; and it was answered him in the same way softly, "Thou and thy wife, with two friends of thine and two of hers, and a famous knight called Don Quixote of La Mancha, and a squire of his, Sancho Panza by name."

Now there was fresh astonishment; now everyone's hair was standing on end with awe; and Don Antonio retiring from the head exclaimed, "This suffices to show me that I have not been deceived by him who sold thee to me, O sage head, talking head, answering head, wonderful head! Let someone else go and put what question he likes to it."

And as women are commonly impulsive and inquisitive, the first to come forward was one of the two friends of Don Antonio's wife, and her question was, "Tell me, Head, what shall I do to be very beautiful?" and the answer she got was, "Be very modest."

"I question thee no further," said the fair querist.

Her companion then came up and said, "I should like to know, Head, whether my husband loves me or not"; the answer given to her was, "Think how he uses thee, and thou mayest guess"; and the married lady went off saying, "That answer did not need a question; for of course the treatment one receives shows the disposition of him from whom it is received."

Then one of Don Antonio's two friends advanced and asked it, "Who am I?" "Thou knowest," was the answer. "That is not what I ask thee," said the gentleman, "but to tell me if thou knowest me." "Yes, I know thee, thou art Don Pedro Noriz," was the reply.

315

"I do not seek to know more," said the gentleman, "for this is enough to convince me, O Head, that thou knowest everything"; and as he retired the other friend came forward and asked it, "Tell me, Head, what are the wishes of my eldest son?"

"I have said already," was the answer, "that I cannot judge of wishes; however, I can tell thee the wish of thy son is to bury thee."

"That's 'what I see with my eyes I point out with my finger,'" said the gentleman, "so I ask no more."

Don Antonio's wife came up and said, "I know not what to ask thee, Head; I would only seek to know of thee if I shall have many years of enjoyment of my good husband"; and the answer she received was, "Thou shalt, for his vigor and his temperate habits promise many years of life, which by their intemperance others so often cut short."

Then Don Quixote came forward and said, "Tell me, thou that answerest, was that which I describe as having happened to me in the cave of Montesinos the truth or a dream? Will Sancho's whipping be accomplished without fail? Will the disenchantment of Dulcinea be brought about?"

"As to the question of the cave," was the reply, "there is much to be said; there is something of both in it. Sancho's whipping will proceed leisurely. The disenchantment of Dulcinea will attain its due consummation."

"I seek to know no more," said Don Quixote; "let me but see Dulcinea disenchanted, and I will consider that all the good fortune I could wish for has come upon me all at once."

The last questioner was Sancho, and his questions were, "Head, shall I by any chance have another government? Shall I ever escape from the hard life of a squire? Shall I get back to see my wife and children?" To which the answer came, "Thou shalt govern in thy house; and if thou returnest to it thou shalt see thy wife and children; and on ceasing to serve thou shalt cease to be a squire."

"Good, by God!" said Sancho Panza. "I could have told myself that."

"What answer wouldst thou have, beast?" said Don Quixote. "Is it not enough that the replies this head has given suit the questions put to it?"

"Yes, it is enough," said Sancho, "but I should have liked it to have made itself plainer and told me more."

The questions and answers came to an end here, but not the wonder with which all were filled, except Don Antonio's two friends, who were in the secret.

The Enchanted Head

On the model of another head, the work of an image maker, which he had seen at Madrid, Don Antonio made this one at home for his own amusement and to astonish ignorant people; and its mechanism was as follows: The table was of wood painted and varnished to imitate jasper, and the pedestal on which it stood was of the same material, with four eagles' claws projecting from it to support the weight more steadily. The head, which resembled a bust or figure of a Roman emperor, and was colored like bronze, was hollow throughout, as was the table, into which it was fitted so exactly that no trace of the joining was visible. The pedestal of the table was also hollow and communicated with the throat and neck of the head, and the whole was in communication with another room underneath the chamber in which the head stood. Through the entire cavity in the pedestal, table, throat and neck of the bust or figure, there passed a tube of tin carefully adjusted and concealed from sight.

In the room below corresponding to the one above was placed the person who was to answer, with his mouth to the tube, and the voice, as in an ear trumpet, passed from above downwards, and from below upwards, the words coming clearly and distinctly; it was impossible, thus, to detect the trick. A nephew of Don Antonio's, a smart, sharp-witted student, was the answerer, and as he had been told beforehand by his uncle who the persons were that would come with him that day into the chamber where the head was, it was an easy matter for him to answer the first question at once and correctly; the others he answered by guesswork, and, being clever, cleverly.

This marvelous contrivance stood for some ten or twelve days; but as it became noised abroad through the city that he had in his house an enchanted head that answered all who asked questions of it, Don Antonio, fearing it might come to the ears of the watchful sentinels of our faith, explained the matter to the inquisitors, who commanded him to break it up and have done with it, lest the ignorant vulgar should be scandalized. By Don Quixote, however, and by Sancho the head was still held to be an enchanted one, and capable of answering questions, though more to Don Quixote's satisfaction than Sancho's.

CHAPTER 24

The Knight Is Overthrown

ONE MORNING as Don Quixote went out for a stroll along the beach, arrayed in full armor (for, as he often said, that was "his only gear, his only rest the fray," and he never was without it for moment), he saw coming towards him a knight, also in full armor, with a shining moon painted on his shield, who, on approaching sufficiently near to be heard, said in a loud voice, addressing himself to Don Quixote, "Illustrious knight, and never sufficiently extolled Don Quixote of La Mancha, I am the Knight of the White Moon, whose unheard-of achievements will perhaps have recalled him to thy memory. I come to do battle with thee and prove the might of thy arm, to the end that I make thee acknowledge and confess that my lady, let her be who she may, is incomparably fairer than thy Dulcinea del Toboso. If thou dost acknowledge this fairly and openly, thou shalt escape death and save me the trouble of inflicting it upon thee; if thou fightest and I vanquish thee, I demand no other satisfaction than that, laying aside arms and abstaining from going in quest of adventures, thou withdraw and betake thyself to thine own village for the space of a year, and live there without putting hand to sword, in peace and quiet and beneficial repose, the same being needful for the increase of thy substance and the salvation of thy soul; and if thou dost vanquish me, my head shall be at thy disposal, my arms and horse thy spoils, and the renown of my deeds transferred and added to thine. Consider which will be thy best course, and give me thy answer speedily, for this day is all the time I have for the dispatch of this business."

Don Quixote was amazed and astonished, as well at the Knight of the White Moon's arrogance, as at his reason for delivering the defiance, and with calm dignity he answered him, "Knight of the White Moon, of whose achievements I have never heard until now, I will venture to swear you have never seen the illustrious Dulcinea; for had you seen her I know you would have taken care not to venture yourself upon this issue, because the sight would have removed all doubt from your mind that there ever has been or can be beauty to be compared with hers; and so, not saying you lie, but merely that you are not correct in what you state, I accept your challenge, with the conditions you have proposed, and at once, that the day you have fixed may not expire; and from your conditions I except only that of the renown of your achievements being transferred to me, for I know not of what sort they are nor what they may amount to; I am satisfied with my own, such as they be. Take, therefore, the side of the field you choose, and I will do the same; and to whom God shall give it may Saint Peter add his blessing."

The Knight of the White Moon had been seen from the city, and the viceroy was told how he was in conversation with Don Quixote. The viceroy, fancying it must be some fresh adventure got up by Don Antonio Moreno or some other gentleman of the city, hurried out at once to the beach accompanied by Don Antonio and several other gentlemen, just as Don Quixote was wheeling Rocinante round in order to take up the necessary distance. The viceroy upon this, seeing that the pair of them were evidently preparing to come to the charge, put himself between them, asking them what it was that led them to engage in combat all of a sudden in this way. The Knight of the White Moon replied that it was a question of precedence of beauty; and briefly told him what he had said to Don Quixote, and how the conditions of the defiance agreed upon on both sides had been accepted.

The viceroy went over to Don Antonio, and asked in a low voice did he know who the Knight of the White Moon was, or was it some joke they were playing on Don Quixote. Don Antonio replied that he neither knew who he was nor whether the defiance was in joke or in earnest. This answer left the viceroy in a state of perplexity, not knowing whether he ought to let the combat go on or not; but unable to persuade himself that it was anything but a joke he fell back, saying, "If there be no other way out of it, gallant knights, except to confess or die, and Don Quixote is inflexible, and your worship of the White Moon still more so, in God's hand be it, and fall on."

He of the White Moon thanked the viceroy in courteous and well-chosen words for the permission he gave them, and so did Don Quixote, who then, commending himself with all his heart to heaven and to his Dulcinea, as was his custom on the eve of any combat that awaited him, proceeded to take a little more distance, as he saw his antagonist was doing the same. Then, without blast of trumpet or other warlike instrument to give them the signal to charge, both at the same instant wheeled their horses; and he of the White Moon, being the swifter, met Don Quixote after having traversed two-thirds of the course, and there encountered him with such violence that, without touching him with his lance (for he held it high, to all appearance purposely), he hurled Don Quixote and Rocinante to the earth, a perilous fall. He sprang upon him at once, and placing the lance over his visor said to him, "You are vanquished, sir knight, nay dead unless you admit the conditions of our defiance."

Don Quixote, bruised and stupefied, without raising his visor said in a weak feeble voice as if he were speaking out of a tomb, "Dulcinea del Toboso is the fairest woman in the world, and I the most unfortunate knight on earth; it is not fitting that this truth should suffer by my feebleness; drive your lance home, sir knight, and take my life, since you have taken away my honor."

"That will I not, in sooth," said he of the White Moon. "Live the fame of the lady Dulcinea's beauty undimmed as ever; all I require is that the great Don Quixote retire to his own home for a year, or for so long a time as shall by me be enjoined upon him, as we agreed before engaging in this combat."

The viceroy, Don Antonio, and several others who were present heard all this, and heard too how Don Quixote replied that so long as nothing in prejudice of Dulcinea was demanded of him, he would observe all the rest like a true and loyal knight. The engagement given, he of the White Moon wheeled about, and making obeisance to the viceroy with a movement of the head, rode away into the city at a half gallop. The viceroy bade Don Antonio hasten after him, and by some means or other find out who he was. They raised Don Quixote up and uncovered his face, and found him pale and bathed with sweat. Rocinante from the mere hard measure he had received lay unable to stir for the present. Sancho, wholly dejected and woebegone, knew not what to say or do. He fancied that all was a dream, that the whole business was a piece of enchantment. Here was his master defeated, and bound not to take up arms for a year. He saw the light of the glory of his achievements obscured; the hopes of the promises lately made him swept away like smoke before the wind; Rocinante, he feared, was crippled for life, and his master's bones out of joint; for if he were only shaken out of his madness it would be no small luck. In the end they carried him into the city in a hand-chair which the viceroy sent for, and thither the viceroy himself returned, eager to ascertain who this Knight of the White Moon was who had left Don Quixote in such a sad plight.

Don Antonio Moreno followed the Knight of the White Moon, and a number of boys followed him too, nay pursued him, until they had him fairly housed in a hostel in the heart of the city. Don Antonio, eager to make his acquaintance, entered also; a squire came out to meet him and remove his armor, and he shut himself into a lower room, still attended by Don Antonio, whose bread would not bake until he had found out who he was.

He of the White Moon, seeing then that the gentleman would not leave him, said, "I know very well, señor, what you have come for; it is to find out who I am; and as there is no reason why I should conceal it from you, while my servant here is taking off my armor I will tell you the true state of the case. You must know, señor, that I am called the bachelor Samson Carrasco. I am of the same village as Don Quixote of La Mancha, whose craze and folly make all of us who know him feel pity for him, and I am one of those who have felt it most; and persuaded that his chance of recovery lay in quiet and keeping at home and in his own house, I hit upon a device for keeping him there.

"Three months ago, therefore, I went out to meet him as a knight-errant, under the assumed name of the Knight of the Mirrors, intending to engage him in combat and overcome him without hurting him, making it the condition of our combat that the vanquished should be at the disposal of the victor. What I meant to demand of him (for I regarded him as vanquished already) was that he should return to his own village, and not leave it for a whole year, by which time he might be cured. But fate ordered it otherwise, for he vanquished me and unhorsed me, and so my plan failed. He went his way, and I came back conquered, covered with shame, and sorely bruised by my fall, which was a particularly dangerous one. But this did not quench my desire to meet him again and overcome him, as you have seen today. And as he is so scrupulous in his observance of the laws of knight-errantry, he will, no doubt, in order to keep his word, obey the injunction I have laid upon him. This, señor, is how the matter stands, and I have nothing more to tell you. I implore of you not to betray me, or tell Don Quixote who I am; so that my honest endeavors may be successful, and that a man of excellent wits—were he only rid of the fooleries of chivalry—may get them back again."

"O señor," said Don Antonio, "may God forgive you the wrong you have done the whole world in trying to bring the most amusing madman in it back to his senses. Do you not see, señor, that the gain by Don Quixote's sanity can never equal the enjoyment his crazes give? But my belief is that all the señor bachelor's pains will be of no avail to bring a man so hopelessly cracked to his senses again; and if it were not uncharitable, I would say may Don Quixote never be cured, for by his recovery we lose not only his own drolleries, but his squire Sancho Panza's too, any one of which is enough to turn melancholy itself into merriment. However, I'll hold my peace and say nothing to him."

The bachelor replied that at all events the affair promised well, and he hoped for a happy result from it; and putting his services at Don Antonio's commands he took his leave of him; and having had his armor packed at once upon a mule, he rode away from the city the same day on the horse he rode to battle, and returned to his own country.

Don Antonio reported to the viceroy what Carrasco told him, and the viceroy was not very well pleased, for with Don Quixote's retirement there would be an end to the amusement of all who knew of his mad doings.

Six days did Don Quixote keep his bed, dejected, melancholy, moody and out of sorts, brooding over the unhappy event of his defeat. Sancho strove to comfort him, and among other things he said to him, "Hold up your head, señor, and be of good cheer if you can, and give thanks to heaven that if you have had a tumble to the ground you have not come off with a broken rib. A fig for the doctor, for there's no need of him to cure this ailment. Let us go home, and give over going about in search of adventures in strange lands and places; rightly looked at, it is I that am the greater loser, though it is your worship that has had the worse usage. With the government I gave up all wish to be a governor again, but I did not give up all longing to be a count; and that will never come to pass if your worship gives up becoming a king by renouncing the calling of chivalry; and so my hopes are going to turn into smoke."

"Peace, Sancho," said Don Quixote; "thou seest my suspension and retirement is not to exceed a year; I shall soon return to my honored calling, and I shall not be at a loss for a kingdom to win and a county to bestow on thee."

"May God hear it and sin be deaf," said Sancho; "I have always heard say that 'a good hope is better than a bad holding.'"

The day for Don Quixote and Sancho's departure came, though Don Quixote's fall did not suffer him to take the road at once. Don Quixote was in traveling gear, and Sancho on foot, Dapple being loaded with the armor.

CHAPTER 25

Six Hundred Pigs

A<small>S HE LEFT</small> Barcelona, Don Quixote turned to gaze upon the spot where he had fallen. "Here Troy was," said he; "here my ill-luck, not my cowardice, robbed me of all the glory I had won; here Fortune made me the victim of her caprices; here the luster of my achievements was dimmed; here, in a word, fell my happiness never to rise again."

"Señor," said Sancho on hearing this, "it is the part of brave hearts to be patient in adversity just as much as to be glad in prosperity; and I have heard say that she whom commonly they call Fortune is a whimsical jade, and, what is more, blind, and therefore neither sees what she does, nor knows whom she casts down or whom she sets up."

"Thou art a great philosopher, Sancho," said Don Quixote; "thou speakest very sensibly; I know not who taught thee. But I can tell thee there is no such thing as Fortune in the world, nor does anything which takes place there, be it good or bad, come about by chance, but by the special preordination of heaven; and hence the common saying that 'each of us is the maker of his own Fortune.' I have been that of mine; but not with the proper amount of prudence, and my self-confidence has therefore made me pay dearly; for I ought to have reflected that Rocinante's feeble strength could not resist the mighty bulk of the Knight of the White Moon's horse. In a word, I ventured it, I did my best, I was overthrown, but though I lost my honor I did not lose nor can I lose the virtue of keeping my word. When I was a knight-errant, daring and valiant, I supported my achievements by hand

and deed, and now that I am a humble squire I will support my words by keeping the promise I have given. Forward then, Sancho my friend, let us go to keep the year of the novitiate in our own country, and in that seclusion we shall pick up fresh strength to return to the calling of arms."

"Señor," returned Sancho, "traveling on foot is not such a pleasant thing that it makes me feel disposed or tempted to make long marches. Let us leave this armor hung up on some tree, instead of someone that has been hanged; and then with me on Dapple's back and my feet off the ground we will arrange the stages as your worship pleases to measure them out; but to suppose that I am going to travel on foot, and make long ones, is to suppose nonsense."

"Thou sayest well, Sancho," said Don Quixote. "Let my armor be hung up for a trophy, and under it or round it we will carve on the trees what was inscribed on the trophy of Roland's armor—

These let none move
Who dareth not his might with Roland prove."

"That's the very thing," said Sancho.

The night was somewhat dark, for though there was a moon in the sky it was not in a quarter where she could be seen; for sometimes the lady Diana goes on a stroll to the antipodes, and leaves the mountains all black and the valleys in darkness. Don Quixote obeyed nature so far as to sleep his first sleep, but did not give way to the second, very different from Sancho, who never had any second, because with him sleep lasted from night till morning, wherein he showed what a sound constitution and few cares he had.

Don Quixote's cares kept him restless, so much so that he awoke Sancho and said to him, "I am amazed, Sancho, at the unconcern of thy temperament. I believe thou art made of marble, incapable of any feeling whatever. I lie awake while thou sleepest, I weep while thou singest, I am faint with fasting while thou art sluggish and torpid from pure repletion. It is the duty of good servants to share the sufferings and feel the sorrows of their masters, if it be only for the sake of appearances."

"I don't know," said Sancho; "all I know is that so long as I am asleep I have neither fear nor hope, trouble nor glory; and good luck betide him that invented sleep, the cloak that covers over all a man's thoughts, the food that removes hunger, the drink that drives away thirst, the fire that warms the cold, the cold that tempers the heat, and, to wind up with, the universal coin wherewith everything is bought, the weight and balance that makes the shepherd equal with the king and the fool with the wise man. Sleep, I have heard say, has only one fault, that it is like death; for between a sleeping man and a dead man there is very little difference."

"Never have I heard thee speak so elegantly as now, Sancho," said Don Quixote; "and here I begin to see the truth of the proverb thou dost sometimes quote, 'Not with whom thou art bred, but with whom thou art fed.'"

"Ha, by my life, master mine," said Sancho, "it's not I that am stringing proverbs now, for they drop in pairs from your worship's mouth faster than from mine; only there is this difference between mine and yours, that yours are well-timed and mine are untimely; but anyhow, they are all proverbs."

At this point they became aware of a harsh, indistinct noise that seemed to spread through all the valleys around. Don Quixote stood up and laid his hand upon his word, and Sancho ensconced himself under Dapple and put the bundle of armor on one side of him and the ass's pack-saddle on the other, in fear and trembling as great as Don Quixote's perturbation. Each instant the noise increased and came nearer to the two terrified men, or at least to one, for as to the other, his courage is known to all. The fact of the matter was that some men were taking above six hundred pigs to sell at a fair, and were on their way with them at that hour, and so great was the noise they made and their grunting and blowing, that they deafened the ears of Don Quixote and Sancho Panza, and they could not make out what it was. The widespread grunting drove came on in a surging mass, and without showing any respect for Don Quixote's dignity or Sancho's, passed right over the pair of them, demolishing Sancho's entrenchments, and not only upsetting Don Quixote but sweeping Rocinante off his feet into the bargain; and what with the trampling and the grunting, and the pace at which the unclean beasts went, pack-saddle, armor, Dapple and Rocinante were left scattered on the ground and Sancho and Don Quixote at their wits' end.

Sancho got up as well as he could and begged his master to give him his sword, saying he wanted to kill half a dozen of those dirty unmannerly pigs, for he had by this time found out that that was what they were.

"Let them be, my friend," said Don Quixote; "this insult is the penalty of my sin; and it is the righteous chastisement of heaven that jackals should devour a vanquished knight, and wasps sting him and pigs trample him underfoot."

325

"I suppose it is the chastisement of heaven, too," said Sancho, "that flies should prick the squires of vanquished knights, and lice eat them, and hunger assail them. If we squires were the sons of the knights we serve, or their very near relations, it would be no wonder if the penalty of their misdeeds overtook us, even to the fourth generation. But what have the Panzas to do with the Quixotes? Well, well, let's lie down again and sleep out what little of the night there's left, and God will send us dawn and we shall be all right."

"Sleep thou, Sancho," returned Don Quixote, "for thou wast born to sleep as I was born to watch; and during the time it now wants of dawn I will give a loose rein to my thoughts, and seek a vent for them in a little madrigal which, unknown to thee, I composed in my head last night."

"I should think," said Sancho, "that the thoughts that allow one to make verses cannot be of great consequence; let your worship string verses as much as you like and I'll sleep as much as I can"; and forthwith, taking the space of ground he required, he muffled himself up and fell into a sound sleep, undisturbed by bond, debt, or trouble of any sort. Don Quixote, propped up against the trunk of a beech tree, sang in this strain to the accompaniment of his own sighs:

> "When in my mind
> I muse, O Love, upon thy cruelty,
>   To death I flee,
> In hope therein the end of all to find.
>
> "But drawing near
> That welcome haven in my sea of woe,
>   Such joy I know,
> That life revives, and still I linger here.
>
> "Thus life doth slay,
> And death again to life restoreth me;
>   Strange destiny,
> That deals with life and death as with a play!"

He accompanied each verse with many sighs and not a few tears, just like one whose heart was pierced with grief at his defeat and his separation from Dulcinea.

326

And now daylight came, and the sun smote Sancho on the eyes with his beams. He awoke, roused himself up, shook himself and stretched his lazy limbs, and seeing the havoc the pigs had made with his stores he cursed the drove, and more besides. Then the pair resumed their journey, and as evening closed in they saw coming towards them some ten men on horseback and four or five on foot. Don Quixote's heart beat quick and Sancho's quailed with fear, for the persons approaching them carried lances and bucklers, and were in very warlike guise.

Don Quixote turned to Sancho and said, "If I could make use of my weapons, and my promise had not tied my hands, I would count this host that comes against us but cakes and fancy bread; but perhaps it may prove something different from what we apprehend." The men on horseback now came up, and raising their lances surrounded Don Quixote in silence, and pointed them at his back and breast, menacing him with death. One of those on foot, putting his finger to his lips as a sign to him to be silent, seized Rocinante's bridle and drew him out of the road, and the others driving Sancho and Dapple before them, and all maintaining a strange silence, followed in the steps of the one who led Don Quixote. Sancho attempted to ask where they were taking him to and what they wanted, but the instant he began to open his lips they threatened to close them with the points of their lances; and Dapple likewise, as if he too wanted to talk. Night set in, they quickened their pace, and the fears of the two prisoners grew greater.

Don Quixote rode completely dazed, unable with the aid of all his wits to make out what could be the meaning of all this, and the only conclusion he could arrive at was that there was no good to be hoped for and much evil to be feared. And now, about an hour after midnight, they reached a castle which Don Quixote saw at once was the duke's, where they had been but a short time before. "God bless me!" said he, as he recognized the mansion, "what does this mean? It is all courtesy and politeness in this house; but with the vanquished, good turns into evil, and evil into worse."

They entered the chief court of the castle, and now two persons of distinction, who were at once recognized by Don Quixote as his hosts, the duke and duchess, came forward to greet him. The duke then gave orders that Don Quixote and Sancho Panza should be conducted to their old quarters.

Sancho slept that night in a cot in the same chamber with Don Quixote, a thing he would have gladly avoided if he could for he knew very well that with questions and answers his master would not let him sleep; and it would

327

have been more to his taste to sleep in a hovel alone, than in that luxurious chamber in company. And so well founded did his apprehension prove, and so correct was his anticipation, that scarcely had his master got into bed when he said, "What dost thou think of tonight's adventure, Sancho?"

"Now I begin to see plainly that there are enchanters and enchanted people in the world"; said Sancho, "and may God deliver me from them, since I can't deliver myself; and so I beg of your worship to let me sleep and not ask any more questions, unless you want me to throw myself out of the window."

"Be it so, and God be with thee," said Don Quixote.

They fell asleep, both of them, and we take this opportunity to relate what it was that induced the duke and duchess to get up their elaborate plot. The bachelor Samson Carrasco, not forgetting how he as the Knight of the Mirrors had been vanquished and overthrown by Don Quixote, which defeat and overthrow upset all his plans, resolved to try his hand again, hoping for better luck than he had before; and so, having learned where Don Quixote was, he got himself new armor and another horse, and put a white moon upon his shield, and to carry his arms he had a mule led by a peasant, not by Tom Cecial, his former squire, for fear he should be recognized by Sancho or Don Quixote. He came to the duke's castle, and the duke informed him of the road and route Don Quixote had taken with the intention of being present at the jousts at Saragossa. He told him, too, of the jokes he had practiced upon him, and of the device for the disenchantment of Dulcinea at the expense of Sancho's backside; and finally he gave him an account of the trick Sancho had played upon his master, making him believe that Dulcinea was enchanted and turned into a country wench; and of how the duchess, his wife, had persuaded Sancho that it was he himself who was deceived, inasmuch as Dulcinea was really enchanted; at which the bachelor laughed not a little, and marveled as well at the sharpness and simplicity of Sancho as at the length to which Don Quixote's madness went. The duke begged of him if he found him (whether he overcame him or not) to return that way and let him know the result. This the bachelor did; he set out in quest of Don Quixote, and not finding him at Saragossa, he went on, and how he fared has been already told.

He returned to the duke's castle and told him all, what the conditions of the combat were, and how Don Quixote was now, like a loyal knight-errant, returning to keep his promise of retiring to his village for a year, by which time, said the bachelor, he might perhaps be cured of his madness; for that was the object that had led him to adopt these disguises, as it was a sad thing for a gentleman of such good parts as Don Quixote to be a madman. And so he took his leave of the duke, and went home to his village to wait there for Don Quixote, who was coming after him. Thereupon the duke seized the opportunity of practicing this mystification upon him; so much did he enjoy everything connected with Sancho and Don Quixote. He had the roads about the castle far and near, everywhere he thought Don Quixote was likely to pass on his return, occupied by large numbers of his servants on foot and on horseback, who were to bring him to the castle, by fair means or foul, if they met him. They did meet him, and sent word to the duke and duchess, who were not two fingers' breadth removed from being something like fools themselves when they took such pains to make game of a pair of fools.

As for the latter, one was sleeping soundly and the other lying awake occupied with his desultory thoughts, when daylight came to them bringing with it the desire to rise; for the lazy down was never a delight to Don Quixote, victor or vanquished.

Some time later, the duke and duchess came in to see them, and there followed a long and delightful conversation, in the course of which Sancho said so many droll and saucy things that he left the duke and duchess wondering not only at his simplicity but at his sharpness. Don Quixote begged their permission to take his departure that same day, inasmuch as for a vanquished knight like himself it was fitter he should live in a pigsty than in a royal palace. They gave it reluctantly, and the conversation came to an end. Don Quixote dressed himself and dined with the duke and duchess, and set out the same evening.

CHAPTER 26

3300 Lashes

THE VANQUISHED and afflicted Don Quixote went along very
downcast in one respect.

"Sancho, my friend," he said, "I can say for myself that if thou
wouldst have payment for the lashes on account of the disenchantment of
Dulcinea, I would have given it to thee freely ere this. I am not sure, however,
whether payment will comport with the cure, and I would not have the
reward interfere with the medicine. Still, I think there will be nothing lost
by trying it; consider how much thou wouldst have, Sancho, and whip thyself
at once, and pay thyself down with thine own hand, as thou hast money of
mine."

At this proposal Sancho opened his eyes and his ears a palm's breadth wide,
and in his heart very readily acquiesced in whipping himself, and said he to
his master, "Very well then, señor, I'll hold myself in readiness to gratify your
worship's wishes if I'm to profit by it; for the love of my wife and children
forces me to seem grasping. Let your worship say how much you will pay
me for each lash I give myself."

"If, Sancho," replied Don Quixote, "I were to requite thee as the importance
and nature of the cure deserves, the treasures of Venice, the mines of Potosi,
would be insufficient to pay thee. See what thou hast of mine, and put a
price on each lash."

"Of them," said Sancho, "there are three thousand three hundred and
odd; of these I have given myself five, the rest remain; let the five go for the
odd ones, and let us take the three thousand three hundred, which at a
quarter real apiece (for I will not take less though the whole world should

bid me) make three thousand three hundred quarter reals; the three thousand are one thousand five hundred half reals, which make seven hundred and fifty reals; and the three hundred make a hundred and fifty half reals, which come to seventy-five reals, which added to the seven hundred and fifty make eight hundred and twenty-five reals in all. These I will stop out of what I have belonging to your worship, and I'll return home rich and content, though well whipped."

"O blessed Sancho! O dear Sancho!" said Don Quixote; "how we shall be bound to serve thee, Dulcinea and I, all the days of our lives that heaven may grant us! If she returns to her lost shape (and it cannot be but that she will) her misfortune will have been good fortune, and my defeat a most happy triumph. But look here, Sancho; when wilt thou begin the scourging? For if thou wilt make short work of it, I will give thee a hundred reals over and above."

"When?" said Sancho; "this night without fail. Let your worship order it so that we pass it out of doors and in the open air, and I'll scarify myself."

Night, longed for by Don Quixote with the greatest anxiety in the world, came at last, though it seemed to him that the wheels of Apollo's car had broken down, and that the day was drawing itself out longer than usual, just as is the case with lovers, who never make the reckoning of their desires agree with time. They made their way at length in among some pleasant trees that stood a little distance from the road, and there vacating Rocinante's saddle and Dapple's pack-saddle, they stretched themselves on the green grass and made their supper off Sancho's stores, and he making a powerful and flexible whip out of Dapple's halter and headstall retreated about twenty paces from his master among some beech trees. Don Quixote seeing him march off with such resolution and spirit, said to him, "Take care, my friend, not to cut thyself to pieces; allow the lashes to wait for one another, and do not be in so great a hurry as to run thyself out of breath midway; I mean, do not lay on so strenuously as to make thy life fail thee before thou hast reached the desired number; and that thou mayest not lose by a card too much or too little, I will station myself apart and count on my rosary here the lashes thou givest thyself. May heaven help thee as thy good intention deserves."

"'Pledges don't distress a good payer,'" said Sancho; "I mean to lay on in such a way as without killing myself to hurt myself, for in that, no doubt, lies the essence of this miracle."

He then stripped himself from the waist upwards, and snatching up the rope he began to lay on and Don Quixote to count the lashes. He might have given himself six or eight when he began to think the joke no trifle, and its price very low; and holding his hand for a moment, he told his master that he cried off on the score of a blind bargain, for each of those lashes ought to be paid for at the rate of half a real instead of a quarter.

"Go on, Sancho my friend, and be not disheartened," said Don Quixote, "for I double the stakes as to price."

"In that case," said Sancho, "in God's hand be it, and let it rain lashes." But the rogue no longer laid them on his shoulders, but laid on to the trees, with such groans every now and then, that one would have thought at each of them his soul was being plucked up by the roots. Don Quixote, touched to the heart, and fearing he might make an end of himself, and that through Sancho's imprudence he might miss his own object, said to him, "As thou livest, my friend, let the matter rest where it is, for the remedy seems to me a very rough one, and it will be well to have patience; 'Zamora was not won in an hour.' If I have not reckoned wrong thou hast given thyself over a thousand lashes; that is enough for the present; 'for the ass,' to put it in homely phrase, 'bears the load, but not the overload.'"

"No, no, señor," replied Sancho, "it shall never be said of me, 'The money paid, the arms broken'; go back a little farther, your worship, and let me give myself at any rate a thousand lashes more; for in a couple of bouts like this we shall have finished off the lot, and there will be even cloth to spare."

"As thou art in such a willing mood," said Don Quixote, "may heaven aid thee; lay on and I'll retire."

Sancho returned to his task with so much resolution that he soon had the bark stripped off several trees, such was the severity with which he whipped himself; and one time, raising his voice, and giving a beech a tremendous lash, he cried out, "Here dies Samson, and all with him!"

At the sound of his piteous cry and of the stroke of the cruel lash, Don Quixote ran to him at once, and seizing the twisted halter that served him for a courbash, said to him, "Heaven forbid, Sancho my friend, that to please me thou shouldst lose thy life, which is needed for the support of thy wife and children; let Dulcinea wait for a better opportunity, and I will content myself with a hope soon to be realized, and have patience until thou hast gained fresh strength so as to finish off this business to the satisfaction of everybody."

"As your worship will have it so, señor," said Sancho, "so be it; but throw

332

The rogue laid on to the trees.

your cloak over my shoulders, for I'm sweating and I don't want to take cold; it's a risk that novice disciplinants run."

Don Quixote obeyed, and stripping himself covered Sancho, who slept until the sun woke him; they then resumed their journey, which for the time being they brought to an end at a village that lay three leagues farther on. They dismounted at a hostelry which Don Quixote recognized as such and did not take to be a castle with moat, turrets, portcullis, and drawbridge; for ever since he had been vanquished he talked more rationally about everything. They quartered him in a room on the ground floor, and when they were settled, Don Quixote said, "Tell me, Sancho, hast thou a mind to have another turn at thyself tonight, and wouldst thou rather have it indoors or in the open air?"

"Egad, señor," said Sancho, "for what I'm going to give myself, it comes all the same to me whether it is in a house or in the fields; still I'd like it to be among trees; for I think they are company for me and help me to bear my pain wonderfully."

"And yet it must not be, Sancho my friend," said Don Quixote; "but, to enable thee to recover strength, we must keep it for our own village; for at the latest we shall get there the day after tomorrow."

Sancho said he might do as he pleased; but that for his own part he would like to finish off the business quickly before his blood cooled and while he had an appetite, because "in delay there is apt to be danger" very often, and "one take was better than two I'll give thee's."

"For God's sake, Sancho, no more proverbs!" exclaimed Don Quixote. "Speak in a plain, simple, straightforward way, as I have often told thee, and thou wilt find the good of it."

All that day Don Quixote and Sancho remained in the village and inn waiting for night, the one to finish off his task scourging in the open country, the other to see it accomplished, for therein lay the accomplishment of his wishes. When evening came, they set out from the village, and that night they passed among trees again in order to give Sancho an opportunity of working out his penance, which he did in the same fashion as the night before, at the expense of the bark of the beech trees much more than of his back, of which he took such good care that the lashes would not have knocked off a fly had there been one there. The duped Don Quixote did not miss a single stroke of the count, and he found that together with those of the night before they made up three thousand and twenty-nine. The sun apparently had got up early to witness the sacrifice, and with his light they resumed their journey.

That day and night they traveled on, nor did anything worth mention happen them, unless it was that in the course of the night Sancho finished off his task, whereat Don Quixote was beyond measure joyful. He watched for daylight, to see if along the road he should fall in with his already disenchanted lady Dulcinea; and as he pursued his journey there was no woman he met that he did not go up to, to see if she was Dulcinea del Toboso, as he held it absolutely certain that Merlin's promises could not lie. Full of these thoughts and anxieties, they ascended a rising ground wherefrom they descried their own village, at the sight of which Sancho fell on his knees exclaiming, "Open thine eyes, longed-for home, and see how thy son Sancho Panza comes back to thee, if not very rich, very well whipped! Open thine arms and receive, too, thy son Don Quixote, who, if he comes vanquished by the arm of another, comes victor over himself, which, as he himself has told me, is the greatest victory anyone can desire. I'm bringing back money, for if I was well whipped, I went mounted like a gentleman."

"Have done with these fooleries," said Don Quixote. "Let us push on straight and get to our own place, where we will give free range to our fancies, and settle our plans for our future pastoral life."

With this they descended the slope and directed their steps to their village.

CHAPTER 27

The Strangest Adventure

AT THE entrance of the village, Don Quixote saw two boys quarreling on the village threshing-floor, one of whom said to the other, "Take it easy, Periquillo; thou shalt never see it again as long as thou livest."

Don Quixote heard this, and said he to Sancho, "Dost thou not mark, friend, what that boy said, 'Thou shalt never see it again as long as thou livest'?"

"Well," said Sancho, "what does it matter if the boy said so?"

"What!" said Don Quixote, "dost thou not see that, applied to the object of my desires, the words mean that I am never to see Dulcinea more?"

Sancho was about to answer, when his attention was diverted by seeing a hare come flying across the plain pursued by several greyhounds and sportsmen. In its terror it ran to take shelter and hide itself under Dapple. Sancho caught it alive and presented it to Don Quixote, who was saying, "*Malum signum, malum signum!* a hare flies, greyhounds chase it, Dulcinea appears not."

"Your worship's a strange man," said Sancho; "let's take it for granted that this hare is Dulcinea, and these greyhounds chasing it the malignant enchanters who turned her into a country wench; she flies, and I catch her and put her into your worship's hands, and you hold her in your arms and cherish her; what bad sign is that, or what ill omen is there to be found here?"

The two boys who had been quarreling came over to look at the hare, and Sancho asked one of them what their quarrel was about. He was answered by

335

the one who had said, "Thou shalt never see it again as long as thou livest," that he had taken a cage full of crickets from the other boy, and did not mean to give it back to him as long as he lived. Sancho took out four cuartos from his pocket and gave them to the boy for the cage, which he placed in Don Quixote's hands, saying, "There, señor! there are the omens broken and destroyed, and they have no more to do with our affairs, to my thinking, fool as I am, than with last year's clouds; and if I remember rightly I have heard the curate of our village say that it does not become Christians or sensible people to give any heed to these silly things; and even you yourself said the same to me some time ago, telling me that all Christians who minded omens were fools; but there's no need of making words about it; let us push on and go into our village."

The sportsmen came up and asked for their hare, which Don Quixote gave them. They then went on, and upon the green at the entrance of the town they came upon the curate and the bachelor Samson Carrasco busy with their breviaries. They were at once recognized by both the curate and the bachelor, who came towards them with open arms. Don Quixote dismounted and received them with a close embrace.

So at length, accompanied by the curate and the bachelor, they made their entrance into the town, and proceeded to Don Quixote's house, at the door of which they found his housekeeper and niece, whom the news of his arrival had already reached. It had been brought to Teresa Panza, Sancho's wife, as well, and she with her hair all loose and half naked, dragging Sanchica her daughter by the hand, ran out to meet her husband; but seeing him coming in by no means as good case as she thought a governor ought to be, she said to him, "How is it you come this way, husband? It seems to me you come tramping and footsore, and looking more like a disorderly vagabond than a governor."

"Hold your tongue, Teresa," said Sancho; "let's go into the house and there you'll hear strange things. I bring money, and that's the main thing, got by my own industry without wronging anybody."

"You bring the money, my good husband," said Teresa, "and no matter whether it was got this way or that; for, however you may have got it, you'll not have brought any new practice into the world."

Sanchica embraced her father and asked him if he brought her anything, for she had been looking out for him as for the showers of May; and she taking hold of him by the girdle on one side, and his wife by the hand, while the daughter led Dapple, they made for their house, leaving Don Quixote in his, in the hands of his niece and housekeeper, and in the company of the curate and the bachelor.

Don Quixote at once, without any regard to time or season, withdrew in private with the bachelor and the curate, and in a few words told them of his defeat, and of the engagement he was under not to quit his village for a year, which he meant to keep to the letter without departing a hair's breadth from it, as became a knight-errant bound by scrupulous good faith and the laws of knight-errantry; and of how he thought of turning shepherd for that year, and taking his diversion in the solitude of the fields, where he could with perfect freedom give range to his thoughts of love while he followed the virtuous pastoral calling; and he besought them, if they had not a great deal to do and were not prevented by more important business, to consent to be his companions, for he would buy sheep enough to qualify them for shepherds; and the most important point of the whole affair, he could tell them, was settled, for he had given them names that would fit them to a T. The curate asked what they were. Don Quixote replied that he himself was to be called the shepherd Quixotiz, and the bachelor the shepherd Carrascon, and the curate the shepherd Curambro, and Sancho Panza the shepherd Pancino.

Both were astounded at Don Quixote's new craze; however, lest he should once more make off out of the village from them in pursuit of his chivalry, they trusting that in the course of the year he might be cured, fell in with his new project, applauded his crazy idea as a bright one, and offered to share the life with him. "And what's more," said Samson Carrasco, "I am, as all the world knows, a very famous poet, and I'll be always making verses, pastoral, or courtly, or as it may come into my head, to pass away our time in those secluded regions where we shall be roaming. But what is most needful, sirs, is that each of us should choose the name of the shepherdess he means to glorify in his verses, and that we should not leave a tree, be it ever so hard, without writing up and carving her name on it, as is the habit and custom of love-smitten shepherds."

"That's the very thing," said Don Quixote; "though I am relieved from looking for the name of an imaginary shepherdess, for there's the peerless Dulcinea del Toboso, to whom all praise is appropriate, be it ever so hyperbolical."

"And," added Samson Carrasco, "Sancho Panza, if he joins this fraternity, may glorify his wife Teresa Panza as Teresaina."

337

Don Quixote laughed at the adaptation of the name, and the curate bestowed vast praise upon the worthy resolution he had made, and again offered to bear him company all the time that he could spare from his imperative duties. And so they took their leave of him, beseeching him to take care of his health and treat himself to a suitable diet.

It so happened his niece and the housekeeper overheard all the three of them said; and as soon as they were gone they both of them came in to Don Quixote, and said the niece, "What's this, uncle? Now that we were thinking you had come back to stay at home and lead a quiet respectable life here, are you going to get into fresh entanglements, and turn 'young shepherd, thou that comest here, young shepherd going there'? Nay! indeed 'the straw is too hard now to make pipes of.'"

"And," added the housekeeper, "will your worship be able to bear, out in the fields, the heats of summer, and the chills of winter, and the howling of the wolves? Not you; for that's a life and a business for hardy men, bred and seasoned to such work almost from the time they were in swaddling clothes. Why, to make choice of evils, it's better to be a knight-errant than a shepherd! Look here, señor; take my advice—and I'm not giving it to you full of bread and wine, but fasting, and with fifty years upon my head—stay at home, look after your affairs, go often to confession, be good to the poor, and upon my soul be it if any evil comes to you."

"Hold your peace, my daughters," said Don Quixote. "I know very well what my duty is; help me to bed, for I don't feel very well; and rest assured that, knight-errant now or wandering shepherd to be, I shall never fail to have a care for your interests, as you will see in the end."

As nothing that is man's can last forever, but all tends ever downwards from its beginning to its end, and above all man's life, and as Don Quixote's enjoyed no special dispensation from heaven to stay its course, its end and close came when he least looked for it. For—whether it was of the dejection the thought of his defeat produced, or of heaven's will that so ordered it—a fever settled upon him and kept him in his bed for six days, during which he was often visited by his friends the curate, the bachelor, and the barber, while his good squire Sancho Panza never quitted his bedside. They, persuaded that it was grief at finding himself vanquished, and the object of his heart, the liberation and disenchantment of Dulcinea, unattained, that kept him in this state, strove by all the means in their power to cheer him up; the bachelor bidding him take heart and get up to begin his pastoral life, for which he himself, he said, had already bought with his own money two famous dogs to guard the flock, one called Barcino and the other Butron, which a herdsman of Quintanar had sold him.

But for all this Don Quixote could not shake off his sadness. His friends called in the doctor, who felt his pulse and was not very well satisfied with it, and said that in any case it would be well for him to attend to the health of his soul, as that of his body was in a bad way. Don Quixote heard this calmly; but not so his housekeeper, his niece, and his squire, who fell weeping bitterly, as if they had him lying dead before them. The doctor's opinion was that melancholy and depression were bringing him to his end. Don Quixote begged them to leave him to himself, as he had a wish to sleep a little. They obeyed, and he slept at one stretch more than six hours, so that the housekeeper and niece thought he was going to sleep forever. But at the end of that time he woke up, and in a loud voice exclaimed, "Blessed be Almighty God, who has shown me such goodness. In truth his mercies are boundless, and the sins of men can neither limit them nor keep them back!"

The niece listened with attention to her uncle's words, and they struck her as more coherent than what usually fell from him, at least during his illness, so she asked, "What are you saying, señor? Has anything strange occurred? What mercies or what sins of men are you talking of?"

"The mercies, niece," said Don Quixote, "are those that God has this moment shown me, and with him, as I said, my sins are no impediment to them. My reason is now free and clear, rid of the dark shadows of ignorance that my unhappy, constant study of those detestable books of chivalry cast over it. Now I see through their absurdities and deceptions, and it only grieves me that this destruction of my illusion has come so late that it leaves me no time to make some amends by reading other books that might be a light to my soul. Niece, I feel myself at the point of death, and I would fain meet it in such a way as to show that my life has not been so ill that I should leave behind me the name of a madman; for though I have been one, I would not that the fact should be made plainer at my death. Call in to me, my dear, my good friends the curate, the bachelor Samson Carrasco, and Master Nicholas the barber, for I wish to confess and make my will."

But his niece was saved the trouble by the entrance of the three. The instant Don Quixote saw them he exclaimed, "Good news for you, good sirs, that I am no longer Don Quixote of La Mancha, but Alonso Quexana, whose way of life won for him the name of Good. Now am I the enemy of Amadis of Gaul and of the whole countless troop of his descendants; odious to me

339

now are all the profane stories of knight-errantry; now I perceive my folly, and the peril into which reading them brought me; now, by God's mercy schooled into my right senses, I loathe them."

When the three heard him speak in this way, they had no doubt whatever that some new craze had taken possession of him; and said Samson, "What? Señor Don Quixote! Now that we have intelligence of the lady Dulcinea being disenchanted, are you taking this line; now, just as we are on the point of becoming shepherds, to pass our lives singing, like princes, are you thinking of turning hermit? Hush, for heaven's sake, be rational, and let's have no more nonsense."

"All that nonsense," said Don Quixote, "that until now has been a reality to my hurt, my death will, with heaven's help, turn to my good. I feel, sirs, that I am rapidly drawing near death; a truce to jesting; let me have a confessor to confess me, and a notary to make my will; for in extremities like this, man must not trifle with his soul; and while the curate is confessing me let someone, I beg, go for the notary."

They looked at one another, wondering at Don Quixote's words; but, though uncertain, they were inclined to believe him, and one of the signs by which they came to the conclusion he was dying was this so sudden and complete return to his senses after having been mad; for to the words already quoted he added much more, so well expressed, so devout, and so rational, as to banish all doubt and convince them that he was sound of mind. The curate turned them all out, and left alone with him confessed him. The bachelor went for the notary and returned shortly afterwards with him and with Sancho, who, having already learned from the bachelor the condition his master was in, and finding the housekeeper and niece weeping, began to blubber and shed tears.

The confession over, the curate came out saying, "Alonso Quexana the Good is indeed dying, and is indeed in his right mind; we may now go in to him while he makes his will."

This news gave a tremendous impulse to the brimming eyes of the housekeeper, niece, and Sancho Panza his good squire, making the tears burst from their eyes and a host of sighs from their hearts; for of a truth, as has been said more than once, whether as plain Alonso Quexana the Good, or as Don Quixote of La Mancha, Don Quixote was always of a gentle disposition and kindly in all his ways, and hence he was beloved, not only by those of his own house, but by all who knew him.

340

The notary came in with the rest, and as soon as the preamble of the will had been set out and Don Quixote had commended his soul to God with all the devout formalities that are usual, coming to the bequests, he said, "Item, it is my will that, touching certain moneys in the hands of Sancho Panza (whom in my madness I made my squire), inasmuch as between him and me there have been certain accounts and debits and credits, no claim be made against him, nor any account demanded of him in respect of them; but that if anything remain over and above, after he has paid himself what I owe him, the balance, which will be but little, shall be his, and much good may it do him; and if, as when I was mad I had a share in giving him the government of an island, so, now that I am in my senses, I could give him that of a kingdom, it should be his, for the simplicity of his character and the fidelity of his conduct deserve it." And then, turning to Sancho, he said, "Forgive me, my friend, that I led thee to seem as mad as myself, making thee fall into the same error I myself fell into, that there were and still are knights-errant in the world."

"Ah!" said Sancho weeping, "don't die, master, but take my advice and live many years; for the foolishest thing a man can do in this life is to let himself die without rhyme or reason, without anybody killing him, or any hands but melancholy's making an end of him. Come, don't be lazy, but get up from your bed and let us take to the fields in shepherd's trim as we agreed. Perhaps behind some bush we shall find the lady Dulcinea disenchanted, as fine as fine can be. If it be that you are dying of vexation at having been vanquished, lay the blame on me, and say you were overthrown because I had girthed Rocinante badly; besides you must have seen in your books of chivalry that it is a common thing for knights to upset one another, and for him who is conquered today to be conqueror tomorrow."

"Very true," said Samson, "and good Sancho Panza's view of these cases is quite right."

"Sirs, not so fast," said Don Quixote, " 'in last year's nests there are no birds this year.' I was mad, now I am in my senses; I was Don Quixote of La Mancha, I am now, as I said, Alonso Quexana the Good; and may my repentance and sincerity restore me to the esteem you used to have for me; and now let Master Notary proceed.

"Item, I leave all my property absolutely to Antonia Quexana my niece, here present, after all has been deducted from the most available portion of it that may be required to satisfy the bequests I have made. And the first disbursement I desire to be made is the payment of the wages I owe for the time my housekeeper has served me, with twenty ducats, over and above, for a gown. The curate and the bachelor Samson Carrasco, now present, I appoint my executors.

"Item, it is my wish that if Antonia Quexana, my niece, desires to marry, she shall marry a man of whom it shall be first of all ascertained by information taken that he does not know what books of chivalry are; and if it should be proved that he does, and if, in spite of this, my niece insists upon marrying him, and does marry him, then that she shall forfeit the whole of what I have left her, which my executors shall devote to works of charity as they please."

With this he closed his will, and a faintness coming over him he stretched himself out at full length on the bed. All were in a flutter and made haste to relieve him, and during the three days he lived after that on which he made his will, he fainted away very often. The house was all in confusion; but still the niece ate and the housekeeper drank and Sancho Panza enjoyed himself; for inheriting property wipes out or softens down in the heir the feeling of grief the dead man might be expected to leave behind him.

At last Don Quixote's end came, after he had received all the sacraments, and had in full and forcible terms expressed his detestation of books of chivalry. The notary was there at the time, and he said that in no book of chivalry had he ever read of any knight-errant dying in his bed so calmly and so like a Christian as Don Quixote, who amid the tears and lamentations of all present yielded up his spirit, that is to say, died.

Such was the end of the Ingenious Gentleman of La Mancha.

DATE DUE

APR 9			
APR 24			
DEC 3			
JAN 29			
MAR 5			
APR 1			
SEP 18			
OCT 6			
NOV 8			

Fic
Cer

Cervantes, Miguel de
The adventures of Don
Quixote, man of La Mancha

B 30-257